D0273124

Julia Gregson's novel *East of the Sun* was chosen for the Richard and Judy TV Book Club and became a *Sunday Times* bestseller in the UK. It was described by the judges of the Prince Maurice prize for Literary Love stories as 'without doubt one of the most simply and profoundly enjoyable books to ever win the prize' – the chairman of the judges was Sebastian Faulks. Previously a journalist for the *Sydney Morning Herald*, *The Times*, *Good Housekeeping*, and *Rolling Stone* in the USA, Julia is married and lives in Monmouth.

To find out more about Julia and her books, visit her website www.juliagregson.net or follow her on Twitter at @juliagregson

Also by Julia Gregson

East of the Sun
The Water Horse
Jasmine Nights
Monsoon Summer

MONSOON SUMMER

JULIA GREGSON

An Orion paperback

First published in Great Britain in 2016
by Orion Books
This paperback edition published in 2017
by Orion Books,
an imprint of The Orion Publishing Group Ltd,
Carmelite House, 50 Victoria Embankment
London EC4Y 0DZ

An Hachette UK Company

1 3 5 7 9 10 8 6 4 2

Copyright © Julia Gregson 2016

A CIP catalogue record for this book
is available from the British Library.

ISBN 978 1 4091 0305 9

Typeset at The Spartan Press Ltd,
Lymington, Hants

Printed in Great Britain by Clays Ltd,
St Ives plc

www.orionbooks.co.uk

For Sarah, Charlotte, Hugo, Natasha and Poppy.

I

Wickam Farm, Oxfordshire

Chapter 1

When I was young, and we were very alone, my mother tried her hardest to make the world seem a nicer, gentler place for me. Once, during a terrifying thunderstorm, she told me I was not to worry, it was only God moving his furniture in heaven, a thought that kept me rigidly awake all night.

Another time, in Norwich, where she was taking care of an elderly widower, I saw, on our way home from the cinema, what I now realise was two people having vigorous sex in an alleyway. They were playing trains, she said, and when I said it looked nothing like the trains we sometimes played, when we put the soles of our feet together and cycled them round and around, she laughed, or maybe she smacked me. You could never quite be sure with her.

But that wet November night, driving to north Oxfordshire, she was fresh out of cheerful things to say. We were going to Wickam Farm, home of Daisy Barker, my godmother, my mother's friend and sometimes employer when all else failed. Daisy had invited us down, 'for reasons we'll discuss when you get here', which was more than fine by me, not just because London, bombed out, boarded up, rationed, was so depressing, but because I loved the farm. For me it was a place of refuge, but for my mother, for reasons I didn't understand, a place of shame.

Sheets of rain fell on our taxi's windscreen faster than the wipers could keep up; on either side of us, hedges as high as small houses narrowed the world down to wet lanes ahead, grey skies above. So quiet there too – just the whoosh of water, the croak of a wet pheasant.

A herd of Jersey cows, steaming from the rain, stopped us at the Roman ruin crossroads. Our taxi driver, a dear old boy who'd earlier looked as if he might die happy under the weight of my mother's suitcases (she had that effect on men), burbled away, trying to catch her eye in the rear-view mirror. Lately, he said, he'd driven all sorts to Miss Barker's: missionaries, schoolteachers, nurses, even some black people. 'Doesn't she run some sort of Indian charity there?' he asked.

I felt my mother stiffen beside me. 'No idea,' she said in her most Home Counties, position-closed voice. 'Haven't seen her for absolutely ages.'

Behind his head, she dug her nails into my hand and rolled her eyes. The impertinence of the common man was one of her themes since the war, even regarding conversations she herself had started. But that was my mother all over, a medley of mixed messages.

We'd come to the iron fences that marked Wickam Farm's boundaries, and around the next corner, when I saw the long drive, the pollarded ash trees, the dark woods beyond, my heart stirred. We were here: Wickam Farm, the closest place to home I'd ever known. Daisy was here.

Daisy, with her large teeth and her honking laugh, had become something of a mother figure to me, though she had no children of her own. It was Daisy who'd encouraged my nursing ambitions: 'Something solid and useful to go back to when the war is over.' And Daisy who, when I was accepted at Thomas's, took me up to Garrould's to buy dresses and aprons, the navy blue suit and little hat.

Daisy, who looked endearingly like an overgrown schoolgirl, had, before the war, run an orphanage in Bombay. She'd written books and political pamphlets, and during the war, she had come home to manage the farm, which had been requisitioned by MI6 and become a boisterous dorm for a cast of artists, bohemians and academics. I'd spent as much of my hospital leaves as I could down here, and when I'd listened to Daisy debating with the clever men around the kitchen table, I'd realised that she was their equal in intelligence and bravery. I couldn't wait to see her.

The porch light went on as we approached the house. Daisy, wearing a man's coat and galoshes, dashed out shouting to the driver, 'Ware! Ware!' An old hunting cry, to warn us of a new and enormous pothole in the drive. She flung her arms around my mother – 'Glory, how wonderful to see you' – which made me happy. I wanted other people to love my mother even when I couldn't. I buried my face in the old tweed coat.

Daisy said the drive was so dangerous now, it was safer to walk the last hundred yards. 'Would you mind frightfully carrying their

4

cases to the house?' she asked the driver. 'Oh, aren't you kind?'
He trotted off happily. It was one of Daisy's many gifts to make
everyone feel they were an essential part of whatever action they
were involved in.

Wickam Farm was a handsome three-storey late-Victorian building with low gabled roofs. Tonight, rain had left a halo of mist
around it, giving it a ghostly look. Its peeling windows wore a shaggy
gown of Virginia creeper through which four faint lights peeped.

A horse cantered to the gate to greet Daisy.

'Bert was demobbed after the war.' She rubbed him between the
ears. 'His owner was killed, so we bought him for nothing, didn't we,
Bert, at the world's largest horse auction, the Elephant and Castle
sale – half the poor loves go for meat now.' She handed me a piece
of bread to give him. I felt the soft velvet of his lips in my hand, and
saw his dark eyes gleaming in the half-light. I took a deep breath.

'I'm so glad to be back, Daisy,' I said with more emotion than
I'd intended because my mother, shivery and taut, was standing
beside me.

'We're a job lot at the farm at the moment,' Daisy said as we
crunched up the drive. 'I seem to be running a sort of ex-Raj
boarding house – I say, do watch out.' She flashed her torch down
another large hole. 'Ci Ci Mallinson's back from Bombay with her
daughter Flora; she's rented the upstairs bedroom, and of course,
Tudor, my half-brother.'

My mother's grip tightened on my arm. She'd told me in a deliberately casual way on the train down about Tudor, aged forty, old by
my standards, unmarried, owner of half the twenty-acre farm; Tudor
who we'd never met and who might, just might, possibly . . . well, I
knew the rest, because as my mother, an incorrigible matchmaker,
never failed to point out, men were a scarce commodity after the
war, and I was approaching the fatal abyss of thirty, when 'a woman
loses her bloom. Not you, though, darling – and don't you dare roll
your eyes at me! I'm only thinking of you.'

'Tudor was at boarding school most of the time I was in India,'
Daisy continued, 'so we're getting to know each other again. We've
delayed supper in your honour.'

'Sorry if we've held you up,' my mother said, on the defensive
already.

'Glory.' Daisy put a steadying hand on her arm. 'I'm just so happy
you're here.'

5

The shadowy hall was as I remembered it. The crunchy fur of a lion skin beneath our feet. The severed heads of foxes, deer, a tiger staring coldly down. (Daisy's father, a civil servant in Mysore, had been a keen shot.) The sweet familiarity of dog smells, bacon, soup and damp raincoats.

'We'll need the smallest room first,' my mother told Daisy, whisking me into the downstairs cloakroom. 'Won't be a sec.' She locked the door and whipped off my hat, then got out a lipstick – a sample with no proper lid – and tried to dab a little on my cheeks.

'Mummy, for God's sake. I can do it myself if I need to.' I pulled away from her, washed my hands and tried to control myself.

'Trust me, darling,' she said. 'You do. You're so pale, we must get you on a tonic soon.'

'Not the tonic!' I said in my pantomime voice, knowing we mustn't fall out now. Her gorgeous black hair crackled like a forest fire as she brushed it, and she was breathing hard. To calm her, I put a slick of lipstick on.

'There.' She straightened my dress, shot her big brown eyes up at me. 'All done. What a fuss you make about nothing.'

Conversation stopped as we walked into the dining room. Three pairs of eyes swivelled to look at us, not in a friendly way.

'So . . . introductions.' Daisy's amiable smile did not falter. 'Before we tuck in.'

'Shut the door first,' said an impatient male voice. 'There's a hell of a draught.'

'Tudor, my love,' Daisy closed the door with her heel, 'this is Kit! The wonderful nurse I was telling you about.' She twisted the knob on the oil lamp so we could see him. A thin man dressed in shooting clothes, plus fours and a green waistcoat, with one of those very pink English skins that looked as if it could peel off in damp weather, a high forehead, and gingerish hair that was already receding. He didn't look like Daisy at all, but then he was only her half-brother.

'Tudor,' she said, 'is frightfully interested in archaeology and knows all the Roman sites around here.' When he raised a languid arm in my direction, my mother gave me a little dig in the back. *Sparkle* was its message.

'Soup, please,' he said to the figure on his right. 'Before it gets cold. Butter when you're finished.'

'And that is Ci Ci passing the butter,' Daisy continued. 'Or Mrs Cecilia Mallinson if she prefers. Recently home from Bombay.'

An old lady, late sixties I guessed, dressed in a lurid kimono, waved vaguely in our direction. There was a King Charles spaniel at her feet. 'I hadn't quite finished with it, Tudor, but as you wish...'

'Kit and Glory,' Daisy continued, 'have kindly agreed to help me with the charity.' My mother's eyes flickered in my direction. Daisy, who'd bailed us out at intervals over the years, was always good about explaining our presence here without denting our pride. 'But Kit's been nursing at St Thomas's,' she smiled at me, 'so she deserves a bit of a break first.'

'Oh well done you. That must have been ghastly,' said Ci Ci. 'Is the mother the Anglo-Indian one?' she added. Clearly Daisy had briefed them before we arrived to avoid any conversational pitfalls. 'Looks awfully white to me.'

I felt my mother flinch. Of all forms of introduction, this was her least favourite. 'And this is Ci Ci's daughter Flora,' Daisy continued smoothly.

A plump girl, early thirties, made her way crabwise to her place and sat down.

'Sorry I'm late,' she said.

'It's the pea and ham again,' her mother said. 'Did you wash your hands?' She took a scrap of ham rind from her plate and put it in the dog's mouth.

'Flora was a Land Girl in Wiltshire during the war,' Daisy explained. 'Fearfully hard work.'

'Hello, both.' Flora, who had a kind, sweet, hopeful face (gormless, my mother said later), held her hand out across the table, her dirty knuckles visible for all to see. My mother, who had a horror of germs, took it gingerly.

'Are you still nursing?' Flora said, passing me the soup. Same old lovely Royal Worcester tureen and battered silver ladle with grape vines on it.

'Yes and no,' I said. 'I'm studying again, hoping to go back to...' I could see my mother shaking her head. I'd promised, on the train, not to mention the midwifery course too soon. 'To London. And you?'

'Well... not actually sure.' She crumbled her roll. 'Now Mummy's back, I'll probably stay with her for a while, which is nice. You see,

I was at school before the war, while Mummy was in India, so tons to catch up on.' Her smile was that of a mongoose left with a snake.

'I like your shoes.' The old lady put down her soup spoon, and looked at my mother, who was sitting very regally, her legs on a slant like a model, displaying the exquisite, almost finicky table manners she'd tried to pass on to me.

'Thank you.' My mother glanced at her snakeskin courts. 'They are rather fun, aren't they? I can't remember where I got them.' I'd last seen the shoes on the high-arched feet of the wife of the solicitor she'd worked for in Norwich.

When everyone had finished eating, Daisy started to pile the dirty dishes on to a tray. My mother and I got up automatically to help her.

'Stay where you are,' she commanded. 'House rules: no work on your first night.'

'It's been impossible getting servants since the war,' complained Ci Ci. 'Everyone thinks they're too good for it.'

Flora looked at her mother uncertainly, and half rose. 'Should I…'

'Sit down, Flora,' the old woman snapped, in a we're-paying-for-this kind of voice. 'Godfrey, my husband,' she told Tudor after pouring herself another glass of damson wine, 'had twenty years in the jute industry, and loved his job. Flora only met him twice, which was sad. You never stop being a mother, you know.' She pronounced it ironically – *muthah* – as if worried she might sound sentimental.

I saw the heat rise in Flora's cheek and thought, poor creature. No father, no husband, no home, no job now that the war had ended; just a future of rooms in boarding houses and cheap hotels with this strange old bird. But then we were all feeling the aftershocks, and the strain; hunger too, with rationing being worse than it had been even during the war.

After another glass of wine, Ci Ci tried to lift her dog into the lamplight, and I saw how strangely she'd put her lipstick on. It extended far beyond the corners of her mouth, and in the half-light looked like a wound.

'And where are all these people going to sleep?' she asked the dog, giving him a kiss.

'In Nannie's old room at the top of the house.' Daisy had

returned with coffee. 'You can see the fields and woods from there.'
She produced all her friendly teeth at once.

'Bless you, Daisy.' My mother sounded every bit as regal as the
old crone. 'It's splendidly quiet, too.'

'I hope you don't mind the attic,' Daisy said to me the next morning
as we were walking across the farmyard. 'I knew you'd want separate
bedrooms, but I've had to rent out all the others since the war, and
you've seen the drive!' This with an aristocratic lack of shame: Daisy
was never furtive about money.

'How did you meet Ci Ci?' I said, circling round a large puddle.

'In Bombay, at a party. She had a splendid house then, servants,
a husband. He died of a heart attack doing up his shoes, and then
of course everything ended shockingly fast after Independence. She
can barely boil an egg, poor love.'

Four geese waddled across the yard, and in the distance, mile
upon mile of fields lay bathed in pale sunshine. Rumour had it that
seven Roman charioteers had burned to death in the valley below us.
A headless man smelling of charcoal was said to haunt the house.

'I'm happy in the attic,' I said, and meant it. I didn't believe in
the ghosts, and I liked my room's whitewashed plainness, with its
sloping ceiling, the washstand, the small soft bed that had once
belonged to Daisy's parents. But what I most liked was the mile
upon mile of open country outside, the silver flash of the river that
ran through it. The quiet of the space (so quiet you could hear an
apple drop from a tree at night) was a blissful luxury after four years
in nurses' dorms in London. My last dorm – spluttering gas fire,
clothes horses crammed with other people's dripping underwear –
was claustrophobically small. Nowhere quiet to cry there, with only
two feet between each bed.

And I did cry, uncontrollably at times, and I needed to think. It
wasn't, I told myself irritably and often, as if I was going through
some special kind of interesting crisis. It was the war, it was life, and
nobody's fault that my cohort at St Thomas's had been catapulted
straight from the classroom into the Blitz. In my first year on the
wards, when London was bombed for fifty-seven continuous nights
of horror and bedlam, the hospital, plum opposite the Houses of
Parliament, was a sitting duck. One night, we'd seen what looked like
the whole of the Thames – houseboats, warehouses, park benches,
trees – on fire.

And now the war was over, and this great quiet blank had opened up. I knew I wasn't the only nurse to still feel extraordinarily tired, in my brain, my spirits, the deep muscles of my legs, as if I'd gone from twenty to seventy in a few short years; or to wake suddenly in the night to the nerve-shredding sound of screaming ambulances; or to find there were times when it took all my mental strength not to give in to the series of gruesome snapshots pooled at the bottom of my mind: the rotting meat smell of burns, the young fireman injured by shrapnel in the gullet, who gargled blood before he died, and, of course, the girl. But I was experiencing something else too. I'd tried for the second time to complete my midwifery training, and I'd failed and that felt awful.

Everyone tells you when you are a nurse or a doctor that mistakes happen, that we're only human, but the girl was the one who took me to the edge, and I can't write about it, can't think about it now. All I can say is I found it hard to forgive myself, and probably never will.

Daisy beamed at me as she unlocked the door to the barn.

'I've been dying to show you this,' she said. There was an immediate smell of dust and hay, and I remembered feeding lambs here during bad weather – the muscular suck of their tongues, the way their eyes rolled when the milk entered their mouths. 'It's been our greatest challenge so far.'

The barn was freezing inside, almost colder than outside. She switched on a naked bulb, festooned with cobwebs, and the first thing I saw was a large blackboard with the words *The Mother Moonstone Maternity Home Fort Cochin* chalked on it in Daisy's slashing hand, followed by a column of figures. Beside the blackboard were two battered school desks piled high with files, and three boxes labelled *Medical Supplies* and *Not Wanted on Voyage*. Tacked to one of the walls was a large chart, one I recognised from R. W. Johnstone's textbook on the internal workings of the pregnant woman at term.

'I do prefer the office to be separate from the house, don't you?' said Daisy, seeing my dubious gaze. This office was arranged like a small stage set in the middle of hay bales and stacks of old gates. 'It's essential to get the house out of your head, at least for part of the day.'

Daisy, I knew for a fact, was often up at five, feeding animals or cooking stews, in order to clear this time for herself. She knelt to light the stove in the corner, brushed a dozing farm cat off her desk.

'That's yours.' She pointed to the chair opposite hers and handed me a rug to wrap myself in. 'But Kit,' she said, looking at me steadily and kindly, 'before I bamboozle you, how are you honestly?'

There was a time when this kind of invitation had led to some of the best and frankest talks of my life. Not now.

'So much better,' I said. 'It's good to be here.' The vague idea I had had about confiding in Daisy already felt like self-indulgence. Sharing the house with dispossessed strangers was no piece of cake, and I thought she looked tired and had lost weight since I'd last seen her a year or so ago.

'I wonder if it was a mistake,' she offered, 'for you to plunge into the midwifery course again so soon after the war. What does Glory think?'

'Not thrilled,' I said. The truth was my mother hadn't spoken to me for a week after I told her. She'd been horrified the first time around, and now her plans for me ran along the lines of something sanitary and secretarial, maybe a doctor's receptionist, a place where you wore nice clothes and met men and flirted discreetly with them.

'Hmm, I didn't think she would be.' Daisy sucked in her lips.

'But I was enjoying the training.' I faltered, furious that my lip was wobbling. 'I was doing well in my exams, I wanted to finish it. It's not that. I got tired, I think,' I added lamely. 'And this awful winter . . . you know . . . normal things.' I closed my eyes tight to blank out the memory that followed me everywhere: the girl. Her screaming mouth.

'Well, we don't have to do any of this today if you don't want to. And don't let me bombard you.' The expression in her eyes was so kind, I had to take a deep breath.

'Honestly, Daisy,' I stood up, 'my brain's going to turn to dust if I don't work again soon, so spill the beans.'

She laughed as if I'd made a splendid joke, and opened the desk drawer. 'Let's get cracking, then.'

Over the next hour, Daisy, intent and serious, sketched out what seemed to me a dangerous plan. 'Do you remember me telling you about the orphanage I ran in Bombay in the late twenties?' she began.

'Of course!' I'd enjoyed her stories about Tamarind Street.

'Well, it was a marvellous time. I set it up with a group of egghead women I'd met at Oxford, and we ran it with Indian volunteers. We all got on splendidly, and I was very happy there, and although it was a drop in the ocean, we did at least do something, though not nearly enough.' Daisy, who never blew her own trumpet, looked sad at this.

'In August, after Independence, we thought we would be kicked out, or worse – but something's cropped up.' Her eyes flashed. 'Something very exciting. I've been asked by my very good south Indian friend, Neeta Chacko, to continue to help a mother-and-baby clinic at a small hospital in Fort Cochin. The plan is to work alongside their Indian staff and develop a short course to share Western knowledge with the local village midwives, the *vayattattis*. So we're on the hunt for English midwives to go out to India. The right kind.'

'The right kind?' I asked cautiously. 'Meaning?'

'Well, not pig-headed know-it-alls. We can learn a lot from the local women.'

'But who would want to go?' I asked. In the last few months, the papers had been full of lurid accounts of the mayhem that had followed Independence: the thirty thousand Muslims hacked to death, the slaughtering of innocent passengers in burning trains, neighbour killing neighbour and so on. 'Don't the Indians loathe us now?'

'Well you see, that's rot,' Daisy said. 'Some do with some justification, but others, we worked with them for years, they were our friends, and besides, they need all the help they can get.'

'Don't they want to cut the apron strings?' That was what my mother had told me, a bitter note in her voice.

'Not entirely.' Daisy put a kettle on top of the range. 'God, it's cold in here, it might even snow tomorrow the weatherman says. It's partly our fault that India still has an appalling infant mortality rate. Tackling it wasn't high on our government's list of priorities when we were there, and sensibly, their government wants foreign midwives from America and Britain to fill in the gaps.'

I must have looked sceptical. Handing me a mug of tea, she said, 'The situation, frankly, is dire. The riots and killings have placed a tremendous strain on local hospitals. Neeta has begged us to come back, to bring equipment, books, money, anything we can.'

She got up and put a piece of rotten gate on the fire.

'Are you going?' I felt my mouth grow dry.

'I can't.' She looked stricken. 'I have to run the farm, otherwise it will collapse, and anyway, it's important that the Moonstone has its own Indian administrator. It's midwives they need. Have a flapjack.' Daisy's flapjacks were good: moist and chewy, with just enough golden syrup in them to make them sweet.

'I'm not a proper midwife yet.' I took a flapjack from the tin. 'When I first did the training, I had two more supervised deliveries to do before I sat my Part Twos.' The rule was that pupil midwives who were qualified nurses had to take responsibility for twenty women during labour in hospital, and ten in the patients' own home, so a total of thirty deliveries over a year. I'd taken part in twenty-eight, and then, because of what had happened, I'd dropped out.

'So, only two more deliveries to go.' Daisy tucked the blanket around my knees. 'I was trying to remember if you'd ever actually been to India with your mother?' she said innocently, while I was chewing.

'Daisy,' I said warningly. I had an inkling where this was heading, and had already decided to say no. 'I was never there, or if I was, I was too young to remember.'

My mother's stories about India were so odd and variable that I always felt, to use her own phrase, 'eggshelly' when the subject cropped up, not wanting to casually blurt out what she had so carefully concealed.

'I think Mummy went to school there.'

'She did,' Daisy said.

'Did she work for some governor or something? A good job.'

'Maybe.' It was Daisy's turn to look wary. 'You'd better ask her.'

A gust of wind made the barn door fly open. Three ducks waddled across the mud, the wind flattening their feathers. Daisy bolted the door shut, put another log in the grate.

'So, back to the Moonstone.' She stood up and wrapped a blanket mummy-fashion around herself. 'What Neeta and I are working on is a simple training programme that won't mystify the local midwives, some of whom are illiterate, and joy! I think I may have tracked down the proverbial needle in the haystack by finding a young doctor at Oxford who speaks Malayalam, the local language in Cochin. He's going to help me with the translations. It is a bit of a minefield out there at the moment, and we must avoid any hint of the English bossing their women about. We want to train their best and brightest, but you know, it can be terribly tricky: some high-caste Hindu women have to go through complicated cleansing rituals if they so much as touch the bodily fluids of another.'

'It sounds insanely difficult.'

'That's what Tudor says.' She smiled sadly. 'He's completely mystified at my spending my time on this, so it's probably best we don't discuss it at mealtimes. It can be an explosive subject.'

'I think my mother would say amen to that, but I'm not mystified,' I said. Daisy was the best person I'd ever met, though she'd have hated me to say it.

She looked at her watch. 'I'll get through this quickly – lunch in half an hour. Our most desperate need is coin,' she said urgently, 'to get the home up and running and show what wonders we can achieve. If we can do that, I'm sure that in time, the new government will support us. I'm sending out begging letters to everyone I can think of. Can you help?'

'Of course, of course!' I felt shamefully relieved that that was all she wanted. 'I can type one hundred and twenty words a minute,' I boasted. My mother had insisted on my attending the Balmoral typing school in Oxford Street. 'When do we start?'

'Today.' She moved a pile of files from the desk. 'Let's begin by making a list of supplies. Nothing too taxing.'

Chapter 2

When the snow came it fell in thick blobs that made the distant hills pillowy and indistinct, and blocked the narrow lanes, making Wickam Farm an island in the middle of whiteness. Every morning, after breakfast, wearing three pairs of socks, every jumper we could lay our hands on, sleeveless gloves, and long johns, Daisy and I crunched across the yard and into the barn. We read textbooks, wrote to student midwives, went methodically through the telephone directory for possible donors and typed begging letters. We wrapped parcels that, when the lane cleared, the postman would take on the first leg of their trip to India.

Some letters got through, thanks to Mr Wills, a neighbouring farmer, who clearly loved Daisy and who, scarlet and puffing, rode up to the door every other day on one of his farm horses. We kept the replies to our begging letters in two old Bath Oliver biscuit tins on Daisy's desk, one labelled *YES!*, the other *NO*. After three weeks, the *YES!* letters didn't even reach the ten-biscuit mark, but Daisy looked joyful as she showed them to me. A ten-bob note and a 'Well done, Daisy' from an aunt. A hard-earned fiver from an ex-India nurse, now retired with stomach problems to Brighton. The promise of twenty packets of swabs and some aspirin from a local chemist. That sort of thing.

The letters in the *NO* tin all but burst with rage at our stupidity at continuing to help an ungrateful India.

'Here's a beauty,' I said to Daisy.

Dear Miss Barker, wrote Colonel Dewsbury (retired) from Guildford, (*am assuming you're a miss*). *In receipt of yrs 20/11/47, am frankly flabbergasted that you still consider India has the right to bleed us dry. I don't know if you read the newspapers, but after enjoying the railways we built for them, the schools we set up, and a thousand and one other advantages we fought and died for,* <u>THEY HAVE KICKED US OUT</u>. He had underlined this so emphatically, he'd gone clean through the sheet of Basildon

Bond. *Two generations of my own family have given their lives to the country (father in Inniskillings, great-grandfather caught in the riots up north, where they holed us up for two days without water or food). So sorry. NO, from now on, charity begins at home.*

His stabbing signature had made another bullet hole in the paper.

'I think we can safely assume the Colonel won't be remembering us in his will.' I shut him firmly in the *NO* tin. 'I can hear you shouting, Colonel,' I put my ear to the lid, 'but you can't come out.'

'Oh Kit,' Daisy said, after a series of schoolgirlish snorts, 'don't leave too soon.'

I didn't want to. I loved working with Daisy, and cocooned by the snow and immersed in this exciting project, I was secretly dreading that the roads would be cleared soon and I'd have no excuse for not returning to St Andrew's, the nursing home where I'd gone to study midwifery after my general nursing training at Thomas's. I wasn't frightened of the study, which I enjoyed, or the exams; I was resigned to the temporary claustrophobia of being back in a crowded dorm. The particular horse I had to get back on was the idea of delivering another child on my own, which made me feel sick and light-headed, not a good feeling for a pupil midwife.

'You can stay for ever as far as I'm concerned.' Daisy patted my arm. 'Your mother's occupied. Tudor likes having you around.'

'So not stinking fish?' I tried to avoid the hopeful glances that Daisy and my mother attached to any mention of Tudor's name. It was an awkward thing, but I'd really taken against him: his languid manner; his prissy way of eating, as if the food was some sort of insult, when my mother was trying so hard; the way he treated Daisy like a skivvy.

Daisy tried to twang my heart strings with excuses for his boorish behaviour: Tudor wasn't used to having so many women around after the army, and before that boarding school and Oxford; Tudor found it hard to make conversation at the table (at which my inner censor sagged and said, oh poor ickle bickle Tudor) because he was fearsomely intelligent and didn't do small talk.

'You could never be stinking fish,' she said stoutly. 'You're family, not guests.'

'It's been good for us,' I said, and meant it. 'Mummy and I were barely speaking on the way down, and being together every day means...' I was faltering as I said this, because it already felt disloyal,

16

'we're at least under the same roof and I'm not so worried about her.'

'That's good.' Daisy's look was steady and kind. 'She loves you, you know.'

'I just wish,' I said eventually, 'she could find something to do that she really liked.'

'It's not ideal.' Even Daisy couldn't deny this. 'But she's saved my bacon with the housekeeping, and she's a wonderful cook.' I felt the old glow of reflected pride when she said this, and it was justified. Maud, Daisy's regular cook, was off with her recurring bronchitis, and when snow had threatened to cut off our food supplies, Ma had performed small miracles with sinister-looking bottles of vegetables she found in the cellar, making them into creamy soups with a pinch of this and that, and conjuring up delicious stews from unpromising scraps of lamb and muddy carrots, or the odd chicken retired from laying.

A shame then that she complained ceaselessly about Daisy's hopelessly inadequate kitchen utensils, the Rayburn, the heating, the dreariness of the grey skies, though I was used to this: my mother had had plenty of practice at nipping the hand that fed her. And at least she and I were talking again.

When I'd tried to tell her a little bit about the charity, she'd crumpled her forehead and said, 'Not now, darling,' maintaining she was too squeamish, but then I'd hear her from another room boasting about my cleverness at school, delighting in the fact that I was typing again, triumphant vindication of her original plans for me.

If I wasn't too tired at nights, I took the battered Remington up to my room and, fingers flying over the keys, wrote to Josie, my dearest friend at St Thomas's, the straight-as-a-die farmer's daughter with whom I'd shared so many laughs, confidences and, when we could afford it, evenings out during the war. It was Josie who was with me the night it happened, and told me endlessly it was not my fault.

Sometimes I wrote in my diary, too, and when I'd finished, I'd cross the landing to my mother's room and kiss her goodnight. If she was sitting at the dressing table, I might brush her glorious black hair, and she'd whimper in appreciation, which made me feel sad.

She was so beautiful, my mother, have I said this? The Indian blood she tried so hard to hide had given her wonderful, smooth pale-caramel-coloured skin and glossy hair. And she was tremendously well dressed considering how broke we were – the quintessential Englishwoman, from a distance, only much, much better-looking. My glamorous princess, green satin dress and diamond necklace (paste). She was my cook, storyteller, exotic travelling companion too: funny and superstitious, with bursts of gaiety that reminded me of a cat dashing up a curtain. The sudden spitting furies of a cat, too.

Some nights, when I went in to say goodnight, she'd slide her tortoiseshell eyes up at me and say in a little-girl voice, 'Read me a story.' She carried with her always a small collection of romantic novels; her then favourite was Georgette Heyer's *The Spanish Bride*. And so, huddled under the eiderdown together, just like in the old days, I did all the voices – Juana, Lord Wellington, Harry Smith – and she was happy again.

Sometimes she'd try to persuade me to put on one of her pretty dresses (some of them donated by rich employers, others – how to put this? – self-donated), saying it would cheer everyone up downstairs, meaning Tudor, I suppose. She pleaded with me to let her polish my nails, too. *A lady is always judged by her hands.*

When I'd told Josie this, she'd said, 'But what about this?' pointing at her wild red off-duty hair. 'Or this?' holding herself erect so the world could admire her bosom. But Josie was working the night shift in London, and not available for jokes, and knowing I'd be leaving soon, I sat patiently (a huge effort) while my mother frowned at my cuticles, and pushed dead skin away with a special little pointed dagger from her shagreen case, and finally held my hand.

The bigger things between us we brushed away under the carpet like so many unpleasant toenail clippings.

There was one night when she walked in and found me wide-eyed at three a.m. I'd been thinking about the girl again – her red hair, her screaming – but said something vague about night shifts at the hospital, and how it was hard now to sleep normally again. Sensing distress, she cut me off with a strange fake laugh that was as bad as a slap, and said, 'Oh Kitty, let's not be morbid. The war's over now.'

On the day when things began to shift and change for me, there was a thaw outside. The cook, Maud, arrived mid-morning, red-cheeked, puffing and with a barking cough, saying it was still blooming cold out there but the snow was melting in the lanes, which made Daisy and me happy. We'd been wrapping parcels of maternity packs, books and wall charts, which could now leave for India.

When I walked in for lunch, Tudor and Flora were framed like silhouettes against a bright window, Tudor behind the pages of *The Listener*, making important rustling sounds. Flora glanced nervously at him from time to time. Poor Flora. Barred by her mother from the kitchen ('We're *paying*, darling. There are people to do that'), it had been made clear to her that she had one job and one job only at Wickam Farm. I'd seen her earlier in the hall, lipsticked and over-dressed, and overheard Ci Ci, who was as subtle as a megaphone, saying, 'Oh for God's sake, Flora, don't make a meal of it. Go in there and talk to him.'

Over lunch, Ci Ci kept giving Flora prodding looks, because Flora, apart from a few timid observations about the thaw, and how nice it was to see green again, and the prettiness of raindrops against the window, hadn't exactly set the table alight. My mother was in a foul mood: the Rayburn was playing up again – something to do with poor-quality coke – and the turnip and carrot soup was well below her usual standard. Ci Ci had pushed hers aside after a few spoonfuls.

Daisy came in late, her pink face and bouncy walk bringing energy into the room. Melting snow, she said, had flooded one of the stables, and William, the carthorse, was absolutely soaked. She'd been drying him. 'Our towels, I expect,' Ci Ci complained.

The phone rang.

'Get that, would you?' Tudor's goldfishy eyes swam up from behind the academic paper he was pretending to read. 'Bound to be for you.'

'Ramsden 587' Daisy's fluting tones came from the hallway. 'How nice. Oh my goodness me, yes! Of course, of course, splendid!' and then, after a pause, 'Lovely, lovely! No, no, no, not at all. That's absolutely perfect.'

'Sounds like we've won the pools,' Tudor said to me, 'but it's probably just another guest.' He gave a ghastly mock-happy grimace.

'Let me get a pen. You can spell it out. No, no, no, no, no. It's gone straight into the book.'

My mother sighed and got up, walked wearily to the kitchen for the shepherd's pie. Tudor threw aside his paper and left the room. He stomped upstairs; a distant door slammed.

'I don't blame him for being cross.' Ci Ci broke the silence that followed. 'Not one little bit. She never says no.' She took a nip of the crème de menthe she drank during meals for her indigestion, and carried on eavesdropping.

'And you're from Tranvancore?' Daisy's delighted voice drifted in from the hall. 'Yes, yes, I know it, of course, a wonderful part of the world. How many nights can you manage?'

Ci Ci was listening avidly, an oily green mark on her lipstick. 'Oh Lord in heaven,' she said. 'She's asking Indians to stay now.' She stroked her dog, breathing deeply.

'Your aunt Ruth's in Eastbourne,' she said to Flora. 'We can always join her there.'

A look of pure panic crossed the girl's face. 'Tudor's promised the house will be quieter soon, Mummy. Can't we wait?' She turned her pleading eyes to me. 'And Kit's going back to London, aren't you?'

I nodded, though I had no clear idea of when.

'I had some splendid news this morning!' Daisy came back with a dish of peas and mashed swedes in her hand. 'My friend Neeta Chacko has found a doctor for us. He trained at Barts, postgrad work at Exeter College, sounds absolutely charming. Speaks good English and Malayalam and is happy to stay with us for a few weeks to work on his thesis and help with the translations. Isn't that marvellous?' She couldn't stop smiling.

'Whoopee.' Ci Ci's voice was slurred. 'More cold baths.'

'Mummy,' murmured Flora.

'Thekkeden.' Daisy spooned shepherd's pie on to Ci Ci's plate. 'That's his surname. Neeta says they're a Nasrani family, well educated, possibly communists. A lot of people from south India are.'

Ci Ci's lip furled. 'Indians. Communists. Better and better.'

'Mummy!'

'It will be nice for Tudor to have some male company in the house,' Daisy said, 'and critical for us.' She had her scheming face on. 'Right, Kit?'

'Right, Daisy.' I smiled back at her, hoping that my mother could cope.

'He'll be here next week,' she said. 'If the snow has cleared.'

Chapter 3

Daisy decided we should welcome the young doctor with a curry. She would drive that morning to Oxford in search of mango chutney. I offered to help my mother in the kitchen because Maud, the previous day, had, on doctor's orders, given in her notice.

Growing up, I'd seen my mother cook the usual ration stodge – rissoles, boiled cabbage, suet puddings – but making curry had a whiff of something secret and special about it, because it only ever happened when we were on our own. She would get out a battered green tin, uncork the small bottles inside it, and, with a finicky, witchy kind of precision that thrilled me, measure out five or six spices. I was under strict instructions never to touch the tin, which she kept in one of the side pockets of her suitcase, or talk about the spices to anyone. When the curry was cooked, she would eat it in a kind of trance, her eyes half closed, very quiet.

But this morning, the old magic wasn't working. Her spine looked rigid as she lashed herself into her apron, a frown line like a sharpened blade between her eyebrows.

'I'll do that, Ma,' I said, seeing a pile of onions and carrots on the draining board. I took an onion and started to chop it, but she snatched the knife from my hand.

'Not like that, like this.' Her hand flew down the onion in a blur. 'There.' She scooped up the tiny pieces and hurled them into the large frying pan. As they sizzled, the air turned blue, and for a second, there she was again: my sorceress, my magician.

Daisy had brought her own spice box home from India, made of carved wood with rows of tiny cupboards inside, each one filled with a different spice. My mother opened it now and sniffed.

'Musty,' she said with an exasperated sigh.

'Tell me what they are.' I was still hoping for a bit of fun with her.

'This is chilli powder, very hot. Fennel seeds, dried coriander . . . I won't put that in, Ci Ci will complain of indigestion. I'll use Daisy's for the chicken curry, and mine for the vegetable. So...' She was lost for a moment, her voice lilting, leaning over the onions, which had started to turn golden at the edges. 'I put the spices in first, warm them nicely... now the lentils—

'Get out! Go away!' Her sudden shout made me jump. It was Sid, Daisy's old black Labrador, who was circling and about to flop down in his usual place in front of the Rayburn. 'No dogs in the kitchen!'

'Keep your hair on, Mummy.' I was soft-hearted about animals. 'He's not the Loch Ness monster.'

'Dogs are full of germs and fleas,' she reminded me once I'd shut him in the freezing hall.

'Now here, come close.' She added a teaspoon of chilli to the lentils. 'These first,' she whispered, 'then the other vegetables.'

And soon it was all lovely in there, with the kitchen filled with smells piquant and strange, the fat hissing, windows steaming, and us absorbed and getting on again. I was accustomed to watching my mother as anxiously as a farmer observes the sky for signs of approaching storms, but now, almost in spite of herself, I saw her whole body soften and relax.

'Stir it clockwise,' she told me, stroking my hand. 'Counter-clockwise is bad luck.'

My mother had a number of strange beliefs like this: don't wash your hair on a Thursday, never shave your armpits on a Monday, things that, when she was in a good mood, I could tease her about.

'Umm.' I closed my eyes, glad to feel the touch of her hand. 'I love these smells.'

'Does Tudor like curry?' she asked out of the blue.

I recoiled from her sly look. 'How should I know?'

'You should make it your business to know.' She dropped my hand. 'Men appreciate these things. And you should change into a dress for dinner, and stop wearing those awful gloves, like some farm labourer, and have you told him about your job?' I had the sense that these reproaches had been backing up dangerously, and now they burst out like steam from a geyser.

'My job?' I dropped the spoon and sat down. 'Why would I talk to him about it?'

'Well Daisy has, because he's mentioned it to me, and by the way, he thinks her charity is madness when the farm is so run down, but anyway.' She'd said what she'd been building up to, and now she continued in her wheedling voice, 'Let's not have a row about it.' She lifted a scrawny chicken from the saucepan. 'Let it cool, take the flesh off it, chop it small.'

But my blood was up. 'Why are you so ashamed of it?' Meaning the midwifery training. 'Why do you hate it so much?'

'Because...' Her hand was on the steaming carcass, water streaming from its bottom. 'Most men hate that sort of thing. They find it squelchy.'

In a better mood, I might have laughed. However infuriating she could be, I loved my mother's odd turns of phrase: 'she's gone all bendy' for a friend who was trying to be feminine and seductive; 'I'm forky today' for when she was cross. Today, I wanted to crown her.

'And I'm just so happy,' she went on in a crooning voice, stirring and sniffing, 'to see my lovely daughter looking healthier. That's all. I was terribly worried about you before. God knows what would have happened if the matron hadn't phoned.'

I chopped the chicken and tried to smile. My night sweats, the insomnia, the bouts of weeping, I'd tried to pass off as the after-effects of the flu that had swept through our dormitory, but Matron Smythe, my no-nonsense superior at St Andrew's, had described my inability to get out of bed one morning as 'a perfectly ordinary case of nervous exhaustion brought on by overwork and the war'. Fourteen-hour shifts and sleepless nights had clobbered quite a few of her girls, she'd said.

A dash of rain fell against the window. Ma's dark eyes filled with tears. 'Please, darling,' she said, 'let's not talk about this any more. It only makes us both unhappy. Soak the rice, and we'll sit down with a cup of tea and try and think what on earth we're going to do next. We can't stay here indefinitely, and honestly,' in a fresh spurt of indignation, 'is it really such a crime to want to see you settled and happy?'

We drank the tea, and when she was breathing normally again, she pulled a copy of *Horse and Hound* from her knitting bag and began the obsessive routine I remembered from childhood. The varnished nail skidding over the results for jumping competitions and advertisements for country homes that, she observed with relish, no one could afford to heat now, stopping at the classified sections at the back that were her employment exchange.

' "Hampshire landowner needs housekeeper to run home and do errands, walk dogs, etc.",' she read aloud.

'No good,' I said. 'Woofers.' She had a deep conviction that dogs were filthy and riddled with disease. She was frightened of them too, even the ones she knew.

' "Elderly widower, Derbyshire, desperately seeks all-round factotum to run house, do accounts for small farm and help with entertaining. No pets, small self-contained flat. Time-wasters need not apply." '

She made a small mark with her pencil. Her stories about the old days were hazy and inconsistent, but she'd told me once, she'd worked as the assistant to some big cheese in Indian royalty, the nabob of somewhere or other. And oh! The balls the polo, the fun.

Poor Mummy. My bad mood collapsed at the sight of her hunched over her magazine, her expression both hopeful and cynical. She was circling another advertisement when Ci Ci's face appeared around the door, her expression stagily dramatic.

'Oh the bliss of curry.' She closed her eyes. 'It does take one back.'

'Keep the dog out,' my mother said curtly. 'Nosy bloody woman,' she added when the door had closed.

My spirits sank. Nothing seemed to work any more: not cooking curry, not being together, and it felt in that bleak moment as though we were trapped in a duet that had once been sweet but now played nothing but duff notes. The spice tin went back in her handbag; I cleaned the counter tops. When I looked up, her mouth was struggling.

'Don't say anything,' she said fiercely.

'Is it the onions?'

'Yes, it's the onions.' She wiped her eyes on her apron and went to the sink.

'You hate this, don't you?' I said at last.

'Don't talk for a bit.' She kept her head down. 'And don't feel sorry for me.'

Patches of white were forming on her cheeks, a sure sign of her strongest emotions, and I disliked myself intensely.

'Would you want this?' She was splashing her eyes with water. 'To do this?'

'I like watching you cook,' I said, but only to soothe her, because I knew in a moment of absolute certainty that I must not end up like this: angry and unsatisfied, dependent on the kindness of strangers.

'Oh, fruit pie' – one of her swear words – 'the flipping Rayburn is low again.' She sank to her knees. 'It will take ages to boil the rice when he comes – and take those awful gloves off.'

'For God's sake, Mummy. It's cold in here.'

'Then don't hang around in the kitchen.'

'I thought it would be fun to cook with you.' I was more upset than the occasion warranted, but I couldn't stop myself.

'Well it's not fun,' she said, a wild look in her eye. 'And for your information, I hate making curry.' She was back at the sink, washing her hands like Lady Macbeth. 'I hate the smell of it, the fiddle of it, and now, with the nig-nog coming, I'm going to have to make it all the time.'

The ugly phrase echoed in my mind all afternoon, mingling with the smell of spices that spread so tantalisingly throughout the house. Over tea, taken as usual in the threadbare sitting room, Ci Ci, hunched on a sagging sofa near the fire, sneered at the Indian doctor's qualifications.

'Some of them make them up, you know.'

Through a mouthful of jam sandwich, she told Tudor and Flora that she personally would rather die than set foot in an Indian hospital. Her beady eyes, glaring at us over the rim of her special teacup, were those of a dishevelled old parrot forced to share its perch. 'Does anyone even know which lavatory he'll use?' she said, as if there were dozens of WCs throughout the house rather than just two – one on her floor, one on ours. 'Some of them don't know how, you know. They squat over the bowl like campers.'

Flora closed her eyes. 'Mummy.'

'Flora, you haven't lived there. I have. Twenty-two years.'

'Twenty-two years what?' Daisy appeared, showing no sign of having overheard this unpleasant exchange. 'Any more tea in that pot?'

'In India. Some of our servants were quite wonderful,' Ci Ci improvised quickly. Daisy had reminded us firmly at breakfast that Anto Thekkeden was a clever young man from a distinguished family. He would be a huge asset to the charity and she would appreciate it if we would all make him very welcome. 'Pandit ran our house like clockwork,' Ci Ci continued with a sneaky smile to Flora.

'Tell them about the Daimler, Mummy,' said Flora, who was a useful prompt when the occasion demanded it.

'Oh yes, our lovely, lovely car.' Ci Ci turned to Tudor, who was looking blankly at her. 'Pandit worshipped the thing. Couldn't stop polishing it, put lovely fresh mints in the glove box. I—'

A knock at the door interrupted her. Maud's husband, Dave, stood there, breathless and important.

'Miss Barker, sorry to trouble you, but a young coloured gentleman has fallen in the ditch. He come on a motorbike, skidded and fell in.'

'Did you leave him there?' Daisy sprang from her seat.

'Well, miss, I didn't know if you'd want him up at the house, like.'

'Oh for heaven's sake, of course we want him in the house,' Daisy snapped. 'Get a torch, and I'll come with you.' She turned to my mother. 'Glory,' she said, 'go upstairs quickly and check the bathroom is presentable. He'll be sopping wet and will need a bath before supper. Honestly.'

She sent me to the barn to finish the invitations to a talk she was giving the following week entitled 'Infant Mortality in India'. I was licking envelopes when I heard the throaty roar of a motorbike coming up the drive, the skid of brakes, and then the opening and closing of the front door.

It was dark by the time I'd finished in the barn. I took a hay net down to Bert, the demob horse, then walked back up the drive. When I got to my room, I saw that my mother had put a blue dress on the bed for me, a pair of pearl earrings beside it. I was struggling with their clips when the lights went out. Melting snow down in the valley, Daisy had warned us, happened every year. As I felt my way downstairs, step by step, I could hear the splash of the Indian doctor having his bath. Daisy was on her hands and knees in the hall, getting oil lamps from the cupboard.

We lit around ten of them, and placed them at strategic points around the house. Golden light pooled round the portraits of the frock-coated ancestors in the hall and gave them a startling intimacy. It bounced off the glass eyes of the stuffed foxes, the eagle bagged near Pondicherry. My mother was frightened of the dark, so I went into the kitchen to help her. She was standing motionless beside the battery of small dishes she'd prepared to go with the curry.

'Oh Mater,' I said, 'this smells nose-toddlingly good.'

It was our joke once to speak like this when the lights failed, pretending that we were toffs in a Georgette Heyer novel. Tonight she wouldn't play.

'It's all gone wrong,' she said, the whites of her eyes showing through the gloom. 'No grated coconut, no mango, no fresh tomatoes. I'm fed up with rationing.'

She plonked a dish of dried-up raisins on the table, along with the WI green apple chutney that Daisy had found in a cupboard under the sink, having drawn a blank in Oxford.

'Is he here?' she said. 'Have you seen him?'

'He's having a bath.'

'In Ci Ci's bathroom?'

'Yes.'

'Oh my God.' She closed her eyes. 'This is going to be awful.'

We'd set the table with white linen napkins, the good plates, and what was left of the Waterford crystal. Did I say that Daisy had bought a beautiful cedar table in India and shipped it home? Terribly impractical, but it looked lovely that night polished to a high conker-coloured sheen. I think it was Daisy who told me once that you never regret your extravagances; this had been one of hers, and it always raised my spirits to see it.

When we walked in with the trays, Ci Ci, Flora, Daisy and Tudor were blurred figures in the candlelight. My first sighting of him was as a vague silhouette against the dark doorway, and when he got closer, a slim man in a too-large jacket that looked peculiar on him, like a boy wearing his father's clothes. His face was in shadow. Daisy leapt towards him.

'Everybody,' she looked down the table towards us, 'I have the greatest pleasure in introducing you all.' She pointed to each of us in turn and said our names. 'And this,' with a drum-roll inflection to her voice, 'is Dr Anto Thekkeden, from south India.'

'And more recently from a ditch near Whitney,' he said. His voice was cultivated, Home Counties clipped, with just a faintly buttery undertone, a purring of the 'r's that sounded foreign. I was surprised by it, expecting the Indian sing-song that Tudor had done as a turn before the visitor arrived.

We laughed politely.

'That corner is a brute,' said Daisy. 'What kind of motorbike do you drive?'

'It's a Norton, twin cylinder. Very old, and the tyres are bald.'

'But frightfully economical on petrol, I expect.' Flora was determined to be kind, or maybe to head off Ci Ci, who'd been muttering about hotels.

Anto sat between Tudor and Flora. I was opposite him. The fuzzy light from the candles meant I couldn't see him clearly at first, but when the light suddenly bloomed, oh Lord, he was handsome: high dignified cheekbones, a wide and tender-looking mouth, and pale cinnamon-coloured skin that made him look more like a Spanish grandee than an Indian. The other striking thing was his eyes: wide-set and almond-shaped and green, and at this moment expressing a polite, faintly quizzical watchful interest in the proceedings.

Daisy had asked me earlier to get the conversational ball rolling.

'I'm Kit,' I said, flustered enough to forget we'd been introduced.

'I'm Anto,' he said as if we hadn't. He stretched his hand across the table and I shook it.

'And you know Mrs Mallinson,' I said, to show I wasn't a complete idiot.

'Delighted to meet you,' drawled Ci Ci, at her most patrician. She'd put on lots of eye make-up, and her silk jacket had a small cigarette burn on the lapel.

'It's a pleasure to meet you all,' he said softly.

Yes, a Spanish grandee, I thought, without the faintest idea really of what a grandee looked like, except from the pages of *The Spanish Bride*. And off-puttingly good-looking, my thoughts ran on: unfair and unnecessary for a man to have cheekbones like that, and as for those eyes ... Josie and I had a theory about good-looking men, based on one or two God's-gift-to-women doctors we'd met at the hospital: they were shallow and unreliable and vain, and usually not very bright. It was like earning interest on money you hadn't worked for in the first place.

'Glory has made this in your honour.' Daisy put a steaming plate of chicken and vegetable curry in front of him. 'No luck with the mango chutney, but this is rather good.'

'Thank you.' He closed his eyes and breathed in deeply. 'I haven't eaten curry for years.' For a moment he looked so troubled, I wondered if we'd got it wrong and he was a strict vegetarian like some of the other Indians I'd read about.

My mother reappeared, dressed defiantly in a green satin shift with jade earrings. Family friend, her outfit signalled, not servant. She spooned rice and lentils on to her plate with her usual slightly finicky delicacy, and then looked around the table, where there was a sudden uneasy pause.

'So, Dr Thekkeden,' Ci Ci said at last, her head at an ironical angle. 'What brings you to our shores?'

He put down his knife and fork and looked at her. 'I've been here for ages,' he said in his soft voice. 'I was educated here.'

'Ah! So that's why you speak such good English.' Ci Ci was quite the Bombay hostess again. 'Do have some more of this rather peculiar chutney.'

'What school?' Tudor looked up.

'Downside.' His reply was clipped. 'My parents are Catholic.'

'Oh.' Tudor sounded surprised. 'Is that unusual?'

'The school or the religion?'

'Well, both.' Tudor was sounding prickly.

'It is most unusual,' the young doctor confirmed. 'But my father loves all things English.' A dry note in his voice as he said this, something a little mocking and public-schoolish. 'He would wear plus fours if it wasn't so hot in south India.'

'And what profession does he follow?' from Cici.

'He is a lawyer. He was called to the bar at Lincoln's Inn.'

'Am I correct in thinking Gandhi practised law in England too?' Tudor asked. 'Before he took up spinning and good works?'

Stop peppering the poor man with questions, I thought.

'Gandhi was called to the bar at Gray's Inn,' Daisy jumped in. 'But he never practised here. I met him once in Bombay, you know, where we ran a children's home. He is a great man.'

'A great man,' Anto confirmed quietly. 'I've been reading about him in the papers.' I noticed that the cuffs on his jacket were frayed.

'Would you like some more rice?' I asked.

'I would.' He looked at me across the table. 'Thank you.'

I walked to the sideboard, where the food was kept warm on a small steel tray with three candles underneath it.

'Sit down.' My mother spoke for the first time. 'I'll do it.'

'The food is very good,' he told her. 'Thank you.'

I saw her considering whether to tell him about her job in India now or later. The governor, the picnics, the polo games.

But Flora said, 'So did you get stuck here during the war?'

'Sort of,' he replied.

'Stuck here!' There was a note of muted outrage in Ci Ci's voice. It was all right for her to hate England, but it was cheek for an Indian.

'My father was keen for me to do my medical training at Barts, and then the war came. I haven't been home for years.'

'So you're practically one of us,' said Daisy.

He didn't answer, just a little smile.

'Did you mind?' Flora asked. She was wide-eyed, like a child.

He put down his fork and stopped eating.

'That's a big question,' he said. 'None of us expected the war.'

'Will you go home soon?' Daisy asked.

'That is the plan.' He looked at her directly and gave an almost smile. 'I'm worried they won't recognise me. And may I ask about you?' He addressed the table generally.

'Oh, us.' Ci Ci's lip furled backwards, showing her sharp little teeth. 'We're empire flotsam and jetsam.' She laughed to show this was a charming and self-deprecating joke. 'We're renting here while we catch our breath.'

After a sip of Daisy's surprisingly potent elderflower wine, she rambled on at length about the Daimler, and Godfrey's factory. How India had taken years off Godfrey's life, and how Gandhi had spoiled things by stirring people up.

'Sorry about this,' she flung a defiant look around the table, 'but I personally thought he was a ghastly little man, sitting there spinning in his nappy.'

Daisy was shaking her head in warning, but said nothing.

'Just a tiny bit more, dear.' When Ci Ci held her glass towards Tudor, I stood up.

'Would you like me to show you your room?' I said to the doctor. 'It's on the first floor.'

My mother shot me a look of pure venom.

'What a splendid idea.' Daisy looked relieved. 'There was only time for a bath before dinner.'

'Thank you,' he said. 'I'd like that.' And to Daisy, and my mother, 'A delicious meal. I can't thank you enough. I look forward to seeing you all tomorrow.'

As we left the room, the door releasing an icy draught, Ci Ci Mallinson said quite audibly, 'Well he's got good table manners – that's something, I suppose.'

Chapter 4

The girl, whose name was Kit, stood up with a forwardness that startled him. She must have thought he needed rescuing. He didn't. He filed all such conversations in his mind under Indya : press the button and you got reams of stuff from the ex-colonials about the railways and the ungratefulness; or rhapsodies about the sunsets! the spirituality! the smells! not forgetting the dust and the fires. Add in the spices and you had Parfum de Partition.

In the hallway, she picked up his briefcase – 'I can take this' – leaving the heavier bag for him. He almost blushed, conscious of the packet of French letters tucked away amongst the few shirts, his cigarettes, the missal his mother had packed with the note inside saying: *Don't forget your prayers*. The condoms were standard issue for red-blooded medical students, but for him an invitation to a dance full of complications.

Walking upstairs in the glow of the lamplight, he did his best to ignore her slim ankles, the straight lines of her stockings, the silk sway of her dark hair. Women were off limits now that he was going home. To make this absolutely clear to himself, he'd gone back to Downside the week before, and spoken in great confusion to his moral tutor, Father Damian: a dear, fat old man with a great sense of humour, who had made his life so much better during his four years there.

Over a glass of port in the book-lined study, he'd started with the smaller sin first: he was addicted to going to the cinema, and it was time spent away from his PhD.

Father Damian had taken a sip, bunched his eyebrows judiciously. 'Exactly how many hours a week do you donate to this pastime?'

'Sometimes a whole afternoon.'

'And what proportion of the week do you devote to your studies?'

Anto thought about this. 'It depends if I have lectures or tutorials.'

'Include both in the sum.'

'Ninety, one hundred, sometimes more, I have to get my doctorate before I go home.'

'I think God may forgive you a little time off.' Father Damian's smile was dry and fond. 'And working too hard is itself a sin, you know. But I hope,' he added with a sly look, 'you have the intellectual rigour to watch Eisenstein and not a lot of old tosh. I do worry about your cultural bearings – remember our night at the opera?'

Anto had never been allowed to forget it: the excruciating performance of *Madame Butterfly* during his first term at the school. His eardrums so tortured by the foreign screeching, he'd sat, hands over his ears, wanting to howl like a dog.

But films were different. A drug, a way of forgetting and finding yourself inside the faces on the screen. He'd sat in the dark, avidly noticing the details: the manners of the handsome men up there, their way of smoking, of greeting women, of leaving rooms, and this close attention had led to him becoming a clever mimic who could make others laugh.

Towards the end of this pleasant meeting, Father Damian had wondered if there was something else troubling him, and suggested that if there was, he might take advantage of his time here and go to confession. Half an hour later, he'd knelt in the school chapel and, breathing in the smells of incense and old velvet, blurted out his confusion and pain.

During the past couple of years, he'd slept with two women, out of lust not love. One of them, a student nurse at Barts, a nice girl, fair-haired, ethereal-looking, had fallen in love with him, and been badly hurt when he couldn't return the feeling. The other, a worldly WAAF, boyfriend in France, had said afterwards, 'I've always wanted to sleep with a foreign man,' making him feel like an exotic pet allowed for one moment into the sitting room.

With his lips close to the grille, he gave an abridged version of these events, and in the silence that followed, felt the familiar cold breath of the chapel floor.

The priest coughed behind the curtain. He said that while God understood that war made many men lustful in ways they didn't comprehend, Anto must now, given the particular circumstances of his life, make an extra effort to control himself.

Was he mistaken in thinking there was a bride waiting for Anto in south India? Not a bride, Anto had said, a young girl, the daughter of a family friend. He'd never met her, or if he had, he couldn't remember her – he'd come to England when he was fourteen. Well, God would forgive him, the priest had said more robustly, but only if he now made a solemn commitment to change. The war had bent everyone out of shape, he added; it was time to return to the old certainties.

The old certainties, Anto had thought later, back in his Oxford digs, eating the cold macaroni cheese his landlady had left on a tray; what a luxury it would be to know what they were. For years, the idea of a God, loving or otherwise, had been slipping away from him, like a small boat unmoored and disappearing on a dark sea.

'This is it.' She opened a carved door at the end of the corridor and lifted her candle. 'Your room.'

When the lights pulsed and flickered into life, both of them jumped.

'Thank God for that,' she said. Her smile was very pretty. 'We have a dreadful time with the electrics here. If you like, I could give you a torch?'

'Thank you,' he said. He'd smashed his own when he'd fallen off the Norton.

He looked around him. He liked his new room. With its tilted floor and cracked ceiling it was shabby for sure, but far more homely than his digs in Woodstock Road. The walls were covered in a lovely old blue Chinese wallpaper; its vines and birds were a little water-marked here and there, but that gave it a kind of faded grandeur. The brass bed with its comfortable-looking blue eiderdown faced the window, from which he could see the dark shapes of the valley beyond.

'Is it all right?' She was watching him.

'It's lovely.'

'Bedside light.' When she leaned and switched it on, the room became a cosy cave. 'Washstand,' pointing at a large jug. 'Basin, towel. You must be tired.'

'No,' he said, 'I'm not.' He hesitated. 'Actually, I spent the afternoon in the Odeon in Oxford.' He didn't tell her about the five a.m. start to study the paediatrics bible. One of the many disguises learned early on at Downside was to saunter into exams saying he didn't know a bloody thing but what the hell?

'What did you see?'

He handed her his ticket. When she peered at it under the lamp, he saw the chestnut gleams in her hair.

'Celia Johnson. *Brief Encounter*.'

'Damn! I missed it! We've been snowed in.' She handed the ticket back. 'Never mind, I've seen it twice.'

'I shall never, *ever* tell anyone else about us,' he said, with Trevor Howard's look of crushed nobility.

'Because all I want is to know that you are safe,' she replied.

Her laughter was velvety and deep. It showed her white teeth. 'What a lot of tosh,' she said.

'Complete pap,' he agreed, although he'd sat there entranced. 'But it passed a pleasant few hours, and I didn't want to arrive too early.'

'The last picture I saw,' she said, 'was a real stinker: *The Steam Railways of Mid-Wales*. I thought I would die of boredom. Do you go to the cinema a lot?'

She was standing next to the bed, looking at him with her direct gaze, and part of him was shocked. Why did her mother allow her to go unescorted to a man's room? Where was everyone?

'When work allows it,' he said in a discouraging way. 'You see, I'm—'

'Kit!' A sharp voice interrupted him. 'Kit, come down here at once.' The voice rose to a screech. 'Where on earth are you?'

'I am twenty-eight years old,' she said, with a conspirator's grin. 'My mother thinks I'm two.'

'You must go at once.' His face was stern in the lamplight, his expression sincere. 'Your mother is calling you.'

Chapter 5

'Ma, stop it!' I said as she practically arm-wrestled me downstairs. 'What on earth are you doing?'

'Taking you outside, so I can talk to you,' she replied grimly.

'Fine with me,' I said, and meant it. She was a shouter when riled, and I had no intention of being a floor show for the other guests. She marched me across the yard and into the barn. I lit the lamp.

'How could you?' she bellowed when the door closed behind us, her face witchy and mean in the storm light.

'How could I what, Glory?' I used her name to remind her I was a grown-up.

'Take that man up to his room and stay with him so long. Everybody was waiting for you to come down.'

Everybody of course meant Tudor.

'You were busy, Daisy was busy, I did it to help.'

'To *help*? By being alone with a man?'

I would have laughed had I not been so angry myself.

'Glory,' I said, as patiently as I could, 'I was a nurse during the war.' I could have told her here about wiping the lips of wounded men, emptying their chamber pots, feeding them, changing their pyjamas, and yes, seeing their most secret parts – what my mother would have called their nooks and crannies – but even in the heat of battle, I needed to protect her.

'And look where nursing got you.' Her eyes were glittering with spite. 'Right back here again.' She looked around at the barn's cobwebby bridles and moulding hayricks, and shuddered theatrically as her eyes settled on a two-foot-high technical drawing, 'The Anatomy of the Genital Tract'.

'Have you any explanation for your behaviour?' she said when she had recovered.

'That foul old bag was attacking him,' I said. 'You know how nasty she gets.'

'Oh, so a world saviour now, like Daisy,' my mother said sarcastically. 'And look where it got *her*.'

I disliked it when my mother sneered at Daisy: a deep mistrust of intellectual women – 'bluestockings' – that came from her own insecurities.

'Get this into your head, Kit.' She held up a finger. 'Number one: you are not a skivvy here – your job is in the office: you're a volunteer, you're Daisy's friend.'

'Can't you see any good in this?' I asked her.

She looked down for a second. 'Oh blast it!' Our walk across the yard had rimmed her suede shoes with mud and melted snow. She set about them frantically with a sheet of discarded writing paper from the waste-paper basket.

'Second' – with a dainty gesture, she dropped the dirty paper back in the bin – 'never, ever go unattended into the bedroom of an Indian man. You don't know them. I do. They are absolute predators, and they see all European women as sluts... Don't look so shocked. I'm only telling you what is true.'

I rubbed my arm where she had pinched it so hard, and pulled away from her. She'd once thrown a lamp at my head in a fury when I wouldn't wear the dress she'd laid out, and now she had the same wild look in her eyes. She'd bathed the cut later and given me a doll as a 'sorry present', and said she loved her little girl more than anything else in the world but it was just so hard sometimes being all on our own together. And I'd hugged her back, flooded with sweet relief at us being friends again, and kept the doll, seeing loneliness for ever after in its glass button eyes.

'I'm a grown-up now,' I said.

'That's exactly the point. I want you to find someone nice, to settle down, have babies, a proper home.'

I had a sinking feeling as she said this; the doll with the glass eyes was back in my arms.

'The thing is,' I replied, 'quite soon, I want... I have to go back to London and finish the midwifery course.' I had to say the word every now and then, as if to inoculate her. 'It won't take long, I—'

'Oh, that.' She squeezed her eyes shut. 'Please, for God's sake, don't talk about that now.'

A sudden wind rattled the barn doors and swayed the flame in the oil lamp. My mother, who was terrified of ghosts, clutched me in genuine terror.

'It's all right.' I put my arms around her. 'There's nothing here.' And then – oh how quickly her moods could change – she gave me a real hug, and I smelled her perfume (Shalimar), and a whiff of cardamom from the curry cooking.

'I'm sorry,' she said in a muffled voice. 'There are too many people here, and it's driving me a little doolally. And I can't stand that old bat either. She never has a nice word to say about anyone.'

She gave a little croaking laugh that I could not return, and then looked around the barn with wide eyes.

'It's stopped raining. Let's go back. I hate it out here.'

'Give me a moment to lock up,' I said. Her nails were digging into my arm.

'I know you're a big help to Daisy,' she continued. She glanced again at the poster. 'It's just such a strange job to choose: I don't know how you can do it.' She shuddered and clutched me more tightly.

'I know,' I said, feeling fraudulent. I was scared of it myself.

Chapter 6

He woke very early, and stood at the window, looking out at misty grey fields, some ghostly cows, a church spire on the horizon. He re-made the view into bright blue skies above the silent green backwaters of the Periyar. He would be there soon, and needed to compass his mind, and not get lost.

It was cold in the room. With an overcoat over his pyjamas, he sat at a desk in the window, working on his PhD thesis on sleeping sickness – *The Care and Treatment of Encephalitis Lethargica* – which had quietly obsessed him for two years. He was paying particular attention to a major outbreak between 1896 and 1906 in Uganda and Congo, in which close to a quarter of a million people had died, and where foreign aid had been patchy and poorly coordinated, leading to unedifying squabbling between the richer nations.

It was a sobering subject to live with day in and day out, and he was desperate to finish. He secretly hoped the work with Miss Barker would not take up too much time, even though it would pay for his rent and food.

Deep in his studies, he worked on, skipping breakfast, until the knock on his door reminded him they were to meet at 10.30.

'I must apologise in advance,' she bounced beside him as they walked towards the barn, 'for making you, temporarily, the lone male in what Shakespeare called a monstrous regiment of women. We didn't plan it that way. In fact, we absolutely welcome the masculine point of view, but Indian doctors who speak Malayalam aren't thick on the ground around here, and we're up to our eyebrows at the moment with fund-raising and speeches and so forth, and ... well, this is it.'

She unlocked the huge door, and together they stared into the cavernous space.

'HQ Moonstone. We've cleared a desk for you near the fire; make yourself at home there. There's rugs in the corner for when we're really freezing,' she added. He liked her already, her big friendly teeth, her air of purpose.

'Miss Barker,' he sat down, keeping his coat on, 'I hope I'm not here under false pretences – my circumstances mean that my Malayalam might be rusty.'

She stopped moving papers and gazed at him sympathetically. 'What a rotten thing, being caught out by the war like that.'

'I was one of the luckier ones.' He had fought against the role of poor Indian boy for years, particularly at school, where chinks in your armour were ruthlessly exposed. 'But my main goal now is to finish my thesis before I go home.'

'May I ask what it's on?'

'Human African trypanosomiasis. Sleeping sickness,' he added helpfully. 'Have you heard about the epidemic?'

'I have, and it was appalling. How very worthwhile.' She peered at him in frank admiration. 'I vaguely remember that a number of foreign powers tried to combine aid, and it led to the usual complications.'

'I'd be happy to show it to you.' He felt a tug of eagerness; it was rare now for people to even know about the disease.

'And when you finish it, you'll be a double doctor. What an achievement. Tell me, are you very swotty, or just naturally clever?'

'Is there a good answer to that?' he asked, with a quizzical smile.

'One that doesn't make you sound like a fascinating big-head?' They smiled at each other. 'You're probably both, but anyway, onwards. Here's the plan. If you can spare an hour or two for translation in the afternoon, you're free to do your own work in the morning. Does that suit?'

'Perfectly,' he said. 'My passage is booked for next November, so it's good practice for me to speak my own language again.'

It was the thing he most dreaded: forgetting his mother tongue. A few months ago, he'd woken in a sweat after a vivid nightmare in which he stood dazzled, excited, on the quay at Fort Cochin. His mother had run towards him – spotless white clothes, soft brown skin, the thick gold hoops in her ears glinting – but when he tried to speak to her, he found that his mouth was sewn up in crude cross stitches.

Inside the barn, there were now three battered desks arranged in a semicircle around the fire. A poster of a gruesomely naked woman was propped against the wall. Not like the naked women sniggered at after lights-out at school, or the anatomical drawings seen at Barts, but the inside of a woman, with all her pipework, her veins, her arteries, her secret caves shockingly exposed.

'That's a work in progress. Do you find it a bit lurid? Do be honest.'

'From whose point of view? Don't forget I'm a doctor.'

'Well...' He sensed her struggling not to patronise him. 'Yes, of course, I don't mean *you*, but this is part of our dilemma. Some of the Indian midwives we'll be instructing may be very experienced, very technically skilled, but they will have absolutely no idea what a woman looks like inside.'

'Miss Barker,' he said after a desperate pause, 'I am at sea here. I left India when I was very young.' *Deliver me from evil, from temptation, from embarrassment* ran in a silly conga line through his head.

'And what about at Barts? Did you receive any instruction about childbirth at all?'

'Remarkably little,' he admitted. The truth was, the war had disrupted and reduced quite a bit of their training – at one point, the hospital had become a casualty-receiving centre. Later, they'd been moved to Cambridge, where, accompanied by much raucous laughter, they'd raced through reproduction and birth in a week.

'Before I start,' she said, 'would you be kind enough to call me Daisy? Miss Barker makes me feel like a maiden aunt. And another thing... Kit, who occupies that desk,' she pointed to the one beside him, 'has a delightful but rather highly strung mother. She doesn't approve of her daughter doing this kind of work, so we try not to talk about it in the house. Does that sound very silly to you?'

'Not at all.' He was amazed she would ever imagine he would discuss such things in mixed company. 'I shan't say a word.'

'So,' she began again delicately, 'I'm to start from the assumption that you know nothing about midwifery in India.'

'Absolutely nothing,' he replied promptly. 'The only thing I know is that the midwives in some parts of the country are called *dais*.'

'Correct.'

'And that when a baby was being born in our house, the men kept out of the way.'

'It's a shame men are kept out of it.' Her clever eyes sought his. 'Sad to say, India has a truly lamentable rate of infant mortality – one of the worst in the world. The British should have done far more to tackle it while they were there. They didn't, and that's a permanent blot on our record.'

She briefed him concisely about the hospital in Cochin, and their aim of combining the best of West and East in its practices.

'Many of your village midwives have more knowledge in their little fingers than our Western-trained midwives will acquire in a lifetime. They come from generations of midwives, who have delivered thousands of babies. Alienate them and we lose a vast sea of valuable knowledge. But some of these women,' she pulled a mournful face, 'are shockers: they cut umbilical cords with rusty knives, jump on bellies to speed births, drag placentas out. We have to teach them that small things like basic hygiene and medical kits will make a vast difference. Our aim is to become an extended family in which we all learn. What do you think?' She gazed at him hopefully.

'It sounds very impressive,' he said politely, while all kinds of alarm bells were clanging in his mind. He'd read in the papers about the tidal wave of fury unleashed after the British had left.

'To date,' Daisy's glasses flashed at him as she showed him an account book, 'we've managed to raise the sum of two hundred pounds for teaching equipment and medicine, which we plan to take to India in three months' time to help maintain the home. Kit's been a marvellous support with our begging letters, and with your help, we can get the training manuals right. Is there anything else you'd like to know?'

'I don't think so,' he said.

The barn door rattled as the girl walked in. She wore a raincoat and gumboots, and an unflattering headscarf. Her cheeks shone with rain. 'God, it's hideous out there.' She wrestled the door closed against the wind. 'Sorry I'm late.'

As she swept off the scarf, her dark hair fell in a cloud around her shoulders. She sat down on a stool near the fire and performed an unintentionally erotic striptease, inching off one gumboot with the heel of the other, revealing her slim lower legs.

'Have I missed the sales pitch, Daisy?'

'Nothing you haven't heard before. How's your mother's head-ache? Did she make breakfast in the end?'

'Not good. I should probably leave early. So, Dr Thekkeden,' she turned towards him with a professional smile, 'how was your night in the Bird Room? Good, I hope.'

'We're going to call him Anto,' said Daisy.

'Anto,' she said.

'And Kit,' he replied shyly.

'Is Anto an unusual name in India?' She unbuttoned her raincoat and set it on a pitchfork near the fire to dry; tugged at her skirt to straighten it.

'Not for a Catholic boy,' he said. 'Most of us have Christian names. My family call me *An*to,' he said, putting the stress on the first syllable.

'*An*to.' Her plump lips cupped the sound.

He took a deep breath, and said, to distance her, 'Does that sound more Indian?'

She gave him a straight, unembarrassed look.

'I don't know, but I shall definitely call you that.'

'Whatever you like.' He gave her a brief smile, and opened the file he had brought with him.

'Well, Anto, don't let me interrupt you,' she said. If she'd registered the slight, she showed no sign of it. 'I have a ton of letters to write.'

They worked in silence until lunchtime. The silence was soothing, giving him time to restore himself amongst his research. Being in the company of women was pleasant too, he reflected, after being alone now for months, in libraries, or in his digs, often working between damp-smelling sheets in bed to keep warm. This must be the reason for the unusual, slightly electric glow he was feeling.

When the lunch bell rang out across the yard, Kit stood up. 'I've replied to most of the letters in the "yes" tin, Daisy,' she said. 'There's a very angry nurse in the other pile. I'll sort her out after lunch if that's all right.' Her blue Fair Isle sweater rose as she stretched – a slim waist, a glimpse of liberty bodice. 'I'm starving,' she said. She turned to Anto. 'How about you?'

Chapter 7

In early March, I got a letter from St Andrew's saying that my course had had to be postponed until the new academic year. The roof of the nurses' home had been deemed unsafe, and with much of London still in ruins, it was impossible to find builders to fix it before the new term began.

When I told my mother, she said, 'So, together again like old times.' She dabbed her eyes and gave me her loving look, and from long habit I smiled back and returned her quick hug. But my feelings were complicated, and since our row, I had become more and more secretive with her.

The truth was that as much as I loved the peace of Wickam Farm, without the Moonstone work, and the challenge of helping Daisy, I would have been climbing the walls by now. There was also something else far more troubling to me, which was the Indian doctor.

For the first few weeks, he'd expressed a preference, in the politest way possible, for working on his own in the Bird Room during the mornings. He also skipped breakfast. I was never sure whether this was due to my mother's chilly treatment of him, or his way of avoiding Tudor and Ci Ci, but it had definitely helped with my mother's worries about having this potentially wild beast housed under the same roof as her daughter.

Daisy tried to talk him out of working in his room, saying, rather shamefacedly, that they could only afford now to light two fires: one in the dining room, the other the ancient solid fuel range in the barn. But he'd insisted, until, during one particularly bitter week in February, the rotten wood surrounding his window had fallen away with a chunk of Virginia creeper, and though, with extra blankets, he could sleep in the room, it was too cold to work there.

For the first few days, we sat several feet from each other at the old school desks that had been brought down from the nursery. I was making sketches and notes from Comyns Berkeley's *Pictorial Midwifery*, and sending out letters. His glossy head was bent over piles of academic textbooks.

Whenever I sneaked a glance at him, I was amazed by his industry and his concentration, because for years I'd heard my mother say that Indians were lazy and stupid, and this was why they'd let the British lord it over them. Ci Ci often sang the same song, recalling servants straining soup through their turbans, or needing a good boot up the 'you know what' to get them going at all.

I felt a spurt of jealousy too sometimes. Men were lucky that way, I thought, remembering how my mother had dragged me away from my school books, saying that if I worked too hard it would ruin my looks. Men, she warned me, were put off by bluestockings, whereas a man's industry was applauded, fed with meals and cups of tea and not interrupted by countless scurrying tasks.

But anyway, it was me who started making him cups of tea; at first because I felt sorry for him missing breakfast, and later because it gave me a queer happy feeling putting the kettle on for him, pouring water into the teapot, adding his spoonful of sugar from the jam jar, and carrying the mug over to him.

When I handed it to him, he would look up and smile at me – the sweetest smile that lit up his face – before going back to his books again. Working together like this felt domestic, contented, even though I was sometimes aware of a deep reserve about him, not exactly shy, but deliberate, and I could never be sure which version of him I would be presented with.

One day, as I was measuring out two spoonfuls of tea, he told me that his uncle grew tea in the hills above Travancore. He had vague memories of his first visit there as a child, and how grown up he had felt when an aunt had found him a special cup and poured him his first taste of tea. When he mimed a child's solemn, serious face, I saw what a dear little boy he must have been, with those long-lashed green eyes. But when I looked at him again, I found him intimidating, with his high jutting cheekbones, that remote Spanish grandee look.

Shadow and sunshine, I thought when, the following day, he put the tea cosy on his head and said in the plummy tones of an elderly vicar, 'Thank you, my good woman, six lumps will suffice,' and I laughed too much and felt light-headed.

He was a very good mimic. One of the reasons, I suspect, why

45

he never complained of any bullying or name-calling at Downside, where, he said, apart from a few twits, he'd made good friends. Daisy told me he had been in the first XI cricket team too, which must have helped.

Our laughter felt shockingly indiscreet, like the piercing of something formal, and afterwards I found myself shaking, and was relieved when Daisy appeared.

I'd started to eavesdrop when he was working with Daisy; I liked hearing him speak in his own tongue. It turned his voice into something buttery and strange, which I felt as a pulse in my stomach. I felt it hurt him too: when he stumbled on simple words, he winced like a man setting out on a familiar walk and finding glass strewn under his feet.

Daisy agreed it must be peculiar to speak your own language again after so many years, and particularly to be discussing childbirth, sexual intercourse, ovulation, periods.

She said she'd let him off translating words like vagina, and nipples. 'The poor boy left home so young, I doubt he even knows them.' These omissions could easily be filled in by Neeta, she said, who would add her own contributions to the notes when they arrived in India.

So far, so purposeful. After a few weeks of this, we started to feel like a good team in the barn. Something separate from the house, something new to rescue us from the dreariness of rationing, and February gales, and the strange silence and even stranger memories the war had left.

Daisy had started to give talks, to the local WI and to some university societies, and these, plus a jumble sale and our begging letters meant that a slow trickle of money was coming in. The refurbishing of the Moonstone home, scheduled for autumn that year, was beginning to look entirely possible.

And then Tudor began to drop in to the barn at inconvenient intervals, in what I can only describe as a proprietorial way.

He sprawled on the edge of my desk and monologued self-consciously about his jazz collection, or his socialist principles, or some archaeological paper he was about to publish. If he spoke to Anto at all, it was antler-clashing stuff about old schools and cricket scores and university results, or else he was noisily sympathetic about Anto having to put up with 'the girls'.

As the days wore on, the sight of his bony tweed bottom on the corner of my desk made me want to scream, or stick a pin in it, but I tried not to show it, both for Daisy's sake and my mother's.

It was my mother, I was sure of it, who was encouraging these visits; her mind leaping ahead to a wedding in St Peter's Church, which was part of the farm, to food for the reception, to manicures, hats, canapés. And why not? Or so she would reason. In the deliberately classless world of Wickam Farm, anything could happen.

But another fly in the custard was Ci Ci, who, noticing Tudor's visits to the barn, began to unsheathe her claws. Poor Flora; poor me: reluctant gladiators for a prize neither wanted. Or maybe Flora did; she'd become so wary of her mother, it was almost impossible to tell.

The storm finally broke one night when Ci Ci was in bed with a hot-water bottle and a tray, because she had a bad cold. Anto was working in the barn; Daisy was in Cheltenham giving a speech and my mother was tidying up in the kitchen.

On that freezing wet day, Tudor had laid aside his socialist principles to swagger off in plus fours to shoot at the Blenheim estate, which was close to us. He'd come back garlanded with dead birds that he wore on a string around his neck. At dinner, when my mother brought in the partridge, nestled in bacon and with a sage and onion sauce on the side, he regarded them with the complacent pride of a man who had just slapped a bison on to the cave floor.

'I took 'em down just behind the Shakenoak Wood,' he said, in his usual careless drawl. 'Lord Clyde was there too, but his dog had a bad day, so they both retired. Here, have some of this. I found it in the cellar – it's Pomeroy 1935, very good.' He looked at me. 'Part of your education.'

He got out a set of Waterford glasses, poured a full one for himself, one for me, and a thimbleful for Flora, who was profuse in her thanks.

The wine was a surprise. Usually, if we drank at all, it was Daisy's carrot, damson or elderflower, combustible and variable brews that might have a thin layer of green mould on the surface, and occasionally went off like bomb blasts in the larder.

I had no idea what the significance of Pomeroy 1935 was, but the taste was good and I liked the warm burr it gave to my bones.

'When you drink a fine wine,' Tudor instructed me, 'you should hold your glass like this.' He put one hand daintily around the stem.

'Never by the bulb. Hold the wine in your mouth for a moment' – his eyes moistly intently on mine – 'then roll it around.' His thin lips rotated. 'And swallow.' His Adam's apple bobbed.

'Don't you love learning new things?' a suitably entranced Flora was saying when Daisy appeared in a wet mackintosh.

'What are we celebrating?'

'Birds,' Tudor said shortly. 'Partridge. Bagged 'em today.'

'Golly, I'm famished.' She unbuttoned her mac. 'This smells wonderful.' She lifted the cover of the silver salver on the sideboard. There was a small amount of partridge left, a few tablespoonfuls of sauce, some bacon, three shrivelled carrots.

'Has Anto been fed?' She stopped helping herself. 'He's still in the barn. I saw the lights on.'

'I thought he went with you,' I said.

'No, too busy. The poor boy must be ravenous. I'll take him some food.'

'I'll go, Daisy,' I said. 'You stay and eat.'

Daisy left the room to hang up her coat, and I put a few morsels of meat and some potatoes on a plate, and what remained of the vegetables. I saw there was about half an inch of Pomeroy left, and picked up the bottle.

'May I take some for Anto?' I asked.

'Don't bother,' Tudor said. 'It'll be against Inky's religion.'

He'd taken to calling him Inky behind his back. When I heard Flora chortling dutifully, I felt a surge of pure rage.

'Don't call him that,' I said.

'It's a joke,' he explained patiently. Some of the wine had stained his chin like a birthmark. 'It's what Billy Bunter calls our tinted brethren.'

'It's not funny,' I said. 'And he does drink wine, you know that.'

'Well, let him bring his own – or take him some of that.' He gestured towards a carafe of damson at the end of the sideboard. 'I don't give a damn.'

The bottle trembled in my hand. I wanted to see wine drip down that smug, taunting face.

'You're pretty when you're angry,' he said, just as Daisy walked back in.

'Oh you angel,' she said, looking at the plate. 'Sure you don't mind?'

*

48

It was misty outside, and very cold, with the moon hanging behind a skein of clouds. I had the keys to the barn in my pocket. We'd had a minor break-in recently, nothing serious: an old typewriter and £8 in petty cash. When I unlocked the door, I saw Anto asleep at his desk in a pool of yellow lamplight, his head resting on his hands like a child, dark hair flopping forward. There was a sheet of paper under his right hand on which he'd written in his small, neat handwriting: *Oxygen exchange system*. A tiny sandstone elephant sat cross-legged on top of a pile of textbooks.

The fire had gone out, and it was cold enough to see your breath. In the stable next door, I could hear William, the farm horse, munching hay.

As quietly as I could, I crept across the room and relit the stove, and when it was crackling and glowing, I put the tray on the edge of the desk, trying to decide whether or not to wake him. Lord, he was beautiful. I'd never thought of a man being so before. The sharp curve of his cheekbones, the softness of his mouth.

The collar of the tweed overcoat he was wearing was up. I turned it down, and then I touched his hair. A puff of air came from his mouth like smoke.

'Thank you,' he said, quietly.

I leapt back, managing to catch the plate of food in my hands, but the tray fell with a noisy clatter on to the floor, scattering knife and fork and wine, which spilled like blood over the hearth.

'Blast.' I was furious and embarrassed. 'I didn't mean to do that.'

I set the plate back on the desk, and we got down on our hands and knees to pick up the fallen cutlery and mop up the wine. And it was then that he put his hands on either side of my face and kissed me.

'I know,' he said, and kissed me again.

We were kneeling, staring at each other like two people about to be executed, when we both heard the clatter of boots outside the door, the horse stamping in his stable.

'Let me in.' A slurred, angry voice.

'Hang on,' I called, scrambling to my feet.

It was Tudor, red-faced, half-cut, proprietorial.

'Why did you lock it?'

'There was a break-in recently.'

'Silly me. I thought the purpose of a key was to keep robbers out.' He smiled unpleasantly at Anto, showing his yellow teeth.

'Boom, boom, boom, boom!' he suddenly shouted, making his umbrella into a gun and pointing it at the sky. 'Did you enjoy my birds?'

He stood close to Anto, less than a foot away.

'I haven't tasted them yet,' Anto said. His voice was very quiet; I could see a muscle twitching in his jaw.

'Well, I can tell you, they're damned good.' Tudor turned to me. 'It's raining, Kit. You can share my umbrella back to the house. Your mother told me to get you.'

'Thank you,' I said with as much dignity as I could muster – I felt weak-kneed, and uncomfortably aware that my hair was mussed.

I looked at the now cold plate of partridge and potatoes on the desk. Then I turned to Tudor and handed him the tray. 'Could you hold this for me?' I asked, as I loaded it with the dirty cups and cutlery Anto had used earlier in the day.

Bullseye, I thought. You wait on him, you horrible man – he's worth two of you.

A small, sweet victory, which I feared could not last.

Chapter 8

One day he would struggle to even remember the name of the pretty girl at Wickam Farm, or the Bird Room, or the barn. He would shut down this part of his life just as he had shut down India on the ship coming here, or at least managed to cram it into some back room in his mind.

But now, the crunch of loose floorboards above him, Kit's faint tread on the stairs, the clink of her bottles in the bathroom, her dress coming off. To corral his mind, he got out the box from under his bed, and laid out letters and photographs of his family on the eiderdown, and switched on the lamp.

His long-ago family: Appan, his father; Amma, his mother; his sister Mariamma; his grandmother Ponnamma. The women who pinched his cheeks, fed him delicious meals, tucked him into bed at night, loved him until they suddenly sent him away. He tried never to be melodramatic about this, to believe in Father Damian's suggestion that it might have been the making of him.

And underneath, more photographs, splayed like a deck of cards: the extended family groups, hundreds of vaguely remembered ghosts from Christmases, christenings, Onam festivals, weddings. He studied them with the expression of a man cramming for an exam he was bound to fail. He picked up a faded snapshot of his father. Studious, bespectacled, grave, he stood a few feet to the right of a group of young Englishmen. A photo taken, as his father had told him many times, on the greatest day of his life: his graduation from Lincoln's Inn. Appan, wearing his dark Savile Row suit, skinny, scared-looking, standing on some grand steps holding a piece of rolled-up cardboard.

Anto's face clouded as he remembered his father: the handsome, authoritative figure at the end of the table. The family ringmaster who could change the emotional temperature of a room simply by walking in. His car, a bullnose Morris, one of the few in the district. Appan on his way to an important court case in Pondicherry, conker-coloured briefcase bulging with grown-up mysteries; shaking Anto's hand in the hall as he left for an overseas conference: 'Look after your mother.'

His hungry desire to keep his father's love with good results, good cricket innings, good behaviour felt like weakness now. When he fell below Appan's high standards, he saw disgust on his father's face. 'You're on the seventh stair, my friend,' before the cane came out of the top drawer of his desk.

When Anto first arrived in England, there was no sun for days on end, grey skies, grey streets, and he'd wondered if this was the eighth stair: a place where you could die from unhappiness. His abandonment felt so unexpected, so complete, that it almost destroyed the balance of his mind. Being happy, being loved, he now saw, had been the worst preparation possible for a life in which nobody knew him. Not a single soul in England.

His mother wrote to him at Downside. Ordinary things: Pathrose, the servant who'd been with them for ever, cooking prawns and okra in the kitchen; the family cricket match on the lawn with, she'd written, 'an Anto-sized hole in the fielding'. The letters, in her impeccable handwriting, faint tang of jasmine oil on the envelopes, had, in his first term, almost destroyed him. He'd snatched them from the basket in the refectory, where milk and biscuits was served, taken them to his room braced for the exquisite misery of remembering. It was only later that their lurid envelopes had become an embarrassment.

Now, in the lamplight, he squinted at a picture of her in the garden at Mangalath, near the small wooden summer house where she tended her orchids. She was dressed simply in the plain white cotton *chatta* and *mundu* she wore at home. Her dark eyes were gazing at the camera with a look that was both distant and scrutinising. Anto was sitting on a tricycle at her feet, his expression pure and trusting as he looked up at her. She was his entire world.

Any moment now she would give up her camera face (she'd always loathed having her picture taken) and scoop him up murmuring, 'My little pot of gold.' Her only son, after years of trying. He could hear her in the kitchen now, barking orders to the servants, clinking the battered saucepans. The spices prickling his nostrils.

He turned the photo over. *Mangalath. Anto. Three years old.*

With a sigh, he picked up his mother's latest letter. It was dated 13/02/1948, postmarked Fort Cochin.

My dearest boy,

I'm sending the pictures taken with my new box Brownie. Sorry to have sliced the head off your father several times. He was the one who gave me the camera for Christmas – not too grateful of me. We had fifty-four family at Mangalath on Christmas Eve, but, as usual, missed you badly. I don't know what I did in a previous life to have suffered without you for so many years, but I hope it will soon make sense to me.

Appan is so proud of you, says the new India needs people like you to show that we can strive and thrive without the British. So I'm proud of you too, and the sacrifices you've made. One day I hope you will be a great man in our community.

I wish I could send you the fresh pineapple we had for breakfast, I know there is still very severe rationing there for you. All I can send is a mother's love and prayers. Your father, up to his neck in a new case, will write separately and send money for your fare.

My love to you,
Amma

PS Today Vidya came with her mother; she asked to see a photo of you, sends hers to you. She says you are handsome!

The sly aside saying the big thing was typical. The girl in the care-fully tinted photograph was slender and shy in what looked like a new sari. She was the daughter of his mother's best friend, beautiful, as his mother had not failed to point out in three of her previous letters. Did Anto remember meeting her when he was a little boy? Answer: not really, or if he did, only vaguely as a shy pair of big brown eyes behind her mother's skirts. It was Anu, her mother, he remembered: the head-patter and bringer of home-made sweets enticingly wrapped in tissue paper, and once a new cricket bat.

This letter, which he'd read anxiously several times, gave Anto a tightness in his scalp, as if part of his brain was shutting down. He was being netted and hauled in, and yet, during the long, lonely years of exile, he'd ached to be home, looked forward to the security of being married to a nice girl, back safely in the bosom of his family again.

Now he lay face down on the pillow, as if to smother his confu-sion and panic. He didn't feel Indian any more, that was the nub of it. During his time in England, he'd got used to freedoms that his family would disapprove of. Going off to the cinema on his own when he felt like it. Having conversations with women who weren't discreetly chaperoned. The one-night stand with the WAAF, a huge and daring adventure before the shame set in. Wearing Western clothes – he had no intention of wearing a *mundu* again; for him it would feel like fancy dress.

But his most pressing problem now was Kit, up there in the room above him in what felt like almost indecent proximity. Knowing she was there, breathing, moving around, was agony, for more than anything else, he wanted to kiss her again.

A rattle from upstairs – her curtains being pulled. Earlier, she'd worn her hair up in a messy bun, stuck a pencil through it while she was working, but now he imagined it tumbling down.

He tried to joke himself out of it, 'My God, Miss Smith, you're beautiful,' because nothing about her had escaped his attention: the curve of her jawline, her dark eyes, her long neck bent over her work, the waterfall of her hair, her flashing smile when he made her laugh.

She was brushing her hair now. She was cleaning her teeth.

'Oh for God's sake.' He looked up, frozen and afraid. 'Stop it, you stupid bastard. Go to sleep.'

Chapter 9

Clearly alarmed at what had passed between us, Anto went back to working in the Bird Room in the mornings. When we met in the dining room, I saw that he looked exhausted, and he would not meet my eye. I kept on working, talking, pretending not to care, but I couldn't stop thinking about him: the satin feel of his cheek, the softness of his lips on mine.

The memory kept me awake, and sometimes, when I crept out of the house at night to see if he was awake too, the light was still on in his window, and hearing my own breathing, I felt myself in the position of a suicide trying to talk myself down from the edge.

I wanted him. My body was racing ahead of my brain like a naughty child, frightening me because everything about it was wrong. He was due to return to India in a matter of months; he would marry a girl there, or so Daisy had said, chosen by his parents. And it went without saying that my mother would be horrified.

But when, in early April, I got another letter from St Andrew's, saying the building was still bomb-damaged, and our course further postponed until the next academic year, I was not disappointed.

Again my Mother's face lit up, and from long habit I returned her fond look, but my feelings were far more complicated and secretive than I let on. What I wanted most was to speak properly to Anto again, and not get caught.

Was it odd to have fallen for him so quickly? Not to me it wasn't. Not really. I was dangerously ready for love after the war, and he was terribly handsome and impressively clever. He already made me laugh, and he called up a maternal feeling in me because he seemed both brave and lost. There was something else too: I wanted to be properly loved, in the old-fashioned way, by a man, a young man who would exorcise a nasty memory.

There was a time, before I was eighteen years old, when I was so wet behind the ears that I honestly thought you could get pregnant

55

if you kissed a man. One of my mother's employers, Mr Frank Jolly, a Yorkshire optician, a widower, had put an end to that by gently sliding a hand down my school uniform in the car one day. I know it's usual for young girls to say they are appalled by such advances. I wasn't.

What I felt, at least initially with Frank Jolly, was experimental. He was not bad-looking, and he was fairly young. He started to pick me up from school, and at first, his advances were mild enough to be called caresses. But then, one afternoon when my mother was at the pictures, I was shocked when a thing like a landed fish leapt out of his trousers.

We were in the sitting room, the curtains drawn, his face all jumbled and mottled, like a jigsaw gone wrong. He said I'd led him on to this, and as he laid me down on a towel on the sofa, he told me I had to go through with it else my mother would lose her job and there would be a scandal. And I believed him, and went through with it, and afterwards I shouted and cried in the bath trying to wash him away.

When I tried to tell my mother later, she blamed me, or maybe she didn't but it felt like it. She said it was not a bad thing to marry an older man who would do things for you, and that Mr Jolly was an attractive man anyway, so how about settling down with him? I said, 'What about school, my exams? My life?'

'Oh don't be so serious,' she said. I didn't speak to her for three days after that. I felt so empty and pointless: a paper cup tumbling down a stream towards a future entirely out of my hands.

Anto had been waiting for ten days to hear whether his PhD thesis had been passed when a letter with an Exeter College monogram on the envelope arrived. Daisy, who'd once played hockey for the county, snatched the envelope from the postman, raced across the yard with it and pinged it on to his desk.

He went so pale, she asked, 'Do you want me to open it?'

'No,' he said. He stared at it, his lips moving silently.

'Prepare for the worst and expect the best,' Daisy said.

He picked up the letter, touched the sandstone elephant, then gave me a strange look and opened the envelope. A few seconds later he said: 'Dammit, dammit dammit!' His head was in his hands, Daisy and I exchanged a look. This was heartbreaking, horrible – all those hours and hours of burning the midnight oil.

'Anto, I'm so sorry,' I said. 'You worked so hard.'

I wanted to stroke his hair, to find words of comfort that wouldn't sound too maddening.

He looked up at me out of his right eye, then grinned and said: 'Double Doctor Anto Thekkeden, please, from now on. They liked my thesis.'

'You absolute fiend!' Daisy whacked his head with a roll of cardboard, and without thinking, I hugged him. If Daisy noticed the quick kiss he gave me, nothing was said.

'Now, Anto,' she continued, when things had quietened down, 'we must definitely have a party. If we dig around the cellar, there might even be some champagne. We could invite a few people from the village too, to make it more fun.'

Anto was still sitting at his desk, staring ahead, in shock, I imagined, at the good news. His normal way was to be very polite and avoid saying no to anything, but now he looked up and said, 'What I'd most like is to go to the cinema in Oxford.'

'That sounds fun,' Daisy said. 'We can have dinner afterwards at the Cardamon. I'm going to suck up to him now,' she said to me. 'He'll be a great asset to the Moonstone when we get him home.'

'Maybe.' Anto sounded guarded. Daisy's *Notes for Indian Midwives* worried him. We'd had a careful conversation about it the week before.

'She knows that Indians aren't exactly in love with the British at the moment,' I'd said.

'Well and good then,' he'd said softly. 'I know she is a kind lady and that her intentions are honourable, but my fear is that she is stepping into a snakepit. It's all changed since she was there.'

The Ritz on George Street had once been a church, but was now a smoky, exciting dungeon with a flaking plaster angel on the roof and the cinema organist hidden behind a faded red velvet curtain.

Later that night, we followed the usherette's torch towards the middle rows, and I sat down with Tudor on one side and Anto on the other. Flora, wearing a dress of stiff purple satin that crackled like fire, was on Tudor's other side.

The film, *To Each His Own*, was about a girl who fell for a handsome pilot, had his baby, and then spent the rest of her life in mourning for him. Watching it in the dark, with Anto beside me, I felt almost unbearably excited, as if this shabby little cinema was charged with life and some promise of excitement that I could sense in the pit of my stomach.

Halfway through the film, I dropped the box of Black Magic chocolates Daisy had given us. Anto and I both sank to the floor to retrieve them, and when I looked at him, and saw a flash of reflected light in his eyes, it was hard not to take his beautiful face between my hands and plead with him, for what I was not sure. I was so aroused, yet so unhappy too, because earlier, when Tudor had asked him, 'When are you going home?' he'd said one word: 'Soon.'

'I hope you're not going to eat any of those,' Tudor frowned, just as Anto put one of the chocolates into my mouth. When we sat down again, breathless and inclined to laugh, Anto was holding my hand, and I felt a high kind of joy that I'd never experienced before.

When the film reached its tear-jerking conclusion, Flora and I dabbed at our eyes with handkerchiefs, and I found I was sweating – my palms, my armpits, my forehead – as if I'd been through some intense ordeal.

Looking back, it was lucky that Wickam Farm had as many digestive groans and gurgles as an old person. The tepid radiators clicked like arthritic bones, the boiler in the basement occasionally roared as if in agony. We were lucky too that Ci Ci often drank herself to sleep, and it was my mother's habit to always make a fortress of whatever bedroom she happened to be in by bolting the door, and sometimes stacking furniture on the other side of it.

Because later that night, with the moon high and the stars bright outside my window, he came to me. I still have no words to describe how inevitable it felt. He stood looking down, and then he took off his shirt and I saw what a perfect young specimen he was, honed by years of cricket at boarding school. Moonlight fell in bars over his sloped shoulders and strongly muscled legs, and I can honestly say I felt not one scintilla of shame about what happened next. As I reached out for him in the dark, what I felt was a kind of singing in my veins. I had no choice.

I was perfectly aware of what a mistake this was, how disastrous the timing and so on, but my body bounded towards his, and once we'd started to touch each other, we could not stop. I was glad I wasn't a virgin, because I didn't want fear or pain to spoil anything.

I lay in the crook of his arm afterwards feeling both wicked and victorious. It felt so right and he smelled so good: sweet and cinnamony. His skin was soft. He stroked my hair. The moon fell very brightly on the Indian quilt. It was only when he reached over me to draw the curtain that I saw he was crying.

'Anto, what is it?' I felt my scalp prickle with alarm. I wanted him to feel the same euphoria that I felt.

He didn't answer, just turned and put his face in the pillow.

I was going to say something else when, across the corridor, I heard the scrape of my mother's door opening; the creak of her foot on the floorboards. The whoosh of the lavatory chain a few seconds later, and then Ci Ci's rusty cough.

I froze until I heard the click of the door closing, then let out the breath I had been holding. We both laughed silently, a scared laugh.

'Don't be sad, Anto,' I whispered when my heart rate had returned to normal. 'It's been a perfect day,' meaning his triumph, the cinema, and now this.

'I know.' He gave a jagged sigh. 'I don't think I will ever feel this happy again.'

'Don't say that.' I had spoken more loudly than I'd intended, and he clapped a hand over my mouth.

'Be careful,' he whispered, and pointed towards the door.

After a while, he got up on his elbow and studied me. He smoothed my hair back from my temples and kissed my forehead.

'I should never have done this,' he said. 'It was wrong.'

'No,' I said. I was like a child not being allowed to eat a favourite sweet, or pet a dangerous beast. 'Don't say that.'

He sat up, and turned his back to me.

'Stop,' he said as I reached out for him. 'Please.'

I hardly heard him. Lying there in the half-light, I felt fantastically, thrillingly alive. I kept my hand on his back, and ignored his sigh. My mind was racing ahead. I could get a job in India. I could go alone if I wanted to.

God, how stupid I was.

Chapter 10

We didn't stop. For the next few months we lived by day like duti-
ful workers, and by night like pagans. He'd creep into my room
after lights-out, and in the dark we made love with a sweetness and
abandon I could never have imagined, or we'd talk in low whispers
for hours about our lives so far, and our families; almost anything
but the future. Everything seemed heightened and either impossibly
happy or desperately sad.

Our time was running out; he was going home. The actual date
was set for 16 November. His mother was disappointed because
he'd miss the festival of Onam. He'd shown me her letter, as if
to make it real for both of us. When I asked what the festival was
like, he said, 'It's something to look forward to, like Bonfire Night,
or Christmas. We play games, have big feasts.' And again I noticed
how his voice sounded warmer and slightly buttery when he spoke
of India; how the word *fire* became a soft purr. It frightened me.

'I thought your family were Catholics,' I said, wanting to make
them sound more normal.

'They're Catholics but they're Indian too,' he said. 'They are
Nasranis, who got their faith from St Thomas the Apostle in the
first century.' When I asked what Nasranis did for a living, he said
that most of the men were now lawyers, or bankers, or doctors;
before that they'd had coconut plantations, or traded rice or tea.

These snippets of information, delivered in his public-school
voice, thrilled me. My Indian with green eyes. My Spanish grandee.
My exotic lover. Oh God!

'What does Travancore look like?' I asked one night. I liked saying
the unfamiliar name, and I was feeling fuzzy and contented after
making love.

'As far as I remember? Lie still, voman. I am giving you a geo-
graphy lesson,' he said in the mock-Indian voice he'd amused the
boys at school with.

'My country has three mighty rivers.' He drew his hand down my breast and rested it on my ribs. 'Beside them are lush paddy fields and palm groves.' His finger travelled slowly from under my chin to my belly and made me shiver.

'You're making this up.'

'I'm not. Lie still. No talking in class. The dark shadows here are the southern ghats.'

'What's a ghat when it's at home?'

'Hush. I'll tell you later. Don't laugh, you'll be tested on this.'

'The western ghats.' He circled my right breast.

'Anto, you're the corniest creature on earth.'

'And here,' in a Pathé News voice, 'is the source.' He ran his hands down my belly, and I was pulling his hair and stifling a laugh when the door opened, and my mother burst in, so angry she'd forgotten she had her hairnet on.

She stood in the doorway, breathing heavily, eyes going like searchlights across our naked bodies, the rumpled bed, the candle we'd lit in a saucer so we could see our flickering bodies.

I pressed my face into the pillow, my heart thumping like a generator, and then turned to look at her.

'May I ask,' she said after a deathly pause, and in her smallest and most terrible voice, 'what you're doing in my daughter's bed?' She suddenly remembered her hairnet, and shot me a look of pure rage as she snatched it off.

Anto sat up and pulled the blanket around him. 'Mrs Smallwood,' his voice, subdued and low, seemed to come from a great distance, 'I am so terribly sorry for this, and it is not how I planned to say it, but I love your daughter. I have prospects now, and was hoping to ask, with your permission, to marry her.'

If he could have clicked his heels under the sheets, he would have. The air went very still around us; we were waxworks in a tableau. I closed my eyes, not sure whether to be aghast or delighted. It was such a strange way to hear a proposal, but in the tick-tocking moments that followed, I found, to my surprise, that I was smiling inside.

The silence lengthened.

'You stupid bastard,' she said at last. It was the first time I had ever heard her swear in public. 'I could have you arrested for this.'

'Don't you dare talk to him like that,' I said. 'He's done nothing wrong, and I love him too.'

'Love?' She snatched at her hair in frustration. 'That's a joke.'

'Maybe for you.' I was ready for a fight. 'What do you know about it? I never even met my father.' My mouth was so stiff with rage, I could barely speak.

'That's just as well,' she said. 'Because if he heard about this, he'd be here with a shotgun.'

'Oh, so he's risen from the dead, has he?' I said, coldly sarcastic. 'Last thing I heard, he'd succumbed to a fever in Hyderabad.'

'I don't know what you're talking about,' she said vaguely, which made me even angrier.

'So where is he? *Where is he?*' My voice rose. It wasn't even a conscious effort to knock her off track, just the way my mind worked, like a blindly flying bird, when it was most disorientated.

Somehow, during all this, Anto had managed to get dressed. He stepped out of the shadows, wearing his shirt and trousers.

'Kit,' he said in a stern voice. 'Stop it. This is not a discussion for now, and your mother is right to be worried for you. We've all had a shock. We should go to bed, unless...' he turned to Glory, 'you would like me to go to Miss Barker and explain everything to her now.'

This, I realised later, was a brilliant move, handing back authority and humiliation in one fell swoop. It worked in a way that apologies never did with my mother.

She pulled her satin dressing gown tightly around her.

'I feel quite sick. I will go to bed and think about it. And you, miss,' she said, 'I'll see you in the morning.'

'Say it quickly,' I said to him before he left. 'I won't blame you. Say it quickly if you don't mean it.' Meaning marriage, meaning me for the rest of his life.

'I mean it,' he said, very quietly. 'I love you.' But he looked exhausted and pale, as if there were other things he should say but couldn't right now.

During the sleepless night that followed, I seemed to run through the full catalogue of human emotions: confusion, and a kind of crazed delight at Anto's unexpected proposal, embarrassment that my mother had caught us red-handed, fury at her for exhuming my father so unexpectedly and then pretending it didn't matter.

Out of this tangle I could only pluck one clear idea: that in the morning, I must tell Daisy before my mother did. Daisy loved Anto; she would understand.

Daisy was in the office the next morning, when I, foolishly happy, dropped the news at her feet, like a cat bringing a dead mouse into the house. She was wearing overalls, gloves on because her chilblains were bad, wrapping up kidney dishes in brown paper. She straightened up, the expression in her eyes moving from her usual look of quiet pleasure at seeing me, to bewilderment, then horror.

'Oh Kit, oh Lord,' she said when I had finished. She clapped her hand over her mouth and stared at me. 'Don't worry,' she said eventually. 'You can still get out of it. Have you spoken to him this morning?'

'He meant it,' I repeated. 'I know he did.'

I was still feeling a kind of victorious expansion, and babbled on for a bit about how we loved each other, and how, in India, I could work at the home, which was what Daisy had wanted all along.

'It won't happen.' Her head was shaking even before I'd finished. She looked ashen. 'It can't. His family won't allow it.'

'But Daisy, they're not *Indian* Indians,' I tried to explain to her. 'They're educated. They're Anglophiles. His father lived in England. He trained to be a lawyer here.'

She sat down and put her head in her hands. 'I know that,' she groaned. 'Oh my dear girl,' she said, looking up, 'you're stepping into a bear pit.'

'I thought you'd be pleased.' I sounded like a child even to myself.

'It's true I'd hoped you might consider working out there, on a very temporary basis of course – you know, a month or two months, part of a team, with a small salary. Not as a wife, not as an Indian wife. And of course Tudor will be desperately disappointed too. He's such a dear.' She put on her glasses and stared at me, looking very sad. Tudor was definitely Daisy's blind spot.

Not in a million years, my mind clanged, only I loved her too much to say it.

'And it will kill your mother,' she added. Unusual for Daisy to try emotional blackmail; it made me realise how desperately she minded.

'She'll come round.'

63

'No, she won't.' Daisy was shaking her head, looking sadder than ever.

'You don't know that.'

'I do.' There was an extra intensity in her gaze, which reminded me of other things I felt I didn't understand: my mother's half-truths, the occasional sly dig from Tudor and Ci Ci.

And I was sick of it suddenly: this unspoken thing that seemed to follow me round like a whiff from a drain.

'Daisy,' I said, 'what are you talking about? If you know some-thing about my mother that I don't, why won't you just say it?'

'You must ask her yourself.' She became very busy rustling papers and putting her pens away in the old Stilton jar she kept on her desk. 'It's nothing to do with me.'

'So there is something?'

'I don't know ... I don't know.'

I'd never seen her look more furtive or trapped.

I ran to the kitchen, where my mother was chopping spinach with her usual economy of movement. Two dead pheasants lay on the table, their necks flopped over, their little eyes all blank. From the door I surveyed her quickly: the neat waist, the trim ankles, the beautiful black hair, caught this morning with a marcasite comb. The apron was the jarring note: an actress cast in the wrong play.

'Mother, I need to speak to you.'

'Well I don't want to speak to you.'

She may as well have added, 'you revolting slut', her look was so shuddery and disgusted. She carried on chopping.

'Mother,' I announced grandly, 'I'm terribly sorry about last night, but we are in love and I'm leaving soon. I really am, you know.' Did I actually believe it then, the grandiose words, the concrete travel plans? I don't think so, but it felt important to make a stand. She stopped chopping and laid the knife down.

'Shut up, Kit,' she said. 'I refuse to talk about it here with all those blasted nosy parkers listening in.'

She was almost levitating with rage as she took off her apron, put on her coat and a headscarf, and we walked out together into the raw autumn morning to have it out with each other.

'Oh don't you bloody well come,' she said when the poor old Labrador tried to squeeze through the door with us. There was a yelp as she slammed the door shut and caught his front paw.

We took the track that led through the avenue of elms and into Shakenoak Wood. Autumn leaves lay in brilliant soggy piles under our feet, and when two fallow deer did grande jetés across our path, and disappeared into the trees, neither of us remarked on them.

At the end of the track, I undid the Hunter's Gate and we stepped into the wood. I was close enough to hear her breathing, which was hoarse and laboured.

'I am going to marry him,' I said. 'Try not to mind too much.'

'Well I do mind,' she said. Her eyes very black, her skin very pale. 'Because if you marry him, you will be dead to me.' Those were her exact words.

'Are you serious? Is it so bad to marry the man you love?' I said.

'Oh love,' she said as if it was some dog mess she'd stepped in. 'It will be an absolute disaster. You know nothing about it.'

My mother always refused to wear galoshes, or wellington boots, saying they made her feel 'elephanty', and now, walking blindly ahead of me, she stepped into a puddle, splashing her good shoes and stockings with mud.

'Don't touch me.' She flinched as I tried to lead her to drier land. 'I'm so ashamed of what you've done.' A tear rolled down her face.

'Mummy,' I said as she dashed it away with the corner of her headscarf. I felt cold, determined to keep myself separate from her in a way I'd never felt before. 'There's something else I must ask you, because I keep thinking people know something about me that I don't know.'

'People will say what they want to say.' Her complexion had gone the sort of khaki green it went when she was really upset. 'They're spiteful.'

'But what is it they're not saying?' I was the tearful one now.

She shook her head violently. 'About what?'

'You. My father. Why is it always so bloody mysterious?'

'Why do you go on like this: on and on and on at me?' She made a stabbing gesture with her hand, as if I was eviscerating her.

'Because I'm leaving and I have to know.'

'You won't like it.'

'Why not?'

'Because it's not nice.'

A mizzling rain started to fall as we stepped deeper into the wood. I stared at the silk headscarf my mother had retied under her chin. It was a hideous but posh thing, patterned with brown and gold horseshoes and very distinctive. I was almost certain it had once belonged to Laura McCrum, the wife of a businessman she'd worked for near Bromley. These items had a worrying way of turning up in her wardrobe after we'd left, a small gesture of revenge maybe, but it shamed me on her behalf.

'Let me tell you one or two things about India,' she said. 'It's the most complicated, class-bound country on earth. Any European putting a toe in the country and thinking they can understand it is a complete clot.'

'I know that,' I said. 'I've talked to Daisy about it.'

She pouffed at this nonsense, and when I protested that I was one quarter Indian myself anyway, she snapped, 'Why do you bang on about that? Your skin is so pale you could pass for English anywhere.' Her face all squeezed under the headscarf, her teeth bared, and then another thought bringing dismay. 'Do you go on about it to Tudor? Because if you—'

'I can't remember,' I interrupted her furiously, 'and I couldn't give a damn. He's got nothing to do with what we're talking about.'

She groaned as if I was the thickest person on earth.

'Tell me about my father.' It came out louder than I'd intended, and a pheasant scuttled out of the tangled undergrowth, clucking and complaining.

She started sighing and pacing around. I looked through the wet autumn leaves at a darkening sky with huge clouds broiling in the west.

'Kit.' She closed her eyes like someone locking herself into a cell, and when she came out, her eyes were very black. 'I'm only ever going to tell you this story once, because it makes me feel like the worst bloody twit in the world, and if you are rude to me, I will stop.'

I waited in terrible suspense. The rain was coming down more heavily, and any moment now I expected her to run for the house.

'God, I hate this climate.' She tied the knot on her scarf again.

'When Tudor marries,' she said, 'he'll own all this wood, plus almost one hundred acres of prime Oxfordshire land. Daisy told me that this morning. She's as upset as I am.'

'Really.' I could not resist the sarcasm. 'Well, always nice to have company in your opinions. And just to make things perfectly clear,

I wouldn't marry Tudor if he was the last man on earth. I don't even *like* him.'

'Daisy knows Indian men as well as I do,' she went on as if I hadn't said a word. After a breath, she spoke again. 'First, I was not born in Wrexham.'

This hardly came as a great shock to me. I'd forgotten, or discarded, the Wrexham version of her story.

'I was born in Pondicherry, on the south-east coast of India.' Her voice took on the queenly drawl I thought of as her telephone voice. 'My father, your grandfather, was an Englishman, a high-up engineer on the railways there. I don't have any pictures of him, so don't ask.' A flash of anger there. 'My mother was an Indian woman.'

I knew that already, but didn't want to stop her.

'My mother died giving birth to what would have been my sister. I don't remember ever meeting my father. I was sent to an orphanage in Orissa, an English convent. I don't know who by, I was just sent. Is this the kind of information you're after?' She gave me a look of muted fury, as if I was an impertinent journalist rather than her child.

'Mummy, I'm sorry.'

'It was a home for half-caste children.'

Half-caste. I'd certainly never heard her say that before, and the words fell between us in an ugly way, like a dead bird, or a turd. For the first time I wanted her to stop, partly because I hated hearing the phrase applied to her, but also because, in a way, it interfered with my dream of her. When I'd thought of my mother in India, I'd imagined cocktail parties, and tiger shoots, and pink and peach skies; and now I remembered a girl I hadn't thought about for years: Dymphna Parry, a miserable little thing who'd arrived mid-term at my Derbyshire school, adopted by the vicar and his wife from somewhere in Africa. Dymphna wasn't exactly bullied, but she was one of the never-chosen: not for rounders, not for special seats on the school bus.

I saw her face again, grey-green with cold, the terrible tweeds she'd been togged out in, the woolly hair pulled into plaits that looked like unshorn sheep, and I felt sick.

'Why didn't you say this before?' I demanded. My mother's eyes looked wild now, and somehow unhinged, as if I'd cut the rope that kept her safe.

'It was nobody's business but my own.'

Yes it was, I shouted inwardly.

My mother's tone was frigid; she had not forgiven me. 'The nuns encouraged the English side of me, just as I have tried to do with you.' She flung me a look of great bitterness. 'We learned grammar and Shakespeare and manners. We ate shepherd's pie, toad in the hole. They were right to do so. The Indian towns around us were filthy places.' She shuddered. 'The people so poor and full of disease. There was a smallpox epidemic.'

'How did you meet my father?'

'I was clever, ambitious. I had good grammar and punctuation, so I secured a job with the British government. I was personal assistant to a resident, a delightful man.' Her voice took on a certain swagger here. 'I've forgotten his name. He was cultivated, kind, good to me. My pale skin, my English name meant my background was never discussed. I went to parties as the spare girl, the decorative girl. I was pretty.'

'And my father?'

'We met at an elephant hunt. Look at me, Kit, I'm soaked, I'm cold. Do you want me to get pneumonia telling you this?'

'Five more minutes, please.'

'All right, an elephant hunt. A horrible affair. They built a cage for this beautiful creature and they smoked him out and stabbed him to death.' She looked at me as if I had personally driven a stake through the elephant's heart. 'That's your Indian. He is two steps away from being a savage.

'Your father was an army officer, good regiment.' Again the showy drawl. 'He was aide-de-camp to General Thompkinson, I thought he was the bee's knees. But why should I talk about him? He behaved appallingly.'

'Please, Ma, I hate feeling other people know and I don't.'

'Only Daisy knows,' my mother said. 'And Daisy won't say either, so don't bother asking her.'

'Did you love him?'

'It doesn't matter. I'm freezing. I'm not going on.' She was like a horse dancing on the spot in agitation.

We had come to a bench in the woods, its seat shiny with rain and old bits of moss. There was a clear view of the hills beyond; the heap of stones that had once been a Roman fort; a farmhouse nestled in a placid field; a farmer on his tractor followed by a sheepdog.

When my mother almost collapsed on the bench, I wanted to put my arm around her and make her better. She was so upset, and I'd always had this haunting sense of something fragile about her that I, her only child, had the power to break. The idea of her as an orphan explained so much: her defensive hauteur, her longing for nice clothes and the outward trappings of respectability, her angry admiration for Englishness, even her mild case of kleptomania.

I'd planned to ask more about my father: specifically, was he really dead, or just dead to her. But instead I said, 'You're cold, Mummy,' because she was shaking. I wished she could have a bath when she got in, but I knew she couldn't – we'd been having trouble with the thirty-year-old boiler again, but Daisy hadn't wanted to call out a workman in case of a huge bill.

As we limped back to the house together, I hated suddenly this feeling of female powerlessness. I wanted action, change; the competence, the money to fix things; a new life, even if it was risky.

'Look at my shoes,' my mother said, taking my arm at last. 'Completely ruined, raking all this up.'

As we stood on the grass verge beside the drive, Daisy drove past us in the Morris. I saw the dim outline of Anto – hat, dark overcoat – sitting in the front with her. We looked at each other, but none of us waved.

'Where do you think they're going?' I watched the glint of the mudguard disappear around the corner.

'To the railway station, I hope,' said my mother. She tightened her grip on my arm. 'It will hurt for a while, but not for long. I've been through it myself.'

'They're probably only going to the post office,' I said. 'They'll be back for lunch.'

She turned on me. 'You don't believe me, do you?' she said. 'You'll be dead to me if you do this. It's everything I didn't want.'

I made myself look at her.

'You don't know the first thing about him,' I said, feeling removed from myself, and heroic, and not a million miles away from Olivia de Havilland in *They Died with Their Boots On*. 'He's clever, he's kind—' I might have added, *and besides, I love him*, but she interrupted me with a jabbing gesture of her hand.

'Mixed blood is like oil and water,' she said, her face very pale.

'Everything bad that has happened to me in my life comes from it. It's a taint.'

'Mother,' I said, 'how many dead people can you afford to have in your life?'

'As many as I need to get by,' she replied.

Chapter 11

'I know about my father,' I lied to Daisy that afternoon. We were sorting clothes for another jumble sale. 'My mother told me pretty much everything this morning.' Daisy's head shot up like a startled horse. She was sitting in a sea of mouldy riding clothes, tennis racquets, pith helmets, and several rotting canvases – her father had been a successful artist before the war, and we often joked about the undiscovered Matisse we'd find in the attic that would change all our fortunes.

'Golly,' she said. She put down the cardigan she was folding and looked at me. 'What a time you're having.'

'She's furious about Anto,' I said. 'Absolutely spitting mad. She's cut me off.' I was trying to sound jaunty and not cry. Her look was steady and kind, the same old safe shore.

'Oh my poor, dear Kit,' she said. 'I did try to warn you.'

'Well, you were right, and I think she means it this time, but I am going to marry him, you know.' The Olivia de Havilland feeling – heroic, dignified, quietly determined – was slipping like an actor's greasepaint under the lights, though I was too proud to say so, and confused. Somehow, my father and Anto had become jumbled in my mind, if only as places of escape.

'Did you know my father?' I'd never asked her before.

'Briefly.' A child's Fair Isle pullover fell to pieces in her hand; she put it in the bin.

'Is he . . . was he a good man?'

'I hardly knew him.' Daisy's eyes stared into mine, terrified of causing me pain. 'I think he tried to make amends.'

'For what? How?'

'Kit, if I could tell you, I would, but it's not my story to tell.'

'I'd like to write him a letter. Do you know his address?'

'I'm sorry.' She put a hand on my arm. 'But why now, after all these years?'

'Because she told me I was dead to her this morning, not once, but twice...' I was having trouble breathing. 'And because I am going to marry Anto.'

Daisy shook her head and sighed. 'Are you sure this is what you want? It's a hell of a thing to take on.'

'Yes... if it's still what Anto wants.'

'It is. I spoke to him this morning.' She gave me an anguished look. 'Forgive me for overstepping the mark here, Kit, but I do understand how addictive physical attraction can be...' She was pink suddenly, and daring-looking, and I was mortified and wanted her to stop. 'It's the most wonderful thing, like being plugged into the universe or something. But it has to be more than that. So are you quite sure?' Her eyes gleaming and moist behind her glasses.

'Yes, Daisy,' I said, frozen with embarrassment at the thought of those sensible square hands touching a man. 'You know the other things about him,' I went on in a steadying voice – we seemed somehow temporarily to have swapped roles. 'How clever he is, and hard-working.'

'Well there is that,' she said uneasily.

And the thought came like a flash of sunlight inside me: *Bugger the lot of them, I love him, I don't have to explain.*

Daisy sighed again. 'Well, if his parents are liberal,' she said after a long and thoughtful silence, 'and if you can work for the home, I suppose you could do worse...' Her voice tailed off. 'And who knows? The new India is terra incognita for all of us, and it's not much fun here, is it?' I could see her struggling and leapt in eagerly.

'Oh Daisy, thank you. You're the first person to sound even slightly pleased. Did he seem happy when he told you?'

She hesitated. 'No, Kit. Not really. He hardly said a word all the way to Oxford. I think he's terribly worried. He wanted to go on his motorbike, but the roads were too slippery. He said he'd take a taxi back.' And then I wondered if he was on the train already, running while he could; some part of me would not have blamed him.

'I love him,' I insisted stubbornly, and then, 'Didn't you ever want that – a husband? Children?'

'Only once,' she said. She hugged the bundle of clothes she was carrying. 'He died young... a fine person.' She looked through me at some dusty ghost beyond. 'He was twenty-five. One day when I've had a few glasses of whisky, I'll tell you about it.'

72

'Oh Daisy.' I took the clothes from her, and said foolishly, because I didn't know what else to say, 'I don't drink whisky.'

'Nor will you ever again.' She recovered her old teasing self quickly. 'Not if you are to be an Indian wife.'

Anto tried to have one sensible conversation with me before we married, in which he warned me how different our life might be in Travancore, and how I mustn't mind if his mother took a while to warm to me, and how Daisy might be embarking on a dangerous enterprise with her Moonstone Maternity Home, but we were lying in each other's arms at the time, him stroking my hair, my hand on his flat stomach, and somehow that dreamy post-lovemaking daze seemed to short-circuit the worry centres in both our brains.

And so we married, more in the spirit of two cars dashing through a green light before it turned red than in the spirit of ... well, what? Thoughtfulness, maybe, or a long and considered court-ship, in which we carefully weighed up each other's assets in the way you might if you were buying a car or a house: value for money, enduring qualities, good workmanship, suitability for the job and so forth. We seemed to be running on our own unstoppable electricity supply, one we could neither explain nor deny. He made me laugh – have I mentioned that? – and I respected him too: the dogged way he worked; the gentle way he deflected Ci Ci's and Tudor's barbs.

But since this is a confession of sorts, I'll admit that part of me opened like a flower at the thought of sunshine and blue skies and new experiences, an escape from rationing and bomb sites and going back to London and into digs with nurses again. I was longing for exciting things to happen.

I wrote to Josie asking if there was any chance she could be my maid of honour. *Dear Dark Horse*, she wrote by return of post. *I'm going to miss you so much. As soon as you have a date, let me know, I'll twist Matron's arm, and get the day off.*

But Matron's arm was not for twisting, and Daisy was, in the end, our only guest. The wedding took place on a cold Thursday afternoon at the Oxford registry office. It cost us one and sixpence to hire it; two shillings extra for the use of a vase of yellow dahlias the last wedding party had left behind.

And I did drink wine at my wedding: Elderflower 1947, as Daisy joked, bringing two bottles from the cellar to wash down some sausage rolls and a fruit cake. My mother had stayed in bed, claiming she had a tight chest, possibly pneumonia coming on. Ci Ci, who'd been noisily sympathetic to my mother, declined to join us, and forbade Flora to come too, all of which was a relief. Tudor, who had suggested to Daisy that both of us be asked to leave the house when he heard, went shooting for the day. My last image of him was standing in the hall, looking like a Victorian rent boy in his plus fours and peaked cap, his father's dead animals all around him. He was so angry he could hardly speak.

'Good luck,' he said stiffly, picking up his gun and making a rattling sound with the cartridges on his belt. 'I think you'll need quite a bit of it.'

'Thanks, Tudor.' I pretended he'd been nice. 'I absolutely can't wait.'

In spite of the guns and the shooting paraphernalia, there was something oddly prissy and flouncy about the way he walked out to the waiting car. It made me think that maybe all the matchmaking females in the house had been barking up the wrong tree.

After the wedding, Anto and I, strangely quiet and shy in the car, went to a guest house, The Culford, where they also bred budgies. It was on the edge of a soggy ploughed field near Burford. Nothing special: we were saving all our pennies now.

I was worried immediately that our landlady, a stout farmer's wife, would notice that Anto was Indian and make a fuss, but he looked very distinguished in his one good suit and grey hat, and was even paler than usual due to the tension of the day. In an upstairs bedroom with a swirly carpet and sagging bed, we stood side by side in front of the wardrobe mirror. He took my hand and turned my wedding ring around my finger.

'I love you, Kit,' he said gravely. 'I'm going to take care of you for ever.'

'Yes,' I said, but perversely, I couldn't stop thinking about my mother, in bed alone and almost certainly sobbing her heart out. 'Thank you.' I couldn't think of anything else to say. It was cold in that room. It smelled of mothballs, and I could hear rain lashing against the window.

'Your ticket came yesterday,' he said. 'My mother sent it to me with a letter.'

'Oh. Good.' It felt peculiar being sent a ticket by someone I didn't know, and I foolishly hoped he'd say something else: that she was happy, that she was looking forward to meeting me.

'Did you say I'd pay her back when I was working again?' The home's trustees had agreed a working wage of £16 a month when I started in India, but I hadn't had enough in my bank account to pay for my passage on the *Kampala*.

'Not yet.' His face in the mirror looked guarded; his voice was distracted. 'It's not the right time now.

'November the sixteenth,' he added, as if the date of departure wasn't blazed on my mind.

'Yes. I love you, Anto.'

'I love you too.'

'You're frightened,' I said as his face swam out of view. He'd grown quieter and quieter over the past few hours. 'I don't blame you. It's all happened so quickly.' I felt a great big blank as I said this, as if we were in a play and acting very badly. He didn't say anything, just held me tight, our two shadows meeting and closing in the mirrored door.

'We've crossed the Rubicon,' he said in his Pathé News voice.

'What exactly is the Rubicon, clever clogs?' I asked him later, trying to keep things light. We'd gone to bed early and were lying in each other's arms.

'A river in Italy,' he said. 'A place of no return. When Julius Caesar crossed it, he said to his troops, "*Alea iacta est*." "The die is cast." He knew that if he didn't triumph, he'd be executed.'

'A cheery tale,' I murmured, half asleep, and then, 'Were you always an egghead?'

'I'm not clever,' I remember him saying sadly. 'Not clever at all.'

We went to sleep and woke to the cheeping of hundreds of coloured budgies singing inside their cages.

II

Cochin, South India

Chapter 12

New husband, new country, new climate, new mother-in-law, and whoopee! one hundred and seven new relatives all speaking a new language. When I opened my eyes in Room 4 of the Malabar Hotel in Fort Cochin, I closed them again quickly. I was lying in an elaborately carved rosewood bed, a dazzling light stabbing my eyes. The fan above me shifted air that smelled of the sea and old drains, and still feeling the sway and tilt of the sea in my blood, I longed to go back to that dreamy, indeterminate place where it was just Anto and me on the ship together.

I could hear Anto splashing around in the vast antiquated bathroom next to our room. The concentrated energy with which he washed every part of his beautiful honey-coloured body was a source of silent fascination to me. Ears, teeth, armpits, toes, nothing was missed, then the fierce scrubbing of the nails, the startling garglings as his tonsils got sluiced.

Once, during our early days on the ship, I'd called through the bathroom door, 'You're worse than a girl.' The door had opened and he'd given me an odd, intimidating look, and I'd made a mental note not to joke about it again.

I looked at my watch. Nine o'clock and I was already slippery with sweat. A slender lizard dashed up the wall. From the bathroom: splash, gargle, throat-clearing, the slap of a towel. We'd made love twice during the night, but now my brain was waking, releasing fear like a drug into my veins.

We'd come alive on the ship. Released from home, from war, rationing, people, we'd made our tiny cabin a secret cave where, on some nights, we'd gone to a level of wildness and freedom with each other that left us both gasping, laughing, speechless and a little afraid. And knowing in some secret cell of myself that we might never be this free again, I'd stored it all inside me: the hours lying in deckchairs on the top deck, dreaming between sea and sky;

the flaming sunsets; the new cities; our cabin on F deck with the salt-smelling sea racing by. Long whispered conversations; the new taste of mangos, bananas, melons; moonlit walks with the night skies so close and bursting with stars; cocktails in the Sunshine Bar.

We lived like kings, and made no new friends on the ship. We only wanted each other; now, the thought of sharing Anto with dozens of inquisitive strangers made me pant with alarm.

It's an adventure, I tried to tell myself, but my insides were swirling. Now that we were back to some sort of reality, I found myself worrying about my mother again. After staying in a more or less permanent sulk since our wedding, she'd promised, in a special cracked voice, to come to Tilbury to see us off. The day we left, she'd worn her tweed travelling suit and a beautiful silk scarf. The paleness of her make-up, the scarlet lipstick, gave her face a startling, almost Oriental look – like a kabuki actress in a play. She'd toyed with her food over breakfast, and later, in the freezing hall, announced, 'I'm not coming to the station with you. I'm too busy here.'

She'd flung me a look of wild accusation – *Thank you for ruining my life*, she might as well have added – and then gathered herself up, pecked my cheek, and said in a stagy drawl, 'So the very best of British, darling,' possibly for the benefit of that old bat Ci Ci, who was peeping around the door, her eyes full of a kind of malicious glee at the horrors ahead for both of us.

'Don't forget to let me know how it goes,' my mother continued in the same vein, as if I'd planned nothing more than a trip to the dentist. 'There's a pet.'

God, I was furious. 'I will. Thank you, Mummy,' I said.

I knew my mother well enough to understand that she became more English than the English when she was scared, but this was more than I could bear. She ignored Anto altogether, didn't even shake his hand, and at the moment when I needed her most, I hated her for playing to the gallery.

Ci Ci contrived an equally stagy farewell. 'Darling honeybun!' she'd cried with more warmth than she'd ever shown me before. The claw-like hands she wrapped around my shoulders smelled of nicotine, and her large ring nicked my cheek. She'd kissed me for the first time ever. 'Give 'em hell,' she'd added, a remnant maybe from some cowboy film she'd watched.

Daisy stood apart and watched us, warily and sadly. She knew the limits of her own embracing hospitality. And it was Daisy who drove us to the railway station, the back seat of the Austin stacked high with our luggage and the boot jammed with medical supplies for the charity. Two large tea chests had gone ahead of us.

The fields were frozen on either side of us, and the sky was without colour. Daisy broke the silence. 'She'll miss you, Kit, I know she will.'

'Do you think she'll write?' I was too shaken to say much.

'I don't know, but I'll keep you informed, I promise.'

Just for that moment, I wished Anto wasn't with us in the car. I'd kept the silly idea in my mind that my mother would crack before we left, and hug me, or give me some kind of blessing; maybe even some more information about my father, because although this trip wasn't like dying, it felt like a point where you wanted to get things straight in your mind. But he was there, looking pensively out of the window, thinking his own thoughts.

During our brief courtship, I was aware that although we'd thought each other soulmates and talked about many things both small and large – books we liked, films, the war, the life we wanted to live – he'd asked me very little about my background. When I'd raised the subject, thinking he must want to know something, I told him my father had died in 1920, a result of war wounds, or maybe pneumonia, but I wasn't absolutely sure because my mother didn't like talking about it. It was, after all, the year I was born, the shock to her had been great. He hadn't pressed me for details – the death of loved ones was a commonplace since the war – and I'd accepted his reticence as tact and been grateful for it.

Later, when I'd tried to take another run at it and be more open, something had always stopped me: a cringe of shame, a sense of guilt, a feeling that my admission might lessen me in Anto's eyes by making him feel he'd been sold a pup, a half-breed at that.

It felt like a long trip to the station. I wiped away a line of condensation from the car window. Anto was still silent, staring at frozen fields, at ponies, breath like plumes of smoke, being fed hay. I told myself: you're a married woman now, you must stop thinking about your parents, because my mind could whirl on this particular hamster wheel for ever and it was quite possible I would never know the truth. I took my glove off and put my hand down on the leather seat, hoping that Anto would hold it, but he was not a natural hand-holder.

*

Three waiters leapt forward with bowls of fruit, offers of tea or coffee, as we walked into the Malabar's cavernous dining room for breakfast. A strange embarrassment came over us – neither of us had stayed in a hotel before – and in between the clinking of our cutlery, I could hear myself making stilted conversation, about the furniture (massive, ugly), the fruit (tiny, delicious bananas), and the heat, which was, even this early in the morning, a startling ninety-two degrees.

I was hungry but didn't want to eat too much. Between us we now had a grand total of £123. He'd counted the notes out on our mattress that morning, and I was aware that if I hadn't been there, he would have already been enfolded in the bosom of an ecstatic family, and spared the expense of the hotel.

He ordered eggs and bacon for me, and something called an appam, a kind of thin flat pancake, for himself. He wrote the word carefully on a napkin as if for a child.

'Is it lovely to eat that again?' I watched him tear it into bite-sized pieces with practised hands and dip it into what he told me was coconut chutney.

'Yes,' he said. In the awkward silence that followed, I looked around the dining room. Four Indian couples sat, half secreted behind palms or wooden posts. They were absolutely silent; all I could hear was the scraping of their spoons, the gulps as they drank their chai, and the bleak thought came: I wonder if he'll stop talking to me now.

After breakfast, he said we should stroll down to the harbour and make sure the tea chests had been taken off the ship. After that, we would find a bank, open an account and change our pounds into rupees. I could feel my spirits lightening, as if this anxious in-between day needed a proper job to give it shape.

'I'll show you around the old town too.' He smiled the sudden thrilled smile that had made me fall in love with him in the first place, the smile that lit up his eyes, a seam of green and tortoiseshell, and the dimples that made him look about ten again. 'And then we shall have lunch, and go back to bed...'

He did his Groucho Marx suggestive eyebrows, and I laughed, and longed to kiss him, but remembered in the nick of time not to: on the ship coming out, he'd warned me that in India it wasn't done for a man and a woman to hold hands in public. Not even married people.

The sun was piercingly bright as we walked, an hour later, towards the Fort Cochin seafront. An old beggar lay half naked under a tree, his eyes covered in flies, and the smell of rotting fish rose periodically from the rubbish-strewn drains.

Anto had the look of an eager boy as he picked up speed, rushing towards the dazzling sea where more ships were coming in. When we reached the water's edge, I heard him groan, and saw him pass his hand over his face.

'Beautiful,' he murmured in a dazed voice. I didn't know what to say. The palm trees, the aquamarine sea, the cloudless blue sky, all looked like stage scenery to me.

'It hasn't changed a bit,' he said softly, sadly.

'I always think a place will change if I'm not there.' I could hear myself babbling nervously as we walked along the seafront, when what I really wanted to do was to hug him, to say, 'How wonderful – you're home,' or some such. I felt uncomfortably surplus to requirements – Not Wanted on Voyage – because there was nothing here that spoke to me, not yet.

'My father had his law offices over there,' he said when we reached the end of a stretch of cracked concrete. 'Just behind the English club.' He pointed towards an elegant building set back from the seafront, and surrounded by lawns. I looked over the hedge at the well-ordered building, with its potted plants and fine shrubs. Now the green, orange and white flag of the new India fluttered from the veranda.

'Look at it.' Anto seemed stunned. 'We thought it the height of luxury when we were children. My brother and I sat in the car while my father had fierce games of chess with his old pal Hugo Bateman, his English barrister hero. My father usually won. We were proud of that.'

'A nice place to come and play,' was all I could think of.

'Not really.' Anto was squinting at one of the placards arranged on the veranda. 'My father couldn't even enter the club without Mr Bateman's permission. That was always made clear to us.' He gave a curious lopsided grin.

'What do they say? The signs?'

'Um … let me see … Malayalam may not come instantly,' he said, a playful mimic again. 'Well, sorry about this, madam, but "Quit India" … and "India is ours again", but you, my beautiful lady sahib, are not to take it personally, please. You're my wife,' he added softly. 'You are most welcome. Do you like it so far?'

'Yes,' I said, my smile quick and insincere. 'Of course I do.' We were passing a group of very old women squatting on their haunches in front of piles of fish laid out on burlap sacking. They stared at me.

'Those,' he told me, 'are the famous Chinese fishing nets.' He pointed towards two skinny old men performing what looked like a lithe and practised dance as they eased down the large stones on pulleys, which made a net full of gleaming fish spring into the air.

'Our physics master from Ignatius College once brought us here to watch them. He said that those nets were "a little miracle of design". A brilliant use of energy and counterbalancing weights. When the stone goes down, the nets come up. No stoney, no fishy.'

I smiled at him. I liked the way he knew how things worked, his good memory for facts and solid things. It felt masculine to me, another kind of counterbalancing weight.

Next, while we were walking around a drain that oozed what looked like oily manure, he told me that India had once led the world in modern sanitation: that its drains, chutes, cesspits and clever devices for moving rubbish out of town would be the envy of the modern world today.

He was warming to his theme when he glanced at me and noticed my expression. 'Good pillow talk, hey?' he said, and we burst out laughing. I was relieved, even for one brief moment, to have my old, clever, funny Anto back again.

On our way back to the hotel, we passed a large Indian family, eight or ten people, padding slowly and companionably down the seafront. The men were dressed in Western suits, their wives in violently coloured saris of the brightest apricots and pinks and lime greens, their arms covered in bangles.

'Most women here don't wear the sari,' Anto explained to me, pointing to another woman in a plain white long skirt and blouse. 'They wear that: the *chatta* and *mundu* – quite boring by comparison.'

The gaggle of children who followed them walked backwards to stare at me: the white woman in the white dress with the white hat. When one of them – a cheeky-looking boy – said something that made the men laugh, a strange little line of poetry (one of my mother's favourites) wafted into my mind.

Oh why do you walk through the field in gloves,
Missing so much and so much?
O fat white woman whom nobody loves.

I kept it to myself, knowing he would instantly assure me of my own slimness, lovedness, and so forth, and also because he'd strode a little ahead of me, pleased to remember a short cut, through a gap in the fence and down a path that took us past the English club.

As we drew closer, I could see that part of the veranda had been damaged, and several windows boarded up. A skinny cat dashed from under the building with something in its mouth. When I asked Anto if the riots had been bad here, he stared at the club and said, 'Nothing like as bad as the riots and massacres up north. But my family were sparing with information, so I don't really know yet.' He picked up an empty firework shell that must have been part of the victory celebrations. 'I only really know what I read in the London *Times*.'

We threaded our way down a bustling street: rickshaws, and stray goats, and street merchants selling buckets and bright sweets, lurid papier-mâché gods, a whole head of lamb buzzing with flies. It felt exciting, and I wanted to explore, but he was intent on showing me the Church of St Francis, where, he said, Vasco da Gama was buried before they moved his body back to Portugal. I trailed dutifully behind him into a large building with curved sides like ship's sails.

He dipped his hand in the holy water near the door and made a sign of the cross – a surprise for me; he'd told me he was a lapsed Catholic.

I felt he wanted to be alone, and watched him from a distance, this handsome stranger – my husband – sitting in soft candlelight, eyes tightly shut, face gleaming with sweat, surrounded by stained glass and stone effigies, and the thought came to me: I hope he's not regretting this already.

Chapter 13

'Do you have an aspirin in your handbag?' he asked me the following day. We were speeding in a battered taxi towards Mangalath, his family home, one hour's drive from Fort Cochin.

'Sorry, no,' I said. 'Headache?' He looked so pale and distant.

'Not really.'

I'd heard him, in the middle of the night, groaning as though in the grip of some kind of nerve storm.

'All right, darling?' I said when he came back to bed, hoping he would confide in me.

'I'm fine,' and then, after a long and expectant pause, he turned his back on me. 'Thank you,' he said politely before he went to sleep.

He'd expected the family car to be sent for us with a driver, but a note had been left at the hotel that we were to take a taxi. It had clearly perplexed and hurt him. I wondered if this was a concealed snub, but kept the thought to myself.

It was so hot in the taxi that my dress stuck to the seat, and I felt sick as our driver, a juicy sniffer, drove hectically, one hand on the wheel, through ramshackle villages and along potholed roads. And then, on the edge of town, quite suddenly, we were in the most spectacularly beautiful country I had ever seen: a dream of water and earth and sky where bright green fields and gorgeously coloured trees seemed to float on a series of lakes and waterways, lagoons and backwaters connected by fragile bridges. Anto stared stonily out of the window, hardly moving.

We were crossing a bridge, approaching the village of Aroor, when he turned to me as if only just remembering I was there.

'Are you nervous?' he asked, at last acknowledging the momentous day ahead. 'You will shortly disappear under a mountain of relatives, and I'm afraid they will be very, very curious about you.'

'Not nervous,' I lied. 'Excited,' and then, 'Is it all very changed?'

'I've changed,' he said softly. He was looking at a small boat adrift in a dazzling stretch of water, sailing towards the horizon.

'It looks like a giant picture postcard,' I said, feeling like a hearty aunt in my startling unoriginality. 'It's nice to see it with you.'

We stopped at a tea shop selling cigarettes and sweets, where Anto arranged for us and our luggage to be transferred to a horse and cart. The horse stood in the fierce sunlight, its eyes obliterated by flies. Its barefoot owner cut the top off a coconut with a machete and offered Anto a glass of its milk, which he downed with an ecstatic look. He told me not to drink any until my stomach got stronger. I said nothing. I was too hot and too anxious to talk, because we were nearly there.

After ten minutes or so, down a dusty road lined with palm trees, Anto gripped my hand tightly. 'We're less than a mile away,' he said when we reached a fork in the road. 'Half a mile ... one hundred yards.' Figures seemed all he could manage now.

And suddenly, there it was: a small stone gatehouse against a lush backdrop of trees, and a wooden sign with *Mangalath* written on it.

Anto exhaled slowly. 'This is it.' He let go of my hand. The horse clip-clopped through an avenue of wonderful trees: as bold and showy as cancan dancers with their waxy blossoms and strangely shaped leaves.

'Frangipani, mango, chembakam, banana, persimmon, guava,' Anto said absently. In a gap between the trees, there was half an acre or so of neatly planted vegetables and a chicken run, all very orderly, and then, through another gap, sapphire-coloured water, blindingly bright in the sun and with the bluest of blue skies above.

Three women weeding the vegetable patch straightened as we passed and gave us a hard bright stare.

'Do they recognise you, Anto?'

'I doubt it,' he said. 'I was so young when I left.'

'Anto.' The words burst from me. 'How could you bear it?' Meaning Oxford, greyness, exile. 'It's so, so beautiful.'

'It is,' he said woodenly, still staring.

At the end of the drive, two large gold lions glowered from gate-posts, their paws resting on shields. Through the gate, an immaculate gravelled courtyard, its low walls covered in geraniums, hibiscus and orchids planted in split coconut husks. At the end of the courtyard, a flight of stairs led up to a large, attractive house – far bigger and grander than I'd imagined – with a bright red pagoda-shaped roof and deep, cool-looking verandas. The house was framed by exuberant tropical trees, and above it, that dazzlingly blue sky, so bright it hurt my eyes to look at it.

The horse stopped. I could hardly breathe, I was so nervous. A woman in a soft white garment was standing on the veranda, looking down at us. Her hand was over her mouth as if to stop herself screaming.

'Amma,' Anto murmured. 'Amma.'

She walked down the steps and broke into a stumbling run. I heard the muffled sob as she stretched out her arms; a long string of words that Anto answered in the same unknown language. I badly wanted him to kiss his mother to match her outpouring of emotion. But he stood there, stiff as a post, while she hugged him. And I wished, for his sake, I was invisible.

When he at last put his arms around her, I saw her shudder. He patted her back awkwardly, then glanced at me, his worried look conveying shock rather than pleasure.

'Amma.' He released her. 'I'd like you to meet my wife, Kit. She thinks this place is lovely.'

I smiled and put my hand out. 'It's good to meet you at last,' and then, absurdly, 'Thank you for having us,' thinking, Oh no! Not *us*. This was his home.

Mrs Thekkeden was tall for an Indian woman and seemed to grow then; I watched her shoulders go down, her neck lengthen. She tidied the tears away with a quick, deft gesture. Now I could see that she had the same fine cinnamon-coloured skin as Anto, the same aristocratic nose.

She held out a gracious hand.

'Welcome to Mangalath.' Her smile was tense, automatic. 'Are you very tired?'

'Oh no, no, no.' I felt the need to reassure her. 'Not at all.'

'My husband can't be here today to meet you,' she said. 'He is involved in a big court case in Trivandrum. You don't mind?' A quick, anxious look at Anto.

'Of course not,' he said. 'Work is work.'

'To him, yes,' she said.

'So, Kit, I must show you our house.' She turned to Anto. 'I've decided to put you in the guest room. The others are coming later. We don't want to bury Kit under a mountain of relatives.'

The exact same words Anto had used earlier. She smiled at me again, but her eyes feasted on Anto as we followed her into an elegant reception room with high white ceilings and heavily carved rosewood furniture. Generations of Thekkedens glowered down at us from elaborately framed photographs: serious-looking people with dark eyes and thick hair, in smart suits and wing collars, and occasionally in their own costumes. We were walking past them when I heard Anto make a sucking sound, and then breathe heavily as if he needed to sob or shout.

'What a beautiful house,' I said, to cover this raw moment.

'Thank you,' said Mrs Thekkeden in a disembodied voice. Her body was angled towards Anto, and she suddenly hugged him hard, and said more words in Malayalam that I didn't understand.

'Tell Kit about the house.' Anto disentangled himself. 'She probably imagined us living in a mud hut.'

'Anto! No!' I protested, although I was surprised at how posh it was.

'What does she want to know?' Mrs Thekkeden asked, and then, like a polite tour guide, 'So, the house and the farm have been in our family for many generations. We have our own granary, where we store rice, a tennis court, a cricket pitch, a schoolroom where the children were educated... I'll tell her more later,' she finished, a faint note of impatience in her voice. 'I can't think...'

An old man, wiry and short on teeth, burst through the door carrying our luggage. When he saw Anto, he put his palms together and bowed low and babbled.

'His name is Pathrose,' Mrs Thekkeden explained with tears in her eyes. 'He has worked for us since Anto was a little boy; now he thanks God that he has seen him before he dies.'

A slender barefoot boy came next, staggering under the weight of my suitcase. 'Kuttan is Pathrose's grandson. He will show you to your bedroom.'

'Thank you,' I said demurely. Mention of the bedroom made me feel oddly shy, as if my new mother-in-law had somehow managed to see us in all our nakedness and abandon.

'May I ask what you would like me to call you?' I added. 'Is there a special name?'

'Actually, you must call me Amma too – it means Mother,' Mrs

Thekkeden said evenly. It sounded more like an order than an invitation to intimacy. 'That's what I am to you now.'

We looked at each other. 'Yes. Good,' I said. 'Thank you.'

'When we were little, we called this the bridal suite.'

Anto stood at the door of our bedroom, still sounding in a mild state of shock. It was a large, whitewashed room, sparsely furnished except for a superb wooden bed carved with fruit and birds, placed centre stage and made up with a white sheet and thin-looking pillows. An old-fashioned wooden fan clanked overhead, but the air felt moist and heavy. The wooden shutters were closed, which gave me a feeling of claustrophobia.

'I've never slept here before,' he added.

'Obviously,' I said, and squeezed his arm, but he was in no mood for joking. 'Where was your room?'

'Over there.' He opened the shutter on to the courtyard. 'Next to Amma's.' He stared at it.

'She's so happy to see you,' I said.

'Yes.'

'Do you mind about your father – not being here, I mean?'

'No,' and then, 'It was always like that. He was either in court or away on cases. I don't mind.'

Sunlight fell in dazzling strips through the shutter. We sat side by side on the bed. 'So,' Anto said, 'I'm home. Prodigal son returns.' He put his hand under my hair and turned my face towards him. 'With prodigal wife,' he added, gazing at me. 'And a cast of thousands coming soon.' His voice – or was I imagining this? – had become more Indian already. That buttery thread running through it.

'I'm looking forward to meeting them.' A complete lie. I was tired and overwhelmed and felt childishly close to tears. I saw the family as a test I was bound to fail. I said, 'Anto, when they come, go down on your own first. I'm sure they'd prefer that.'

'Do you mind?' His whole expression brightened.

'Not a bit. Honestly.'

'Sure you don't?' He hugged me properly for the first time that day.

'No, really, just don't leave me for hours like the princess in the tower.'

'I won't,' he said.

I hoped he'd kiss me. Instead, he showed me the bathroom so I could wash while he was away. This odd-looking room had a large copper cauldron of cool water in one corner. Above it was a shelf holding a bundle of twigs, and what Anto said were Ayurvedic oils for hair and skin. Thin towels that didn't look like towels, just strips of cotton, hung on hooks on the wall.

'Be careful with water – we're often short in summer – and don't drink it. I'll bring boiled water up later.' The lavatory, he said, was a short walk outside the house, next to the chicken run. He could show me now if I liked. Later, I said, paralysed with shyness at the thought of going downstairs.

He went to the bathroom to wash his face, and when he came out, his hair still damp, I lay on the bed and watched him change. He took off his shirt, dusty brogues, dark London trousers, white shirt, and folded them neatly. When he laid them in a pile on the chair, the empty garments fluttered like ghosts under the fan. Naked apart from his underwear, he went to the rosewood wardrobe and took out a white shirt and a strip of white cloth with a gold border.

'Home clothes.' He glanced at me shyly. 'This is the Cochin version of the dhoti.' He wrapped the white cotton around his waist, like a sarong. 'It feels odd,' he murmured. 'Most peculiar.'

I couldn't tell if he was embarrassed or moved to be wearing again the clothes he'd grown up in. All I knew was that Anto, bare-legged, half-naked, had in one startling moment become an Indian husband.

I didn't know what to think. I ran my hand down his spine, wrapped my arms around him. His back made a drum of my voice. 'You smell different. What is it?'

'Coconut oil, from our own trees. There's some in the bathroom. You can use it too, on your skin and on your hair.'

'Umm.' I clung to him: my anchor in a shifting world.

'That's enough of that, woman,' he said, disentangling me. 'They're waiting for me downstairs. I'll come up and get you before lunch.'

I'd expected him to say half an hour, an hour at the most.

When he was gone, I put on my nightdress, and with nothing else to do, lay down on the bed and slept, wishing in a way I could sleep for ever, astounded at my own naivety at not thinking this through.

*

A couple of hours later, at the sound of a car horn, I leapt to my feet and, through a slit in the bamboo blinds, watched my new family arrive. A group of women stepped out of the car. They were dressed in dazzling clothes in every colour of the rainbow: cerise, emerald, ochre, gold. They were chattering like jays, jiggling up and down on the spot as if they could barely contain themselves. They love him, I thought with a childish kink in my heart: my Anto. I'm not the only one.

I watched him walk his easy, athletic walk towards them and stand between the two gold lions at the entrance. The sight of my husband in a *mundu* would take some adjusting to, but Anto at least had good legs: long and well muscled, not spindly like Gandhi's, though I decided not to tell him that. The old jokes wouldn't work here.

A youngish woman in a peach-coloured sari detached herself from the crowd and ran towards him. She put her head on his shoulder and sobbed, wiping her eyes with the corner of her stole. Mariamma, I thought. The clever older sister.

Next, a plump old lady – the grandma? – waddled through the courtyard: mouth half open, gait eager, a little off centre. Ponnamma, Anto had told me, was Amma's mother – a little doolally, spoke her mind. He'd warned me in the same breath that some members of the family abbreviated her name to Ponnae but until I knew her better this would be disrespectful.

Three children then skipped across the courtyard followed by a young woman in a pale lilac sari who hung back and looked uncertain. I've no idea who any of you are, I thought. There were only so many family members I could keep in my head at once.

Now the old lady stood in front of Anto. She patted his cheek like a blind person reading Braille, and when her face crumpled, Amma gave her a handkerchief. Watching these tender scenes, my stomach began to knot and coil. In England, Anto had reduced his family to a few colourful or touching anecdotes – his grandma's startling outspokenness, Mariamma's bossiness when young. Sometimes, when I was slow to eat, he'd assumed a high falsetto mimicking Amma's admonition to take a hanky or finish my rice. Now they were real and about to inspect me. I shrank behind the half-opened blind, my heart thumping as I listened to their voices rise and fall, swell into gunshot exclamations. And over this happy commotion came suddenly the sound of Anto laughing uninhibitedly. I'd heard

92

him laugh before, at silly films, at jokes, but this had a new clear and childish note to it.

The gargling sound of their conversation grew louder as they moved towards the veranda. And then, like a shoal of fish, they all stopped, turned and looked up together, towards our window. I dropped the blind and blushed a fiery red.

Anto was mouthing indistinct words and waving at me in an encouraging way. 'Come on down, come on,' he shouted, and I wanted to kill him. Come and get me, I thought. Don't make me do this on my own.

I'd had years of this with my mother. Standing on the outside, marvelling at families I would never be part of. I'd hoped that marriage would mean never feeling like that again, which was obviously absurd. And then I disliked myself intensely.

Shut up, Kit, I told myself brutally. You wanted this.

In the bathroom, I looked at myself in the mirror. Sister Smythe, the most feared matron at St Andrew's, came back to me. Brush your hair, girl. Straighten that dress. Smile!

'Grow up.' I said it out loud. I was ready for my inspection.

As I hovered in the doorway to the dining room, trying to smile, twenty-four pairs of Thekkeden eyes swivelled towards me. En masse, they were an exceptionally handsome family: large dark eyes, soft brown skin, their high-cheekboned faces a fine blending of East and West, well dressed, cultivated. They examined me now with a frank but not unfriendly curiosity.

They were sitting comfortably around a fourteen-foot-long rosewood table. I had been told (in bed, in Oxfordshire) about this table by Anto. He said it had been made from wood salvaged from the deck of a splendid ship that the family had owned when his great-great-grandfather was one of the principal spice traders on the Malabar Coast, taking coriander and green and red peppers to Africa, to northern India, to China. It was set with copper cups and jugs of water. In front of each chair there was a green banana leaf.

Anto jumped up. 'Kit,' he said. 'Sorry, I've been . . . Everybody, this is Kit. My new wife.'

The family greeted me with beaming smiles and perfect politeness. When the fuss had died down, his mother, waiting tensely by the kitchen door, raised her hand, and two servants arrived carrying dishes filled to the brim with chicken and ginger-scented prawns, elegantly spiced rice and lentils, fish and creamy coconut curry, each one giving off its own tantalising aroma.

'All Anto's favourites,' she said.

Anto was seated at the head of the table. My place beside him was the only one set with a bone-china plate edged in gold, a crystal glass, and a knife, fork and spoon.

'You must say grace, Anto,' Amma said, a deep emotional throb to her voice. 'You're the head of the family today.'

When the old woman said loudly, 'Where is Mathu?' Amma put a reproving finger against her mouth. 'Go on, Anto,' she insisted.

He glanced at me. 'Well...' He closed his eyes and mumbled, 'For these and all thy gifts, may the Lord make us truly thankful. Amen.'

'And thank you, God, for bringing Anto back to us,' Amma said. 'Kit too,' she added politely. She pronounced my name Keet, to rhyme with meat. 'And now,' she looked at me, smile wobbling only slightly, 'it's time to introduce you properly to your new family. Not everyone, of course: Anto has one hundred and ten cousins.' She said this with evident pride. 'We had to tell some people to stay home today, which was a bit awkward. All my husband's family and mine grew up together.'

'Thresiamma is sulking badly,' boomed the grandmother, and everyone laughed. 'Amma's in the doghouse.'

'We couldn't have them all,' Amma snapped, throwing her mother a dark look.

'It wasn't possible,' Anto consoled. 'We can visit them some other time, can't we, Kit?'

He helped me to some of the food. 'Try this, Kit, it's called meen molee. The best fish curry you will ever eat.' He sniffed at it ecstatically. 'It's all cream and coconut, and this is a roast pork dish ... and vegetables, and have some pickles, and rice and buttermilk – I'll teach you all the different names later. This is wonderful, Amma. All my favourite things,' he told his mother, who was so overwhelmed with emotion she couldn't speak.

'She's been cooking for days,' Ponnamma yelled. 'Nothing better than feeding your children.'

I must learn to cook for him too, I thought. I could barely boil an egg; once we'd joked about it, now it didn't seem so funny.

When the pickles, the rice and the appam, the lacy coconut

pancakes, had been passed around, it surprised me to see these exquisitely dressed people eating with their hands.

'You must teach me to do that,' I said in a low voice to Anto. I meant later, but he took the fork out of my hand and put a thick green banana leaf in front of me.

'Here.' He squeezed my right hand into a pouch. 'Your right hand is your eating hand, so put your elbow on the table. It will give you a firm plank. Now compact the rice with your fingers, and use your thumb to push it into your mouth.

'I'm undoing twenty-eight years of her mother's teaching,' he joked with Mariamma.

'She is twenty-eight! Old!' roared Ponnamma. 'I was married at fourteen,' she confided to me, and then, 'Your left hand is to wipe botty with, so don't use.'

I saw Amma flush with anger and wondered if it was Ponnamma or the spectacle of her son teaching his wife to eat that had made her cross.

'Make your rice into a neat tight pile like this.' Anto closed his hand over mine. 'It tastes better that way. Add in a little of the lentils, a piece of chicken, and there!' He smiled at me. 'Now try it for yourself.'

I put my hand into the bright sauces and the sticky rice, and immediately thought of my three-year-old self holding out food-splattered hands to my fastidious mother and saying 'Dirty' in tones of deep disgust.

'Like this?' The whole table watched, fascinated, as I dropped a blob of sauce on my blouse, half a handful of rice on my new skirt. Halfway through this mortifying spectacle, Anto got up and washed his hands in a sink in the corner of the room. On his way back, he looked at me and said something in Malayalam that made the family rock with laughter.

'What did you say?' I asked.

'Nothing,' he said. 'We're not laughing at you, I promise.'

I believed him – he was too kind to mock me in a situation like this. Besides, I liked seeing him laugh and dab his eyes, the sharp planes of his face relaxing.

'You'll get the hang of it soon.' Mariamma, my new sister-in-law, had placed her plump, sweet-smelling body beside me. She picked some grains of rice from my lap and told me in faultless English that she was so happy to meet someone from England, and that she was a great fan of English literature: 'George Eliot is my particular favourite, and Mr George Orwell speaks to us especially since Independence.'

At this, several heads were raised and looked in my direction. So far no one had said a single sausage about Independence, or the British, or the massacres up north, and though I'd been bracing myself for this conversational cliff, I'd been grateful for their tact. But when Amma came back from the kitchen, I took the plunge.

'Anto was sorry to miss Independence,' I said. 'It must have been a tremendous moment.'

'It was,' Amma said with a quelling look. 'Let's talk about that later. Did he seem homesick in England?' she said, her eyes very bright, very hurt.

'He was brave,' I said after a confusing pause. 'He must have missed you so much, but he was never self-pitying about it – he simply put his head down and worked.'

'He had no choice.' Amma gave me a level look. 'Did he?'

She ate in silence for a while, and then continued, 'He broke many hearts while he was away.'

I felt a surge of panic at these words. If I'd known her better, I might have asked, 'Do you mean here, or in England?' But I was dimly aware that these were the dangerous spaces between us, so I kept my mouth shut and she went back to the kitchen.

We had coffee on the veranda, twenty or so of us sitting around a mother-of-pearl-inlaid table. Anto gave me some slices of pineapple, and then plucked a few leaves from a saucer.

'These are betel leaves,' he said, 'good for digestion and palate-cleansing.' He opened a small brass pot beside them. 'Take a bit of this lime and smear it on the leaves, put some chopped betel leaf on the pineapple, then pop it into your mouth and chew – nicer than a Mars bar,' he assured me.

I chewed away dutifully despite the horrible taste. Thank you, Anto, I thought: bright red teeth to add to the humiliation.

When everyone's coffee was poured, the granny said, 'So, what I am waiting to hear is how the two lovebirds met.'

'Nosy.' Mariamma gave her a reproving tap on the shoulder as the table fell expectantly silent, and one or two people were shushed. I saw Anto's head go up like a nervous horse, and my mind leapt to the first night we'd made love. The speed with which we'd ripped off each other's clothes felt positively indecent in this setting, and because Anto had never once mentioned it again, I'd sometimes worried that he'd found my behaviour worryingly fast. I didn't understand it myself. My body had decided, and morals had lumbered on behind.

'Well . . .' Anto crossed his legs.

'It was very romantic, I'm thinking. Was it?' prompted the old woman, head on one side. 'A love match maybe. Come on, young lady, how did you meet this *themmadi*?' The table notably sucked its breath in, but nobody stopped her.

'Bad Granny.' Mariamma smacked her hand softly, but her eyes gleamed with curiosity too. '*Themmadi* means rascal,' she translated helpfully.

'Well, why else would he bring her all this way?' the old lady protested boisterously.

'Actually, it was not romantic at all,' said Anto. 'It was terrifying.'

'Terrifying?' Amma's eyebrows rose.

'Yes, terrifying. I didn't tell you this before, but we were together in St Thomas's Hospital on the night it was bombed. Actually, it was bombed several times; the first time, fourteen people died.'

'Oh dear Lord.' Amma crossed herself, her hand flying to her face.

'This time, not so bad,' Anto said. 'The roof fell in, there was a lot of shouting and running and I met Kit. We were both covered in soot, so she had no idea I was Indian.'

No one laughed at his little joke.

'And why were you there?' Amma asked me. 'Were you ill?'

I took a deep breath. Most of this was the truth, but a strange version of it: the fact was, he told me once that he'd been seconded to Thomas's that night, but I had absolutely no memory of meeting him then, and we'd never discussed the coincidence, not even with Daisy. My mind seemed to have blanked out that awful time, and I hated talking about it, mainly because of what happened next. Now when I looked at Anto, he shrugged and nodded as if to say: 'Go on.'

'I was a nurse. I am a nurse.'

'A nurse.' A dribble of red betel juice ran out of the old woman's mouth. She grimaced at the others in an unguarded way.

Daisy had warned me in advance that it would be best to call myself a medical researcher or some such, until I got to know the family better. Nurses, she'd said, were considered a low form of female life in India. When I'd protested that Anto's family were well-educated Catholics, from the more progressive south, she'd said simply, 'Trust me, darling, no woman in their family will ever have been a nurse.'

But now the point had come, and I wasn't going to lie about it.

'An English kind of nurse,' said Anto in the incredulous silence that followed. 'Kit did her three-year training at St Thomas's. She nursed during the war. She has a war medal to prove it.' No mention of the midwife training, I noticed.

'Oh,' Amma said doubtfully.

'So more like a doctor, or a missionary?' Mariamma supplied helpfully.

'Not really,' I said. 'In England, doctors are doctors; we look after their patients.' When I saw Anto giving me his 'stop now' frown, I frowned back. He'd led me into this particular landmine, and I found this level of surprise ridiculous.

'The Thames was on fire the night we met,' Anto continued doggedly. 'The entire hospital had to be moved down to the basement.'

I remembered that part, of course: the flames, the sirens, the meaty, coppery smell of blood in the wards. The girl screaming and yelling at me, her dead baby inside an air raid helmet.

'And were you hurt badly?' Mariamma, the peacemaker, wanted to know. She placed a warm hand on my arm.

'Only a bump on the head.' I found I couldn't say any more. When I looked at Anto, he gazed back blankly, as if we'd just met.

'So . . . are you thinking of working here?' Amma's face arranged itself in polite enquiry. 'As a nurse, I mean?'

So Anto hadn't told them. Wonderful. I felt the shock of betrayal, and then the suspicion that I might have to lie about myself here, over and over again, and that made me suddenly furious with Anto, who was staring down at his cup.

I was about to tell them about the Moonstone when I looked across and saw Anto frowning and shaking his head.

'It is good you have a training,' said Mariamma, filling the even more awkward silence that followed. 'My years of study were the happiest of my life.'

'First-class honours in English and history,' said Uncle Yacob. 'And she played the piano to a high standard.'

'The family brainbox,' Ponnamma shouted.

'Before children,' Mariamma reminded them, biting into a sweet-meat. And looking at this plump, complacently smiling woman, I thought: is this my future?

Chapter 14

'You were the one who brought up St Thomas's,' Kit said to his bare back. 'Why should I have to lie about it?'

The big old fan whirled arthritically above his head. Its sound would keep him awake for hours, and he longed for sleep.

'Forget it.' He stretched an arm behind him but didn't turn. 'It's your life, your work. I understand.' Liar, he thought. He wanted to scream with frustration.

Because she was right. It was his fault for deliberately bringing up, and distorting, the bomb incident at St Thomas's, imagining that the thought of his possible death would mitigate against the sin of him bringing an English girl back. A cheap trick. And he should have warned her about the status of nurses in India, not left it to Daisy to sugar-coat it.

But with that cat out of the bag, she could have helped him by sounding less determined. It was not the way things were done around here.

He'd also had the vague hope – one he wouldn't admit to himself, let alone her – that back in India she'd change her mind about working at the Moonstone, or find the job too overwhelming, or that a baby of their own would change her priorities.

She thrashed around beside him for a bit, turning and bashing her pillow, and then, hearing her breath grow even, he covered her gently with a sheet, tucked the mosquito net around her and sat by the window trying to untangle his thoughts.

He was home. This day, so dreaded, so eagerly anticipated, had brought with it a rush of sensations: the joy of seeing Mariamma again; the relief of hugging Amma; delight at seeing the new children, eating his own food, breathing that moist, blossom-scented air – it was like slipping into a warm bath after the long, lonely years away. His father's absence had been the only disappointment of the day. Mariamma had said he couldn't wait to see Anto too, but 'you know' – a humorous rolling of the eyes – 'that man can't ever stop working. It's his drug. Don't know how Amma puts up with him.'

Oh Kit. He looked down on her as she slept. *How will we do now?* The risk suddenly felt enormous, like bringing home a large and unmanageable animal thinking it would thrive here. Had he lured her into a trap?

He thought of the day he'd drawn the map of south India on her belly with his finger. How full of love he'd felt creating his child's picture, with its promise of exploding sunsets, exotic fruits and smiley faces – everything in stark contrast to blitzed-out, worn-out Britain. He'd needed her so badly then: her warmth, her succour, the outspoken fun of her. Now he tried to remember if they had even come close to one sensible conversation about how hard this would be.

It was dark outside their window now, a dense, perfumed darkness occasionally pierced by the screech of an owl on the hunt, the chirping of crickets. Kit was asleep, her hair in damp tendrils against her cheek. She's brave, he thought. I can't not love her now. She'd looked after him in England; he would do the same for her here. He crawled back into bed and put his arms around her.

He was drifting off when she rolled over and touched his shoulder. 'Anto, they're horrified, aren't they?'

'Umm . . .' Feigning sleep.

'And you know, we didn't actually meet that night at the hospital.'

'Well, we might have – it was chaos.'

'I was much too blasé.'

'About what?'

'Everything.' A note of desperation in her voice. 'What was the name of the other girl – the one they thought you'd marry.'

'Vidya,' he said after a tense silence.

'What happened to her?'

'No idea. I was only a boy when I left, and then I met this crazy woman in Oxfordshire.' He ran his hand around her stomach. 'This wonderful, crazy woman who stole my heart.'

'Do they mind? Terribly, I mean.' A plaintive note in her voice. 'Amma, the others?'

He kissed her shoulder. 'I love you,' he whispered, 'and they will too when they get to know you.'

She accepted his embraces in silence.

'Were you sad not to see your father?'

'We'll meet him soon; you'll like him. We all look up to him.'

'Amma was telling me about him – he sounds terrifyingly perfect.'

'He's . . .' Several possibilities ran through his mind. 'He'll think you're swell,' he said in his Humphrey Bogart voice. 'Now go to sleep. I can't talk any more.' He smoothed her damp nightdress over her thighs.

'I'm trying, I'm trying, and don't you dare, Anto, it's too damn hot.'

Chapter 15

I was dying to start work, but an inexhaustible supply of relatives began to arrive in horse-drawn phaetons and in rickshaws to welcome Anto home and give me a discreet once-over. After days of smiling at people I didn't know, my mouth was rigid, my reserves of small talk dangerously low, and I understood how a caged animal might feel claustrophobic and overstimulated all at once.

'Anto,' I said, towards the end of the second week, 'I've got to start work soon.' I didn't add 'or else I'll go mad', but my meaning was clear.

In the silence that followed, I heard the scrabbling of the family of bats that lived in the attic above us, and Anto's sharp sigh.

'Kit, listen.' His voice was stern. 'I'm going to Fort Cochin tomorrow to see a Dr Kunju, an old friend of my father's. He's a bigwig in the new medical directorate. Lots of new appointments since Independence, so the timing seems good. Do you mind?'

'Mind?' I could hear my voice rising. 'Why on earth would I mind? That's what we're hoping for. It's exciting.'

'Depending on what's available,' he continued, 'I may have to travel for a while.'

'That's fine, I—'

He put his hand up to stop me. 'I haven't finished.' He turned my face towards him. 'Listen... while I'm away, I'd like you to stay at Mangalath, for a few more weeks at least, and give my mother a chance to get to know you.'

'What?' I sat bolt upright in bed. 'No, Anto, I can't. We've already been here a week. I promised Daisy I'd get cracking as soon as possible.' Because the thought of delivering babies so frightened me now, I'd told Daisy before I left that I could only be counted on to do administrative work or research at the home. I'd dreaded her examining my reasons, but she hadn't. She'd simply looked at me and said quietly, 'Give it time, then see how you feel,' and we'd both tidied the conversation away quite quickly.

'I've been thinking about this.' Anto sounded uneasy. 'I think I should go to the home first.'

I stared at him. 'Why?'

'Do I have to explain?'

'Oh, sorry, forgot. Me white woman nurse, you Indian man, that sort of thing.' I was breaking my own rules now: be nice. Be calm. Give it time.

'That's below the belt, Kit.' He was smiling cautiously, hoping I was joking. He stroked my shoulder. 'We're part of a family now. Try to see it from their point of view.'

'Anto, I have a job that I get paid for. I can't not do it.'

When my voice rose, he put his hand over my mouth and glanced towards the wall, beyond which were dozens of sleeping Thekkedens.

I pulled his hand away. 'Tell the absolute honest truth. Do your parents mind me working? I mean, will I have to lie about it more or less continuously?'

I saw him take a deep breath.

'No, no, no, no,' he said, but with no conviction. 'They know, through the church, some fine missionary women who help the poor here, and they respect them. But here's the thing: we need to take it gently.' Holding my hand, stroking it. 'If I start by telling them you are part of a British organisation that trains our midwives, it gets tricky. The British are not the most popular people in the world right now ... you know that, Kit.'

'Anto ... please stop.' He was stroking my head now, as if I were a feverish child, and it felt like the worst kind of blackmail. I got out of bed and put my dressing gown on.

'This isn't how we said it would be.' I was determined not to cry. 'We both promised Daisy that I'd go to the home as soon as possible. I absolutely can't leave it for weeks.'

'I'm only asking you to stay here for a few weeks more. That's all.'

'Please, Anto ... at least take me to the home for one day.' I heard a note in my voice I didn't like: a wheedling, wifely one, and it took a great effort of self-control not to add, 'before I go into purdah'. 'Let me at least introduce myself to Neeta; I promised Daisy I'd unpack the boxes with her and tick them off the inventory.'

'So what should I tell Amma?' He sounded grumpy.

I don't give a damn! my rebellious heart shouted.

'I don't know. That we're having a sightseeing trip before your work begins, a few days off. Would that seem so unreasonable?'

His head was pressed between his hands. 'If we're having a sight-seeing trip, she'll want us to go and visit our Travancore family. I know she will.' He'd warned me of this in a jokey aside in London: that holidays meant family reunions. If you stayed for less than a week, the relatives took umbrage.

'So tell her straight that I am going to work at a home that trains midwives. That I get paid for it and that I am expected to turn up.'

He gazed at me incredulously, as if I had no idea of the intricacies involved in this simple explanation. Then he scratched his head, and gave me a cold look that in another person I might have taken for hate, before leaving the room with a firm click of the door.

I fell into a feverish sleep, and when I woke, an hour later, I found myself less than a foot away from a hideous monster. A bat, caught in the mosquito net around our bed, was staring down at me like an angry old man. It let out a horrible high-pitched squeal – purple gums, little yellow teeth – and I screamed back into its open mouth. Then, shuddering with disgust, I prised its claws from the fine gauze and flung it on to the windowsill, where it stared at me with large panicked eyes.

Chapter 16

Amma heard the girl scream from her room, watched him sprint upstairs to investigate, listened to the sobbing that followed. When he explained, somewhat shamefacedly, that it was only a bat, she expected him to laugh with her about it. But he looked at her sternly and said, 'Amma, Kit needs a day out. This is all very strange for her. You have to understand that.'

As if she was a heartless creature. So *Kit needs a day out*, she repeated to herself sarcastically, watching the family car disappear in a cloud of dust. Didn't they all? Perhaps Kit should inform herself about the price of petrol in Cochin since Independence. The cost of paying their driver extra. The great privilege of the car, since there were only ten or eleven of them privately owned in Travancore. The thought of Vidya, who would need more than a day out to recover from her change of plans.

She knew she was being unfair, couldn't help it. So far, the golden boy's return had proved a crushing disappointment. The girl was a handful; all the relatives, even the servants, were already talking about her behind her back, and Anto himself seemed permanently in flight, leaping upstairs at every opportunity to make sure she was all right.

The table Amma was sitting at was scattered with the remains of their breakfast. And suddenly, as she swept his crumbs into her palm, relief seeped into her bones, a shaft of sunlight, at the thought of having the house to herself again, and then she wanted to weep or shout: relieved to be away from Anto – could she ever have imagined such a thing when he'd lived in England and seemed closer to her?

And now the next big hurdle was Mathu's return. Prodigal husband, she thought, throwing the crumbs over the veranda rail and into the garden. He'd telegrammed that morning to say his case had concluded satisfactorily; he'd be home on Thursday to meet the happy couple. Calm as a cucumber, as if nothing had happened. He wouldn't be pleased about the car being used in this way.

Drinking a cup of chai without tasting it, she had a brisk mental conversation with Mathu. *This is all your fault* – the thought came as vicious and unbidden as a dirty punch. *You've destroyed the best thing in my life.* After having Mariamma, she'd been slow to conceive, and after five years of waiting had been told it was doubtful she'd have another. But on the day she'd been sure the new baby was inside her, she'd come to the prayer room, carefully prostrated herself in front of the Virgin Mary, and prayed, 'Make it a boy. Make it a boy!' Afterwards, she had taken a boat out on the water. She'd felt the sun on her shoulders, and seen kingfishers skimming, the egrets, the green fields, the banana palms, and had known for absolute certain that this was the happiest day of her life.

Her little pot of gold: this curious, infuriating child, with his almond-shaped green eyes that everyone commented on, his clever, inquisitive face, his way of listening hard, even when young, as if trying to discern the meaning behind what you said. Aged two or three, he'd toddled around the grounds with her while she supervised the women threshing rice, and on down the winding path that led to the backwaters beyond. When she'd shown him the birds and the trees, he'd screwed up his dear, solemn little face in concentration, repeating the names: first in English (*flame tree, banana, coconut, tulsa*) and then in Malayalam; or they'd sing songs, and sit on the swing and close their eyes, and dissolve in sunlight and sweet smells.

Before Anto, no child in their family had been sent away. Never, never, never. It was unthinkable, like throwing away the most precious gift of your life. It would never have happened if Mathu hadn't met Hugo Bateman, his English barrister hero: so flatteringly genial, so well read. Bateman had played chess twice a week with Mathu at the club, filled his head with posh dreams of a Thekkeden going to his old Oxford college. His easy charm had turned Mathu's head (*My dear chap! The one person I'm longing to see*). At lunch, at their house, he hadn't bothered to hide his patronising surprise at the extent of the farm, her orchids, the glistening stretch of water beyond. (*My God, this is paradise on earth*). He'd recommended Mathu for a role in the fevered preparations for India's first budget (*The shrewdest lawyer in Travancore*). Then a month after Independence, Bateman had packed up his house – a Tudor pagoda mess called The Larches – and scuttled back to a cottage in Dorset with Pru, his hearty tennis-playing wife, leaving poor old Mathu to find he'd been batting for the wrong team all along.

That was when an embarrassed Mathu had suggested they change the name of the house where the family had lived for one hundred and twenty years, from The Anchorage to Mangalath, which meant happiness, auspiciousness. He also suggested Parappurath, a Malayalam word meaning built solidly on the rocks – another joke now they seemed to jog along in a dizzying whirlpool of events: new government, new flag, new leaders, new friends and, most bittersweet of all, a new son (one who had lost his marbles with this new wife).

She rubbed her forehead vigorously as if it were a blackboard from which unthinkable thoughts could be erased. This dislike of her husband was new and hateful to her.

They'd had another nasty row last month when she'd begged Mathu not to be away when Anto came home. Mathu had asked her with a patient smile if she had any idea how much money it cost to run this place.

'So go to Madras,' she'd shouted, meaning the opposite. Anto would be heartbroken not to see him. 'And if your fancy woman is there, I hope you'll see her too.'

She was referring to Jaya, who'd been his legal secretary once; an educated, unlikely love object whom she privately called the mongoose on account of her long face, short legs and solitary, predatory ways. She'd found her love letter to him twelve years ago, emptying his pockets for the wash. Mathu had confessed, bought her orchids and sent her a long, sweet letter of love and contrition, and knowing he was a good man at heart, she'd tried to forgive, but the memory was a thorn that worked its way to the surface, particularly when they were going through a bad patch.

Climbing the stairs towards Anto and Kit's room, she turned detective again, with the same old feeling of dread and self-disgust. At the door of the bridal bedroom, she stood and looked in. It was too early for the servants to have tidied the room. The bed was crumpled, the pillow on the floor, the girl's peach silk nightdress flung over the chair.

In the bathroom, she panted softly as she ran her fingers through his shaving brush and held it against her cheek with a feeling of anguish that he'd grown up without her. Now her fingers touched the girl's toothbrush, still damp, her Pond's cold cream, her lipstick.

Why couldn't you wait? she asked him. Was this our punishment after all these years?

Three dresses, one blue, one made of thin flowery stuff, hung in the cupboard, drab-looking things, she thought, though it wasn't fair to judge after the war in England. The girl had no dowry; she'd already asked Anto.

Vidya's family was wealthy, and since they had no sons, she and her two sisters would one day inherit twenty acres of beautiful rice paddies and grazing near Ernakulam. Vidya, who was studying at the Women's Christian College in Madras, was pleasingly traditional: no silly bobbed hair like some local girls who fancied themselves modern, hers in a thick plait down to her hips. She bought her saris from the new shop on Broadway in Ernakulam, and wore the exquisite jewellery her mother had been collecting for the girls since the time she was born. To put it crudely, she was a catch.

Amma's hand had moved to Anto's tweed jacket when her eye was caught by a blue folder on the floor of the cupboard, just behind a row of shoes.

English Notes for Indian Midwives, the label read, and scrawled underneath it: *Neeta Chacko – Mother Moonstone Home, Fort Cochin.*

A page fluttered to the floor; she picked it up, turned it round and around, and when she saw what it was, hurriedly shut the door, her heart making a sick pounding in her ears.

The most disgusting thing she'd ever seen: a close-up picture of a woman's spread legs, her yoni there for all to see, with a huge bulging extrusion the shape of a split pear. The caption read:

Fig. 76 – Oedema of the vulva. May precede labour, and may then be an indication of pregnancy toxaemia, chronic Bright's disease, or gonorrhoea. It may also occur during labour in those cases in which the head of the child is impacted in the pelvic cavity, because the head is too large, or the pelvis is generally contracted.

Her hands trembled as she turned more pages of more naked women, one, legs apart, sitting on a bench demonstrating something called Walcher's position. Women kneeling with their naked behinds in the air. Women with babies drawn inside them in coloured pencil;

beheaded women on their backs like insects, legs raised; one with a terrible-looking condition called varicose veins of the vulva, which the notes said might rupture during the delivery of the child and cause fatal haemorrhage.

I am not a prude, she told her new daughter-in-law furiously, putting the notes back in the cupboard. What woman is after having two children? She'd enjoyed the physical act of love with her husband; still did, in spite of all their disagreements over the years. But these disgusting things had no place in a bridal suite, where dreams and hopes, joy, purity should be celebrated. Had Anto been made to share these terrible images?

She tucked the folder back where she had found it, on the wooden floor of the wardrobe behind Anto's London brogues. And now what? First she heard this girl was a medical researcher; next she learned she was a nurse, something no Thekkeden would ever stoop to; now the even more unbearable thought that she might be a midwife swooped into her mind like a black bat and flew around wildly.

Closing the cupboard with trembling hands, she decided she must never tell Mathu, or anyone else in the family, about the contents of the blue folder. Mathu, for all his alleged liberal views, was an old-fashioned man: he would be disgusted; he would express his distaste forcibly, and then Anto, so obviously besotted by this creature, might leave for ever – more heartache for her. For a brief moment she considered confronting Anto, or the girl, but the bats flew around again: if she did, she would have to admit to snooping, or pretend and blame one of the servants, who would be dismissed. Ergo: she was caught in her own trap.

Chapter 17

Anto sat beside me in a pool of sunlight, freshly shaved, smelling faintly of limes, ridiculously handsome in his smart linen interview suit.

We were colleagues again, that was how it felt: friends, with unfolding but richly connected adventures ahead of us. In a voice low enough to exclude our driver, Anto apologised for what he thought had been his overbearing manner in the last few days, said he was feeling his way here too. I said I was sorry for being a sissy and for crying; that it wasn't just the bat-in-the-net incident that had so thrown me, but the general strangeness of everything.

We laughed like young lovers again, silly and inclined to giggle at anything as he made a bat face. We held hands surreptitiously in the back of the car.

'This place is paradise.' I watched a flock of parakeets fly over soft green fields, towards the floating water and up into the huge blue sky.

'I can't wait to show you everything,' he said. He put his cheek close to mine, said in a low voice that Amma hadn't turned a hair at the thought of my visiting the home.

'Visiting? Is that how she thinks of it? Does she know it's a job?'

'With Amma, the drip-drip approach is best,' was his unsatisfactory answer. 'She'll know when the time is ripe. Look, look!' He pointed towards a blurred green horizon. 'That's where the tea plantations are. When I was eight, my father took me there on my own for a special treat. We stayed at a beautiful rest house in the Cardamon Hills. Down there,' he pointed south, 'is Trivandrum; that's where the monsoon arrives. You'll never see anything like it in your life: first a massive cloud, then this roar. It comes over the horizon like a wild animal. Makes you feel so small; makes English rain look like the dribble from a tap.'

Oh Lord, he was sweet lit up like that: eager and boyish, longing to show me things, and his excitement was infectious. As we drove through the landscape of inlets and coves and bays and backwaters, we laughed like children at the adventures ahead.

On the outskirts of the city, birdsong and lapping water gave way to the mad, jumbled music of the streets. An old woman with a skeletal baby approached us at the traffic lights and put one wrinkled palm through the window. The baby's face was covered in flies and dried snot. Anto felt my shudder as our car sped off.

'Those are the people you'll meet at the Moonstone,' he said quietly. 'No disgrace if you decide it's too much.'

I forced myself to sound confident. 'I'm actually sort of ... really looking forward to it. I mean ... obviously, well ... I'm a bit on edge about it, but ...' Aware that I wasn't making a good case for myself, I turned to him. 'You must be nervous too.'

He gave an incredulous huff, but didn't answer directly.

'For you, there's no shame in giving up. It's different for me.' He squeezed my hand. 'And I'm only saying this because I love you.'

There were so many baffling and contradictory answers to this odd declaration of love that I remained silent. It wasn't just Daisy who made me want to do this; it was more twisted and deeper than that. My failure of nerve that night at St Thomas's, my cackhandedness, haunted me. If I didn't have the motor skills and the kind of quick thinking it took to be a midwife, I wanted at least to use my training to be useful again.

I also knew that much as I appreciated the peace, the timeless beauty of Mangalath – the unhurried meals, the gently padding feet, the exploding sunsets – my motor (forward, quick, now!) was set at a different speed, and it was clear to me already that I could never be an Indian wife if that meant being the kind of smiling, docile presence I saw in, say, Mariamma or Amma.

'I can't go back on my promise to Daisy,' was the easiest way of explaining it. I had to shut up then, or be sick, as our driver, Chandy, swashbuckled his way through a broiling mass of pedestrians, ancient trucks, gharries, donkeys and, alongside us, a hand-pulled rickshaw carrying a woman with three tiny children in her arms. I saw the hem of her sari flirting with the wheels, sparks flying, babies wriggling, and couldn't bear to look.

'It can't be!' were my first words when we arrived at the Moonstone ten minutes later. We'd parked on the edge of a crumbling pavement.

The home, once the offices of a spice merchant, or so Daisy had told me, was a tumbledown pagoda-shaped slum. Its dangerously sagging roof was missing tiles. The mess of electric wires that bulged from the roof and crossed the street looked like a bad hernia. A skinny dog flopped in the bare front garden, exhausted.

Anto looked at the piece of paper again, reeled off a question in Malayalam to Chandy, who shrugged and pointed at the house.

'This is it,' he informed me curtly. 'The Moonstone.' He touched my arm. 'Listen, Kit. I can't come in – I'll miss my appointment – but promise me you won't leave here until I pick you up. I'm not sure yet when that will be – I'll come as quickly as I can. Promise; you must promise.'

'That's fine, Anto,' I said. 'I understand. I promise. Good luck.' And to show how perfectly all right I was, I gave him a cheery wave as he drove away.

And truthfully, I didn't want him there as I walked towards the house. It felt easier to absorb the shock alone. There were goats in the garden, munching at overgrown weeds, a rusted bicycle, a sign – *The oonstone* – hanging from a dusty palm tree. To be fair to Daisy, she had described the place as 'modest but serviceable', but I'd foolishly imagined it pink-bricked and full of light (an image supplied by an old India print in the lav at Wickam), rather than a worn-looking shack.

I was walking down the path when a slight figure on the veranda stood up and waved me towards her.

'I'm Kit Smallwood,' I said when I reached her. I'd decided to use my maiden name to save the family embarrassment. 'I'm Daisy Barker's colleague from Oxford.'

'We've been waiting for you,' she said in a shy whisper. She wore a medic's coat and had a broom in her hand. 'I am receptionist.'

She led me through a beaded curtain into the dim recesses of the waiting room inside. Its cracked floor was painted in red oxide; the walls were covered in a selection of fly-blown posters showing pictures of various bloodthirsty-looking gods and goddesses. Propped up on an artist's easel was a crudely drawn cardboard sign that read, in English: *Happy Birthday, Healthy Mother, Healthy Baby at the Matha Maria Moonstone Baby Clinic, Fort Cochin.*

On low benches around the wall, ten or so local women in various stages of pregnancy sat with an air of weary resignation, surrounded by children, grandmothers, mothers. All talk ceased when I walked in, feeling large and conspicuous and white.

'I've come to speak to Neeta Chacko,' I said to the girl. She stared at me for a moment, then shook her head vigorously and pointed towards a door with a sign on it: *Dr Annakutty*.

'Neeta Chacko is not here,' she said.

'Are you sure? I think she is waiting for me.'

'No.' Gently, firmly. 'She's not here, definitely. She has another job now.'

From behind the door, two voices were clearly audible: one a hectoring machine gun, the other soft and sad and submissive, then the rat-tat-tat again. The girl tiptoed to the door, opened it an inch or two, listened to a hail of words, then shut it again quickly with the air of one crating a dangerous animal.

'Dr Annakutty very, very busy today,' she told me. 'She says you must wait. Sorry, madam.' She grimaced.

So much for Daisy's 'Darling, they will welcome you with open arms.' I waited for over an hour, cushioned on either side by pregnant women, whom I examined furtively. Looking down, I saw cheap leather sandals, one or two held together by string; careworn toes garnished with a silver ring. I saw one woman unwrap a picnic for her child that consisted of minute quantities of rice and vegetables wrapped in a leaf.

But what struck me most after the war and the greyness of London was their colourful clothes, their beautifully kept hair. To use one of my mother's favourite (often furious) phrases: they'd made an effort.

The woman on my left wore a flame-coloured sarong-type garment with a tight short blouse, her eyes carefully made up with kohl, a flower in her hair. Poor as poor, but her own work of art. The girl beside her, who looked no more than thirteen, was heavily pregnant and had huge purple rings under her eyes. Her pallor suggested anaemia, but her hair was plaited as carefully as a show pony's, and Mother (why did I keep thinking of her?) would have applauded her book-on-head posture.

It was hard not to compare them with the slovenly, exhausted women we saw in London. The grey aprons, the scuffed shoes, the threadbare underwear.

I mentally slapped myself. No romanticising. Anto had warned me of that, and so had Daisy. To fall into the trap of pink-light thinking would be fatal for me now.

I sat, I listened (padding feet, low voices, the grizzling cry of a newborn in some distant room) and I started to panic as a stained clock on the wall ticked to 10.30, 11.00, 11.30. My hours of precious freedom were being gobbled up and I was still not called.

Hearing my impatient sigh, the woman on my left turned and smiled at me, and if a smile could pat your arm and massage your neck and give you something soothing to eat, she'd smiled it.

I was a sweating heap of frustration when Dr Annakutty finally appeared, wearing a white doctor's coat, a stethoscope around her neck. She was a heavy-shouldered, mannish woman with a short neck. 'I can see you now,' she said curtly. She lowered her head and scowled – the first Indian woman to give me the evil eye. 'Follow me.'

I followed her large bottom down a curry-smelling corridor and into a dimly-lit office-cum-storeroom.

'Hello,' I said heartily, when she'd closed the door behind us. 'I'm Kit Smallwood,' and then, like a twit, 'Daisy sends greetings.' Very Dr Livingstone.

'I can't shake your hand until I've washed mine,' she said, making me feel like a contaminant when she was probably simply being hygienic. That was my problem already: trying to judge each situation according to rules I didn't understand.

Her office was tiny: no fan, no outside window, and the floor blocked by the three large packing cases, the same ones Daisy and I had packed up so carefully in Wickam, what felt like a lifetime ago.

She switched on a naked bulb, then sat behind the desk looking at me and breathing deeply. A big woman, with a big pockmarked nose, a big frown and a big presence. You wouldn't want to put her back up, and it seemed I already had.

At first, she spoke so fast it was like being lashed with hailstones, and I could pick out only the odd phrase: *closed down, too late, not happy*.

'I'm sorry,' I said, overwhelmed by this avalanche. 'I can't... could... would you slow down, please?' And then, rather ridiculously, 'Has something gone wrong?'

'I – am – sorry – too.' She spaced her words now as if to a complete imbecile. 'Because we have a catalogue of woes. First,' she held out a stout finger, 'when Independence came, we were given many prior promises from your Oxford ladies that they would not pull out as quickly as the British pulled out of India. Then we heard nothing, not for months, then this comes.' She pointed towards the packing cases. 'And I am given orders, from England, that I cannot open a single box until you arrive.'

Her eyes bulged with fury. 'So we are left like dogs with the food up on a shelf: we can see supplies, we cannot get them. And the new government is telling us to cut our ties with you, so what to do? Close down this place that has taken us years of work to build? Tell the women to go home to their village midwives and take their chances? You're here now, you tell me.'

Daisy had warned me to expect 'a few dicey moments', but being told something and experiencing it were very different things, and in that stuffy room, I was getting my first inkling that this woman saw our fund as a necessary and compromising evil and myself as its condescending representative: a white maharani determined to keep hold of the purse strings in the new India.

'Why isn't Daisy Barker with you?' she asked suddenly. 'She is the one I must speak to.'

I explained that Daisy had urgent business at home; it was impossible for her to come.

'Who are you?'

'I'm an English state-registered nurse, trained at St Thomas's Hospital in London.'

'You have midwifery qualifications?' She sniffed and looked at me.

'Not quite. I've done my Part Ones and most of my Part Twos bar a few deliveries.' *Flunked one*, my guilty heart added. 'But I plan to stay here, and I would like to work with you, Dr Annakutty.' (Was this even true now I'd met her?)

When I stumbled on her name, she snapped, 'Call me Dr A. I don't have time for all that.'

Her chin made a bristly sound as she rubbed it. She tapped her fingers on the desk.

'What we need most is money to run this place. Do you understand that?'

'Yes, I do.' (Rude bitch. She was really starting to put my back up.)

'If we give you a job, it will be for creating funds and writing reports.' Dr A's important nose quivered. 'Nursing will come when I have assessed you. If you want to help now,' she added, 'you can open the boxes – we have almost nothing left.'

'Of course,' I said sweetly. 'Happy to help, but first, may I ask if Neeta Chacko is here? I think Miss Barker thought... she said she—'

'Neeta is gone,' she interrupted, eyes beady and cold. 'She has another job – I don't know where.'

When I said I didn't think anyone had told Miss Barker about this, she gave that most ambiguous of Indian gestures: the sideways head wag, the yes that could mean no – the one Anto confused me with sometimes.

'So who... Forgive me... sorry, but have you taken over from her?'

'I've told you,' she snapped. 'My name is Dr Annakutty. I am the acting official head of the home, put here by the new government.' She reeled off a string of qualifications: a medical degree from Madras University, obstetrics, midwifery course (Trivandrum Hospital), six hundred and fifty-six deliveries – the full deck of cards. 'Plus, I am now senior lecturer to the village courses we run with the *vayattattis* – the local midwives.'

More muscle-flexing followed from her side of the desk – she declared that she could be a full professor in Bombay at this point in her career were it not for her political ideals – then she opened the door and yelled something in Malayalam into the darkness.

'I'm calling for a knife,' she said. 'Because you are here,' she gave me a quizzical look, 'we can open the boxes.'

I mumbled that the committee's rules were none of my doing, *big, fat, bully girl*. I was getting hot and bothered myself.

A boy arrived and removed the packing case lids with a knife and hammer. Dr Annakutty lowered her considerable bulk to the floor. 'I'll take things out,' she said curtly. 'You write,' handing me a pencil and a pad.

We worked in silence for a while, just the rustle of paper, a man crying *pani, pani, pani* in the street outside, while Dr A unpacked the Petri dishes, rubber enemas, thermometers, forceps, swabs, sanitary pads and cord clamps we'd wrapped in back issues of *The Spectator*.

At the end of an hour, my entire body prickled with sweat, but the job was done: the packing cases were empty, my inventory covered five pages, and Dr A and I were surrounded by piles of nightdresses, baby clothes, medical supplies and three copies of Comyns Berkeley's *Pictorial Midwifery*.

She signed each page of my inventory in a slashing hand, a big circle of sweat underneath her arm.

'Is this enough to last for a while?' I asked.

She gave a big sigh. 'No. Not really. I was turning women away last week.'

I made murmuring sympathetic noises.

'There was so much killing up north that medical funds and staff have been diverted, plus it's hard to get women from good families to train with us. We had to send two away. Their families did not approve. One has promised to come back, the other I don't know.' Dr A's frown made a huge V in her forehead. 'Her husband won't allow it.'

'Is it dangerous to be short-staffed?'

'Of course, and I don't know yet if I can use you. I must check with our own government officials first,' she said. 'British people can't just walk in now and work.'

She put some of the equipment back into the cases. 'I'm taking these home tonight,' she said. 'There are bandits in the streets around here, and this building is not safe. Tell your charitable ladies this. We need better locks on our doors.'

'Look, I live here now,' I said. 'I need a job.' I'd made up my mind.

'Why?' I could hear her thighs sucking as she heaved herself off the floor and sat behind the desk. 'Are you married?' She was looking at me thoughtfully.

When I told her that I was married to an Indian, a Nasrani whose family lived at Mangalath, I swear it was like the sun coming out. 'The Thekkedens,' she said, her face visibly brightening. 'A well-known family here, though not personally known to me.'

'I met my husband in England. He's a doctor. He did his training there.'

This slight thaw between us encouraged me to add, 'He worked on the translations with Daisy Barker in England. Both of them feel this home could do great work.'

She gave me a hard look, as if to say, 'What would Miss Barker know about anything here?'

'Great work is our aim,' she said after a considering pause. 'But we have two big obstacles to overcome. Number one.' She stuck a large finger in the air. 'In some people's minds, a nurse is like a prostitute – sorry for the word – and some doctors here do use them like that. Not good information for you, but if you are going to join us, better you know the facts.' She adjusted her enormous bosom.

'Number two. If a girl becomes a nurse here, she has a very bad showing in the marriage market, despite all our efforts. Even the married ones have difficulties: one of our best midwives was beaten badly by her husband last week. Even though she supports him,' she added with a dark look.

'But I thought the Christian community here felt differently.' I was anxious to prove I was not a complete novice. 'And that women from south India were well educated and encouraged to work.'

'Up to this point.' Dr A made a small and not very encouraging mark on her desk. 'And only to here. Our biggest problem with employing Hindu girls is they do not like to handle the bodily fluids of another, they think it pollutes them, so we do prefer Christians to work here. Some fathers will hand their oldest daughters over to us for training, but the families are not always happy about it.

'We're trying to start a revolution,' she said tiredly, rubbing her eyes, 'with not enough soldiers.'

In that moment, I felt I could forgive the rattiness, the inability to give anything but the unadorned facts. Charm, jokes, emollient words took it out of you when you were working the long shift.

'So,' she smiled at me for the first time, 'you're a Thekkeden. Sorry for the confusion at first. Now I can show you the work we do. If you come back on Friday, we'll take a boat out from Alleppey to the villages where we train some of the midwives and you can see it first hand,' as if this had been decided all along.

Oh Lord, I thought, excited and startled. I had no idea what Anto would think about that, or Amma, who was now frigidly polite to me. It seemed that part of me was already thinking like an Indian wife, except the other part was promptly and eagerly replying, 'Thank you: that sounds perfect. What time should I come?'

It was the tail end of dusk when we got home to Mangalath: cows munching hay beside rose-coloured backwaters, evening fires being lit on the edge of the village of Pookchakkal. As we turned the last corner in the road, the house rose out of the trees, a tangible welcoming presence with oil lamps glowing on the veranda.

It was then that I saw a grey-haired man standing motionless on the steps. He was staring at us as we drove up. We got out of the car.

'Appan,' Anto said, rooted to the spot. I saw his face twist as his father walked towards us.

When he drew closer, I saw that Mathu Thekkeden looked eerily and disconcertingly like an older, wearier version of Anto. The same abundant springing hair, though his was grey now; the same languid, slightly aristocratic bearing; the same jutting cheekbones and finely shaped green eyes, though his were wrinkled and deep-set.

He walked straight up to Anto and put his arms around him, and hearing his sobs, the muffled words in Malayalam, I hung back, not wanting to spoil things. There were more anguished-sounding words, a keening sound from Anto, and then Mathu turned his wet face to me and after a jagged pause said in a kind but formal voice, 'Forgive me, I am forgetting all my good manners. Welcome to Mangalath, you are Kit?'

'It's lovely to be here,' I said. 'I've heard so much about you.'

In fact, I knew surprisingly little, except the bare-bones stuff about him being one of only a handful of Indian judges in south India, a clever man, an Anglophile with a tiresome predilection for cards (played bridge for his Cambridge college during his four years there; tried to teach Anto, aged ten: a disaster). On the rare occasions that Anto had talked about his father, he'd adopted a lightly ironic tone, referring to him as 'Pater', as if he was some spat-wearing character out of a Wodehouse novel – the kind of man who went on tiger hunts with English toffs, who ordered his cravats from Bond Street.

It was hard to connect these fragments with this anguished man who now stood hugging my husband as if he was the last person alive on earth.

Chapter 18

In the study after supper, Anto felt like someone surfacing from a long dream. It was all still there: his father's curved captain's chair, the magnificent cedar desk, the green lamp casting shadows on the teetering piles of books his mother was not allowed to touch – in French, Italian, Malayalam, English, Hindi, all languages his father was fluent in – the complete works of Shakespeare and Dickens, the ancient texts on agriculture that had been in the family for years.

And Appan: a little more stooped, but still handsome, the usual cut-glass decanter of whisky beside him. Soon he'd pour his one glass per night in a special Waterford crystal glass given to him by Mr Bateman, smoke one of three cigarettes taken from the tin with *Player's No. 3* on it – Anto used to be allowed to light them.

'Can I offer you one?' Appan pushed the tin towards him.

'No thank you.' He'd been beaten for less once.

Appan lit up in the old, methodical way: long brown fingers placing the cut-glass ashtray just so, click with the silver Dunhill lighter – another present from Bateman – the slow drag that made his cheekbones pop out.

The bookshelves behind him were crammed with files on the thousands of court cases he had taken part in. When they were young, Anto and Mariamma would hide, and Mariamma, in a thrillingly hoarse whisper, would relate the lurid details of the serial killer from Bangalore who chopped his victims into little pieces and threw them in the Ganges. The new bride strangled with her own hair. Rex versus Colonel Thorn, the Hampshire-born colonel who'd poisoned his Indian mistress.

The schoolroom, which they'd nicknamed the Torture Chamber, was once in the next room. He and Mariamma were taught by a Scottish woman named Ann McGrath; they'd privately called her Hoots Toots and imitated her mercilessly. It was the place where

Mariamma – whip thin and sarcastic in those days – had effortlessly shone.

On his infrequent visits home, Appan would appear there to check with thrilling gravity on their progress, or sometimes to wind up the gramophone and play them his scratchy recordings of Shakespeare. He was a many-headed god in those days – a pincher of cheeks, a flyer of kites, but unpredictable: if you crossed the line, he'd appear with a face like thunder and a strap in his hand.

Anto was fourteen years old when his father had called him into the study and told him he was to be sent away to school. He still cringed at the memory of how he'd wept and pleaded to stay. Later he heard his mother sobbing and shouting in their bedroom, saw her red-rimmed eyes at the dinner table.

He'd stayed awake all night trying to make sense of this catastrophe. He loved the farm, with its animals and tree house and warm sheds, the cricket hut where he and his friends smoked, the spangled lagoon outside, the shrine, the temple, the village where everyone knew him. The pattern of his life was fixed here, and he didn't mind. Even the vague notion that he might one day marry Vidya had not alarmed him. She was happily linked in his mind to her head-patting mother, Anu, who'd given him the cricket bat he treasured, and who'd brought him sweets wrapped in bright tissue paper. All things that mattered to the half-formed creature he was then.

'Sure you don't want one?' It was unusual to see his father light one cigarette from the stub of another. The second whisky was new, too.

'No thanks.' In the glow of the lamp, he saw how Appan had aged: the permanent mark on his nose from his spectacles; the slump of defeat in his demeanour, or maybe he was just bone-tired – Amma said he never stopped working.

'Is it funny being back, Anto?'

'Yes.' Neither of them smiled.

'So much to catch up on.'

'Yes.'

His father fiddled with the notebook on his desk.

'How did your interview with old Kunju go?' he asked after a pause. 'I haven't seen him properly for years, but I think he is quite a big nob now in the medical world.'

'He is the Chief Medical Officer: big desk, staff of eighty, or so he told me. He hopes he can find me something.'

'Only hopes?' his father said sharply. 'Did you not show him your qualifications?'

'Of course.'

'Was he impressed?'

'I don't know.' It felt too early to explain everything, so he took a cigarette instead, thinking, to hell with it, I'm a man now. His father passed him the Dunhill with trembling hands.

'We need all shoulders to the wheel at the moment. The estate has taken quite a dip in profits since the war.'

'I'm aware of that, Appan. I want to work too.' Anto exhaled, took a piece of tobacco from his tongue. His father was looking anxiously at him through the smoke. 'Dr Kunju hasn't got a job for me. Not yet.'

Dr Professor Kunju, he thought privately, was a pompous prick of a man, with his walrus moustache and his office wallpapered with medical certificates and back-slapping photos of him taking tea with Gandhi, and he'd caught the distinct whiff of old scores being settled.

'How long since you saw him?'

'Oh God.' Appan plunged his fingertips under his glasses, rubbed his eyes. 'Let me see, quite a while. We used to play squash at the English club. I don't suppose he wanted to be reminded of that.'

'No. He is a fully paid-up Indian now.' They exchanged an awkward glance. 'And when I told him where I'd been, he said preference must be given to those who stayed behind and fought the good fight here.'

'I see.' His father rubbed his forehead rapidly. 'So, nothing?'

'Nothing immediate,' Anto said wearily. 'A few things in this.' He handed his father a copy of *The Hindu Times*.

Appan peered at the two ringed advertisements: ' "Junior doctor wanted for TB sanatorium." '

'Look below.'

' "Urgently wanted, forty doctors for service in refugee camps in East Punjab. Pay 300–400 rupees per calendar month plus camp accommodation." '

'Dr Kunju peppered me with questions about Independence,' Anto continued. 'A kind of test: which politicians did I personally support? How many people were slaughtered? He was horrified at my ignorance, and now I feel as though I was in a dream while all this happened. I had no idea of the extent of it.'

'It was a bloodbath,' his father gasped. 'Don't you read the papers?' His eyes were huge bruised plums, shining in the lamplight.

'The English papers were not so detailed.'

Appan was holding his head in his hands like a balloon that might burst.

'Don't go away again, not now. Surely he has a local job for you.'

'Nothing, Appan, not yet. You see, another awkward thing cropped up in our talk. Vidya. He knows her family well and told me what a wonderful girl she is: beautiful, clever, kind.' The Doctor Professor had delivered this encomium in a voice dripping with regret.

Appan drew a hairless head on his pad. He blew his nose vigorously and took a sip of whisky. 'Well, he is Vidya's auntie's cousin. Look, Anto, I can't lie about this to you. It's an awkward situation, you coming back ... you know ... not single.'

'What did you expect, Appan?' Anto tried not to raise his voice. 'After so long away.'

'That was never our intention. It nearly broke your mother's heart. But we did hope ...' Appan was trembling with emotion.

'Hoped what?'

'That you would have the self-discipline to wait for a wife. Would that have been so hard?'

'Kit is my wife.' He knew he should say more – about her intelligence, her kindness to him in England, her bravery in coming here – but the words didn't come.

His father was holding back tears, teeth bared like a dead animal, eyes screwed tight.

'Your mother was so excited. She had planned your wedding with Anu and Vidya, told all her friends, and then ... it was too much.'

Anto sat and tried to breathe.

'Is this really so hard for you?'

'It will be if you can't work.' His father took a deep breath. 'I took out a big loan to finance your time overseas. Bateman promised to help with your fees. But you know, once he got back he had other priorities, and of course this family is top heavy with women. That's why I'm working night and day.'

'I'll find a job, I'll do whatever I can.'

'Thank you, son.' He'd never seen his father look so blank, so obedient. 'Don't tell the others what I am telling you.'

A tray rattled outside the door. Amma with their nightcap: camomile tea for Appan, vetiver for Anto, just like in the old days.

'Goodnight, Antokutty, goodnight, Mathukutty. I'm going to bed, son, don't forget to say your prayers.' When her cry woke a crow, which squawked from a tree outside, his father, who was superstitious, made the sign of the cross.

'And you, Ammakutty. Goodnight. God bless. Leave the tray outside the door, we're busy.'

Anto took a deep breath. 'Father, could you call her in for a moment? There's something I need to say to both of you. I've been putting it off.'

Amma brought the tray in looking sleepy but pleased.

It was then he told them that Kit would be starting work soon.

'Where?' His father's voice was suddenly sharp.

'At a home for expectant women in Fort Cochin.'

'How will she get there?' Appan's face was rigid with surprise.

'We'll have to use the car, until we get our own place in Fort Cochin.'

His father's frown deepened. Amma was staring down at the tea, which lay untouched in the cups. 'Who will pay for the car?' he said after a lengthy pause.

'Kit will,' Anto improvised. 'She'll be paid sixteen pounds a month.'

'Is she nursing?' A dark note had appeared in the old man's voice.

'No . . . I mean to say . . . I think her duties are mainly administrative. That was the work she was doing in Oxfordshire. They are carrying out an important survey on infant mortality here, and how it can be improved.' He noticed that he had swerved around the word 'midwife' or even 'midwife training', and was not proud of the fact. 'Look, I'm sorry, I know it's not what you want, but she has to do it.'

'What do you mean, she has to do it? She is your wife now. Do you let her dictate?'

'It's not a matter of dictating. I want her to do it too.' Even to himself he sounded unconvinced.

Appan sighed deeply. He shot a quick look at his wife, who was trembling and shaking her head, but he did not ask for her thoughts.

'What will happen if I say no?' His father stared into the cold tea.

'Don't ask that question,' Anto said grimly. 'I've only just come home.' He heard his mother give a small groan.

'Make sure she pays for the petrol,' his father said at last. His face had taken on some of the greenish colour of the lamp, and when he raised his exhausted eyes and looked at Anto, they were so full of frustration and foreboding he might as well have added, *This woman will ruin your life.*

Chapter 19

He came to our room that night, lifted my nightdress and made love to me as if it was our last night on earth.

'I love you, Kit, I love you.' He said it over and over again. My head was jammed against the headboard. 'Never forget it.'

'I won't.' I was startled by his tone. 'I love you too.'

'This is hard for you,' he said. 'You're being brave. Do you trust me?'

'Of course I trust you. Now pass me a glass of water and let's get the mozzie net properly tucked.' I was trying to make things sound normal because he sounded different in a way I couldn't put my finger on. When he didn't respond, I put out the oil lamp, squirted the Deet, and tucked the net around us.

He said in a muffled voice, and without turning over, 'I'm going to sleep now.'

He went off quickly while I lay awake feeling the heat bear down on me like a soft, soggy cloak. I was getting more and more confused by him. When he woke in the middle of the night, I put my hand on his shoulder. 'Anto, something's wrong, isn't it?'

He didn't turn over. 'Nothing's wrong.' His back was a drum I could feel words through. 'I just meant to tell you that Appan said you can start work whenever is right for you. He thinks it's good for women to work.' He might have been reading from a report.

I was even more confused. 'Anto.' I pulled on his shoulder. 'Was it that easy? What did you say?'

'Nothing. It's just that I may have to travel soon. I must get a job.'

'Of course, that's what we planned, and then we can get a house of our own.'

'We'll try.'

I felt my life being organised behind my back and I hated it.

'Anto,' I said. 'Something's wrong. I know it is. I can feel it.' But he was gone, as quickly as if someone had stuck a chloroform mask over his face. I knelt beside him and in the slatted silvered moonlight studied him: the curve of his cheekbones, his lips, his fine soft skin. Was it a simple case of lust that had led me here? Before him, I'd never known the matchless intoxication of sexual attraction, how it powered you with an energy you could neither predict nor control. If another man had asked me to take this journey, would I have been more clear-sighted, less idealistic, less delusional?

For the next few days, I had the sense of him drifting away. He went out early, going for every job he could find, and then one day there was a note saying he'd had to leave suddenly: an interview had come up in the north. He wasn't sure he would get the job, but he had to try. He was sorry not to give me the message in person, but would I stick to our agreement of staying for two weeks at Mangalath?

Mariamma handed the note to me at the breakfast table, with the possibly kind embellishment of: 'And he said we were to look after you, and have lots of fun.'

'How far north?' I was trying not to look as shocked as I felt. We'd never once discussed the possibility of him working up north, plus it was so unlike him to leave without a word, a kiss, some reassurance.

She patted my hand, said, 'Bombay, I think, but dinna fash yourself, the men in our family are always on the move. This morning I am going to show you how to tie a sari.' She had Anto's quick and irresistible smile. 'A surprise for Anto when he gets back.'

Threatened now by the shapeless days ahead, I was grateful for any kind of plan.

After breakfast, Mariamma's daughter, Theresa, a sweetly solemn plump child, with huge brown eyes, and the early beginnings of a moustache, sat on the veranda staring at me without a word until Mariamma came downstairs, her arms covered in stoles and saris.

The saris smelled delicious. Mariamma explained how, depending on the time of year, she and Amma would take them out and refold them with different herbs: jasmine in spring, attar of roses or lemon grass in summer, mitti or lavender during the monsoon. She laid them out for me over the wicker chairs, explaining how the *chatta* and *mundu*, the simple white blouse and soft white skirt she and Amma wore every day, was more or less the Nasrani woman's uniform. These more elaborate jewelled and coloured saris were usually for weddings or for kitty parties, when all the women got together for fun and gossip – God save me from one of those, I thought in a panic.

'I hear you are starting official duties with a charity soon,' she dropped in casually, giving me the feeling she had been part of a family discussion I hadn't been party to. 'So this would be most suitable and cool.' She held up the Nasrani outfit: the white draping skirt with the pleats at the back, the simple cotton blouse. Her smile was friendly, her hands busy folding, stroking, unfolding saris, tucking one or two into the tissue paper she explained was acid-free and protected them from termites, from sweat.

I liked Mariamma: she was funny, and affectionate, and proud of the Scottish sayings she'd learned from her governess. If she felt any sibling protectiveness about Anto and me, she hid it well.

She wrapped the cloth around me with neat and practised hands, part of me was thinking, this must be what it's like to have a sister – getting fizzy about clothes, rolling our eyes about boys, confiding things. When we'd been talking about Anto earlier, she'd told me, 'As a boy, he was always sneaking off. He was quite a solitary soul.'

'Really?' I'd said, thinking of our all-too-brief courtship at Wickam Farm, and how we'd craved and plotted for more time together.

'We used to play tracking games.' She wound the cloth tighter. 'I would leave a trail of clues in the trees, the flower pots, on the jetty, once behind the donkey's ears. Anto and his friends would follow them, for miles sometimes, by canoe or bike. They had wonderful fun. They were so free.'

'I bet you loved that, too!'

'I stayed home with Amma,' she said serenely. 'My job was to set the clues. I enjoyed that,' she added, a little defensive. 'From an early age here, we're in training to be good wives.'

It was tempting to ask how this fitted with her three years of intoxicating freedom at university. But she, focused, serious, was lifting another sari from tissue paper and putting one end of its length on my shoulder.

'So has he changed much since he was away?'

'Very much,' she said.

'In what way?'

'He's more serious. He makes a lot of jokes, but he's sadder.'

I was quietly devastated to hear this, and she, glancing quickly at me, changed the subject, lifting up a sari of gossamer-fine white silk gauze with a gold border that sparkled like sunlight on water.

'This was for my wedding,' she said. 'I was covered in gold jewellery, too.' Her eyes gleamed at the memory. 'Such a wonderful day: feasts, fireworks, the wedding parties arriving by boat, and the jetty, the garden all lit up with flaming torches – so beautiful you wanted to cry. I wish you'd been there,' she added politely. 'What did you wear for your English wedding?' The question I'd dreaded.

'Nothing fancy.' Thinking of the freezing registry office, the sausages and fruit cake, Daisy's frantic efforts to compensate for the absence of my mother. 'A tweed suit, a hat.' The look of pleasure in Mariamma's eyes turned to disappointment, even disapproval.

'Did Anto mind?'

'No.' But I didn't know any more. 'Clothes are still in very short supply in England.'

To cover the awkward pause, Mariamma, wafting rose water, made me try on another sari. Usually I hated the feeling of being dressed – memories of Ma smacking me, spitting on her hanky, saying brooches out, belts in etc. but Mariamma's expression was gentle as she patted me and moved me around, adjusting a fold here and there.

'What sort of clothes did you wear in England as a very little girl?' She smiled over my shoulder at Theresa, who was watching with rapt attention. 'Our Scottie governess wore tweeds even in the heat.'

'Anything my mother chose – usually in wool,' I answered. 'Yes, even my bathing suits. Mother knitted them, and they had buttons on the front, and when we went to the seaside and they filled up with water, I looked like a larva on legs.'

'A larva!' Mariamma started laughing, and when she flapped her arms and translated this for Theresa, who cackled and threw herself around, we were all laughing. I was hungry and could smell spices and herbs coming from the kitchen. I was thinking I could be happy here.

'Yes,' I continued, mainly now for Theresa's sake, 'woollen hats, very prickly, woollen skirts, even woollen knickers.'

'Woollen food also?' Theresa spoke in English at last. She beamed, showing her sharp little teeth.

'Definitely woollen food: woollen sausages, woollen potatoes.'

A stream of words followed from Theresa.

'She wants you to come to the ladies' party next week,' Mariamma told me. 'She says you're...' She stopped and drew in her lips. Amma had just appeared on the veranda, so quickly she might have been watching us all along.

'Of course, we must ask Amma first,' Mariamma continued smoothly. 'We start with a lot of prayers, which you may find boring, so maybe later.'

Amma didn't say a word, just took a long, appraising look at me half draped in a pale pink sari, another kind of larva about to shed, or add, a skin.

'Can you walk in it?' she asked at last, trying for a smile.

I tried, a sort of graceless hobble to begin with; then, remembering how Mariamma did it, smaller steps, greater awareness of posture. Theresa clapped her podgy little hands.

'How does it feel?' Amma's face was expressionless.

'Quite different,' I said, which was true: I felt taller, more womanly, and, once I'd got the walk right, almost stately. I also felt bandaged, swaddled, held in, like someone in a three-legged race, but thought it best not to mention this.

'She looks pretty.' Theresa closed one eye, screwed up her funny little face like a Paris seamstress. When I looked at her, I imagined the children I would have with Anto – though please God not yet.

'Very pretty,' said Amma faintly.

'We were thinking she could wear this for work.' Mariamma held up the plain white outfit.

'For work, yes.' Amma was sort of smiling and sort of frowning. 'Anto says you start soon. Are you happy with that?'

'Yes,' trying to sound humble, but clear; sure of myself, but not obnoxious.

'Good,' Amma said drily. 'So you got your own way at last. You do know I'm not happy about it, don't you?'

'I sort of guessed,' I said. 'And I'm sorry.' Her expression froze.

Later, when I was walking back to my room, she stopped me in the corridor, pinched my arm and glared at me, a hard, bright look full of intent.

'You must never discuss your work within the family,' she said. 'That's one thing I insist on. Do you understand?' I told her I did, but I didn't, not properly, not yet.

Chapter 20

Terrified that I would oversleep, or that Amma would forbid it at the last moment, I hardly slept a wink before my first official day at work. I got up at four a.m. and read for a while, and arrived an hour early at Alleppey, where, at 7.30 in the morning, the wooden jetty buzzed with fish sellers, coconut juice vendors, and a sleepy child selling fried crisps and wooden snakes.

I found Dr A sitting in a wicker chair outside the ticket office, looking very grand and impersonal, and not much friendlier than the first day I met her. The anxious-looking bespectacled woman beside her, she introduced as Maya, 'Our fully qualified midwife.'

Maya gave a wincing smile, and when she looked at me, I saw, underneath an impressive pair of men's glasses, a fading green and purple bruise.

Our boat was a battered old rice boat with *Moonstone* written on its side in faded red lettering. It was a beautiful, romantic-looking thing with gracefully curved lines and a bamboo roof that flung patterns of sunlight on the floor. Dr A explained to me, in a bored monotone, that its deck was tied together with rope coated with resin from cashew nuts and fish oil, and that the boat was both an urgent necessity – the only way they could visit some villagers – and a serious drain on finances, since it needed complete restoration.

While it was being loaded with boxes of medical supplies and cardboard signs for the midwife classes, Dr A settled back in her chair and withdrew into the magnificent citadel of her mind (either that, or she'd fallen asleep), and Maya, who had the sweet, shy smile of a child, became more and more animated as she showed me around.

In a tiny, squalid kitchen at the end of the boat, she pointed to a stove, 'where you may cook your rice and chai'. Then, indicating a duck innocently floating by, she mimed strangling him. 'For our dinner.'

When I asked what our plan for the day was, Maya beamed at me through her swotty glasses and produced a map from under the saucepans.

'Our first port of call,' she said, 'is Champakulam, where we will have a confab with some local midwives to try and persuade them to do our training. Next we'll go to see a post-partum mother who has had a big, *big* baby: twelve pounds, poor thing. The biggest ever in the village.' Query diabetes, I thought, but said nothing. 'We'll also see a mother on the point of delivery.'

I was getting used to the lackadaisical rhythms of India by now – the chai, the chat, the *hawa khana*, which Anto had told me was Hindi for chewing air – but this seemed an awful lot of work to get through in a day, and I'd promised, actually sworn, to Amma I'd definitely be home that night. I tried to disguise the panic I felt.

'How long will it take?'

When she replied, 'Oh, two days, definitely,' my scalp prickled with alarm, and before the boat left, I had to jump ashore, yell for the driver (glares from Dr A, whom I woke up) and scribble a grovelling note to my mother-in-law saying that I might be delayed but no one was to worry about me.

When the boat's bell rang, I was hauled aboard by Maya's surprisingly strong arms. Dr A watched me, frowning, from the prow of the boat: a huge black shadow framed by the sun. But I soon forgot her and my worries about Anto and Amma and all the rest of it, it was so wonderful being out on the river. I was here, I was working. It ran like a song through my head all that morning. Plus, the first shy shoots of friendship had sprung up between me and Maya, whose general demeanour was so sweet and friendly, and whose English, like that of so many other locals, was excellent.

As the boat chugged through the narrow waterways, I felt a sense of relief. I was entering a wonderfully new and secret world, one that was separate from the Thekkedens, with all their rules and expectations and disquiet about me. Around the first bend in the river I saw a whole family – parents, children, dogs, buffaloes – washing in the water, then a row of rainbow-coloured women walking in single file through a rice paddy with water pots on their heads. There were colourful shacks and tiny neatly planted gardens; a fierce old lady peeling her vegetables; a Hindu temple, so close that its incense prickled my nose, with a priest waving at us from the bank. Around us, rice paddies and palm trees were reflected in the water; soft hills beyond that looked like clouds, and clouds looked like hills. Families of ducks that virtually ignored the gentle splash of our boat. The flash of a kingfisher wing; the leap of a fish. I don't think I had ever been so spellbound or so happy.

A large canoe passed carrying a load of giggling schoolgirls, hair plaited and tied with white ribbons, long blue skirts, white shirts, smart enough to go to Roedean.

'I know them all.' Maya returned their waves. 'I delivered two of them. One took two days and nearly killed me.'

On the opposite side of the river, a pathetic scrap of a girl – no more than six or seven – stopped washing clothes when she saw us pass. When she waved a skinny arm at us, her collarbone popped out like organ stops. Maya told me that the poor people were poorer than ever around here, what with the war and the rice crop being bad last year. That girl was an orphan, but I was not to worry about her. 'In India, the children belong to everyone – grandmas, aunties, friends.'

So why had my mother fallen through this particular net, I wondered, and ended up in an orphanage? The jagged pain of wondering if she missed me as familiar as an old injury by now. On the ship coming over, I'd written her two letters, half hoping to hear that she still loved me, that she forgave me. I'd followed up with another letter and two postcards from Mangalath, but the silence from her end was deafening, and I was starting to believe that I really was dead to her.

To stop my gloomy thoughts, I asked Maya about her training, and if she would mind my taking notes. She told me that after delivering babies for many years with no formal training, she'd been persuaded by Dr A to do three years of general nursing in Madras, followed by one year of midwifery.

'My family allowed me to do this because my husband is ill with a heart problem, but now he hates what I do,' which was pretty obvious from the green and purple shiner. 'Most nurses here,' she added with a shrug, 'are life dust: widows, orphans or deserted wives. Until recently there was no formal training of midwives at all. We caused a very big stir,' she added with a wide smile. 'But now there is a government push towards it.'

I marvelled at her calm, cheerful presence; it made my blood boil too. Every bloody religion in the world pretended to care about mothers, children, the sick and the lame – but they didn't mean it, not really.

As we were talking, Dr A rose like a large whale from the prow of the boat. She pointed towards a cluster of mud shacks on the riverbank, the spire of a white church.

'Champakulam,' she said, adjusting her sari and picking up her large doctor's bag. 'Two local midwives will see us there.'

Only two! Daisy had led me to believe there'd be a classroom crammed with them, but I followed her meekly off the boat and down a dirt road (filthy drains, lots of stinky rubbish, an old woman with milky eyes selling fish) to a small whitewashed convent on the edge of the village, where an old French nun greeted us.

The nun led us to a windowless room at the back of the church where two women were waiting. The first, Amba Kannan, was a small, wiry, aggrieved-looking woman, about thirty-five years old, arms covered in cheap gold bangles. The other midwife covered her face when she saw us, and told us in a reluctant mumble that her name was Latika.

Amba greeted Dr A politely with a namaste, but then let go a torrent of words. Dr A listened silently, wagging her head sympathetically, then turned to me. 'Her biggest problem is this: some of the people in this village have stopped paying the local midwives for their work because they hear that you are paying them now. She says...' she listened to another blast of invective, 'they are being treated like criminals.'

'Please tell the village people we only pay for training,' I said.

'This I have explained to them, but they are angry and do not trust British people any more.' Dr A snorted non-committally. 'She would like some money now to make up for what she has lost.'

'May I ask how much they charge for each delivery?' I asked.

'It's very meagre: twelve to sixteen rupees is standard.' In English money, between one and two pounds. I made a note of it in my new notebook, as if I knew what I was doing.

'How many deliveries does Amba do on average each month?'

Another torrent of words.

'Last month, five. In total, three thousand.'

'Three thousand. Good God!'

'Yes, three thousand,' came the firm reply. 'Maybe more.' Amba's eyes darted towards me, a proud curve to her lips.

Now Maya translated as Dr A addressed the midwives.

'Dr Annakutty is proud to announce that now that Independence has come, Travancore will be the best place in the world to have a baby, and that we have only come to show them simple things.' Dr A's head was waggling fit to fly off her shoulders.

'More hygienic methods.' Maya rubbed her hands like Lady Macbeth. 'Example: not moving from baby to baby without washing our hands, or leaving the—' She didn't finish the sentence. Dr A was shaking her head forbiddingly and looking at me. 'They are talking about the afterbirth,' she mumbled at last. 'I will explain this later.'

'So.' After another majestic snort, Dr A clapped her hands loudly. 'Time to begin.'

The two midwives sat cross-legged on the floor as Dr A produced a plastic pelvis and a stained wooden doll from her bag and demonstrated various angles of delivery. It was beastly hot, but it was good to feel my brain engaged again.

After a half-hour talk, Maya, like some obstetric Father Christmas, unpacked brown paper parcels full of sterilised maternity pads, feeding bottles, rubber gloves and jars of lubricant. While these offerings from the wonderful world of modern medicine were laid out on the stone floor, I reminded myself to tell Daisy that Dr A had the rest of the supplies at her house.

Maya was demonstrating how much lubricant she used on a rubber glove when the door flew open and the old French nun appeared. She said there might be a baby on the way.

Dr A turned to me.

'You must go with Maya. She knows this girl and will know what to do.'

As we rushed in searing heat down the dusty street, I was sweating with alarm. The memory of the red-haired girl was always there, lying behind some sopping black curtain in my mind, and I honestly didn't know if I could cope.

'Miz Kit,' Maya said. 'No rush.' She steered me around an old man sitting on the pavement with his sewing machine, and told me the girl we were going to see was sixteen years old. Her name was Prasanna and she was having her second baby. Five weeks before delivery, she'd moved into her mother-in-law's house.

'Her relatives sell fish, like these people.' She pointed to an ancient couple sitting on the other side of the lane. Beside them, a bamboo mat was covered in shiny fish and bunches of chillies.

'When we get there,' Maya reached into the canvas bag she was carrying and handed me a stethoscope, 'put this round your neck and I'll tell them you're an English doctor. They will think you bring good luck.' When I shook my head, she put the stethoscope back into her bag and patted me reassuringly. 'For later, then,' she said. 'You may stay and watch.'

We found the girl inside a dirt-floor hut, lying on what looked like a pile of packed sand with a few dirty rags scattered around. The sand, Maya told me, was a good way to soak up blood. Two women were cooking over a smoky wood-fire stove – one chopping onions, the other stirring a pot of rice gruel. There was no sense of panic here.

The girl was half asleep when we arrived, beads of sweat gleaming on her forehead. She smiled when she opened her eyes and saw Maya. The pains, she told her, were coming *vegan* and *adupichu*. Thick and fast, Maya translated.

'I thought you said the village midwife would do this delivery?' I said.

'Maybe.' Maya shrugged. 'We'll have to see.'

The mother-in-law padded silently into the room, barefoot and holding a saucepan of unappetising-looking lentils in her hand. Her hair was grizzled and grey; she looked tired. As I took out my notebook, I saw that my hands were shaking.

When I asked her to confirm Prasanna's age, she looked blankly at me and scratched her head.

'She's not sure,' Maya said, adding that that wasn't particularly unusual around here. I carried on down my list: how many other babies did Prasanna have? One. Length of labour: ten hours.

When half an hour later the girl's tummy started to tense and strain, Maya pulled the thin sheet back and told me to stand in a spot in the corner.

'This we call thinking with our fingers.' She brushed them over the pulsating dome of Prasanna's belly, prodding here, listening intently, feeling the sides with questing hands. 'The baby is in a good position,' she said. 'No need for fuss.' A cockerel crowed through the open window; a bicycle rattled through the lanes.

We both smiled when a small foot suddenly popped under the skin, as if the baby was saying, 'Hear, hear!'

Maya put on her rubber gloves, lubricated her fingers and did an internal exam. The quiet economy of her movements, her calmness, reminded me of old Jack, a horse-breaker who came to Wickam

Farm, and the sly, almost unconscious way he could slip a horse's head into its first bridle almost before it knew it.

'Close now,' she murmured, patting Prasanna's arm. 'Now you will learn some new words,' she told me. 'Write them down. *Vellum kondu vaa*, bring some water. *Choodu vellum*, hot water. *Tulle* means push. *Mukkeh*, bear down.'

She told me to step outside the shack for a few minutes to give her more room to administer a massage. When I did, I realised I had almost stopped breathing. I knew of course that I would almost certainly have to watch a delivery again, and was prepared for that, but that hut, with its fug so thick you could slice it, plus its smells of sweat, smoke, human bodies and ancient meals, was making me sweat and even heave a little.

When Maya joined me again, she was eating a dosa and smiling. The girl's cervix was well dilated. She had given her a light massage with coconut oil. Prasanna was happy.

When, an hour later, the baby's head started to crown, I was ashamed to find myself almost on the point of fainting. It was as if my mind had blanked out the twenty-eight deliveries I had been part of and taken me back to being a knock-kneed novice. But when the hut had stopped wobbling, I saw from a distance that Maya was completely in command. A loud shriek, a full head of dark damp hair suddenly visible, then Prasanna, puffing, blowing, shouting, gave one last almighty thrust and pushed a new person into the room. The mother-in-law yelled, *Ente daivame aan kunju!* Oh my God! It's a boy! And Maya held it up so the girl, who was crying with happiness, could see it.

I was bundled out of the room for the cutting of the cord and disposal of the afterbirth. The baby was washed when I came back, and Maya was kissing him. She looked him over slowly from his wriggling toes to his tufted head, then said something that made all the women laugh.

'Why are they laughing?' I still felt sick.

'I said lovely hair, good fat legs and a nice packet between his thighs.' Maya wiggled her head, delighted with her own joke.

As I walked wobble-legged out of the hut, I experienced an almost tearful rush of emotion I could not name. Today had shown me that if I could get over the faintness, I might at least work my way round to being a helpful pair of extra hands at the clinic. That was a start. Whether I could still be a midwife was debatable – the thought was enough to make my heart pound again, so to avoid my mind going down the usual rat holes, I asked Maya if Prasanna would have been very disappointed had the baby been a girl. She gave me a sharp look.

'Of course,' she said. 'Girls cost too much: their dowries ruin families.' After she herself had her second daughter, her mother-in-law had refused to talk to her for weeks, but then, thank God, a son came.

'His name is Shiva,' she told me proudly. 'He is only eighteen, but he rules the roost.'

Proud grandparents stood at the door when we arrived at our next stop to see the whopper: the twelve-pound baby who had become a local celebrity. We found him sleeping serenely in a cloth cradle suspended from a rod that hung from the ceiling – a great big plump, smiling Buddha of a baby, coffee-coloured and with deep creases around his wrists and neck. He shone with coconut oil and was festooned with a faded marigold garland. He also had what looked like an infected umbilical cord.

'Did this happen in a hospital?' I asked Devika, his mother, when she lifted him up proudly. Maya had pleaded with me to put on the doctor's coat for this examination, and since it was not a delivery, and seeing no great harm in it, I had done as she asked.

'No.' Maya explained that Devika, who had had her first baby at fifteen, didn't like hospitals. She went once and they were rude to her and jumped on her stomach to make the baby come.

'So her usual midwife came,' Maya continued. 'She trusts her. There was much bleeding and yelling,' she translated, as the woman's voice rose dramatically, 'but Devika is all right now.'

She peered more closely at the baby's umbilical cord, which was red and weeping. 'This one does it with a rusty knife,' she told me in a mutter, while keeping a neutral expression on her face. 'She is stubborn about that. Now put your stethoscope on, look at it, and *frown.*'

I studied the cord, wondering why the baby wasn't screaming blue murder. Even when Maya cleaned the wound, he merely kicked two legs the size of hams and looked at me with his huge brown eyes. No squealing.

When I handed the mother a small bottle of potassium permanganate, she thanked me with a fervour that made me feel ashamed.

'What did you say about me?' I asked on our way back to the convent.

'That you were a fine English doctor.'

'Oh God, you mustn't say that. I feel like the most awful fraud.'

'It will help her, and her baby,' Maya said simply. 'The power of the mind is very strong.'

I didn't argue. We were late for lunch and both of us were hungry.

'That child was a baby elephant. Poor woman!' As we ran down the towpath together, I was laughing.

Fish curry for lunch, and afterwards Maya showed me my bedroom – a small whitewashed room above the church with an iron bed and a crucifix on the wall. The air smelled faintly of incense. Later that evening, when I crawled under the mosquito net, my head was reeling at all I'd seen. I heard birds singing as I drifted off to sleep, the lapping of water from the river. I was too tired to worry much about whether Amma would mind me being here. As for Anto – what a wicked wife I was: I'd hardly given him a thought all day.

Chapter 21

Before she took her breakfast, Amma went into the prayer room, determined to find some rest from the furious thoughts that kept her awake at night. Anto's new wife had been staying with them for close to two months now, and Amma had started to hate her. She blamed her for Anto's new reserve, when he was once so open and jolly with her; she blamed her for his frequent absences to find work. She was sure that by now he would have been deluged with job offers had he not come home with the impediment of an English wife.

Kneeling at the cedar altar, breathing in the mingled smells of beeswax furniture polish and incense, she wrestled her mind into a state of weary numbness. This is your favourite time of the day, she reminded herself: no relatives to talk to and placate, nothing to disturb you, only the discreet twittering of birds; and from the kitchen the silky sounds of Pathrose pouring water through muslin into the earthenware pots; the flash of spices hitting hot fat.

Soon she heard the swish of Satya cleaning cow dung from the steps. Later, three other women would come to pick stones out of the rice stored in the granary on the left of the courtyard. They would fold at the waist like ballet dancers, murmuring as they worked; she might hear them giggle. If she heard the low drone of complaints, she'd go out to see what was wrong. That was her job: keeping the house running like a well-oiled machine. Mathu, at his most unreasonable, behaved as if any fool could do this – let him try.

'Heavenly Father, make me an instrument of Thy works. Don't let me be proud, or hard, or unkind. God help me, please...'

Often nowadays, her formal prayers seemed to break down into a desperate pleading, because when he was home, Anto had almost stopped speaking to her, and it was grinding her down. Ashamed of her weakness, she wiped her eyes, got up stiffly and went into the kitchen, where Pathrose, standing in a pool of sunlight, was measuring out rice, dhal and fenugreek seeds for breakfast dosas.

For dinner that night, she planned a beef ularthiyathu, a stir fry, a spinach thoran, and a dish of the fiery red fish curry that the girl had praised extravagantly the day they arrived, before she had a coughing fit. Anto had loved it, licking his fingers in sheer bliss. This much she could do for him at least.

'Don't make it too spicy for the English girl,' she told Pathrose. They shared a brief look of malice and exasperation before she moderated hers into one of studied calm. Pathrose knew her too well, how she faked sunniness sometimes to keep this house on an even keel, just as she knew how he and Satya rolled their eyes behind her back and mimicked her sayings – *Aana karyam parayumbol aano chena karyam*. 'Must you talk about the yam when I'm dealing with the elephant' – or complained about her tongue lashes. They shared her shame, too, when on entering the young master's bedroom they saw the blatant display of stockings, the silk slip on the rattan chair. They were simple people; to them, the English girl was like an exotic harlot.

After breakfast, she slipped on her sandals and walked into the garden.

Anyone watching her padding serenely towards the summer house would think her a fortunate woman in full control of her little world, but today, she felt she'd like to smash or throw something. She was fed up to the back teeth with being the family's pet chameleon, cheerfully adapting to Mathu's moods, pretending she wasn't hurt by Anto's sudden disappearances, or the arrival of new wives, tiresome relatives, badly timed illnesses, when the truth was that, like the weather, she had her own moods.

The path on either side of her was lined with orchids planted in coconut husks. Mathu brought them to her, these beautiful, useless plants – the Singapore orchids, the Painted Ladies, the Vandas – from all over India: his apology for his many absences, his pipes of peace. Each year, she chose with finicky precision the exact spot to plant them, the right amount of cow dung to dilute with water for their flourishing.

Once these plants had seemed a poor substitute for him, but over the years she'd come to find something erotic and freeing in their pointless, flapperish beauty: they did nothing but flower and dazzle and attract insects; they gave nothing back.

From the summer house she could see the lagoon, flushed pink in the dawn light, and hear the cry of the postman who came from Ottappuram with packages and letters. Every morning, she watched the English girl walk down to the postbox at the end of the drive, returning alone and empty-handed. And, God forgive her, she did not feel one iota of sympathy for her. The girl was a pest, a nuisance, and her list of crimes was growing. Every day, she was driven in the Austin to the women's home in Cochin. An unforgivable liberty. True, the arrangement had been agreed in principle by Mathu and Anto, but Amma had expected her to make only occasional visits, in the same way she herself went to call on the poor children's school in the next village as a representative of the Thekkeden clan.

When the girl offered to pay for petrol from her own funds, as per the arrangement, Amma, trained to demonstrate hospitality even when she didn't feel it, had, from long force of habit, smiled and waved away the suggestion as if it was a gnat. But in a ritual she hated, she was the one who had to go to her husband's study once a month, and nod and smile as he got out the leather-bound ledger in which she had to write down every single rupee spent while he was away.

Other crimes: the girl added her opinion during meals when the men were talking about world affairs. She ate with her hands now, but badly, not using the fingertips as delicate prongs as they did, but holding the food in a sticky mass in her palm. Amma had seen Anto wince at this, the last time he was home. Why didn't he correct her?

She wore lipstick, not a lot and not always, but some, and powder, and a few days ago, without permission, showed Theresa how to apply it. Admittedly, they practised on a doll, but Theresa, although too young to properly understand, might get wrong ideas. When Amma herself had reached puberty, a whole list of instructions had come with it from her mother. She wanted them passed on untainted.

Next, Kit, responding to the frosty atmosphere, had turned to Amma and asked her about her own beauty routine. When Amma protested that she didn't have one, Theresa interrupted, 'Yes you do, Ammamma.' And she had described to Kit how every day Amma's maid beat the bark of a soap nut tree until it was soft, so Amma could scrub herself with it and remove dead skin before she oiled herself. Personal things. Amma had stood by, nodding, smiling, nodding, smiling, just like a good Indian woman, but inside she was a tornado.

The worst crime, though, had come last week, when she'd seen Mariamma and Kit on the veranda, talking in low voices and glancing furtively in her direction. She'd taken Mariamma aside, pinched her arm until her daughter mumbled that Kit had been asking questions about menstruation, childbirth, attitudes to marriage. Embarrassing questions.

'What a cheek,' Amma said, expecting Mariamma to agree, but Mariamma had said that Kit wasn't being nosy, she was writing a report, and besides, she would need to know local attitudes herself when she and Anto had children.

Children... that was another wound – theirs would be half-breeds, whereas the ones he would have had with Vidya...

Stop! She pulled at a clump of weeds around her moth orchid, so violently that she splattered her slippers in soil. She must try with all her strength to put an end to these horrible thoughts, but for now, let God tell her what she had done in a previous life to deserve this.

It's your fault, she wanted to tell the girl. You should have controlled yourself; you should never have married him. Her last thought felt like the ultimate blasphemy. It would have been better for them all if Anto had stayed in England.

When Pathrose found her, he picked up her sodden handkerchief from the bench and made no mention of her red eyes. When she sent him off to check the postbox, he came back looking stricken. 'Madam,' he said, 'sorry. No letter comes.'

Chapter 22

It was clear that the driver, Chandy, was sick of having to drop me at the Moonstone every weekday morning when he would rather spend leisurely days polishing the car and waiting for Appan's return. When we reached the first village, Karappuram, he threaded his way through it, hand on horn, swerving to avoid a fruit stall, or a chicken, or a man being shaved. He sighed a lot and occasionally glared at me in the rear-view mirror. But I didn't care, because as we headed out into the immense skies, the green fields, the pearly water, I felt I could breathe again. In spite of all my terrors, this was the first step. I was going to work again. *I was going to work.*

I'd never understood before what a salve work was in times of trouble. It stopped me minding about Amma, particularly at meals, when she was so silent. It gave me less time to worry about Anto, who was still trying to find a job and was away as much as he was home.

All of us, I suppose, have parts of us that are like foreign countries even to ourselves, but I kept remembering our first day at Mangalath, and that strange new look, both embarrassed and challenging, he'd given me when he dropped his suit on the floor and wrapped the strip of cloth around his waist, as if to say, this is who I am now, like it or lump it.

And then I would think of my mother and how much I'd hurt her. I'd try to remember the conversations we'd had before I left, but I couldn't exactly, only her tears and silences and my absolute determination to leave, and perhaps my cruelty to her.

My only other outlet during this time was letters home to my old friend Josie – married now to her childhood sweetheart Archie, a newspaper journalist, and pregnant with her first child, saying that she was thrilled, but hoped one day to go back and nurse at Thomas's. *I'd go potty if I thought I would never work again, though it won't be the same without good laughs with you.*

And of course, I corresponded regularly with Daisy, who, after my first three months in India, wrote asking for a) an account sheet, and b) a full progress report – 'warts and all'.

I headed my reply 'A Cure for Warts', to make her laugh but to warn her too that the Moonstone operated on a knife edge. We needed money to patch the leaking roof and mend the rotting veranda (termites), parts of which were so soft you could crumble the wood between your fingers. We desperately needed more staff.

The official letters I wrote for the Moonstone were sent out, via rickshaws, battered buses, barefoot boys and bicycles, to everyone Dr A and I could think of: Indian businessmen, maharajas, teaching hospitals, charitable funds.

Our only significant response so far had come from a Mr Namboothiri, a noisy, emotional paint manufacturer who supplied materials for the fabulously lurid lorries seen on the roads here. The day after we'd treated his maid at the home for a late miscarriage, he'd arrived with what Dr A described as 'a small cash donation' (she wouldn't say how much) and designs for a new sign painted in gleaming yellows, reds and purples announcing: *The Matha Maria Moonstone Home, First-Class Treatment for Expectant Females.* He also brought a tub of hibiscus and geraniums to put beside the veranda steps.

Money worries and begging letters aside, safe in the knowledge that my role here was administrative, I was starting to relish the rigour and the challenges of the work; the sense, however misguided, that I was living under the skin of India.

After the shapeless days at Mangalath, I enjoyed the routine. At 8.30 sharp, Maya would arrive in a rickshaw, chaperoned by her son, Shiva. Recently, she'd confided in me that her husband and son had turned over a new leaf and were now happy for her to support the family. That was her version. I hoped it was true. No more bruises that I could see, but huge plum-coloured circles under her eyes made her look permanently exhausted.

Her son sported the same large swotty glasses that Maya wore, but his face had none of her sweetness of expression, and he dropped her off with no more ceremony than a man delivering a parcel, leaving without a word or a backward glance.

This was painful to watch because Maya was a gem: highly intelligent, loved the work, and, best of all, open-minded about the need to connect the best birth practices of East and West without letting the 'pig heads', as she called them, get in the way. Her kindness and her quiet air of competence with all forms of living life was wonderful to behold. The first thing she did every morning was to peer at the new hibiscus and geraniums through her huge specs, then measure out water into an old Petri dish and give them all a careful dose.

At nine o'clock, a bell rang, the doors opened and the straggling line of women that had formed in the garden surged forward. They came with every imaginable female problem: early and late miscarriage, pregnancy, incomplete abortion, gonorrhoea, trouble breastfeeding. My job was to move between the consulting rooms and take notes.

Their numbers were growing, Maya told me, because the home, despite all our financial woes, had a reputation for cleanliness and kindness, and (great selling point) it was free. Some women were picked up by Moonstone volunteers in local slums and factories. We had to be extremely careful about the latter group: men controlled the women there mostly, and some were very suspicious of the work we did.

Some of the women arrived holding hands, or the tips of each other's saris, like terrified children.

'Women here aren't used to going to the doctor,' Maya explained. 'It makes them uncomfortable to show their private parts.' When she told me this, I thought of the erotic statues in Hindu temples – the bare breasts, the bristling penises – and wondered if I would ever understand this country. I couldn't see a common thread here and probably never would. I longed to be able to discuss such inconsistencies with Mariamma, or Amma even, but I'd seen the lemony look on Amma's face when I asked any sort of personal question.

Sometimes, because we were so short-staffed, patients had to wait for hours to see us. Time moved at its own stately pace here, but no one complained and no one apologised.

The morning that my role changed without any warning began normally enough. 'Chandramati Achari,' barked Dr A, standing at the door, list in hand, calling for our first patient.

A tiny, immaculately clean-looking woman stood up. Her sandals were held together by string, but she walked towards us with the kind of long-necked, straight-backed posture that would not disgrace a principal of the Royal Ballet School.

She lay on the consulting room couch, eyes closed, dusty sandals on the floor. I sat beside her, notebook at the ready. Dr A washed her hands at the sink. A dim electric light hung over the examination table. When the light failed, we were dependent on a wonky generator.

Dr A sighed, put on her glasses, and talked to me over the prone body. 'This woman suffered from eclampsia last time and nearly died. She began fitting, and had a blood pressure of 180 over 110. It was frightening, wasn't it, Chandramati?' The girl nodded, eyes tightly closed. 'But when she went to the hospital, they treated her very roughly, then left her on her own in a corridor until the baby was almost come. Correct, Chandramati?'

'Correct, ma'am.'

'Now we'll take a look.' The rubber gloves went on and were lubricated. I watched Dr A insert two fingers into the girl's vagina and feel around for several minutes. Her imperious face was calm.

'This baby,' she announced at last, 'feels very happy; it will be beautiful.'

The woman gasped; tears rolled out under her lids, and a spurt of passionate words followed.

'She's telling me God is good,' Dr A said. 'That she likes coming here. That she's going to be brave about having this baby, and that she would like you to deliver it.'

I felt the news as a swell of nausea in my stomach. When the room was empty again, I reminded Dr A that I didn't have my full midwifery certificate yet. She gave me a blank look and said with her usual humility, 'I will watch you, and if I feel you're ready, you're ready. When that time is come, I will ask the gorement' – that was how she pronounced government – 'for full accreditation.'

In hindsight, I would have saved myself a great deal of distress and humiliation had I said something then, or, later, insisted on seeing the relevant certificates, but instead, I froze. If Anto had been home, I'm almost sure I would have discussed it with him, but he wasn't. He'd been away for a couple of weeks and we didn't yet know where he was. The sense I had of being about to step off a cliff made me sleep badly that night. I was, if possible, even more frightened than before, because every day the stream of patients was teaching me how little I knew about this country, with its mind-boggling complexities of religion, of caste; its ideas of purity and pollution.

Anto had tried to warn me, Daisy too. She'd told me once that

Indians were the sweetest and kindest people on earth, until they were the angriest. If I got it wrong this time, I had no doubt that revenge would be swift.

After morning clinic the following day, Dr A pulled another alarming rabbit from the hat. She stomped off, with me trailing behind her, to visit the in-patients, who were housed in a ramshackle brick edifice, once a barn, at the back of the main building. It had six emergency beds, and a nest of rats in the roof.

To follow the ample buttocks of Dr A on her rounds was to feel like a queen's bridesmaid – even the sickest of patients attempted to smile or salute her. In one bed, an underweight child of fourteen showed the whites of her eyes at our approach. Dr A told me she'd been admitted with a threatened miscarriage in the second trimester of her pregnancy. Her mother sat on the floor beside her with a small spirit stove to cook on. In the next bed, separated by a small cloth screen, a woman bleeding heavily from incomplete separation of the placenta was being prepped by Maya for a transfusion.

After a very late lunch – some rice and lentils, and the inevitable fried fish, delivered from a street stall across the road – I was changing to go home when Dr A appeared, her large nose quivering with importance.

'Come to my office, please,' she said. 'Don't look worried. Good news has come.'

I was about to tell her that my driver was waiting – Amma got quietly furious when the car was late – but when I opened my mouth to speak, Dr A held both palms up.

'Don't speak!'

She opened the office door. Maya was inside, plus two new nurses who smiled at us timidly. No one introduced us.

Dr A sat down at her desk and opened a letter. Her expression was one of rare joy.

'I have two special announcements,' she said. 'The first is that Nurse Kit Thekkeden can start delivering her first Indian babies.' I heard Maya's little grunt of pleasure, hands clapping; felt a rapid fluttering in my chest, but there was no time to absorb the full impact, or to ask whether I'd been officially cleared, because Dr A had another announcement. 'We've done it,' she said, her eyes fixed on me. 'A year's grant from the new Cochin Medical Foundation to support our work. I told you our own people would support us,' she added, in a 'same to you with knobs on' kind of way.

The new nurses beamed. Maya made a funny sound with her tongue. I felt sick.

'How much are they giving us?' I asked, to play for time.

Dr A shot me a dark look. 'That information is between the Minister and myself.'

'But I'll need to tell Miss Barker,' I said. Her requests for itemised accounts had so far been ignored.

'I have no time for this now.' Dr A's tone was chilly. Our priority, she said, was to enrol as many village midwives as we could and bring them to the Moonstone for a ten-day training session. All the important national newspapers, as well as the locals – *The Malayala Manorama, The Mathrubhumi* – would come for their graduation ceremony, and we could show them the future of obstetrics for Indian women.

I saw Maya nodding her head, smiling serenely, a splendid idea, until Dr A added, 'But there is one string attached. If we succeed, the gorement will extend our lease by a year. If we fail, we must hand our premises back for other purposes.' There was a combined gasp at this.

I put my hand up. 'Forgive me. I think these premises belong to the Oxford charity.' I'd seen the deeds at Wickham Farm.

'Not since Independence,' Dr A replied. 'It's gorement-owned now.'

We looked at each other with deep distrust. This would have been a good time to clarify my official position here, but Maya jumped into the tense silence. 'So, Doctor, please may we know when courses start?' Dr A opened her diary, planted a finger on the page. 'In one and a half month's time. I have already certified the date.'

'Good Lord.' I was aghast. This felt like an impossible deadline. Where in God's name would these women sleep? What about a cook? Proper training equipment? Transport?

'Does that give us enough time?' I asked.

Dr A frowned and rubbed her bristly chin. 'This is my decision now,' she said. 'Our gorement and God will provide.' She clapped the diary shut and stood up. 'Our first course will begin as stated on the third of April, for ten days. And important to note too, we have an official inspection coming up, so everything must be right. If it's not, they can close us down overnight. Now, no more questions, please.'

After the meeting, Maya stopped me in the corridor. 'I am very worried,' she whispered. 'Why is she rushing, rushing, rushing?' This from Maya, who never said a word against Dr A.

'I don't know,' I whispered back.

Maya pinched her nose in thought. 'Maybe she is worrying about the monsoon. It will be coming soon. The streets do flood round here.'

'I don't know.'

'We must patch the holes in the roof to stop the drips.'

'And kill the rats – they've just had babies.'

'Beds for the vimmen?'

'Food and a cook.'

'A blackboard, somewhere for them to sit.'

We exchanged a look of terror.

'But I think you're happy to be a proper midwife again,' Maya said, patting my arm. 'Not a secretary.'

There were no words to tell her how terrified I felt, because she assumed that I, being English, was better trained, more knowledge-able. But even thinking about it brought that trapped bird feeling in my chest again, as my mind tripped back to the baby inside the government-issue tin helmet, its lips turning blue as it gasped for breath. I knew I wanted to try again. I knew it would kill me to get it wrong again.

Chapter 23

A fortnight later, Amma called me downstairs.

'Anto has written,' she said tonelessly. She pulled a letter from the folds of her skirt and handed it to me.

'It's open,' I said.

'Of course,' my mother-in-law replied. 'He wrote it to all of us.' There was no mistaking the look of triumph in her eyes.

The letter, postmarked Madras, was in a cheap brown envelope, the kind you could buy in a bazaar, with a red frill around its edges. I read it in front of her, trying to control my expression.

> Dear Appan, Amma, Kit and Mariamma,
>   My apologies for not letting you know sooner that I went for a few days to Madras to find out whether I could get immediate employment there. While there, I was asked if I could volunteer to work at a refugee centre (Chengalput) near Madras, where there was no functioning telephone line. I did not mean to be away for so long, or to stay here, and I hope I have not worried you all too much, but the need here was so great it was hard to refuse. I shall come back on the Egmore to Quilon train, and get a taxi to Trivandrum hopefully around Thursday the 8th. Will wire you exact times later. If convenient for Appan and Amma, perhaps Kit could come down with the driver to collect me at the station.
>   Your loving son,
>   Anto

'Why has he had to go to Madras?' Amma asked me, her look turning spiteful. 'What is he running away from?'

'I don't know,' I said. I didn't want to cry in front of her, but I was so confused that Anto hadn't even managed a postscript for me.

'Were you getting scared he wouldn't come home at all?' she

added. *Of course I was bloody well scared*, I felt like saying. *Weren't you?* We looked at each other.

'Because you hid it very bravely.' Amma smiled, a strange, hard smile. Appan, she continued, had travelled for most of their married life, but when he was away, she'd stayed home, prayed, made sure the house was extra clean. I, on the other hand, rushed around like a mad thing, caught up in my own work.

'Things have changed so much.' She tucked the letter into her blouse. 'In my day it was considered disrespectful to even say your husband's name in mixed company.'

Upstairs, I closed the door, ripped off my dusty shirt, lay on the bed and cried like a child. I was cut to the quick by Anto's curt letter, and furious with him for writing to everyone and not just to me. Fed up to the back teeth too with Amma and her wonderfully subtle talks about how a wife should behave.

When I heard the supper gong clang, I cleaned myself up, changed my blouse and went downstairs. Outside, the night with its purple sky and brilliant stars, was beautiful, but I was dark inside.

Chapter 24

On the train that took him south, Anto was buttonholed by a Mr Patel, a cotton manufacturer from Lahore. His new friend, in a shiny tight suit and sprawled plumply over two seats, had noticed English shipping labels on Anto's suitcase. He'd opened an array of greasy packages and offered to share his lunch, and before Anto could decline, Patel had spoken for twenty minutes without drawing breath. The market for cotton was diabolical: Independence, the famine up north, Gandhi's assassination had put a spanner in everyone's works, he personally thought, and on and on, while Anto tried to control a mounting distress.

He couldn't stop thinking about Habi, the two-year-old orphan in bed nine at the refugee centre where he'd spent the last three weeks. Habi weighed nine pounds, and had been found in a rubbish tip close to the track where the Bombay express flew past. Someone had flung him from the train before or during the massacre that had occurred after partition, when many Muslims from what would become India had fled to Pakistan, and Hindus and Sikhs from what would become Pakistan had fled to India.

Now he lay in his narrow cot, blank-eyed and with the loose, dry turkey skin typical of malnutrition. Above his head a sign: *My name is Habi, please pick me up*, because as the nurse had explained when they'd first tried to hold him, 'he didn't know how to put his arms around us. When he slept, he used to clutch his own head.' Anto had been assigned to Habi, visiting him twice a day and sometimes leaving a sugar ball on his pillow. The first time he'd touched the child's shoulder, he'd felt him wince, but ten days ago, for the first time, Habi had squeezed his hand. The nurses had counted this as a great victory. 'It's a big improvement,' one of them had said. 'He won't die now.'

Habi had shown him in the starkest possible way what it felt like to be alone, and by extension how he himself had been before he met Kit. Before her, it was normal for him to go to sleep hugging himself. He'd been so hidden, in spite of the superficial ease, and she'd coaxed him out. Now he seemed to be retreating again into some kind of emotional igloo, and it was desperately unfair to her. These thoughts were muddled up with a kind of anguish about Habi, who would be waiting for him that morning, for his touch, for his sugar ball, and he was on a train going south, once again whizzing between two worlds.

Guilty. He felt so guilty. The camp was run by one doctor, two nuns and some volunteers; three doctors had died. At the height of the crisis they'd admitted seven hundred patients to fill three hundred beds, sometimes two or three to a bed.

'I'm telling you,' said Kanchana, the female doctor, 'it was like Scutari before your Florence Nightingale moved in.'

'Not my Florence Nightingale,' he said. 'I'm Indian.'

'Oh, sorry,' she'd teased. 'A very posh one, I'm thinking.'

In this place, the admission that he'd spent the whole of the war in England felt like something to hide. Everywhere he'd looked he'd seen glimpses of misery: a woman with a ravaged child at her breast, rags hanging out to dry, a dimly lit tent with four people staring out slack-jawed. Overnight, they'd lost everything.

At first, he'd gone into a state of wary numbness that he recognised from the London wards, but once he'd adjusted, his time at the camp had passed in a dizzying round of examining, dosing, stitching, injecting: patient after patient with stab wounds, dysentery, cholera, malnutrition, burns, pneumonia. The director of the camp had begged him to stay on, and he would have, but he had to get home, to a wife who couldn't possibly understand. Why should she? He wouldn't have believed it had he not seen such horrors with his own eyes.

The train was moving through a tangle of electrical wires and weary shacks on the outskirts of a town whose name he could not read. Out in the open again, the brown dirt horizon blurred and dissolved like a dream, and the world looked liquid and insubstantial. His feet squelched in his shoes, and he had developed a stinging prickly heat rash on his back. He'd forgotten how unbearable the weeks leading up to the monsoon could be: last week, the glass had reached 110 degrees for four days straight. His romantic account of the monsoon to Kit now struck him as another deceit. No mention of the suffocating nights before the rains came, the dying birds, the athlete's foot, the bad temper. What a tour guide he'd turned out to be.

As the train steamed into the station, he spotted her standing near the chai stall on Platform 1. Some part of him had hoped to see her in Indian clothes, as a mark of change, but instead she wore the blue dress he'd once loved. He could see the curve of her patrician nose under the brim of her hat. Her hands were clasped together tightly. When she first turned towards him, she squinted, whether to protect her eyes from the sun or in distress, he couldn't tell.

He'd booked a room at the Ambassador Hotel, a peeling two-storey edifice on the seafront. Aching, sweating, he sat beside her in the family car, close enough now to see the soft down on her cheek, the purple flashes in her brown eyes. He wanted to kiss her, but it was she who turned away, and said, with a wary smile at the driver, 'Chandy's come down to see his family.'

Later, in their room on the second floor, they stood awkwardly opposite each other. She put her hand on his hair, and said, 'You've lost weight.' When she touched his hip bones, he pulled away involuntarily.

'What's the matter?'

'I don't know,' he said, bewildered by his flash of antagonism. Five minutes ago, he'd longed to take her to bed; now he felt anger at her easy assumption that she could touch him whenever she felt like it. He moved towards the window and lit a cigarette.

'It's very good of you to drive all this way.'

'Don't be silly, it's what we planned.' She looked confused. 'I haven't seen you for three and a half weeks. I was starting to think you would never come home.'

'Well,' he tried to smile back, 'I'm here now.'

'Yes,' she said after a long silence. 'You're here now.' She shot him a look of pure exasperation. Her voice heated up. 'And that's all there is? No explanation needed about where you've been, or, I don't know, a job, or where we're going next?'

He'd never seen her so angry.

'Oh Kit.' He sat down heavily on the bed. 'Do you think I could possibly have a bath first, and something to eat? Would that be too much?'

'No, Anto, naturally, whatever you want.' She sat down on the opposite side of the bed and pinched her nose.

'Can we talk about it later?'

'Fine.'

'Kit, give me a moment.'

'Whatever you want.' She breathed out noisily. 'I'm sure it would be fine with you if I took off for weeks and didn't let you know.'

'Please, Kit.' He tried to take her hand. 'I'm sorry. I'm so tired. Was it terribly hot on the way down?'

'Oh really, Anto.' The ghost of a smile as she glanced at him. '"Was it terribly hot on the way down?" You sound like the King.'

'Christ, I hope not,' he said with sudden savagery. He stubbed out his cigarette and threw it out of the window.

'Anto,' her voice was tight and as airless as the day, 'what in God's name is going on?'

Through the window, he could see purplish clouds gathering at the edge of the horizon. The monsoon would be here in a matter of days, and he had a sudden wild wish that it would swamp them all.

'Do you want to stay?' he asked. 'Here, I mean.'

'Of course I do.' Her voice faltered. 'Isn't this our holiday?'

He gazed at her, lost and miserable. Was it a trick of light or time that the glow he'd once felt in her presence had gone. The Wickam Farm memories – the long whispered conversations, the childish jokes over whose turn it was to have their toes on the hot-water bottle, the dream version of India he'd laid out – felt like pure self-indulgence.

He hated this room, too – the sagging bed with its stained mosquito net, the uncarpeted tiles. It had been all he could afford, a miserable place for what he'd once promised would be a proper honeymoon.

'Kit, I'm sorry, but I want to go home,' he said. 'The monsoon won't come for a couple of days. We still have time.'

'What home?' She lifted her chin and stared at him defiantly. 'Mangalath? Oh, so that's our permanent home now, is it? Thanks for letting me know.'

'I'll need money for our own house, a proper job.'

'I thought getting a job was the point of your going away. Would it be too forward of me to ask about that?'

'I'm sorry, Kit, I'll explain later. It's complicated.' He had a sudden irrational longing for Downside, the neat line of beds, the company of men, the suppression of violent emotion.

'And I'm sorry too.' She pointed her finger at him without words for a moment. 'Because the thing is . . .' Her eyes were flashing, her blue dress patched with sweat. 'The thing is, I have my own work to do, and this may be my only chance for a holiday for a long time, so if you want to go home, you carry on; I'll join you later under my own steam, because I'm not going to simply meekly,' she was running out of words, 'trot home after you ... like a ... like an Indian wife.'

'What do you mean, like an Indian wife?'

As the air between them grew electric and thrilling, he felt a loosening inside him. If she wasn't prepared to hold back, neither was he.

'Well, the waiting, for one thing; the giving up any sense of yourself, the not taking decisions, the being told what to do, the boredom of it all.' Her smile was bright, sarcastic.

He sat for a long time looking at the floor. 'Kit, have I ever told you to give up your job? Have I? That's so bloody unfair ... so ...' He was too angry to form proper words. 'You've been allowed to work,' he burst out at last. 'All I asked was for you to stay at Mangalath while I was away.'

'Allowed to work,' she repeated. 'Lucky old me!'

He put his head in his hands. He wanted to hit her. 'What a lot of rot,' he said eventually. 'Really. Complete and utter poppycock.' He shook his head. 'But since we're talking about it now, how long do you intend to stay there?'

'As long as I can.' Her voice was hard and defiant. 'I promised Daisy, and ... I haven't told you this yet, but quite a few of the things that the Oxford ladies sent out have gone missing. I need to get to the bottom of it.'

'You're heading into murky waters.' He wiped his sweating face with a handkerchief. 'I advise you to stay out of it.'

'Really? Thanks for the advice.'

'These are violent times,' he continued in a low voice. 'The home is a controversial place. If things are disappearing, the men who are involved will almost certainly have weapons: guns, knives, lathes, boxes of matches, whatever they can lay their hands on.'

'Anto,' she said, 'the midwives are coming.'

He blew out air, chewed the inside of his lip. A gust of wind rattled the window. Black cumulus cloud was tumbling in the sky. He turned and looked at her again. 'So is Mangalath that bad? Is there absolutely nothing you like about being here, apart from your work?'

'Nothing.' She put her face in her hands. 'Actually, not a thing, now I come to think about it,' she said in a muffled voice. Eventually he heard her jagged sigh. She went to the basin in the corner of the room, ran some rust-stained water and splashed her face.

'Kit.' He handed her a towel. 'This is a terrible time to argue. Before the monsoon – everybody does it.'

She dried her face and looked at him. There was a long silence. 'You're right,' she said in a small, expressionless voice. 'Let's not.' And after a considering pause, 'But it's not just the monsoon. Mangalath is beautiful, but I would have died of boredom in the last month if it hadn't been for work. The work you seem to want me to give up now.'

'Unfair, Kit.' He walked towards her and took her hand. 'Definitely below the belt. All I'm asking is for you to make the family important.'

'Compared to what?' She sounded very weary.

'To work.'

'Anto,' her voice softened, 'we can have both, but not if you keep running away and writing your blasted communal letters.'

'Come here.' He drew her into his arms, and she laid her head against his chest.

'Was it awful in the camp? I haven't asked you a thing.'

'Not awful for me. I could get out.'

She smoothed his hair and wiped his face. 'Let's stay,' she said gently. 'Let's talk.'

'Later,' he said. 'Not now.' He hated the idea of crying in front of her.

There was a high round window above her head, shaped like a ship's porthole. Outside, dark purple clouds growing darker, a bird flung across the sky.

'We won't have much choice soon.' He swallowed. 'Monsoon is coming, madam.' His Indian voice. 'And by the way,' he added drily, 'when you talked earlier about going home under your own steam, what steam were you planning: magic carpet, the jet stream? Who owns the car?'

'Don't make a joke of it, Anto. I still hate you.'

'I know.' He tightened his arms around her. 'Poor me.' He felt oddly revitalised by the purity of her anger, as if he was coming out of an anaesthetic. 'Kiss me.' He held her hair in a bunch behind her head.

She took his face between her hands. 'Why should I?'

'Because you love me, because you're beautiful, because you smell beautiful.' He touched her hair. 'Is it rose water?'

'Don't try and get round me. So hot,' she murmured. 'Feel my dress.' It had stuck to her back like glue.

She took him by the hand and led him into the old-fashioned bathroom. It had a red oxide floor and a large pot of water in the corner. A pane of coloured glass set in the ceiling flung jewelled patterns on the floor. Her dress made a sucking sound as he drew it over her head.

'Sit down.' She guided him towards a small stool with a cork seat. She stood in her slip and bare feet and washed his back and arms, then kissed the nape of his neck.

'It's mad hot,' he said. 'No one should speak before the rains come.' He lifted her slip and sponged between her breasts. 'This is a very ancient monsoon custom.'

'Bloody liar.' She leaned towards him and closed her eyes.

The purple sky was humming when they went to bed, the light dappled, distorted. A line of sweat ran down his cheek as he kissed her, and afterwards, lying on his back and looking at the ceiling, he was dimly aware of the swelling sounds of a procession passing in the street outside. Drums, cymbals, a cracked trumpet, the gobble-gobble sound of human voices.

'Feast of Indra,' he told her sleepily. 'The god who makes the monsoon come.'

An hour or so later, rain rattled against the window panes.

'Is that it?' she asked. 'Has it come?'

'Not yet.' He was longing for its release. 'The newspapers predict in two days' time.'

'How will we know?'

'The sky will get even darker, the birds grow quiet, the air is electric.'

'If only we were so predictable,' she said.

He thought about this silently. From certain angles, human beings *were* that predictable: the wild changes of adolescence, the longing for children, the nine-month gestation period, the loss of hair and teeth in old age.

'When the rains come,' he was falling asleep, 'the beaches will be crammed with people dancing... shouting... celebrating... It is...' His voice became a vague blur, and then tailed off.

When he woke an hour or so later, they made love again, with a violence and abandon he had never experienced before. When it was over, he got up, sat on the side of the bed and smoked a cigarette.

He went to the window, where a thin muslin curtain was fluttering. From there he saw black skies, more wildly flying birds. He could feel the sea vibrating the floor beneath his feet. The monsoon was gathering force.

Chapter 25

At breakfast the next morning, our waiter, with an air of barely suppressed excitement, brought a copy of *The Hindu* to our table, so we could keep up with news of the monsoon, which the front-page story confidently announced would arrive 'in full power and glory' at around 3.10 that afternoon. The town, it said, was 'full to bursting' with visitors: there was no more room at the government guest houses. There would be parties tonight, and bonfires, great celebrations.

Anto listened to all this, his eyes gleaming. He looked film-star handsome that morning, his hair still wet from the bath, and a white shirt on – restored, or so I thought, by our lovemaking. I sat for a while enjoying the sight of him, my limbs heavy and sweet, but then, aware that I knew so little of what he'd been up to in the last few weeks, I asked him again what the work had been like at the refugee centre. When I saw the light go out in his eyes, I regretted it immediately. Bad timing. He played listlessly with the eggs and bacon he'd ordered, pushed his plate aside.

'It feels wrong to describe it, eating all this food,' he said.

'Oh come on, Anto.' I felt anxious again, and ready to be irritated. 'It's me you're talking to. I think I should have some idea.'

So he told me at least some of it, looking, but not looking, at me, as if there were a pane of glass between us.

'I had no idea how bad it was: thousands of homeless people crammed into tents. Gunshot wounds, cholera, TB, smallpox, women having babies. We did three clinics a day. Shit up to our knees.'

'Why on earth didn't you tell me you were there?' I said. 'Do I really strike you as being that selfish?'

He ignored this, and put his hands on the table between us. 'We were living in a fool's paradise in England, all that guff about the happy end to the Empire. It was a shambles. These people have been left with nothing.'

'Fools maybe,' I said, 'but not in paradise. There was the small matter of the war in England.'

'I didn't ask enough questions.'

'No one here asks us about the war; it's what people do to get by,' I said to comfort him.

'Maybe.' His hands were twisting; he was unconvinced.

'Will you go back?'

'I don't know, because here's the point,' he said, still not looking at me. 'There are jobs up there. I was hoping you might come with me.'

And then he did look at me, so hopefully that I knew what I was supposed to say: that I would go with him to the ends of the earth, if necessary. But we were not in a film.

'When were you thinking that might be?'

'As soon as you could.'

The waiter darted towards us with more chai and was waved away impatiently.

'I can't,' I said. 'We start our first midwife classes at the Moonstone next month. I've promised to be there.'

'Ah.' I could not read his deliberately blank stare, but I suddenly felt like Maya, a woman doing a distasteful and unpopular thing.

He heaved a big sigh, put his chin in his hand and looked at me.

'Well this is a nice holiday,' he said. 'Two hearts beating as one.' I was shocked at his childishness.

'Anto, be fair,' I burst out, to the considerable fascination of the waiter, ostentatiously dabbing a table nearby. 'I promised Daisy that I would see this through. I told you that last night.'

'I know,' he said, and gave me a look of such bafflement and misery that I felt like the worst heel on earth.

We were so sad and ill at ease with each other again, it felt good later that day to join the crowd of mildly hysterical people on the seafront.

Clutching the railings, we moved down to the beach, where the wind was making a singing noise in the flagpoles and the sky was dark and electric. At around 3.15, there was a combined gasp, and Anto grabbed my arm as the drums started to pound. It was the most astonishing sight I had ever seen, this cone of blackish cloud starting to mass and change shape and charging now like a live animal towards the shore. Birds were spiralling round and round like feathered tops; children were held tight in case they blew away. My dress was flapping like a sail, and my feet were moving to the sound of drums, and cracked trumpets, and crashing waves, and the louder and louder whine of the wind, and I was lifted out of myself. When I looked at Anto, his eyes were shut and his face twisted as if he was drinking it in.

Buckets of rain started to fall. 'Do you mind getting wet?' Anto shouted. His hair was soaked, his face ecstatic, his shirt clung to his ribcage. I felt a great wave of desire for him.

'Not at all,' I shouted back. 'I love, love, love it, and I love you.'

And there we stood, two dumbfounded savages, watching the rain pelting down and the wind roaring and the birds going backwards and the great waves crashing on the beach. Soaking wet, we ran back to the hotel, towelled each other off and spent the rest of the afternoon in bed. I knew he was still upset, and so was I, so our lovemaking didn't feel like a truce, or an escape, but something deeper, sweeter: an acknowledgement that human beings had their own weather, and couldn't always control it. Something like that, anyway.

Afterwards, as he lay back on the pillows with his arms above his head, I could almost see the thoughts travelling from his unblinking eyes to his mouth.

'Don't start thinking again, Anto,' I pleaded, partly to make him smile. 'I like it better like this.'

'I have to.' He squeezed my hand. 'I wish I didn't.'

'So try talking to me.'

With his face partly concealed from me, he said, 'Do you miss your mother?'

'Yes,' I said, surprised. I thought for a bit. 'More than I thought I would.'

He put his arm round me. 'Write to her.'

'I've tried; she doesn't answer.'

'Keep trying. It's only pride in the end.'

'D'you really believe that?' I was on my elbow now, looking at him and feeling so sad.

'I do. You know, Kit, you can't escape it. I've tried with my own family, and now I know how deeply embedded in me they are.'

He went on to tell me he would be away again for the next

month. He would be working in the camp. It was work he would be paid for: not much – two hundred and fifty a month – but he could save all of it, and send some home. After that, he'd come back to Travancore and take any job he could find.

'There must be something for you here.' I was trying not to cry: I felt he was in flight and there was nothing I could do. 'And I know it's hard, but why have you stopped telling me things? In England you told me things, and I liked that. Isn't that the point, of being in love: a sort of unveiling, someone to tell your secrets to?'

He looked at me and gave a small smile.

'Do you keep secrets from me?' he said at last. 'I think you do.'

'I try not to.' I hedged. But it wasn't entirely true.

The air had cleared, around us and inside us, and during the next sweet night we made love, made promises, made up names for children we might have. It didn't last: over breakfast the next day, Anto told me we must go home the following morning. When I looked surprised, he said, 'Some roads will be flooded already. We can't get stuck.' A peremptory Indian husband, firing out orders.

'Two days!' I said after a long and fuming silence. 'For a holiday!'

Anto looked up from his dosa. 'Kit, I tried to explain this to you: Mangalath is losing money, and we must all save for it now.'

The air between us sizzled with unsaid things, and I hated his patient expression. I told him in a tight voice that I was more than happy to contribute to the family coffers, but we deserved a break occasionally. He blew out air, looked out of the window, chewed the inside of his lip. We went up to our room in silence.

It got worse. An hour later, while I was packing, he came out of the bathroom with my diaphragm in his hand. I'd washed it, powdered it, and, in the excitement of the night before, left it in its plastic box on a high windowsill.

'Why didn't you tell me?' He put the box on the bedside table.

After a long silence I said, 'I wanted to wait until you'd found a job closer to home. I didn't know how much of a Catholic you were. I was a coward. I'm sorry.'

He barked with frustration and flew apart from me. *He's going to hit me* raced through my mind, he looked so angry. But he just blew out breath and put his head in his hands.

'And you say I keep secrets from you!'

*

It couldn't have been that much of a secret, I thought, sitting in the back of the car on our way home, feeling like a criminal – an angry criminal. When we'd made love during our first days at Mangalath, he'd sometimes withdrawn abruptly as if terrified of what might follow, and I'd understood, knowing how confused things were between us. Also, I raged inwardly, had he never wondered during the times he'd stayed inside me why I hadn't got pregnant? He was a doctor, after all, he must have known. While I seethed, the car skidded and sloshed down a broken road with waving wet palm trees on either side, trying to stay ahead of a monsoon that was moving north-east now. Chandy, angry, or so I imagined, at having his own holiday cut short, had his foot down.

The car stopped. Chandy got out to pee. Anto, who'd hardly spoken a word, turned to me and said, 'So what are we going to do?' He rubbed his eyes, looking so weary and confused that my rage disappeared and I felt his sadness.

'Give me a month or two,' I said. 'That's all.'

I told him in a rush what was true, that I loved him, that I longed for his babies. All I needed was a little more time. He took my hand and squeezed it tightly. 'If you mean that, and I hope you do,' he whispered urgently, 'I am begging you not to stay beyond the point of safety at the Moonstone. You don't know the country well. Kill one baby and they'll kill you.'

He stopped talking. Chandy had appeared from the bushes and was jogging back towards the car. When he was close enough to see our faces, he stopped and stood waiting in the rain.

Chapter 26

A letter was waiting for Anto when we got home, offering him a two-month locum at the TB clinic near the refugee centre at Quilon. Because it offered a proper working wage of four hundred rupees a month plus accommodation, he decided instantly to take it. He was to start in four days' time.

The offer of a job would normally have been a cause for celebration, but we took the news warily, both of us still badly shaken by the row in Trivandrum.

Two days after Anto left, Appan called me into his study at Mangalath, where we began with a cat-and-mouse conversation about his son. Appan hoped that I would support him, 'because family is at the core of everything we do'. He knew it was hard for a young wife to be left alone so much; it had been for Amma, which was why she was so sensitive.

He lit a cigarette, looked at me with his hooded eyes and said I was lucky that I had a career in south India, which was advanced in its support of women gaining professional qualifications. It was the future, but everyone had to be sensitive to the changes.

Finally he grilled me about the home, my work there, the training. 'I'm assured it's a place the family can be proud of,' he said, fixing me with the famous stare. 'And that your work is mainly administrative.' In his next breath he told me I would be allowed to stay for two weeks in a family house near Fort Cochin beach. The house belonged to Appan's cousin Josekutty, another lawyer, who only used it as a holiday home. He showed me the location on a map, and I could hardly stop smiling when I noticed it was on Rose Street, two blocks away from the Moonstone, and not far from the Chinese fishing nets – a lovely part of town. Two trusted family servants would look after me there.

When he saw me smiling, he became stern. Two conditions were not negotiable: number one (rigid finger in the air), that I come back to Mangalath every weekend. Number two (finger pointing at me), that I never discuss my new freedoms outside the family.

'I don't want any gossip about you,' he said.

The terrifying eagle-like glare reminded me of Anto's stories about the strap in the desk, the thunderous rages. As urbane and charming as he could be, you would never want to cross this man.

When I saw the house on Rose Street, I fell in love immediately. Here was the perfect place for Anto and me to live together and have the new start I longed for.

It wasn't a bit smart: it had the look of a tiny, slightly dilapidated Chinese temple, with its sloping tiled roof and a deep veranda with a swing on it – a piece of wood fixed with thick coir to the roof. A cool corridor led straight through the house to a central courtyard scented with jasmine and mimosas.

The two servants, Mani, the odd-job man, and his wife Kamalam, cook and maid, together with their seven-year-old son Uni, were very sweet and proud of the house. They showed me a primitive but adequate kitchen and the four bedrooms, all of which had carved wooden beds, plain furniture and tiled floors.

The timing, for once, was right too. On the day after I moved in, and after much consultation with astrological charts, Madhavan Thambi, the new Minister for Health and Family Welfare, came with the promised year's grant from the Cochin Medical Foundation (Dr A still wouldn't say for how much), which he handed over in an envelope after a short ceremony. He also gave us a shiny plaque for our waiting room, noting wryly that it hung next to a picture of the goddess Bhadrakali; with three eyes, twelve hands, flames flowing from her head and a small tusk protruding from her mouth, she had been created to kill demons with a largely female army. 'I won't cross her,' he said roguishly, and we all laughed politely.

Thanks to our new funds, we now had a staff of twelve: Dr Annakutty and myself, Maya, four nurses, four staff for general cleaning and cooking, and Sister Patricia, a raw-boned Irish nun of about forty who came twice a week from a local convent.

To prepare for this day, Maya had mounted a fierce raid on the rats in the roof, which were now mostly dead, while the home's new purple, red and yellow sign was clearly visible from the road. Most importantly, Mr Namboothiri, our tireless donator of paint, had left in the middle of the night in the smoking, paint-spattered bus we called Cyclops – one headlamp was missing – to collect our first ten midwives, who arrived five hours later looking dusty and petrified. Most had never been in a bus before, or left the network of small villages where they practised. One tiny pockmarked woman wrestled an enormous bedroll; several carried tiffin boxes, worried that they might not get enough to eat here.

Some local musicians had been drafted in to give the ceremony a bit of oomph, and after drums and twiddly flutes, incense was lit, petals strewn. During Mr Thambi's long and droning speech, the midwives sat at his feet on the new coir mats, staring at him in frank amazement.

Dr A jumped up next, her nose quivering importantly, and, in her usual rat-tat-tat delivery, gave a stirring speech, which Maya translated for me.

'You women are the future of India – some of you have more knowledge in your little fingers than the male doctors at the hospital.' (Shy giggles at this; a tremendous frown from the Minister for Health.) 'But we have new things to teach you here: hygienic methods, greater understanding of physiology. Crisis alleviation.'

When they'd finished the course, she told them, they would gain this certificate – she brandished a crackling sheet of cardboard – plus their very own sterile midwife kit. Maya opened a small tin box to show a tantalising glimpse of its contents: scissors, swabs, a bottle of iodine, soap and a clean towel.

Sister Patricia watched this with her head on one side and a fond smile on her lips. 'Look at their little faces,' she whispered to me. 'Trilled to bits, poor dears.'

Shortly after this, Mr Thambi, who'd been furtively checking his watch since the ceremony began, roared off in his government car. The midwives were given a small breakfast of steamed bananas with uppuma, a semolina-type dish, and the teaching part of the day began.

Each pupil was asked to give their name and age; to state the length of time they'd practised, the number of babies delivered and their marital status.

A few looked mulishly suspicious at this and refused. Then a small, stooped woman with dust on her elaborately tattooed bare feet stood up and said in good English (what a relief) that her name was Subadra and she came from Nilamperur, where she was a senior midwife. She had learned her English at a mission school there. So far, she said, she had resisted the government's attempts to retrain her, because, she added, with considerable pride and a hint of challenge, she had delivered 'hundreds and thousands of healthy babies'.

'Hundreds and thousands?' Maya peered at her over her big specs. 'For our study, how many exactly?'

'No idea,' said the woman. 'Maybe four thousand.' She sat down heavily, and muttered something under her breath to the woman next to her, who immediately tried to hide her face.

'You?' Dr A pointed to her. 'Stand up. No need for shyness.'

The woman cast a fearful look towards the door, and when she found she could neither flee nor speak, she whispered something to Subadra, who translated for her.

'Her name is Bhaskari. She is from a Dalit family. Her only job is to cut the cords and to dispose of after-baby.'

A low grumble broke out at this among one or two of the mid-wives. In some communities, I already knew, these women were regarded as the lowest of the low.

'You also have an important job, Bhaskari.' Dr A bestowed one of her rare smiles. 'We will teach you here how to do it sweetly and cleanly. We must all learn to work together.' The one woman still muttering was given Dr A's famous basilisk glare and visibly shrank.

'Sit down, Bhaskari,' Dr A continued smoothly. 'We're very glad to have you with us.'

One by one we took their histories, from fat, thin, young, old, bright and stupid-looking. They were, as Sister Patricia whispered to me, a bit of a job lot. Each midwife was then given a piece of paper and a pencil.

'Your first task,' Dr A announced, 'is to draw what you think is inside a woman's body. Take your time. This is not a test, it's for knowledge sharing.'

I saw Bhaskari take her pencil and paper and strike off immediately in a series of confident slashing circles. One woman tucked her pencil inside the folds of her sari and gave me a truculent why-should-I-tell-you look.

After twenty minutes or so of scratching and sighing and worried looks in our direction, Maya collected the sheets, adding names to those of the six women in the class who were illiterate. Some drew childish circles with eggs inside, some drew women with random pipes and squiggles for ovaries.

Rosamma, who said she delivered up to thirty babies a month, piped up indignantly: 'No one really knows what is inside the human body – you can only imagine it.'

Sister Patricia whispered, 'Well I wouldn't want that one to intuit me baby out of me.'

At the end of the day, I left the home exhausted and conscious of a mountain to climb.

The women returned to the classroom the following morning looking far more relaxed. Rosamma, a fat woman with an exuberant smile, made everyone laugh when she said she would like to keep dancing all day because she was so happy to get away from her husband for a while. Her good English and self-confidence had already made her the group's leader and translator.

We had asked them to describe the work they did in their own villages. It was possible that no one had ever asked them to do this before, because they listened to each other with open-mouthed fascination. Rosamma, settling in a comfortable cross-legged position and adjusting her large bosom, began.

There were two kinds of midwives in her village, she said: the visible ones, the *vayattattis*, and the invisibles, who washed the mother after delivery and buried the afterbirth. Her voice dropped confidentially at this, and when one or two of the other women frowned, she said, with a note of defiance, 'We are here to talk about these things.'

It was the *vayattattis*, she went on, who were blamed for everything.

'Many things stop a woman having a baby,' she said, her voice warm with indignation. 'Lack of good food for the mother to eat, and this year our rice crop failed.' She addressed this directly to Sister Patricia. 'No proper place to have the baby. In my village, some are sent out to cow sheds.' The gold bracelets jangled on her right arm as she lifted it to cover her eyes.

'Can you remember a time when you felt you were blamed for something going wrong?' Maya asked her softly.

I saw the expression on the women's faces change as they waited for her reply, and wondered if Maya had made a mistake by asking for these intimacies too early.

'Last month,' said Rosamma after a long silence, 'a woman died in my arms. She was in labour for nearly eighteen hours, and the baby got stuck. There was no bullock cart to take her to the hospital; it belongs to the head man in our village, and he needed it that day. The family blame me now; they refused to pay me and avoid me in the street. This is not fair, and this is why I am here, to get more government protection.'

The other women murmured sympathetically, and Rosamma added, 'In my village, there is also much suspicion of me because I have the freedom to travel.'

Another said, 'Some will never forgive me if baby comes and it is a girl, or if it is crippled or dies; they think maybe I'm bad luck and they should have gone to another *vayattatti*. I am a poor woman,' she continued, breathing heavily. 'I don't do this for money. I do it because God wants me to.'

Chapter 27

Anto wrote to say that his old tutor at Exeter College had recommended him for a year-long research project at the Holy Family Hospital in Kacheripady. *It sounds*, he wrote, *almost too good to be true, so only dare to be cautiously optimistic. But how wonderful it would be if it happened.*

I burst into tears when I got the letter. At last, what sounded like the perfect job for him. I was missing him badly: my days were crammed with activity, but nights at Rose Street were long and lonely. I wrote straight back, happier than I'd felt in weeks, with an edited version of events in our midwife classes.

We'd had such a funny morning when Maya announced: 'Today we're going to have our first Mother Moonstone baby. Who will be mother?'

Rosamma lowered her considerable bulk to the floor, where she lay on her back and groaned like an injured calf. Maya chose Kartyani, a frowning, dark-skinned girl, to be midwife. So far she'd refused to join in with any activity, and when I'd tried to persuade her, she'd said angrily, 'My head is bursting with new information. It is not helping me.' Maya thought she was homesick. Sister Patricia said she was dim.

Maya ignored Kartyani's scowl. 'Our patient is having her first baby. She's been in labour now for fourteen hours, and nothing is happening.'

Rosamma rolled her eyes convincingly and clutched her belly. 'Owwwwwwww. Oh dear. No baby comes.' The class tittered.

'What will you do now to progress the baby?'

'I don't know,' Kartyani said sulkily, and shook her head.

'Hurry up,' Rosamma commanded from the floor. 'I am paining badly.'

In a mutinous drone, Kartyani began, 'First, I would go to her house.'

'Of course.' Rosamma was irritated by this glimpse of the obvious.

'I would loosen her hair and her bangles,' Kartyani said in the same unwilling monotone. 'I would open all her cupboards and doors.'

Maya peered at me through her big specs. 'This is psychologically helpful to a woman – it opens everything up.'

'Then this.' Kartyani sank to her knees and rubbed her hands expertly around the rim of Rosamma's belly.

'What is she saying?' I asked. Rosamma was rolling her eyes lasciviously, shimmying her shoulders.

'That I can't translate.' Maya was blushing. 'Too crude.' Even Kartyani couldn't resist a faint smile at this.

Before the lesson ended, *pop!* Rosamma produced a plastic baby from the folds of her sari, and everybody cheered except Kartyani, who ran out of the room.

'She is not happy here,' Maya whispered in the corridor later. 'She says the teaching is too Western, and that she doesn't want to share her secrets with us or with low-caste village people. I think she is a spy from the government.' She laughed to show me she was joking, but nothing would have surprised me.

I wrote to Daisy about what happened next, but left it out of my letter to Anto.

Kartyani refused to leave her room. She reiterated that her head was bursting with all this new information, that she wanted to go home.

'Stay there then, *mundi*' – stupid idiot – Dr A barked at her. '*Nee orikkalum nannavilla*. You will never improve.'

'Write that down,' Maya instructed me. 'It's a good insult.'

Kartyani missed that afternoon's lively debate on menstruation and contraception. Shanta, a sprightly young woman who had delivered umpteen babies, stood up and said in her piping voice, 'I will share my knowledge with you. Monthly bleeding was originally given to the man, but God found it was too hard for the man, so he gave it to the woman.'

'Do you all think this?' Maya asked the other women. They bobbed their heads in the yes–no Indian gesture.

'How you behave with your monthlies will depend on what caste you are in,' said Subadra, noticing my confusion. 'A Brahmin woman must stay apart from her family, wash many times, and not meet with her husband. She cannot take part in celebrations. A Dalit, an untouchable, will go about life as usual.'

'In our family, we are very careful not to stop the period,' Shanta continued, unwilling to relinquish the floor. 'If you do, you could become poisoned and lose your sight.'

Maya listened patiently. 'So now I am going to show you what really happens,' she said. She opened the cupboard and took out the wall chart of the naked woman Daisy and I had christened Vera. Her Fallopian tubes, womb and major arteries were clearly marked in red; stomach, heart, liver and kidneys in blue. Her face was concentrated and thoughtful, as if it was hard work keeping all this complicated machinery going.

'Is this an Englishwoman?' Shanta asked as if this might explain Vera's elaborate plumbing.

'No,' Maya said. 'This is what we are all like inside.'

'No we're not,' Subadra contradicted immediately. 'I have seen other drawings done by Ayurvedic doctors, and there are many, many more blood vessels.'

One or two of the midwives looked defiantly towards me, as if I was the snake oil salesman here. When Maya took off her glasses and polished them, I saw that her eyes still had dark purple bags under them. She worked far too hard. She put her specs back on and took a deep breath.

Maya was five minutes into her menstruation talk when I looked up and saw Dr A standing at the door. She was beckoning to me.

It was the wrong end of a long, hot day. I wanted to go home for a bath, an early supper and to finish my letter to Anto. But Dr A's gesture was insistent, excited.

In the corridor, she whispered in a quick cinnamon-scented blast, 'We have a patient, Laksmi, in labour. Maya is busy; Sister Patricia's gone home.'

I assumed I was to assist her. Laksmi, with her slender child's body and her history of miscarriage, was anything but a straightforward case. Admitted to the home the week before, very anxious, she had had a show of blood. Her husband was a local policeman.

'She asked for you this morning,' Dr A continued as we sped down the corridor. 'She said she wanted the English doctor lady to do the delivery.'

I stopped, aghast. 'But I'm not a doctor.'

'I am not the one saying it.' Dr A handed me a starched white coat with a bland stare. 'And neither are you. But she needs a good delivery this time. With this we can make her confident.' She put a stethoscope around my neck, patted me on the back. 'Don't look so frightened.'

I should have said no. Instead, I buttoned the coat with shaking hands and walked towards the delivery room on rubber legs. I could already hear Laksmi's weak cries coming from behind the door.

Anto once told me he believed everything we were was the result of what we had thought, so I knew that in one sense I had led myself down this corridor and towards this test. Half of me had wanted it all along. I knew too that if this was a normal vaginal delivery, I had the skills to do it. After all, firemen and panicked husbands had managed in the past. Caesareans were very rare here.

'Maya will be finished with the class soon,' Dr A said, at the door. 'She'll come and take over.'

'So I'll call if there are any complications,' I said in what I hoped was a calm voice. She was already walking away.

The first thing I saw was Laksmi's small feet sticking out from under the sheet, clenching and unclenching in pain. When her head reared up, I remembered her better: a small, undernourished woman with a two-inch scar from a burn on her right cheek. I recalled that she suffered from anaemia, which was not unusual amongst the local women. Please God, don't let her start bleeding again.

Her mother – a wizened woman dressed in a widow's white sari – sat beside her, fanning her with the neem leaves thought to keep angry spirits at bay. Then Subadra walked in.

'Dr A sent me,' she said. 'I know this girl and speak her dialect.'

She took a damp flannel from the table and wiped Laksmi's forehead, which was filmed with sweat. The girl's eyes fixed on mine, and with a desperate expression, she poured out words.

'She is very afraid,' Subadra said. 'She thanks God you have come.'

'Tell her I am glad to be here,' I said, trying for a confident voice. 'I'm going to have a look now, to see how her baby is.'

When I rolled back the sheet, her taut belly was covered in grey ash.

'Don't touch it,' Subadra said quickly. 'Ash is put there for a boy.' Another gush of words from the girl made the mother nod vigorously. 'She says she will kill herself this time if she doesn't have a boy. She has conceived' – she shot a question at Laksmi, got a tearful confirmation – 'six times in the past eight years; only two children survived. She says if she has another girl, her mother-in-law will take it away and harm it.'

The girl's eyes moved from Subadra to me like someone watching a tennis match. Tears poured down her face; another fusillade of words followed.

Subadra murmured a string of the phrases Maya had taught me. '*Saramilla pottey ellam sheriyakum, njaan illay*' – it's all right, let go, don't worry, everything will be OK – but Laksmi was still crying.

Subadra wrung out the flannel and sponged the girl's face and arms.

'She says she should have taken a drink of hot chillies, killed the foetus and herself before coming here. She knows it will be another girl.'

Laksmi let out a groan like that of a tree before it loosened from the earth and crashed to the ground. The tight brown dome of her tummy strained, and I could see the clearly defined shape of a baby's foot kicking out.

'Can you stop her crying?' I was terrified of hurting her. 'Get her to breathe evenly?'

After the internal exam, I estimated she was two fingers dilated. If all went well, the baby would be born in a matter of hours.

By five past six, a buzz of insects was whirling around the light, and beyond the barred window, the sky was growing dark. I could hear rickshaw wheels turning, a tea vendor yelling, but the outside world felt distant and unimportant. What I most felt was the gathering of energy and concentration inside this small room, the glug, glug, glug, of my own heart thumping.

Twenty minutes later when I examined Laksmi, my hand felt steadier, my head less swimmy. She was nearly three fingers dilated, and her contractions, every eight minutes or so, lasted forty to sixty seconds. I mentally revised her delivery time to 7.30.

At 8.15, some rackety music struck up in the street outside. A dog was barking somewhere. Subadra left the room and came back with food from a village stall: some pappadams and lime pickle, spiced buttermilk and a roll of banana leaves to use as plates. She washed her hands ostentatiously and, after a sneaky look at me, ate in the corner of the room near the sink. Maya, who'd spent yesterday morning lecturing the midwives on hygiene at the point of delivery, would have had kittens at this, but Maya had gone home, and I was so grateful for Subadra's presence, I said nothing.

As darkness fell quickly outside, Laksmi's breathing between contractions became more relaxed and she seemed to sleep. Subadra put her fingers around the girl's birdlike ankle, and with her eyebrows waggling told me that this girl's mother-in-law was a very hard-hearted lady – she'd starved her of food.

'Why?' I was scandalised.

'She lost too many babies,' Subadra replied. She waved an index finger from left to right. 'She thought the evil spirits were there.'

My old matron from St Thomas's appeared in my mind, warning me never to gossip about patients in their presence. Here it seemed par for the course.

'She's slow.' Subadra looked down at the girl, whose brow was now corrugated and sweaty. 'I would like baby here soon. This will bring it on.' She produced a small bottle from her sari filled with an inky blue liquid.

'No!' I leapt forward. 'You can't do that.' I pictured the headlines – *Local girl poisoned by English midwife* – and was wrestling the bottle out of her hand when Dr A stepped into the room, so quickly I wondered if she'd been there all along. She looked shattered, and her normally neat grey bun was all mussed up.

She took the bottle from my hand. 'This is good.' She sniffed it with her voluminous nose. 'It's castor oil, gherkin root, cumin and other things. We use it.' This surprised me – she'd told me earlier that the British had banned the use of local Ayurvedic medicines, and that she'd agreed with this.

She shuffled out again, saying in a sleepy voice that she'd be in her office if we needed her. When she was gone, the girl's mother got down on her knees and began to pray.

'She's asking Mother Goddess to please give them a boy,' Subadra said. 'Not long now.'

I knelt beside Laksmi, who was now having three or four contractions every ten minutes. At last she gave a hoarse cry, the muscles on her forehead corded and the baby's head started to crown.

'It's coming, Laksmi,' I said. 'Hooray!'

Subadra smoothed oil between her hands and rubbed the girl's tummy with deft, gentle strokes, first clockwise, then counter-clockwise, and finally, more firmly, down the sides of her waist.

When I examined her again, she was fully dilated, and had the intense look of concentration I'd seen on other mothers at this stage of their labour.

'Push now,' said Subadra. 'Push hard. *Tulleh pennay, nannayi tullek-kay*. Soon the baby will come.'

Laksmi let out a guttural roar. Her legs started to tremble violently. The fluff of the baby's head appeared in the birth canal, then the forehead, nose, mouth chin of a perfect little boy shot out in a rush of blood, so fast we almost dropped him. He started bawling.

The mother had torn her perineum on delivery, and I was good at stitching – Matron Smythe had once told me I would always have a job in upholstery if I got fed up with nursing. I threaded the needle and quickly put in two or three stitches with Laksmi barely noticing. She was covering her son in kisses, sobbing with relief. His life would save hers. I was crying too as her mother put a smear of soot on the baby's cheek to ward off the evil eye, and then the child began to suckle.

Afterwards, I sat on the veranda, all emptied out with happiness. I'd done it! The thing I never thought I'd be able to do again. The air was like warm milk, and there were a million stars. Subadra sat beside me, her hennaed feet on the step. When a servant brought us a cup of chai and some coconutty sweets, we devoured them ravenously.

Relief kept flooding through my body and I was too tired to censor myself. Over the next twenty minutes, I told Subadra more than I had ever told anyone about the last time I had delivered a child: how I felt I'd made a mess of it, and how it had taken me a long time to get over it.

She listened to me so quietly that I wasn't sure she'd understood, but when she took a sip of tea and patted my arm gently, I realised she was just doing what she did so well in the delivery room: listening, taking everything in, not trying to hustle things along.

'Your stitches were beautiful,' she said. 'You are a very fine doctor. She didn't even know you were doing it.'

After a long pause, she continued, 'I couldn't say this in class, but I had a mother, only one month ago. She was too weak, she died. Nobody blamed me, but I was not happy with myself.' Her worn hands pleated the skirt of her sari as she talked. 'Don't tell this to the others,' she said, and I promised I wouldn't.

I wasn't naive enough to think that delivering this baby was the magic wand that would miraculously banish all my fears. But it did feel like a momentous night for me. Later, undressing for bed, longing to have someone to share it with, I wrote five pages to Daisy, telling her about the delivery and about Subadra, knowing how pleased she would be. This was exactly the kind of collaboration she had dreamed of for a long, long time. While I was writing, a piece of paper fell from my lap to the floor. I picked it up and smoothed it out. It was Subadra's picture of what a woman looked like inside – a few random squiggles inside a child's body with pipe-cleaner legs.

I'd planned to send it in a letter to Josie for a cheap laugh. I knew better now.

Chapter 28

He was packing to go north again when Amma appeared carrying two ironed shirts. She looked down at the bed littered with his things: khaki trousers, spirit lamp, steel tray, scissors, antiseptics, painkillers. 'When are you going to stop running away?' she asked.

He sighed. 'Amma,' he said, 'I have three hours left in which to pack, go to Cochin, see Kit and get the train.' His nerves were so shredded, it was hard to keep his voice steady. He'd been sure he'd get news about the research job at Kacheripady, the job that was made for him, but no letter had come.

Amma shook her head. 'So why bother coming back here at all?'

'To pick up my clothes.'

'So, that's good.' She tried another tack. 'She gives you ten minutes at lunchtime. Lucky for you.'

'Don't blame her, Ma.' He hated her sour expression. 'It's not easy for her either.'

'I've been checking the papers. They're still looking for people at Palluruthy; she could go with you, or you could talk to Dr Kunju again. I can't believe there is nothing here.' She put her head in her hands and gave a strange bark of frustration.

'Ma, please.'

'If you wanted to leave her,' she said softly, 'we would understand.'

'Leave her! What in God's name are you talking about?'

This was a blasphemy, particularly coming from Amma. The Thekkedens didn't divorce. They knew that marriage was hard work sometimes: that Josekutty drank too much, that Mathu, the family saint, neglected Amma for his work. But that was life, your karma. Accepting hurt was part of growing up.

'You do know that I'm properly married to her?' he said, thinking she might have imagined some counterfeit English arrangement, easily dissolved.

'You call it a proper marriage? A registry office, no relatives, no celebrations?' He saw in her face contempt, and also a kind of bitter enjoyment at finally being able to let fly. 'Look at yourself.' She snatched a mirror from his shaving kit. 'Skinny, sad – it's horrible seeing you like this.'

Their reflections shimmered and merged in the mirror – her huge brown eyes brimming with tears, his face all strain and bones.

'Work is all she wants to do,' Amma spat. 'And that place where she works – I don't think you know the first thing about it.'

'What are you talking about? I did some translations for them, for the charity, in Oxford.'

'Oh, Oxford.' She flapped the place away with her hand. 'I'm talking about here. It has a very bad reputation. People are gossiping about it.'

'What people? What gossip?'

'I can't give you their names. What does that matter?'

This shrill, tale-telling voice was new to him, or perhaps it had always been there, and before he'd had a wife he'd never heard it, but it diminished her and saddened him.

'And you know,' she shot a look at him, 'there are already good government-trained midwives in Travancore. This charity is only interested in dirty, illiterate women full of disease.'

'That's quite an assumption, Amma. I thought you were a liberal.' He made a great effort not to raise his voice. 'All for progress, for new ways. Have I got that wrong?'

'Yes, you have.' She was shaking with pent-up rage. 'Because the new progress you are talking about sounds like the very old progress to me: foreign women coming here to teach us about something so private. How dare they insult us like this? What do they know of our ways? Maybe I should go to England now and tell your Daisy Barker how to have her baby.'

He knew he should defend the Moonstone's aims, or at the very least Kit. But the moment passed: another plate spinning out of his hands, like his work, his life, his wife, the train that would shortly leave without him.

'There's another thing, Anto,' she said. There was something bunched and venomous in her face. 'Something I wasn't going to tell you about her.'

'Go ahead, Ma,' he said wearily. She'd already complained about Kit's untidiness, her lateness, her unseemly conversations with

Mariamma. 'What crime now?' He sat down heavily on the bed and stared at his shoes.

'We had a ladies' party while you were away. Mariamma and I thought it would be a good opportunity for Kit to meet our friends.' He knew this wasn't true: Mariamma had talked Amma into asking her.

'So I asked Appan if the car could be sent for her,' Amma continued.

He looked at his watch. He was desperate to see Kit before he left.

'We said prayers, as we always do.' She was settling into this. 'We laid out all the special food, nothing too spicy for her.'

'Ma, you don't have to do that. She loves our food.'

'Anyway, we waited, and waited, and waited. When she comes, she is one and a half hours late, and as white as a sheet. There is blood on her sleeve.' Amma's mouth was strangely twisted. 'Mariamma says, "She is delivering babies at the home. She is not a report writer, she is not a social reformer. She pulls the babies out."' An expression of horror on her face. 'This is the woman you have brought into our house.'

He waited several moments before looking up.

'Amma, listen to me: she is part of a charity, and she is a midwife too. Try and understand that this is not a job to be ashamed of in England. We should be proud of her.'

'Proud of her.' His mother's look was one of angry incredulity. 'That is too much. The situation grows worse and worse.'

Driving back to Fort Cochin, he felt a dull anger settle inside him. He was angry with Amma for being so small-minded; at Kit for upsetting his mother; at Mariamma, who he suspected stirred things up, partly because she didn't have enough to do; and furiously disappointed at not hearing any more news about the possible job.

To shield himself from the piercing brightness of the day, he pulled the curtain in the back of the car. He should have known the Thekkedens would never accept a midwife as a daughter-in-law. However much they might give lip service to the new India, and its shiny new ideas – the banishing of the caste system, better lives for women and for widows – privately they wanted things to stay as they always had been for them: peaceful, privileged, content. Kit was an unexploded bomb in their midst, at least in Amma's mind.

Anto had brought her here, and now he must find ways of limiting the damage.

The row with Amma had left no time to go back to Rose Street. Instead, they sat opposite each other in the railway's restaurant.

'Anto,' Kit looked pale and wary, 'how long can you keep doing this?'

'Until I get a job here,' he said.

'I'm sure you'll hear soon. It's tailor-made for you,' she said. 'How long will you be away this time?'

'Two weeks, and then I'll come back.' He was close to tears. 'I'm sorry about this. It's just much harder than I thought.' He didn't have the heart to tell her how many applications he'd made.

'Everything is changing here,' she said. 'It's not your fault.'

He was grateful to her for saying this, because a clammy feeling of guilt had taken root in his mind.

'I love you, and I have a wicked plan. Let's ask your uncle if we can rent the house in Rose Street as soon as you get back. It's perfect for us. You'll get work in Cochin eventually, I know you will, and we can be a proper old married couple together.'

'I like that idea,' he said, knowing Amma would hate it. 'A lot. I love you too. This has been a sort of fugue, you know, all of this, coming back and feeling, I don't know, like a stranger, and then feeling so at home again. I'm so sorry.'

'I'm not sorry.' She drew close to him. 'I'd like to kiss you,' she whispered, 'but don't worry, I won't.'

The other passengers were staring at them openly.

'So, how are things at the Moonstone now?' he asked in a neutral voice. She glanced at him, and then at her cup.

'Good,' she said. 'Actually, more than good. We've got ten more midwives coming next month, and . . . drum roll announcement.' She glanced at him quickly. 'I helped deliver my first baby here. It felt like a big step.'

'So I hear.' He'd hoped to sound glad for her, but his voice was weary and flat.

'Who told you?' Her smile faded.

'Amma.'

'Amma! God! What does she know about it?' She moved away from him.

'Did you really think they wouldn't find out?'

'No.' Her voice was tight. 'I thought they would, which is why I wanted to be honest with them right from the start, remember?'

He sighed, and his glance travelled to the next table, where a plump man sat with his much younger wife and a clutch of beautiful long-lashed children. They were poring over a travel guide together.

'Poor Anto,' Kit said. 'I don't know why I expected you to be pleased. Nothing is easy now.' They smiled unhappily at each other, and in some treacherous corner of his heart, he agreed with her.

He watched the family leave, then looked at his watch. 'I have ten more minutes, Kit, so I have to say this quickly.' He drew a deep breath. 'I'm happy, really happy the work is going well, but I worry about you all the time. If something goes wrong, the consequences could be terrible for you.'

'What consequences?' A bright look of accusation.

'Angry people, nationalists, those who think we should drop British charity now.'

'I can't do anything about them, Anto, because I don't meet them. The women I meet mostly smother me in kindness.'

'They will until something goes wrong.'

A train screamed through the station, rattling their saucers.

'So how long are you going to keep working?' he said, when they could hear each other again. 'The last time we spoke of it, you said a month or two.'

'I can't say exactly – as long as it takes to get things up and running. I'm loving it,' she finished helplessly.

Another train drew in and disappeared. When he started to cough, she patted him on the back. He waved her hand away and kept on coughing until his eyes watered.

'How long?' he said when he'd stopped.

'I don't know!' She had to raise her voice against the babble of passengers swarming off the train. 'Must I give you a date?'

'So, no children of our own?' He was suddenly furious again. 'Is this your command also?'

'My command?' She looked shocked. 'Don't be so bloody horrible. You know that's not what I meant. I can do both.'

'You know best,' he said. 'You're making all the rules now.'

That was the last thing he said before his train shrieked off in a cloud of smoke.

Chapter 29

The row with Anto churned me up badly. I sat brooding about it on the veranda that night, and thought about it all through the following day's training session.

After the usual prayers, the midwives sat down on the coir mats, and Maya posed the question 'Who owns your body?'

'You start,' Rosamma encouraged Kartyani, who had barely spoken for two days.

Kartyani glowered at her beautifully patterned feet. 'I don't want to talk of such things in a public place.'

'So I'll start.' Rosamma was impossible to offend, soaked up knowledge like a sponge. 'I have plenty to say.

'In my village, men own our bodies. As girls, we are given away young, often to older men, for sexual pleasure, or we are used as cooks, as beasts of burden.'

'Why complain?' Kartyani picked sullenly at the folds of her skirt. 'A man's life is no picnic either.'

'No.' Rosamma waited several moments before replying. 'But let me ask you this: who eats first in your house, your husband or yourself?'

'He does, of course, but that is my choice.'

'Really? And who gets the best food?'

No one bothered to answer.

'Who is the most educated? Sons or daughters?' Rosamma had her pouncing legal face on.

'Sons, of course,' Kartyani said. 'They have to run the household. What is your point?'

'Here's my point.' Rosamma brandished her finger. 'I want a daughter of mine to be educated to live outside the cage, like this person.' She pointed at me. 'To be educated, not to pretend to be shy.'

Oh God, I felt like a twenty-one-carat fraud. I did so much shyness-pretending at Mangalath, and at the moment, I felt I did nothing but placate Anto.

'A woman should be shy.' Kartyani's small fists bunched. 'Shy and obedient, that is the way of the world.'

'You are not shy and obedient. You contradict everything.'

Kartyani joined in the laughter reluctantly.

'So, Miz Kit,' Rosamma asked me, 'who owns your body?' Which set me back on my heels.

'As a child,' I said at last, 'I think you could say my mother owned it.' Colonised it, I thought, as her little fiefdom, to feed, smack, clean, dress.

'But you are a married woman now?'

'Yes.' I showed them the cheap gold wedding ring Anto had bought in Oxford. 'This is how we show we're married. It's like your bindi,' I said, referring to the red spot that married women here put between their eyes.

'Children are there?'

'No, but when I have them, my body will belong to them.'

My stumbling answer had confused some of the women. I had another run at it.

'I think a woman should . . . that she . . . that there are times in a woman's life when she should be brave. It's important to be brave.'

'Otherwise, other people will use her up.' Rosamma, who'd been examining my wedding ring, dropped my finger. 'My own mother died at thirty-six years old, worn out with trying to please. Her last words: "Thank God for the rest."'

We all laughed at this, except for Kartyani, who was still looking sour and perplexed, but I found it painful too. I felt I'd lost the easy confidence that came from Anto's love and support, and I hated that. I missed the jokes, childish as they were; the sense of being lucky, lucky, lucky to have found each other, and I wanted him back.

Wickam Farm, 11 April

Dear one,

Your letter gave me great joy. Your first Indian baby delivered! Golly, I'm impressed; so pleased for you too: there's nothing like being really scared of a thing and finding you can do it. Subadra sounds like a wonderful woman. We have so much to learn.

You don't give much news about the rest of your life in India. When I lived there, I knew my time would end, but you've given up your Western life — much more difficult, and I hope rewarding too.

187

Don't say it's none of my beeswax, but I don't suppose anyone has ever solved it: the sense of never being exactly sure where one belongs; one's heart and mind seem a mix of such different things.

Nothing of great moment to report from this end. Tudor has found a local farmer to manage the land. He's moved to London and is doing sterling work on a treatise he is publishing on the archaeology of our Roman remains. House full of usual waifs and strays. Ci Ci, very much the grand dame, has moved into the Bird Room. Flora has gone to London, living in digs and doing a typing course. We have two new residents, so I'm happy to say that your sainted mother is back here, after working for a family in Warminster. I'm sad to hear you no longer correspond.

In great haste, blackberry and apple jam on stove and about to bubble. Will write longer, later...

All love,

Daisy xxxxxxx

Chapter 30

When Uncle Josekutty said I could, with Appan's permission, stay a few weeks longer in Rose Street I was overjoyed, but I stuck to our agreement of going to Mangalath every weekend. It was there, one afternoon, while the servants were asleep, Mariamma took me into Amma's immaculate kitchen and showed me how to make karimeen mappas, Anto's favourite fish curry. We were chopping up garlic, ginger and green chillies when she turned to me and said in her mocking sing-song voice:

'So, don't be a stuffed shirt, Kit, tell me some juicy stories from the home. What are they like? Salacious details, please.'

She teased me like a sister now. I was no longer the foreigner, to be kept at a polite distance, and when Amma got tricky, which she could even about something as innocent-seeming as our cooking together, Mariamma would roll her eyes, wobble her head, and do her mother's voice to a T: *You can stoop and pick up nothing.*

'Come on.' She brandished her knife in my direction. 'Get on with it. More information please.'

'What are they like?' I teased her back. 'I assume you're talking about the midwives... Well, here's a surprise. They're all different. Some are highly intelligent, very skilled, brilliant in fact, and some are – how shall I put this?'

'Thick as bricks?' Mariamma supplied.

'I didn't say that,' I was trying not to laugh. I liked it so much more when she dropped the veil of formality. 'I would say that some are confused by what we're saying, and of course, we do have one or two awkward customers, who don't want to change at all.'

I told her about Shanta's theory about men menstruating first, and God taking it away from them because they moaned so much. Mariamma laughed and said she was glad not to be a Brahmin woman, confined to a dark room at the back of the house each month because you were considered impure. It had stopped one of her friends going to university.

'Do you think you have made the women you teach happier?' The innocent mockery in her eyes had changed to something more challenging. 'Or have you caused family problems?'

'No idea. It depends what you mean by happier.' Now that the conversation had veered into seriousness, I wondered if this was a not-so-subtle dig at me and my strangely absent husband. 'Some have loved the teaching and the company so much, they dread going back to the isolation of their villages; others can't wait to see the back of us.' I told her about Kartyani, her sighs, her sulks, her refusal to take part.

'How rude,' said Mariamma in her Scottish brogue. 'Very clarty behaviour.'

She pushed the chopped garlic into a neat pile and began to peel the ginger into parchment-thin slices.

'So, have you learned anything from them?'

'Masses,' I peered at the long list of ingredients in Amma's hand-written recipe book, hoping to steer the conversation away from me. 'So we fry the garlic and ginger in oil, then what?'

'What have you learned?' she insisted.

I stopped and thought for a while, and then a new feeling bubbled up from nowhere: something like exhilaration, or pride, or maybe it was just belonging that loosened my tongue. 'Oh, I don't know... so much: to think with my fingers; how to watch, how to wait. I'm still scared, but nothing like as much as I was. How to shut up.' I stopped suddenly. This was exactly what I should be doing. I liked Mariamma, but I didn't trust her not to tell the others.

'Show me something you've learned,' Mariamma said with a glint in her eye. At moments like this, I could see why Anto called her the family bossy-boots. My mind raced through several possibilities. Something that would emphasise my role as observer. Nothing to frighten the horses.

'Well, last week, a girl came in whose labour was very slow, and Rosamma, one of the women, taught me the circular massage.'

Mariamma slid the fish into the fragrant liquid. She washed her hands, and lay down on the floor. 'No one will see us. The servants are asleep, and Amma is out.' I hesitated, then closed the door.

'The pressure is like this.' I pushed gently on her abdomen. 'You do it clockwise first.' I swept my hands to the right, and then the other way. 'It relaxes the mother and helps the midwife feel the baby. Rosamma told me that "God is the doer, the hands are mine." ' It suddenly seemed a good idea to introduce a religious element into the discussion.

'God is the doer, the hands are mine,' Mariamma murmured. Her plump, beaming face grew thoughtful, as if another bit of the jigsaw had fallen into place.

'Your own midwife must have done something like this,' I said, feeling stupid.

'Yes,' she admitted. 'But we only ever use one midwife, Rema. She is properly trained, we all trust her . . . but good to know the nitty-gritty of these other things,' she ended vaguely.

She stood up, washed her hands again and went to stir the curry, which had come to the boil.

'And you must have to touch them,' her back was turned to me. 'I mean . . . you know . . . in their private parts. It's so intimate,' she added a sprinkle of salt, 'so . . .' her shoulders hunched as she searched for a word to describe the squalor of it, 'so odd.'

I felt a flash of impatience. This was life we were talking about. Why make the source of it such a taboo?

'It's thrilling to watch a child being born,' I said.

'And even more thrilling to have one,' she said pointedly.

Pathrose and his grandson, Kuttan, rescued me. If they noticed the strange atmosphere, they didn't show it as they smiled and sniffed appreciatively at the fish curry. Mariamma, after rapping out instructions about when it should be taken off the heat and what should be served with it, put a protective arm around me and led me into the garden, to a bench underneath a banana tree.

When we were seated, she said, 'I like listening to you talk about your work.' She patted my arm reassuringly. 'I think you're brave.'

'No,' I said, 'not brave at all.'

'Hmm.' There was still something watchful and guarded about her expression. 'I'm happy for you, but I must give you some serious advice.' Her eyes flickered towards the house. 'You've been married for six months. You should think about your own babies soon.'

The following Friday when I arrived at Mangalath, Amma came rushing towards me through the courtyard like a little steam train. I assumed she was angry, but when she stopped, I saw she was beaming.

'Kittykutty, Kittykutty,' she said – the first time she'd ever added this endearment to my name – 'we've had a telegram from Anto. He's coming home soon, God willing.' Her eyes were full of tears.

She watched me while I read the dog-eared telegram – *Job offer from hospital. Home soonest, love Anto* – then embraced me properly for the first time, murmuring, 'Thank God, thank God.' I cried too, feeling a flooding relief, as if some vital stability had been restored, not just to me, but to the house. Now Amma would stop blaming me for his absence, he'd have a proper job, we'd get our first proper home together and be happy again. Life is never that simple, of course, but on that night, it felt that way.

We feasted, and Appan, who was home, drank more whisky than usual before dinner, and the whole house floated on a cloud of relief and delight.

'We'll have a party to celebrate,' Amma decided when we were drinking tea on the veranda. She patted my arm. The grumpy vertical line had gone from between her eyes, and she looked a decade younger. 'We'll ask Thresiamma, Ammamma, Sadji, Aby...' She wrote the names down on a list. Appan mock-groaned. He'd been in Delhi – another conference on the shaping of India's new laws – and come home with a mountain of work to do.

When Father Christopher arrived to say a special mass of thanks, I knelt in the chapel and felt, for the first time in a long time, profoundly happy, a soft billowing rising inside me. It wasn't God who brought it to me – or if it was, I was not aware of it. It was Anto coming back, having work to do that fulfilled me, and, strangely, the presence of Amma on one side of me, Mariamma on the other, with Theresa beside her. I looked around me at the samplers I'd watched Amma stitching, breathed in the smell of the incense, heard the lap of the lagoon outside, the melodious call of the koyal bird in the jackfruit tree and Appan's sturdily male 'most grievous fault' as he thumped his breast. Tonight I felt anchored in a way I wasn't used to feeling, and it came to me that home was not, in the end, a place, or a country, but something much deeper and more lasting.

Chapter 31

For a while, it seemed that it was the old Anto who came home – the one who made me laugh, who confided in me, the one whose beautiful tortoiseshell-green eyes would squeeze shut when he laughed and open in a gleam of mischief – rather than the in-flight Anto, distracted and grumpy, who was beginning to make me feel like a dangerous pet. His new job paid a decent salary of four hundred and fifty rupees per month. His title: junior physician at the Holy Family Hospital at Kacheripady in Ernakulam. He was also to work with Assistant District Medical Officer Dr Sastry on a newly funded research trial, the details to be supplied later.

Later that week, Uncle Josekutty, the distinguished-looking Thekkeden who owned the house in Rose Street, asked if he could call on us. Our arrangement with him had never been formalised so we were both shockingly nervous, thinking our good luck had run out, but when, at the end of a leisurely conversation, Anto asked if we could possibly secure a year's lease, Uncle Josekutty, who was childless and recently widowed, said, 'That's what I came to say. I think you should buy my house at a peppercorn price.'

When Anto politely protested, Uncle Josekutty patted him on the arm. 'That's enough! I believe in giving gifts warm, not when I am frozen in the ground.'

We danced around the kitchen once he had gone. Shortly after that, the deeds were handed over, the house was blessed, and I asked Dr A for a week off so I could unpack and settle in. She sighed mightily and agreed, though she made it clear that it was at great cost and inconvenience to her.

The entire family swung into action, not stinting with advice or help. Amma spent a day in the storage room behind the granary at Mangalath, a room crammed with rosewood and teak furniture, linen chests, mosquito nets, old mangles and cricket bats. She found a beautiful old rosewood table for our main room, and a carved four-poster bed for the guest room that would only need a few repairs before it was serviceable.

She was fantastically bossy about where to put everything, rapping out orders about how much air to leave around the furniture; telling us our bed should face either south or west for health and luck, and I was suddenly reminded of my own mother and her fierce high standards about carpet cleaning, and the right hangers, and mothballs, and mattress turnings.

Uncle Josekutty's workman came over to repair a couple of loose struts of wood planks on the veranda. Thresiamma brought us a kindy, a brass utensil with a spout, filled with water, for cleaning the feet of those who entered the house. Pathrose came with fresh soil and cow dung and planted up the little courtyard with hibiscus and jasmine and frangipani.

When this whirlwind of advice and people finally left us alone, we sat exhausted on the swinging chair on the veranda. Anto put his arm around me. 'Just us at last. Thank God.'

After a while, we got up and walked slowly around the house together, admiring our bed, freshly made up with scented sheets; our whitewashed kitchen full of sparkling pots and saucepans from Amma's house; our courtyard with its freshly watered plants; our guest room. Anto turned to me with glowing eyes. 'Can you believe this is all ours?'

Anto was high as a kite when he got home from his meeting at the hospital. Dr Sastry, he said, was young, progressive and unblinkered. He took a great interest in Ayurvedic as well as Western medicine, and was about to undertake a funded three-year research project into the efficacy of both systems. Right up Anto's street. He was to start work immediately.

On his way home from the hospital, he tried to buy a bottle of champagne to celebrate, but only managed to track down one dusty bottle of German wine at the Malabar Hotel. We gave the servants the night off, ate supper together and drank all the wine, which Anto described as playful without being impertinent. Afterwards, we wound up the gramophone and played the Louis Armstrong and Chick Chocolate records that Mariamma had given me. She had the best music taste in the family.

While we were dancing, he touched the salwar kameez I was wearing. 'I like you in that.'

I joked that there were whole days now when I forgot I was English.

'Mostly English,' he reminded me.

'Well, OK, three quarters English, Mr Pedant,' I said. 'But it's strange. Yesterday, I was in the market and about to buy myself a marigold-coloured shawl, but when I held it up to my face in the mirror, I thought, "Crikey, I'm white, this won't do." It was the oddest feeling.'

'I used to feel like that when I was buying plus fours in Harrods,' he said. 'I'd see this impertinent brown face in the mirror and think, "Maybe not."'

'Liar!' I said. We were both a little drunk; we hadn't had wine in the longest time. 'You never bought plus fours in your life.'

When we got too sticky to dance, he said, 'Let's go down to the waterfront. I want to see our house lit up from the road, and think, "What lucky brutes own that palace?"'

It was lovely down there: a crescent moon, coloured lights bouncing on the sea, some stalls still open selling fruit and vegetables and fish. Two fishermen waved at us as we passed, their faces reflecting the glow of their paraffin lamps.

As we sat in a little café, I was intensely, almost painfully aware of him: the sheen of his hair, his arm resting on the table, his hands around a glass.

He took a bath when we got home. Mani had come in to fill it while we were out. We were like children with new toys as we admired the huge claw-foot tub with its beautiful brass taps. I washed his back, and later, we lay in our new west-facing bed and enjoyed each other as never before.

'That has never left us, has it, KK?' Anto said in sleepy satisfaction afterwards. KK: Kittykutty, Kitty darling.

'Can't talk,' I said, 'too happy, no brain.' I was lying in the crook of his arm, looking through the curtains at a sky bursting with stars.

'Not fishing, but do you mind it's just us here?' I asked him sleepily. 'Will you miss Mangalath?'

He took so long to answer, I thought he'd gone back to sleep.

'I couldn't live like that again,' he said eventually and a little sadly. 'Anyway,' he stroked my breast, 'with any luck, we'll have company soon, won't we?'

Chapter 32

Breast: *sthanam* (singular), *sthanamgal* (plural). Womb: *udaram/garba paatram*. Stomach: *vayar*.

My Malayalam notebook was beginning to fill up, and I was growing in confidence, but when I returned to work the following Monday, Dr A was in such a stinking mood, I felt as though I was back at square one. Ten deliveries had, she said, made the previous week their busiest ever. The emergency midwife they'd had to call in from the Victoria Gosha Hospital had been expensive, and there were three more training classes on the cards. I must write immediately to Daisy and see whether the Oxford ladies could tide us over. Without funds, the home was once again on a knife edge.

This time I plucked up the courage to tell Dr A straight that I was sorry, but I didn't think that would be possible without turning over the Moonstone books. Daisy had asked three times for the home's accounts and I had not been given them; I doubted there would be more money without them.

Dr A's right nostril widened into an incipient sneer when I said this, and she bundled me into her study and locked the door. I wouldn't have been surprised if she'd slapped me, as I'd seen her do this to one or two of the nurses.

'You are forcing me to tell you a very unwelcome thing,' she said, in full finger-jabbing flow. 'Something I have been keeping back in respect of staff morale, and in respect of gorement funding.'

'What is it?'

'Someone is taking money from the home and I don't know who.'

'That's horrifying,' I said, remembering the other equipment that had gone missing. 'We must contact the police immediately. Why didn't you tell me before?'

'Because I don't want any gossip about this at the home, or to your family. It could ruin us, and we have so much good work to do.'

'Does Maya know?'

'Maya knows, of course.' She closed her dark eyes.

'I have to tell Daisy,' I said.

She gave a shrug. 'It will be a shock, so tell her also what great work we're doing.'

'It will be more than a shock.' I found myself shaking with rage at the almost blasé look she was giving me. 'She's put hours and hours of work into fund-raising. You may think of her as a rich white woman. She's not.'

'Listen!' She was glaring now too. 'I have two hours' sleep a night trying to run this place, and I am doing everything I can to find the miscreant. Tell her that.'

I offered to help her find the accounts, but her scowl deepened and she told me to stop going on about them – she had far more important things on her mind. She would write to Daisy herself.

I didn't believe her, and wrote to Daisy that night telling her about my strange conversation with Dr A and asking for advice. Several weeks later, I was relieved to see, on a brass tray in the hall, Daisy's familiar slashing handwriting on pastel-blue Basildon Bond notepaper. Our letters must have crossed on the high seas, however, as hers answered none of my questions. Instead, it was uncharacteristically full of bad news. Wickam Farm was on its last legs: high winds had blown most of the roof off the barn, flooding the office; a ceiling in the main house had collapsed, narrowly missing Ci Ci's bedroom. *Also*, she wrote, *I'd been hearing a strange munching sound for ages, but had no idea it was the death watch beetle. Did you know they have fierce little jaws; you can actually hear them?*

I did sense a sort of panic beneath the jocular tone, but nothing prepared me for what came next.

So, Kit, I am so sorry, but we've had to move all our boarders out for the duration, and I am in a quandary about your mother, who has had a very nasty bout of flu, and who, I fear, can't go on working for much longer in this climate.

I almost stopped breathing when I read what came next.

She is now planning a trip to India, with money she has been saving. I am not sure how you will feel about this, but the sun, to put it bluntly, may save her life. For God's sake, Kit, don't tell her I've warned you, Daisy concluded. *You know how proud she is.*

Another letter, in a sealed envelope, lay inside Daisy's, my name written in a beautiful italic script that I recognised immediately. But now the writing, taught to my mother by the Pondicherry nuns, had a slight tremor, as though penned during a minor earthquake.

Wickam Farm, 5 May

Dear Kit,

This letter is to let you know that I have come into a little windfall – the details later. I plan to use some of it to come out and see you, and maybe look up a few old chums at the same time, and get some SUN. It has been a vile winter here. I've been staying off and on at Wickam Farm, where we've had the usual dramas of burst pipes, and, of course, the barn roof.

Daisy, who is getting more dotty by the year, tries to laugh at it all, but it's no joke, particularly with three guests staying – Ci, plus Flora again after a broken engagement.

I hear from Daisy that you're doing well and are up to good works, and tip my hat in your general direction. I've had flu but it was too cold to stay in bed as Daisy demanded. If she writes making a fuss about it, ignore. More news later when I hear from you.

Your mother,
Glory

I didn't know whether to scream or laugh or cry when I read this. Not a dicky bird from her since I left home: no reply to any of my letters, no messages via Daisy, no telegrams. A big fat nothing, and now this odd missive, so blasé and peculiar-sounding that I wondered if Ci Ci hadn't helped her write it, making her sound more like a person wanting to be asked to a cocktail party than a mother who had told her daughter she was dead to her.

But I knew too that she was always at her most peculiar and unreal when she was ill, for the simple reason that she hated me to see her like that.

I stood in shock, the letter in my hand. She was coming, and the timing felt so cruel. Things were finally settling down between myself and Anto, who was loving his job and was very busy with a research paper, and in spite of my anxieties about the Moonstone, I was learning all the time. Wicked of me to confess this, but being dead to her had become, in itself, a kind of freedom.

My mind raced about for the rest of the day. How had she financed her trip? I wondered in sudden panic, knowing her predilection for helping herself from other people's houses. Shoes and scarves, the odd pilfered belt, was one thing, but a windfall big enough to get her to India sounded unlikely. Dear God, I hoped it hadn't come from Daisy, who could least afford it. And what if this flu of hers was something more serious?

'I'm terrified,' I told Anto at dusk when we'd joined the slow, peaceful crowd that strolled along the waterfront most evenings. The sun, melting like a fat peach, would soon flop over the horizon and the breeze was soft and silky. I could imagine only too well my mother walking with us, paying attention to all the wrong things: the broken drain near the park with evil-smelling fish heads stuck in the grille, the skinny dogs, the beggars. She'd be remembering why she hated India – its mess, its muddle – and she'd be restless, wondering where all the amusing people were. Much as I'd resist it, I knew I'd feel her confusion too, and feel responsible for her, because, dammit, I still wanted to make things right for her.

When we sat down on a bench to talk, he put his hand next to mine.

'This is the first chance we've had to be properly together,' I moaned. 'And I'm quite sure she'll hate it and make us miserable.'

He didn't answer for a while.

'Make us miserable,' I repeated, thinking he might not have heard.

'Come on, Kit.' He looked at me almost in surprise. 'She's your mother. You have the power to make her happy.'

'Really?'

'Really.'

I looked at him suspiciously in case he was teasing me, but he wasn't. His face, coloured by the setting sun, looked weary, after a long day at the hospital, weary and infinitely precious to me.

'Now I feel like a heel,' I said, relieved he was taking it so well. 'It's just such bad timing, and I've never heard her say a good word about India. *Ghastly place*,' I added in her voice.

'You're making her sound like Margaret Rutherford, who never said anything horrid about anyone', he said in a plummy Rutherford voice.

The small boy who ran up and down the seafront every night

with his arm full of bangles was delighted by our laughter, and joined in with a loud cackle.

'Anto,' I warned him when we'd stopped. 'I'm not laughing inside. I'm frightened, and I wish I wasn't. There's just so much about her I don't know.'

Chapter 33

On the front of our calendar at home, there was a beaming lady in an orange sari floating down the Ganges advertising Horlicks. Whenever I looked at her (*Horlicks is good for you!!*), I went cold inside. Now it was only two months until my mother hove into view aboard the *Strathdene* from Bombay. Our brief idyll was over, and I felt like a selfish bitch for minding, but I did.

One of the new freedoms I particularly relished was my daily commute from Rose Street to the Moonstone. I liked the feeling of the sun on my arms and saying good morning to the knife sharpener who sat outside the hardware shop on the corner, then to Murali on the next corner, the fruit seller who loved to instruct me on what to eat and how to cook it, and who sometimes chased me down the street with a ripe mango or passion fruit, shouting: 'Madam, your ladyship, stop! Special treat for you.' The mangos tasted of roses, of honey and summer.

I liked the view from the seafront, the ships from China and Europe and Africa, laden with cedar and spices and oil; the sight of the Chinese nets rising and falling like prehistoric creatures against the sky; saying hello to the old lady who cooked for the fishermen, who now waved and beamed at me toothlessly when I passed.

Mind you, I was still sometimes an object of curiosity, and occasionally followed by overzealous traders, who were irritating rather than frightening, so I didn't worry much that morning when I noticed three young men who seemed to be walking with deliberate casualness behind me. When I stepped from the kerb into the road, I could hear the flip, flap, flop of their sandals.

When I stopped at a small kiosk on the corner of Fort Street to buy some of the sweets Anto liked, one of the men stopped too. He was wearing a cheap shirt, and had a thin moustache and an odd, emotionless stare, as if he was looking straight through me.

'Take care of yourself, Mrs Queen,' was all he said, yet it sent a brief spasm of fear through me.

But one of the bonuses of working at the Moonstone was that the work was so intense that as soon as I'd stepped over the pile of dusty sandals in the doorway, I'd forgotten all about the encounter.

We had five soon-to-be-delivered mothers on the ward, and eight new midwives in training. That morning, as I put on my overall, I could hear them singing with a fervour and joy that was humbling.

Dr A had encouraged dancing, too, and when I walked into the room, I saw our new group of trainees waving their arms luxuriously above their heads, worn hennaed feet moving for nothing but pleasure. I knew by now that Achamma – eyes ecstatically closed, wheeling, stamping – usually slept on the floor of a cramped hut shared with ten other people in a nearby fishing village. Her thin friend Suleka, who hadn't said a word so far during training, had once done backbreaking work in the paddy fields. Rama, from Quilon, now making beautiful sinuous movements with her wrists and fingers, had produced five children in rapid succession. Watching them dance was like seeing their secret selves come to life, and it always moved me.

This morning, after a tiffin of soft rice idlis and coconut chutney, the question posed was: 'What was your quickest delivery ever?'

'Two minutes from waters breaking,' answered Rama, who had delivered hundreds of babies. 'Slowest, three and a half days.'

Low sympathetic moans at this.

'Did you take her to hospital?'

'No.'

'Why not?'

'Doctors jump on you there.'

Raucous laughter from some, timid shushings from Rama, who seemed wary of upsetting me – the English memsahib taking notes. This worry about hospitals cropped up again and again, and was probably why, according to Dr A, 99 per cent of all births in India were home births.

'Be serious now.' Maya gave them a stern look through her swotty glasses. 'Mother has been in labour for over twenty-four hours, what will you do?'

Rama said, 'I would put ginger in her chai. I would get her up and walking. I would observe her vital signs, by taking pulses.' Some of the midwives followed the Ayurvedic principle that the human being had seventy-seven pulse points, all of them vital to health.

A short but violent debate on contraception followed.

Madhavi, a stout woman whose nose ring made her look like a stubborn old bull, listed various methods on her fingers: a stone placed in the vagina, sponges, and, for many women, anal sex. Achamma piped up that she thought contraception was fine for city people, but she didn't feel country people needed it. A furious discussion then took place, lots of finger-pointing and flashing eyes.

In the lunch break, Maya filled me in. Achamma was, she said, talking codswallop, of course, but contraception was 'a big blank' for many of these women.

'What was making them so angry?' I asked.

'Abortions,' she said. 'In country areas, many have to do them, and some are very primitive: sticks in the womb, stones, poisonous concoctions. We must stop them,' she said simply. 'Bad for their conscience, worse for the mothers.'

At the end of the day, Maya and I flopped in the dispensary room and drank chai together. When she took off her glasses and polished them, I saw large blue circles under her eyes.

'You look tired, Maya,' I said. 'Is everything all right at home?'

'Yes thank you, ma'am,' she replied politely. She hardly ever called me ma'am nowadays. 'My son has not been well, but he is getting better.'

'Does he still drop you off in the morning?'

'No, ma'am.' She looked at the floor.

'How do you get to work?'

'Boat and bus and walk.'

'But isn't it miles away?' I had only the foggiest memory of where Maya lived. 'Couldn't we ask for some extra money from the kitty to get you here?'

'No.' She was always nervous of rocking the boat. For her, being singled out for education, for training, had already been a magic carpet ride powered by Dr A. 'Don't do that. If I lose this job, I have nothing.'

She closed her eyes; she didn't want to talk any more. I took our cups to the sink. I was getting water from the old Ascot heater when I looked up and saw, from the corner of my eye, the backs of two young males scrambling over the wall that separated our land from the alleyway leading to the street.

My shout was heard by Dr A. She came rushing in with the nightwatchman, who bared his teeth convincingly.

'What happened?' Dr A had what looked like a hockey stick in her hand.

'I saw two men jumping the wall. I could only see their backs.'

'Anyone hurt?'

'No, Doctor.' Maya had leapt to her feet; she was trembling.

'No crisis,' Dr A told me. 'Just local boys.'

'But shouldn't we call the police?' I asked.

'No!' she snapped, with her position-closed face on. 'We'll put up more barbed wire later.'

I understood her reluctance better than I would have done a few months ago. Calling the police might mean a bribe we could ill afford, or long negotiations with the new health officials, who already watched us like hawks. And for me there was a new fear – one that brought me out in a cold sweat when I thought about it. I was here, officially, to write reports, not deliver babies. I was two deliveries shy of my full midwifery certificate. Dr A had assured me she would write to the relevant examining bodies in England to see if an Indian delivery would be accepted, but I had never asked if I could see the actual papers. Now I wondered if the letter had been sent at all, or whether staff shortages, and her new respect for my fine stitching, meant she'd chosen to ignore it. If the rubber-stampers found out, I could lose my job and my reputation, and the home would be closed down.

I seemed to be making a habit of secrecy, and didn't mention the intruders to Anto when I got home, even though the sight of their skinny backs, the speed with which they'd shimmied up that wall, had replayed itself several times in my mind.

Walking up the path through the mild peach-coloured air of early evening, I saw Anto on the veranda playing chess with Uncle Josekutty, and the sight of them – whiskies, bare feet, dark heads bent together – was a comforting one. Later, after Josekutty had gone home, Anto and I sat in the courtyard at the back of the house and enjoyed the soft jasmine-scented breeze. I loved this time of day with him: the thrill still of our own house, the talk, him smoking a cigarette with the long fingers that would later touch me there and there.

'Do you mind being the new boy at work?' I asked him.

'No,' he said. 'Though I'm very much on probation still with some of the doctors. They think I chose to live in England, so I'm beta minus minus with them at the moment, but trying hard.'

Anto was strong like that: he'd learned how to be a survivor in a non-mean way; it was something I admired tremendously about him. He went on to talk eagerly about his work with his new boss, Dr Sastry, whom he revered. 'I can really achieve things with him,' he told me. They'd had a long conversation that day about African sleeping sickness, and Anto had promised to dig out his PhD thesis and show it to him.

When he asked about my day, I gave him selected highlights of the group discussions, and he told me he was surprised at how open the women were with us. I took a puff of his cigarette and immediately put it down, it made me feel so sick.

'There are definite no-go areas,' I said when I'd gone to get myself a glass of water. 'Like today, when we talked about the imbalance of boys and girls in their villages, they were close as clams about it.'

'I'm not surprised,' Anto said. 'Laws are changing all the time, and these women will be useful scapegoats; some could even be had up for murder.'

He put his hand on my hair. There was a long, considering silence. 'It would never bother me to have a little girl,' his voice soft in the darkness. 'Or a boy, for that matter, if he came. It would be the most wonderful thing.'

And I felt like the worst sneaky wife in the world. I was still using my diaphragm, though not every time. I longed for children too. But not yet, not now, with things so very interesting at the home.

Four days after this conversation, I was properly sick in the morning. Kamalam had brought in fresh bananas, a mango, some dosas. Instead of eating them, I felt sweat break out along my hairline. Five minutes later, I was panting beside the commode. I did a few sums in my head, and if I hadn't been feeling so lousy I would have laughed, or cried. I was going to have a baby!

On my way to work, I decided I would tell Anto in a day or two. I wanted time to collect myself, to feel as thrilled as he would, because now everything would change.

Amma had already warned me that Thekkeden women always spent the last six weeks of their confinement at Mangalath. This might drive me mad. Who owns your body? Not me. Not now. I was excited, but fizzing with nervous tension.

Later, calmer, and at home again, I sat on the swing on the veranda, and it came to me in a blaze of happiness that this dazzling spot of consciousness inside me would soon be my first child.

I was in this strange jumble of emotions when I arrived at the Moonstone the following morning. Before I had time to unlatch the gate, Maya ran out to meet me, sunlight bouncing off her specs.

'Quickly!' she said. 'Come! Mrs Saraswati Nair is here. Her waters have broken, she's in a state. She is calling for you.'

'For me?'

'She says she wants the Englishwoman.'

'Are you sure?'

'Absolutely.'

My heart sank. All of us were a little scared of Mrs Saraswati Nair, who had already attended two antenatal clinics. Small, politically passionate, and of a peppery disposition, she was a lawyer and cut from a different cloth than most of our patients. Originally from a high-caste Brahmin family, she had declared herself a feminist, and a campaigner, before Independence, and had married, for love, a prominent local lawyer.

During an early examination, she had asked Dr A rather peevishly what I, an Englishwoman, was doing there. Dr A had, for once, inflated my importance.

'She is part of worldwide gorement initiative to improve standards for village women, a highly trained midwife.'

'Are you quite sure she wants me?' I asked Dr A now, before she bustled off to another appointment.

'Definitely,' she replied.

As I changed into my white coat, I tried to control a wave of panic. Mrs Saraswati Nair, with her clever, shrewd look and her legal training, had the power to raise my pulse without me even thinking about it. I knew she'd throw the rule book at me if anything went wrong.

I found her sitting in a chair by the bed with a small suitcase beside her. Apart from a light sheen of perspiration on her forehead, she looked composed. Anusha, a new nurse, came in, and together we helped Mrs Nair put on a hospital gown. While I was tying the straps behind her, her stomach bucked vigorously and we both laughed.

'So definitely a boy this time,' Mrs Nair joked. She already had a much older girl who was away studying at university. Her husband, wanted a boy.

She was only one and a half fingers dilated and her contractions were coming irregularly, so I took her arm and encouraged her to move around the room.

'I had no wish at first to become a lawyer,' she said as we walked. 'It was my father who insisted on educating me, but now I am glad.'

She stopped, blew out air, smiled, spoke again. 'I approve of what you women are doing here' – puff, groan, puff – 'but you must be very careful.' She sat down heavily, her face gleaming with sweat. 'You can't just take the traditional form and put a hammer to it. That's a dangerous thing to do, particularly now.'

'Are any of your family members coming in?' I asked when she was two fingers dilated.

'No.' Her mouth turned down. 'My family don't speak to me now.'

'Why not?'

She'd begun to pant softly like a marathon runner who knew there could be miles and miles ahead. I relaxed a little: she was a good patient.

'They are very traditional, so many rules...' She wiped her face with a towel. 'Before my daughter was born, I had to stay with my mother-in-law for three months. Very boring, and I was not allowed out after dark. After baby was born, I had to stay in for forty days. My parents-in-law wanted many children so the whole thing would take up months and years of my life and make it impossible for me to work.

'My husband and I have both broken with the past,' she continued after a pause. 'We made our own wedding, and he supported all my law studies. Law is my language now,' she added fiercely, and then, after a wince, 'And this is my last baby.'

By 11.25, Mrs Nair, who at thirty-nine was an ancient mother by Indian standards, was still not in active labour. She lay on the bed, eyes wide open, looking pale and sweaty. After missing breakfast, I was starting to feel light-headed myself, and for one spiralling, panicky moment, my mind emptied as if I knew nothing, before I pulled myself together again. I made myself breathe and wait.

'How is it going?' Maya poked her head around the door.

'Slow,' I whispered. 'Contractions every ten to twelve minutes, lasting about fifty seconds. When will Dr A be back?'

'Don't know. Do you want food? Your face is pale.'

'No thanks, not hungry. A glass of water.'

But Maya sent a nurse for tiffin anyway. 'I'll sit with her for ten minutes,' she said, 'if you need to rest.'

It felt too early to tell anyone at the home that I might be having a baby too, but Maya was looking at me anxiously.

'It's very hot in here. Nurse – a fan,' she snapped at Anusha. Like Dr A, Maya didn't waste her charm on underlings. 'More towels, too.'

I took a short break. When I got back, Mrs Nair was crouched beside the bed, head resting on her arms, howling like a dog.

'A word, please,' Maya said curtly. We moved towards the end of the bed, out of earshot. 'The baby has turned. I have a mother and daughter in the class,' she whispered. 'Name of Charu and Ammini. They are very experienced in massage. I'm going to get them.'

The door closed, I turned to Mrs Nair. I held her damp hand. 'How are you feeling?'

'Horrible,' she gasped. 'Worse than last time.'

'So listen.' My heart was flipping around in my chest. 'Everything is going to be all right, but your baby's bottom will come out first unless we try to turn it.' I blew out a couple of puffs of air.

When Charu and Ammini came silently into the room, they put the palms of their hands together and bowed low. Once they had scrubbed up at the sink, they moved without panic towards Mrs Nair, who was now rolling her eyes in agony. They told Mrs Nair to lie on the bed again and poured coconut oil into the palms of their hands. I watched in awe as they performed their massage with the confidence of two pianists who had duetted together for years. It was a beautiful thing to see, but after a while, Mrs Nair pushed their hands away.

'I want to get down.' Her mouth a rictus of pain.

When we'd helped her out, she got down on her knees and began to hug herself and howl.

'Try not to do that,' I told her, peeling her arms away. 'Keep your tummy open,' an instruction I'd learned from the Moonstone midwives. She gave me a look of ferocious dislike, and was sick all over the floor.

'Check that we have enough sterilised implements in the autoclave,' I told Maya.

When Mrs Nair was half lying on the bed again, breathing in short, anguished gasps, Charu gave the baby one last beefy shove, and joy of joys, I could feel through her tummy the knobs of a spinal cord. The baby had turned itself like an eel in a basket.

Less than twenty minutes later, Mrs Nair gave a guttural cry and her legs began to tremble.

'You're doing wonderfully, Saraswati.' I rubbed her legs. '*Ippo varum* – good girl, you're almost there.'

She closed her eyes. I thought she was going to give up, then came a string of words that sounded like desperate pleas to the gods she said she'd abandoned. It was the longest three or four moments of my life before she started to push violently.

'Slow it down,' Maya told her. 'Hold for a moment and then push.' A few seconds later: '*Tulleh umm! Tulleh onnum! Loodi ippo varum!* Push once more, about to come!'

After three more contractions, the baby's head appeared. Nose, shoulders, a tiny hand: a perfect baby boy with a shock of black hair.

I suctioned his mouth, felt around his neck for the umbilical cord and cut it; then, because he wasn't crying, Maya held him up by both heels and slapped him briskly on the bottom, and he bawled. It was a beautiful sound that made everybody laugh. Finally he was anointed with gold and honey. Maya said that if he'd been born in his Brahmin home, a lemon would have been tossed out of the window.

Mrs Nair lay in an ecstasy of exhaustion on the bed, her baby's naked breast on hers. 'My boy, my baby,' she crooned.

It was late by the time I left the Moonstone. I was charged with energy: I had delivered a perfectly formed baby in difficult circumstances. I was having a baby myself!

My legs felt leaden and achy when I started to walk, so I took a short cut home, through the iron gate that led into the English club and out on to St Francis Street. The guards who sat near the gate usually let me through with a quiet 'Goodnight, madam', but there was no one there tonight, and it looked deserted inside the gardens, the shadows lengthening.

In the tufty grass at the edge of the once manicured lawn, I saw a pile of rusted croquet hoops, an old wooden tennis racquet press and a faded cap. Some of the veranda's rails had been chopped down, presumably for firewood. A mournful sight, like a still life for summer's end, except I wasn't feeling mournful at all. I was in a semi-ecstatic mood, thinking of the new baby, feeling a part of the abundant trees springing from the earth around me – the palms, the banyans, the Indian bean trees with their fat waxy flowers – reflecting on how beautiful this country was and how much had changed in my life.

When I reached the club house, I sat down on a bench in front of it, wanting to savour the moment. It was then that I felt the light changing behind me, the sound of an opening door.

'Madam.' The boy with the thin moustache who had called me Mrs Queen the other morning was standing over me. I gazed up at skinny thighs in wrinkled trousers, a smiling face with cool, calculating eyes.

'Don't be frightened.' He saw me jump. 'I've been waiting for your return.' He handed me the light muslin scarf I often wore to protect my head from the heat. 'You dropped it this morning.' He smiled as I took it.

I wasn't too alarmed. I'd grown used to being tracked in India. Only the week before, I'd been cashing a cheque at the bank when a voice behind me barked, 'Wrong date, madam.' A funny story saved for Daisy, but not now.

'How very kind,' I said in what Anto called my toff voice. 'Thank you so much.' I put the scarf in my handbag and got up to walk away.

'Do you come here often, madam?' His sandals clattered down the steps behind me.

'No,' I said, walking a little faster. 'My husband is an Indian man. He's very strict.'

'That's good.' He fell into step beside me, shot me a glance. 'You are too pretty to walk on your own. Please don't run, I only want to talk to you.'

'My husband is waiting for me.'

'Lady, stop running!' His voice rose. 'You're safe with me. There are bad men on the street who can hurt you.'

'The guard on the gate knows me.' I tried to sound calm.

'There's no one there,' he crooned in a sing-song voice. When he jerked his head towards the club, the line of angry pimples on his neck made him look younger than I'd thought at first: seventeen, eighteen at the most.

'Look.' I fumbled in my bag for my purse. 'You've been awfully kind to find my scarf. I'd like to—'

'Put it away, madam,' he said, very offended. He smiled and looked down at the bulge in his trousers, which was growing, grabbed my arm and pulled me towards a large banyan tree. Its thick leaves and impenetrable roots formed a small, dark room, with a bench where I sat sometimes to read a book or shelter from the sun.

'This is what I like from English girls.' He pushed me down on the bench and sat beside me. With the sly smile of a dog about to steal the Sunday joint, he put his arm round me. I thought my best bet was to be polite, to talk him out of it, until his free hand dived up my skirt and pulled at the edge of my knickers. In the scuffle that followed, the contents of my handbag scattered in the dust: purse, mirror, notes for Daisy.

Maya had warned me about Eve-teasing, the practice of groping women in the street. 'If it happens,' she'd advised, 'slap the miscreant hard, I mean *really* slap him.' She'd demonstrated with a sharp crack on her palm.

'Doesn't that make things worse?' I'd asked.

'No.' She'd cracked her palm again with a stinging sound. 'If you give in, they'll hurt you.'

When I hit him hard on the side of his face, *biff* went crazily through my mind, *biff, biff, biff*, as if I was Desperate Dan in *The Dandy*. I used the worst swear words I could think of, and I had plenty to choose from after nursing in the wards. When the mark of my hand bloomed on his face, I was shocked. He looked towards the street, hesitated, his head wobbling on his neck, and then hit me back, *thud, thud, thud*, on my arms and head.

'Don't!' I shouted. 'Stop it! I'm having a baby.' He raised his fist, and when it came towards my stomach, I grabbed his wrist and shouted, 'You bloody bastard! Don't you dare!' He shook me off and landed a punch just below my ribs.

'I know who you are,' he sneered. 'You are the foreign lady who teaches our Indian girls bad things. We don't want you. Go home!'

He saw my purse in the dust and dropped to his knees, scrabbling crab-like towards it.

'Take it.' I kicked the purse towards him. He tore the few rupees out of it, then ran off through the iron gate in the direction of the town, leaving me shaking.

Chapter 34

It would have been so much better if I'd confided in Anto that night, but I didn't: the habit of keeping hard and potentially shameful things to myself was so ingrained. This was no excuse, but the handful of times I'd confided in my mother had not been a rousing success.

I was bullied once for weeks at a new school in Edinburgh, where my mother was working as a companion to a polio victim. A girl called Celia McIntyre – wild red hair, an undershot jaw – had on my second day there pulled my hair and called me a Sassenach pig. She began to ambush me after school and push me off my bike, or throw my homework in the bushes. When I finally plucked up the courage to tell my mother, who'd been worrying about my grazed knees and the occasional patch of hair missing, she listened gravely at first, then rushed into the bathroom and turned the taps on hard. Over the sound of running water I heard her shout, 'Oh God! Why does *everything* go wrong for me?' or some such. She returned from the bathroom, eyes red-rimmed, voice all echoey and sad, and said, 'Don't worry, Kit, ignore that pig of a girl.'

And I'd said, 'It's all right, Mummy, I don't mind,' because I had a growing sense of us both being swirled down a plughole of female powerlessness and rage, and this was the voice that frightened me most. Going, going, gone.

So the lesson learned was that a trouble shared was frequently a trouble prolonged till bedtime, and often beyond; and anyway, in later years, my mother had recast the whole incident.

'Do you remember that vile girl who hated you? The one who looked like a rugby player? We gave her what for, didn't we?' No mention of 'ignore that pig', or the shouting.

I lay in the dark that night, eyes open, thinking of the boy: the saliva on his teeth, his skinny Douglas Fairbanks moustache. I was hugging Anto hard. When he'd seen my bruised cheek earlier, I'd sat on a footstool between his legs and he'd bathed my face with warm water.

I knew I should tell him, but instead I played the daffy woman.

'Silly me, I took a short cut through the club garden, and had a tumble down the steps and hit a geranium pot. Nothing serious.'

And it wasn't, except I had a new fear now that our baby might have been harmed, and that Anto might blame me if anything happened to it.

'Poor Kittykutty.' He stroked my head in the way I loved; it made me want to butt my head against his hand like a cat. 'You should take a rickshaw. I don't want a falling-down wife.'

'It's only a ten-minute walk,' I protested, but I still felt shivery and out of sorts. 'I like it.'

'Do it for me.' He tucked a strand of hair behind my ear. 'Your scaredy-cat husband who would die of misery without you.'

We laughed and we cuddled, and then he undressed me, and I almost told him as he ran his fingers gently over my breasts and belly, but I kept my eyes wide open instead, checking the exits, the windows, the doors, thinking of the boy, his mocking smile, the line of pimples on his neck.

Over prawns and rice at supper, Anto talked some more about his new job at the hospital, the inspirational boss who had been so pleased with the work he had done on their research project. Funds would be provided soon for him to travel to the areas of India where doctors were reinstating Ayurvedic principles into their work. Dr Sastry had also read his thesis and thought he should publish it as a book.

'I feel I'm on a journey now,' Anto said. 'One of striving, and of happiness. I can say...' He closed his eyes and thought. 'I can say I feel whole for the first time.'

He looked boyish, happy. The extra skin of irony and detachment he'd had to wear in England seemed gone. When he asked me about my day, I told him about Mrs Nair and her new baby, and all she'd told me during our time together: how she'd given up following the rules of her own caste, and burned her sari when she met Gandhi and became politicised.

'Is she a terrifying harridan?'

'Anto!' I said. 'Why on earth would you assume that?'

'Because Appan told me about her only recently. He said he was in court with her and was very taken with her sharp brain.

She would be a handful if things went wrong,' he added, looking troubled. 'Why on earth did she go to the Moonstone? She has plenty of money.'

'It's not to do with money. She's left her family home, and she hates the thought of hospital: very simple really.'

'Sorry, Kittykutty, but Appan says she is an angry woman. I'm only thinking of you if anything happened.'

'Well it didn't.' I gave an enormous yawn. 'Everything went well. I must go to bed.'

But before I did, I made him check every single shutter and door and window, my mind flipping back to that rank-smelling hand over my mouth; my skirt being clawed. And now this extra terror, that the boy's punch had harmed our child, and that it was all my fault for taking a stupid short cut.

Chapter 35

When I wrote to Daisy and my mother to tell them I was pregnant, I was heartily relieved when my mother, who was still living at Wickam Farm, cancelled her proposed trip with the vague explanation that she didn't 'do' babies, and would keep out of our hair until ours was a little older.

Yes, I was relieved, but if I'm honest, I was hurt and disappointed too – in some locked corner of myself, I must have been looking forward to seeing her.

I worked on at the Moonstone for eight months of my pregnancy, and was told I could come back at any time after the baby was born – Dr A assured me there would be plenty of willing and experienced hands at the home who would help.

Work was a good thing: like many midwives in their first pregnancy, I found plenty to worry about, and had to stop myself looking up stray symptoms in old textbooks. I took comfort from Anto, who was radiant with happiness, and who said I was as strong as an ox and not to worry about a thing.

And he was right – almost. Halfway through my pregnancy, I felt as physically strong as I'd ever felt, but the memory of that boy's punch stayed in my mind like a bad bruise that would not fade.

When, at Mangalath, on the veranda, I felt the first cramps of labour, I felt as apprehensive as any woman having her first baby, and mightily relieved when Rema, the family midwife, trained in Madras and wonderfully efficient, came cycling up the drive and walked into my bedroom. She had no idea I was a midwife too, and I didn't care. All I wanted was her comfort and guidance, because once my own labour properly began, I felt swept away by forces that I could neither control nor understand. It was the difference, say, between knowing the chemical composition of snow, and taking a bobsleigh ride at breakneck speed down a steep mountain. The sheer force of it shocked me: my own womb clenching and unclenching like a great jaw, and then the joy, the soaring sense of triumph, bigger, better, deeper than anything I had ever experienced, of having put a new human in the room who wasn't there before. Such a very ordinary thing to happen, but for me, my first miracle.

When, at three minutes past two in the morning, my son Raffael was born, after a twelve-hour labour, the midwife part of me checked him over neurotically – two working legs, round little tummy, perfect toes like Jersey new potatoes, a face at first like a furious tomato – while the mother part was ablaze with happiness. I'd known nothing about this: the helpless love, the vulnerability, the joy and, in a weird way, the strength. If I could do this, I could do anything.

After he was born and we'd moved back to Rose Street, Anto raced home every night to see him. Raffael was like a little fire burning in the house, and it was a happy time. I took a photograph of him and sent it to Josie, asking if she'd be his godmother, and she wrote back saying what a little corker he was, and she'd be proud to keep him away from damnation.

The only fly in the custard came six months later, when a telegram arrived at Rose Street saying that my mother had booked tickets on the *Strathdene* and would be arriving in Bombay in two months' time.

'So, how do you feel about *Mummy* finally coming?' Mariamma asked me with sugary emphasis. We were at Mangalath for the weekend, sitting in dappled sunshine, side by side on the summer house veranda. I had the telegram in my handbag and was still experiencing its aftershocks.

'Terrified, since you ask,' I said. 'I don't know what to think.' My milk was slowing down, and Raffael was on my lap, sucking manfully on his new bottle. When he saw us watching him, he flung the bottle away, his eyes bulging and affronted.

'Give that young man to me.' Mariamma took him from my arms and burped him. 'I don't blame you,' she said, putting him back on my lap, where he lay watching the sky through his fingers. 'Mothers are terrifying – too much power is the problem.'

I ran my hand through Raff's soft, thick hair. 'It's awful to admit this, but I was almost glad when she couldn't come. It's not that I don't love her, it's just— Damn!' I could feel the slow trickle of Raffael's pee running through my skirt. He didn't wear nappies, because Amma believed babies should be trouserless until they learned to potty-train themselves. In Raffie's case, and to my surprise, it worked

217

about eight times out of ten, and I was learning how he paddled his legs, and stretched his arms towards me when he wanted to use the potty.

Mariamma called to Theresa to take him to the house. There was no shortage of willing slaves at Mangalath. Amma spent hours walking him round the garden, showing him the new Leghorn chickens and collecting eggs, throwing alfalfa at the donkey, topping up the water for Appan's new Tibetan mastiff dog.

As we watched Theresa walk importantly towards the house with Raffael in her arms, I told Mariamma that I'd never even held a real-life baby until I was eighteen.

'Don't be silly!' She simply wouldn't believe me. 'You must have had relatives with babies – sisters, brothers.'

'Honest truth,' I said. 'I was an only child and my mother worked for a living; we travelled a lot.'

I'd said almost nothing to Mariamma about my strange upbringing, because if I'm honest, it still gave me a queer sick feeling when I thought about the dead-to-me row I'd had with my mother when I'd married Anto. The family would be mortally offended and I didn't want that, plus it only seemed fair to let her arrive with a clean slate.

And also, now that I had my own baby, so many of the things that had once driven me mad about my mother – her anxious protectiveness, her hovering, her fudging of the truth – I now understood and felt a sort of anguish about. I should have been kinder.

Theresa came back with Raffie wearing a strip of cloth tied like a loincloth, both ends tucked into a silver chain clasped around his waist. She put a rug underneath the mango tree and he lay in the shade testing his fat legs for pinginess and stretch. He put a thoughtful toe in his mouth, and took it out again so he could imitate the sound of one of the birds. *Brrrr brrr, cheep chee.*

He was a sublimely contented child, with a filthy chuckle. He liked nothing better than to be here at Mangalath, handed from lap to lap. On the day he was born, Amma looked at him and then at me with tears in her eyes and said, '*Entey kochu rajakumaran!*' – my little prince. Anto asked Appan to dab gold and honey on his tongue, saying he hoped the baby would inherit his father's brilliant mind, his tenacity and generosity. On the twenty-eighth day, the silver chain was clasped around his waist to tuck the loincloth in.

Happy days, but it was Mariamma I was most grateful to. She was the one who insisted on staying up with me on the first blurry and alarming nights of having a baby of my own to keep alive. She brought me tea and little snacks. When I needed to bathe, Theresa sat with him. When Anto came home, weary often from the hospital, we were free to spend hours lying with him between us, floating in the sweetness of his presence. Nourishing meals arrived, helping hands at every turn. When I thought of my own mother in her isolation, I was ashamed.

'So tell me more about your mummy.' Mariamma threw the ball again, soft but insistent. 'What part of India did she hail from?'

I'd shared this fact with her in the early days, but said almost nothing else. Mixed blood, as I was perfectly aware by now, was not a great calling card in India.

'Well...' I dipped a finger in my coconut juice and put it in Raff's mouth. 'She's lived for years in England, but I think she went to school in Pondicherry, and married my father over here. It's all a bit fuzzy.'

'A bit fuzzy,' Mariamma crooned, running her fingers through Raffie's thatch, and pretending it was his hair we'd been talking about. 'We can question Grandma when she comes,' she told him. She smoothed his hair down, kissed the back of his neck.

And this was my dread. I could too easily imagine my mother's cornered looks, the strange replies that could sound so haughty.

'Will you show her around the Moonstone?' A quick glance.

'Maybe,' I said. My mother had agreed to arrive with some new obstetrical equipment for the home. Nothing big: scissors, forceps, Petri dishes, to be packed and stored in the hold. 'But maybe not. She never liked me nursing.'

'Even during the war?'

'No.'

'Will she mind your work here?'

'Probably.'

'She wanted you to be ladylike?'

'The exact words she would have chosen,' I said. In the silence that followed, I had the small revelation that I had chosen a profession guaranteed to make me least like my mother.

'Do you miss it?' I could feel Mariamma watching me.

'No,' I said, 'because I'm definitely going back to work soon.' I'd decided it was time the week before, when I'd made an appointment to see Dr A. 'I'll do two, maybe three shifts a week. They're short-staffed and they have a government inspection coming up. I can take Raffie if I want to, and Kamalam is at home all day and like a second mother to him.'

'Oh dear.' She could not hide her dismay. 'Do Amma and Anto know this?'

'Amma, no, not yet,' I said. 'Anto, yes, of course! He's happy about it.' Not entirely true, but at least he understood. 'He's told me to go ahead.'

Chapter 36

I started with only two shifts a week. Raffie, who often came with me, enjoyed holding court to a circle of admiring women. Maya was glad to see me. Numbers had grown at the clinic, and her husband was angry with her again because she was often home late and his own mother had to come over and cook his rice. Sometimes she looked so weary and crushed, I wondered if he was beating her again. By these standards, Anto was a peach of a husband, except that, three days into our new regime, we had a shocking row as sudden as a summer storm.

Anto was lying on the bed, Raffie on his chest, playing the game the baby loved: 'Atishoo, atishoo, we all fall down'. Anto, who still liked teaching me things, was explaining that the song derived from when people were falling like flies from the plague. Raffie, who hated attention being given to anyone but him, flung his arms around Anto's neck and covered his face in kisses, steering him away from me.

'I love my boy,' Anto crooned, 'but he's getting spoiled – he needs six brothers and one or two sisters.'

'Why not twelve?' I said. 'Enough for a cricket team.'

He held Raffie high above his head. 'I'm serious, Kit. We're in another phase of our lives now.'

He'd explained this to me before: the Hindu belief that a man's life should fall into four distinct stages. The first was Kaumaram, the south Indian word for youth; the next Brahmacharyam, or the celibate student phase – well, Anto had missed that boat then. This was followed by Grihasthashramam, the householder stage, in which a man devoted himself to earning a living and having his children, and finally Vanaprastham, the hermit stage, when you left off worldly ties and pleasures and lived as an ascetic sage in the wilds. As a blueprint for life, it sounded intriguingly tidy and purposeful, but from a Western wife's point of view – how could I put this? Claustrophobic.

'So next stop sackcloth and ashes,' I said.

'Don't joke about everything.' Raffie had fallen asleep, so he kept his voice low.

'I'm not,' I said. It was no surprise to me to learn that he wanted lots of children. The Thekkedens saw them as one of life's greatest gifts. I liked that about them, and agreed. Up to a point.

When he added, 'I want as many as possible,' was it wrong of me to suddenly feel like a great big breeding cow? The argument that followed was loud, and when Raffie started to bawl, we continued it in angry whispers in bed.

Me: 'Of course I love him, of course I love you – but can't I have any other life at all?'

Him: 'You're being dramatic, you have a different life now. Can't you change?'

Me: 'Why must I change? For you, life is the same with Raffie here, but better.'

Him: 'Rmmmnnnnpph.' The Indian version of *harumph*. 'Don't play games with me, Kit. You're a woman, I can't have our babies.'

Me: 'I'm not so different from you, or at least, not as much as you'd like to think: I like challenges, I like excitement, I like getting better at things, I like seeing things grow. I'm proud of what we do at the Moonstone.'

It was true. This scruffy, frustrating, life-giving place, with its inadequate facilities and bewildering days, had connected me to India in ways I didn't even understand. I wanted to stay part of it, to watch it grow.

Him, shouting now: 'Watching your own children grow, what could be better than that?'

There was more, and it hurt us both. What I should have said loud and clear was that I had seen in my mother the fury and the fate of the untrained woman moving from one menial job to another and hating them all.

And he would have said, 'But you're not your mother, and I love you, and I won't leave you.' I wouldn't have believed him, because my sense of men being abandoners was so deep-rooted. The father who left me, whom I was forbidden to talk or think about, had followed me through life like a bad smell. I'd tried my best to ignore him – it made no sense to miss someone you'd never met – but he was there.

*

I was examining Valli, a village woman who had presented with premature leaking of her amniotic fluid, when I heard a tremendous crash in the street outside, as if someone had dropped fifty trays. The windows trembled, and Valli shrieked and disappeared under the sheet.

When I ran into the hall, Ajala, one of the midwives, yelled, 'Ma'am, they're cutting down a tree.'

Outside, I saw Maya shaking her fist at three men stripped to the waist and sitting in the tree's branches. She looked white as milk, and very frightened. 'It's the neem tree; a government department sent them. No one told us they were coming. They said disease was there and the tree is unsafe.'

'Don't they need to tell us?' The tree, strictly speaking, was on the boundary between our land and the empty building plot next door.

'Very definitely we should know.'

I had no strong feelings about the tree losing one or two branches. I enjoyed crunching its pods underfoot because they gave off a refreshing aroma, and it was a nice tree to sit under at lunchtime, but for Maya, this was a catastrophe in the making. The neem, she'd already told me, was a god amongst trees, a shade-giver, a maker of creams; rags soaked in its oils were used as contraceptives. Now, on the verge of tears, she said that the workmen had ignored vital rituals. If the whole tree was to go, the axeman must pour ghee over the stumps and say, 'May you grow with one thousand shoots,' otherwise they would offend the powerful spirits that lived there.

'But what if it's only a branch?' I said, stupidly, because I was not sure how to comfort her.

'Then you must beg pardon for its injuries,' she said. 'I have done that now.'

As we stood in the blinding light, looking up at the tree, my eyes moved to the right, and a strange jangling began in my brain.

A small crowd of curious onlookers had gathered to watch. Standing apart from them was the boy with the thin moustache. He wasn't looking at the tree; he was looking at me.

I told Maya I was going inside, but she didn't hear me. She was praying distractedly, as if something terrible had already happened.

Chapter 37

And then my mother arrived. Predictably unpredictable, as usual, she was a day early, blaming a telegram that hadn't arrived, and full of complaints about the appalling service aboard the *Strathdene*. The food was awful, the staff were rude, her cabin was next door to a couple who had rowed constantly. She'd hardly slept a wink the whole voyage.

When she showed me the bags under her eyes, almost as a mark of honour, I thought, yes, of course, once again it all goes wrong for you, and was distressed by my instant meanness.

Her first highly perfumed tentative hug reminded me of a nervous mother burping a new baby, and I can honestly say I felt a big blank nothing.

'Darling, this is perfectly sweet,' she said, when she first stepped into our house.

'We like it a lot. You look well, Mummy,' I said, the safest thing I could say, and the most dishonest. She was as carefully dressed as ever – blue silk suit, feathered hat, stockings, even though the heat was 105 degrees, crocodile shoes polished to a high shine – but I was shocked by how much older she looked, and somehow shrunken. Her voice was higher than I remembered it too, and lighter, as if it was an effort to talk.

I'd looked forward to showing her Raffie, and when he woke, Anto appeared with him tousled and blinking in his arms.

'Your *perakutty*,' he said. 'Mr Raffael Thekkeden.'

My mother, in the middle of ranting about the horrors of the ship, stopped. 'My grandson,' she agreed. She closed her eyes, and held Raffie apart from her as if he was a wet cat. Raffie, who was teething, let out a thin wail and flung his arms towards me.

'Oh! Oh! Oh!' My mother practically threw him back. 'I'm no good with babies,' she said.

We exchanged a look. Anto rescued us.

'He's always a crotchety old devil after his sleep.' He took Raffie in his arms and gave him one of the smacking kisses on the tummy that made him laugh. 'Give him time.'

Because my mother loathed any kind of muddle, we'd had a major spring clean before she arrived. We'd also made an anxious inventory of what Anto called Mummy food: prunes and oatmeal for the digestion, which had Babu, who owned the general store, scratching his head; lemons for the early-morning hot water and lemon juice regime she followed strictly; bread from the roaring oven of the old-fashioned baker up the street who had once supplied the Raj; English breakfast tea from a supplier Amma knew in Fort Cochin.

We'd moved from our bedroom into the guest room so she could have the larger bedroom at the front of the house. It was a lovely room now, whitewashed and spare, with a comfortable double bed and a chair with long arms and dainty mother-of-pearl inlays on the headrest that had been in the shed at Mangalath before Amma had it cleaned up and re-caned.

She slept for twelve hours on arrival. I crept about the house, relieved already for the break from her, and for the next two or three days we danced around each other – polite self-conscious strangers. Careful avoidance of the rows we'd had about Anto, no mention of the dead-to-me decree, or Daisy, or my work at the Moonstone.

In the early mornings, I fed and played with Raffie, often taking him to the park, where he could be noisy and not annoy my mother. She got up around eleven and sat looking dazed on the chair facing the window, saying gentle, admiring things about the house, the street, the sky, the trees. As I accepted compliments and made bland conversation back, I thought about those nuns who, at mealtimes, must only talk about birds, or trees, or flowers, to avoid anything controversial.

During the day, she sipped, very daintily, on lime juice and soda and ate very little. At night-time, after I'd bathed Raffie and told him a story, she and I drank weak whisky and soda, or gin and it for her, and waited for Anto to come home. This, normally, was the time I most looked forward to with him: catching up on each other's day, hearing the gossip from the hospital and telling him about the Moonstone. But on those first nights with my mother, I observed him like a stranger. He always washed when he got home, and changed his clothes, and in his linen trousers and white shirt, his good looks still had the power to take my breath away, but now it was his kindness I marvelled at. He angled his chair towards her, he listened to her with sympathy and respect, as if it was a privilege for him to be talking to her, while she chattered gaily as if she'd never said any of those terrible things about him.

Some nights Kamalam would appear, smiling, proud, to present Raffie for a goodnight kiss. Often my mother's glance would flicker over him and she'd carry on talking, and I would feel I hated her.

After one such night, lying in bed in the spare room, Anto repeated his instruction to me. 'Give her time. This is very shocking to her, being back in India again, and don't forget, you're speaking to her from the grave.' He meant it as a joke, but that was how I felt with her – frozen and cold.

The next terror came in the form of an invitation from Amma. She wanted the family to get together for a special welcome lunch.

When Anto told my mother this, she said, in a small, trapped voice, 'How lovely,' and then, turning to me as if he wasn't there, complained, 'But I'd rather hoped to have a few days to lie low. I've been talking to strangers for weeks.' Again I felt that prickle of dislike rising like a thorn in me.

Anto said there was no rush, whenever she felt like it. The man was behaving like a saint, but it wouldn't last – he had his limits too.

On the morning we left for the Mangalath party, Glory, in spite of another twelve-hour sleep, still looked tired and seemed to have shrunk to half her normal size. For the first time I felt truly sorry for her, and a little alarmed. Dressed in a new and very smart black and white silk polka-dot dress and small hat, she winced in the blinding sunlight as she left our house. Her arm felt twig-like and breakable as I helped her into the car, and she sat gasping for a few moments.

I was enough of an Indian wife by now for a ride in a car – loaned to us by Appan for the day's outing – to be something of a treat, and I'd grown to love the drive from Fort Cochin to Mangalath: the rowdy markets, the green paddy fields, the huge sky, the sunlit lakes, on which houses and bridges seemed to float. But today I felt sick and tense about the day ahead.

My mother sat in the back with her eyes closed. I sat beside her with Raffie on my knee. Anto broke the silence.

'I don't think you've been to this part of India before, have you, Mother?' She'd asked him to call her Glory, but he couldn't. In his family, to call an older person by their Christian name would be unspeakably rude.

'No,' she said in the echoey voice I recognised as a No Trespassing sign. 'Further north.' When Anto's eyes swam into the rear-view mirror, I shook my head slightly.

'It's awfully pretty, though.' She opened her eyes briefly, the perfect guest again. 'Lots of lovely water and birds.' A line of herons flew in a straggling ribbon across the lake, leaving a ruffle of water behind them. Raffie, who watched everything, let out a shriek, but turned back quickly to the pattern on my mother's dress. He moved one podgy finger from dot to dot, examining each forensically as if it was a complicated logarithm he must solve.

'Do you mind that?' I asked.

'No.' She put her hand on his head, and let it stay there for a while.

'This must be strange for you, Mummy,' I said.

I saw her lips moving, her hand grasping the car's leather safety strap.

'It's not very strange,' she said. 'I'm fine.' Then, in the silence that followed: 'I don't want you to worry about me.'

When Mangalath emerged from the red dust of the road, my mother immediately perked up, and became someone sociable and fun. I must say, it did look lovely. It had rained briefly on our way over and left big fat diamonds winking on the leaves. Glints of silver from the lake beyond.

At the house, Amma stood between the gold lions waiting to greet us.

'It's so good to finally meet you.' She gave her sweetest smile as she took Glory's hand in hers. 'I can see where your daughter gets her good looks from.' I saw her cast a shrewd and appraising eye over my mother's clothes and jewellery – that was the way her mind worked; it was the dowry obsession most mothers had here.

At the sight of Amma, Raffie let out a longing cry and flung his arms towards her. He buried his face in her shoulder.

'So, what do you think of this rascal?' Amma asked as we walked towards the house. 'Your very first grandchild, Kit tells me.'

'Yes,' my mother agreed, her heels click-clacking on the path, and breathless with the effort to keep up. 'My first ... he's awfully sweet.'

Only nine of us for lunch, so Glory would not be swamped. We took our places in the dining room. Appan at the head of the table next to Anto; Ponnamma and Mariamma in their usual places, and a couple of elderly aunts whose names I'd forgotten. I sat next to my mother, who was at her most delightful, exclaiming and smiling at everything. Feeling her sharp bones beside me, I hoped she could cope with all the food; her appetite had been so poor.

In her honour, a magnificent meal was served on fine bone-china plates: the pearly spotted karimeen fish that was a delicacy of the area, a tender mutton stew, soft, fluffy boiled rice with chicken curry, and the usual thoran and sautéed okra, crisp fried pappadams and lime pickle. I'd forgotten to have breakfast, and my mouth watered at the sight of all this food.

Glory had been given a knife and fork, just as I had on my first day here. I could feel her stiffen beside me as I ate with my fingers. Below the general bubble of conversation she said, 'Don't you find that frightfully messy?'

'I like it now.' I added some buttermilk to my rice, crushed a pappadam into it, and popped it into my mouth, to demonstrate how elegantly I could do it, and then laughed at myself. Do we ever stop showing off to our mothers?

Appan pulled up a chair beside us and peered at Glory through his glasses. 'We're so happy you're here,' he told her with apparent sincerity. 'It's like a dream come true.'

She gave an embarrassed laugh. 'How kind,' she said, very much the colonel's lady as she began to sprinkle compliments like hundreds and thousands.

'Goodness me, Kit was right, so clever,' she murmured in shock when he told her he'd been in Delhi, drafting new government legislation. Appan, an essentially modest man, deflected the compliment.

'It's my son I'm most proud of, working his socks off at the hospital. It's a great joy to have him home again.'

This courtly dance continued for a while: the passing of dishes, the tentative questions, the knitting together of a holey blanket that must, for now, be my mother's vision of her new family. While

Glory charmed Appan, Ponnamma swapped places with Mariamma so she could follow their exchange more easily.

She patted my mother on the arm. 'Come on,' she said. 'Eat up.' She put some of the mutton curry on her plate, spooned a little dhal on the side. 'You need feeding up.'

As I watched my mother take a forkful, I felt a piercing sadness. For the first time I could ever recall, she was the centre of attention. And maybe she felt it too, because when Ponnamma suddenly blurted out, 'Why did you delay your trip here?' she launched into a surprising story.

'Well,' she pushed her chair back, took a delicate sip of water, 'it's rather wonderful, actually. I have a great and dear friend in Oxford. Her name is Daisy. She lives in a very grand but rather run-down house – the war, you know – which she is hopeless at doing up, so I help her sometimes.'

That's it, Mother, I thought. Still a master at biting the hand that feeds you.

'Anyway . . .' She wiped the side of her mouth with her napkin, to make sure no stray piece of spinach interfered with her look. 'I must tell you what happened there . . .' The thread of excitement in her voice and the deliberately held pause reminded me what a good storyteller she was. Every eye at the table was now trained on her. Ponnamma's mouth agape.

'It was shortly before Christmas, a dark night, and very rainy – the kind of rain that seems to be poured in buckets rather than drops. I was sitting in the sewing room, making some new curtains' – she flung a smile at a mesmerised Appan – 'when suddenly I dropped a pin. When I kneeled down to pick it up, I saw, through the floor-boards, a light shining up at me. A shaft of light.' She sketched it out delicately in the air.

'From the room below?' Appan was applying his legal brain. 'Which room?'

'Ah, well you see, aren't you on the ball? That's the exact point,' said Glory. 'There was no room below. Only what we had always assumed was a solid staircase.' She quelled any more questions with her hand. 'I called to Daisy,' she continued in the same thrilling voice. 'We got a torch and went downstairs together.'

'Oh my God.' Ponnamma clutched her throat. 'You were very brave.'

Glory ignored this. 'Downstairs, on the side of this staircase, we found a small door. When we opened it, there was . . .' her eyes swept the table, 'a room that we never knew existed. A whole new room.'

'What was inside?' Amma asked.

'Well, this is the wonderful thing,' Glory continued, her finger in the air. 'And the dreadful. Before the war, Daisy's father was an artist. He studied at the Slade in Paris; he was taken around all the studios and met all the gang. So . . .' Another long pause. 'What we found in this very dusty room was a pile of pictures, leaning against a wall. Now, does the name Picasso mean anything to you?' She slid her eyes up at Appan.

'Of course.' He was slightly exasperated. 'Square ladies with round heads and such things. One of the most famous artists in the world,' he explained to the aunts.

'Well, behind two very ordinary seascapes, we found one of his paintings.'

The table let out a collective gasp.

'When we picked it up, the whole thing crumbled in our hands. Heartbreaking – woodlice, woodworm, who knows? As I said, Daisy is not the world's best housekeeper. So I wrapped up all these shards, and I took them to a restorer in Cirencester.

'He looked at them and said, "Terribly sorry, they're beyond hope." I begged him to try and save them, but all we could salvage were bits of hands and feet, a skew-whiff smile, and, tantalisingly, the name Picasso, beautifully preserved.' She gave a small sigh, then collected herself.

'So how did this situation resolve?' Appan, ever practical, wanted to know. My mother looked confused for a moment.

'Oh, I took the chap back to the house, and we found one or two other bits and pieces. Minor artists, nothing special. We took them to an auction, got some money for them – some of it helped pay for my journey, all very exciting.' Her smile was flung about the table like a sunbeam. 'But it delayed my trip.'

'Your friend was kind to give you the money,' Ponnamma said. 'It was her house. A very good friend to give you the money.'

'That's true,' my mother replied. 'But don't forget, I found the extra room.'

In the applause that followed, I was in awe of her: her verve, her daring. It was good to see her smiling, too, and the haggard, hunted lines of her face soften, at least for now.

Was the story true? No idea. Honestly none. She'd never divulged to me the origins of the little windfall that had brought her to India, and I hadn't dared ask. If she was embroidering the truth, I thought Picasso was a mistake – too obvious, too unlikely – but if she wasn't, why hadn't Daisy mentioned a shred of it?

Chapter 38

Later that day, when Anto saw Amma go into the garden, he followed her down the narrow path and towards the potting shed. He knew that lunch with Glory had been an ordeal – this exotic hybrid appearing from nowhere, needing knives and forks and special conversation, with the linked thought of how much easier and more fun it would have been with Anu in her place, and Vidya sitting beside him.

'Hello, stranger,' she said when she saw him. She was on her knees, planting an orchid.

'Hello, Amma.' He sat down on the bench. 'Thank you for lunch. I know these things aren't easy for you.'

'Did I show it?'

'No, you were kind.'

'Kind.' She examined the word as she settled the new plant into its bed of bark and soil; a trickle of moisture from her jug coloured the grey earth red.

'This one's called lady's slipper,' she said at last in a tight voice. 'It came from my specialist grower in Madras. He said, "If anyone can charm flowers from buds, you can, madam."'

'Well it's true.' When he touched her hand, he saw her eyes fill with tears. 'People bloom here too; it wouldn't happen without you.'

She brushed the tears away with a quick, efficient gesture.

'What else can I be but polite?' She gave a little gasp. 'Life happens to you; you can't control it.'

She put away her trowel, and they walked down to the bench facing the lake. They watched the sun gild the water with shining bars of light and slowly melt behind the trees in a fiery glow. Across the lake, early-evening fires were being lit outside the scattering of huts. There was the thump of drums from the Hindu temple, voices singing evening prayers.

'Just like old times,' he said.

'Yes,' she replied. Her face golden with reflected light. 'But not really.' He wanted her to add something comforting, but her expression was both sad and proud.

He knew he confused her now: the jokes, the deep reserve, the uneasy look he gave her before he answered simple questions, as if trying to filter out what would offend her.

Over lunch, he had looked at Glory through Amma's eyes and known what she'd be thinking. A strange kettle of fish, that one: so confident, so instantly vivacious, ever so slightly flirtatious. Skinny, too – must be ill – and very . . . What was the word? Slippery about her own past. Where was she from? Why had she stayed away? Where was her family? Underneath Amma's tranquil gaze, these questions would have seethed.

'Your father seemed to like her,' she said now.

'Yes.'

'But men are like babies: feed them the sugar of flattery and they bloom too.' She smiled to show she didn't care.

'Do you mind him being away so much?'

'Of course. I think he is working himself to death, but what can I do?'

Anto didn't have an answer.

'But I will tell you one thing.' Amma broke the long pause that followed. 'He and I agree about one important matter, and so, by the way, does her mother. We would like Kit to have more babies and spend less time at work.'

A swarm of confused feelings rose up in him at this. How to explain to his mother without being disloyal to Kit that this was what he wanted too. How to explain to himself the resentment he felt at these old biddies butting their noses into her reproductive life.

'When did this discussion with her mother take place?' he asked.

'We were alone after lunch; you and Kit were upstairs with Raffie.'

'What did you say?'

'Well . . .' Amma began, innocently bland. 'I began by saying, "Your daughter is a wonderful mother. I hope more are planned." She said, "Amen to that. I'd like her to have tons of babies and give up that work she does. I think it's a horrible job." ' She brushed invisible crumbs from her lap. 'She told me she blamed the war for getting her into it. The war changed girls, she said, and not for the better: it got them almost addicted to danger and responsibility.

When it ended, she begged and begged her to stop. Don't look at me like that! You asked me what she said. I'm telling you.'

When his mother had finished her outburst, with a firm closing of her lips, he felt a moment of dull rage on Kit's behalf: addicted to danger! What insulting claptrap, what a reduction of her spirit and her bravery and her dedication – of the other nurses' too. He said nothing. The two grandmas were talking – for everyone's sake, this truce must be preserved, for the time being.

'So you covered a lot of ground.' He shifted away from her.

'Not really. It's probably the only thing we have in common.' She gave a bitter smile and stood up. 'I'm tired, you know. I'm going to go to bed early.'

Chapter 39

'Is there anything you'd particularly like to do while you're here, Mummy?' I'd asked her when she first arrived, thinking there must be an old school, a village, a district she'd want to visit; one that might bring the big blank of her past alive, not just for her, but for me too.

'Not really, darling,' came the disappointing answer. 'You decide for me,' adding, 'Unless there are some amusing people you'd like me to meet.'

When she said this, I felt myself sinking into the bog of her inertia, her disappointment, the lack of concrete plans I'd dreaded as a child. But then I was ashamed of my meanness: the shadows under her eyes were growing, and in the mornings, when I opened her bedroom door, she often looked as still and dead as a wax dummy. Then I'd hear her laboured breathing, or the long coughing spells that were frightening to listen to.

Anto took the day off and borrowed the family car from Appan so we could tootle around Fort Cochin. She was perfectly polite about its churches, the monuments, the covered market, the Chinese nets, but when we stopped for a lemonade overlooking the harbour, and Anto was out of earshot, she said to me, 'It is quite a limited little town really, isn't it? And the pong! Why don't their new lot do something about it?'

After ten days, I couldn't bear this drifting any longer, and one afternoon, I told her I had to go back and do my two shifts a week at the Moonstone. The house was running smoothly now, and Kamalam would be a willing supplier of tea and toast – the only thing Glory ate in the morning. I'd come home for lunch, and spend the afternoons with her.

To my surprise, she made no protest. Instead, she stroked my fingers and said, 'It's nice being together again, isn't it?' And I wished with all my heart I could say yes, and mean it.

On my first day back, there were thirty women waiting outside, many of them new patients. After clinic, Dr A drew me aside to tell me we were dangerously short-staffed and I was to write to the Oxford group asking for funds for a new trainee midwife and two nurses. I felt discouraged: I wanted to function as a midwife now, not a cash cow.

I wrote the letter, then raced home down the seafront, arriving breathless to find my mother peacefully knitting – knitting! – in a patch of sunshine. Raffie was playing with his coloured blocks nearby, with Kamalam looking on.

She didn't ask me about my morning, and I said nothing. Instead she showed me an out-of-date copy of the Army & Navy catalogue, which she enjoyed despising.

'Urgghhh, look at this.' Her perfectly buffed fingernail stabbed at a tweed shooting skirt. 'You'd have to pay me to wear this.'

'You won't get much,' I teased her. 'Not a big run on tweed since Independence.'

'Silly asses,' she murmured softly, 'kicking us out.'

I looked at her in silent amazement. Had she completely forgotten what she was?

'Oh, darling, I forgot to tell you.' She looked up and frowned. 'A funny little lady came while you were out this morning. She wanted to talk to you. She seemed in a bit of a state.' She picked up the magazine again.

'Any idea what her name was?'

'Let me think . . . Sorry, darling, it's gone . . . Oh, hang on.' I watched a thought form in her head. 'I wrote it down.' She picked up a scrap of paper and handed it to me.

Neeta Chacko! The woman Daisy had revered as a midwife; the woman Daisy said would greet me with open arms – except she'd disappeared into thin air before I'd got there.

'Neeta Chacko! How strange. Are you sure?'

'Yes, at least I think so.'

'What did you say?'

'I said you were busy. She said she'd come back.'

'Any idea where she went?'

'No, sorry,' and then, seeing my expression, 'Darling, in India, you can't just ask any old Tom, Dick or Harry in off the street, you must know that by now.'

Neeta Chacko was sitting in the baking sun on a wall in front of a vacant house when I found her. There were two cloth bundles in the dust at her feet. I'd seen a photograph of her at Wickam Farm, but had she not leapt up when she saw me, I wouldn't have recognised her.

'Ma'am, please, I must talk to you,' she said, her eyes frantic. 'Somewhere quiet, not here.'

'Neeta!' I said. 'What a surprise!' I'd heard nothing but praise about this woman: her energy, her tact, her competence. It was hard to connect this with the woebegone creature in front of me.

She looked like she needed something to eat. I decided on a modest fish café on the harbour, away from my mother and other flapping ears. Ropes of coloured beads covered its dark entrance, and a Bovril advertisement hung on the wall outside.

As we sat down at the wobbly table inside, Neeta, half covering her face with the end of her sari, glanced fearfully at a group of men at the next table drinking beer and eating sambals. When I tried to wedge a piece of paper under the table leg that was causing the wobble, I saw her toes were scuffed and bleeding.

'Have you walked a long way?' I asked.

'Yes, ma'am, I needed to see you.'

I ordered chai for both of us, and when I asked if she was hungry, she shot me a desperate look, somewhere between shame and desire.

'Yes, ma'am,' she whispered.

'Please don't call me ma'am,' I said. 'My name is Kit; we're colleagues.' But she could not meet my eye.

She ordered modestly, rice and some lentil thing, and when I ordered two extra dishes, she apologised in instant gratitude.

'Please don't say sorry,' I said. 'I'm glad to meet you; Daisy spoke so highly of you. I was disappointed when I came here not to meet you.' I heard her take a deep breath.

When the men left and the café had emptied, she looked at me over her cup, her eyes brimming with tears, and talked about how much she'd loved her time at the Moonstone.

'I felt I was growing every day.' She wiped her eyes on her shawl. 'I was learning in my profession, feeling part of our new country.'

I told her I felt the same. 'It's a very special place.' And then I

237

had to ask, 'Are you ill, Neeta?' thinking this could be the cause of her distress.

'No, ma'am.' She shook her head. 'I'm back at my home now, because my family wanted me to leave here. My son was badly hurt.'

'Where is your home?'

'Near here. Not far,' she answered with a vague flap of her hand. 'I don't want to say exactly.'

'Is your son better now?'

Neeta looked around the restaurant, then whispered across the table. 'Yes, ma'am.'

'So do you want your job back?'

She backed away from me and shook her head. 'No, ma'am. I can't pay the men the money.'

'What men?'

'I will tell you in a minute.'

Her desolate look brightened for a moment at the approach of two plates of rice with curried goat scattered untidily on top of it. A small boy placed vegetables and chutneys on the table beside them. When she'd eaten ravenously for a while, she wiped her mouth daintily and looked at me.

'My son was beaten by some bad boys. They came to see him last week. They think he knows more than he does because I used to work at the Moonstone. They told him there will be big trouble there soon.'

'What boys? What trouble?' The rice I was eating sank like a stone in my stomach. 'I don't know what you're talking about.'

'They don't want you there. They want their money. When my son said he couldn't pay them, they beat him again. It's not safe.'

It took a while for her words to sink in. 'What do you mean, not safe? Are you talking about the home in general or me in particular?'

'Everything,' she whispered.

'So who is paying this money?' I said. 'And how much? And why are they bothering your son?'

She shook her head vigorously. 'I don't know. They don't believe him. I can't say any more. They are bad, bad men.' She pushed her plate away.

'So we must tell the police,' I said at last.

'They won't care. They're part of it.'

I thought for a while. It was hot, very hot inside the café, which had a tin roof. My brain felt fried.

'My father-in-law is a lawyer, a very honourable man,' I said at last. 'He might be able to help us.' Neeta looked sceptical.

'Ma'am, if you say these things, they will close the home down.'

'You must tell me who gives the men the money.' I was pleading with her. 'I can't keep asking Daisy for it if I don't know where it's going.'

'I can't say; they will hurt me badly, and if you tell Miss Barker, she'll stop sending it.' Neeta gave a ragged sigh. 'She wrote to me, but I knew I must not reply.'

She pushed her chair back and raised her eyes to me. A drop of blood fell from her right foot on to the floor.

'So what would you do, Neeta? Help me. Tell me honestly.'

'I don't know, ma'am, you must say.'

A gust of wind, warm and smelling of fish, slammed the café door shut. Neeta jerked as if she'd been shot.

'I can't stay,' she said. Scrabbling in one of her stained bundles, she pulled out a piece of paper folded into four. 'My address. Don't show it to anyone, and please don't fix my name to the information I have given you.' Her foot made a bloody print on the floor as she stood up.

'You're hurt,' I said. 'Come back to my house, I'll dress it.'

'I can't,' she said. 'I've got to go home.'

I gave her what I had in my purse – only a few rupees left over after paying the bill, but enough I hoped to buy a little food or get her a rickshaw or a bus home.

'One day,' she said before we parted, 'I pray God will let me do the work I'm trained for.'

I wanted to shout: it's not God who bloody well forbids it, but said instead, 'I'd back you up if you decided to go to the police. You know where I live now.'

She shook her head. 'I can't do that. I give my blessings to Miss Daisy Barker, and to you.' She bowed her head, put the palms of her hands together, and after a quick *namaskarin* was gone.

Later, much, much later, when I tried to piece this conversation together, I was amazed at how I could have been quite so stupid, ignored so many fire bells. Neeta had spelled the dangers out clearly, but in the ten minutes it took me to walk home, I had decided to agree with her plan to do nothing. Why did I do that? One thing, but no excuse, was that Neeta's warning made me feel like a foreigner again, out of my depth in a country in a period of violent change, in a city whose deeper machinations I would probably never understand.

I was also, and maybe this was uppermost in my mind, now part of a family whose honour must be preserved. Any publicity about the Moonstone with my name attached to it would be a social nightmare for them. We were also two weeks short of the government inspection Dr A had warned us about, the one that could close the home down at a moment's notice. No, it didn't wash, not really. I should have listened. Should have acted.

I was so deep in thought that I jumped when a boy leapt out at me. His skinny arm was festooned with bracelets: crude wooden things shaped like snakes, with cheap-looking mirrors for eyes.

'Madam, madam, stop!' He said. 'I love you, thank you, please don't run.'

But I was running, down the path, under the banyan tree and out into the sun, the tarmac burning through the thin leather of my shoes.

I thought about Neeta's surprise appearance on and off all that night, and might have mentioned it to Maya the next morning except there was a new crisis brewing at the home and it involved me. With only two weeks to go before our government inspection, two of the midwives stood up and announced that they wanted to go home.

Janamma and Madhavi were both from small villages north of Trivandrum. Madhavi was a small, fierce, wiry woman with wide-set eyes, and smallpox scars on her cheeks. Maya said she'd looked unhappy from the start, refusing to dance or to tell the stories of birthing that the other women enjoyed. This morning, during prayers, I'd caught her looking at me with a hard, blank stare. Later, during a session on birth control, she stood up in a fury, let forth a fusillade of words in Malayalam and jabbed her finger at me.

'What is she saying?'

Maya held up her hand to stem the flow. 'She is cross.'

'I can see that. What did she say – and no soft-soaping.'

'It's nothing, Kit.' Maya blinked at me through her glasses.

'Come on, please.' My conversation with Neeta had made me nervous.

'She thinks,' Maya said reluctantly, 'you should go back to your own country and sterilise the women there. She says this teaching is a government plot from your country and you are a spy.' Maya's expression was caught halfway between merriment and embarrassment, but for one brief, paranoid moment, I wondered whether she wasn't expressing a thought that she'd had too.

'What shall I say?' The other women were staring fixedly at me; one or two were muttering in a way that made me realise how quickly the mood could change here.

Maya, keeping a serene smile on her face, muttered, 'Tell her that's poppycock.' She loved this word and used it as often as possible.

I took a deep breath and faced the women.

'None of us are spies; that's a horrible thought, and nothing will happen unless we learn to trust each other. Let the men do the fighting.' Maya smiled encouragingly. 'Also, I am married to an Indian man; he is a doctor.'

They were still not convinced. Janamma, from Vaikkom, a stout, self-righteous woman, stood up, jabbed her finger at me and began a shrill rant that went on and on – squeak, squeak, rant, rant – with Maya growling back when she could get a word in edgeways.

It was hot. The fan in the reception room had broken, and I felt a sudden primitive urge to strike the woman round the head and let loose myself. *Ungrateful bloody baggage, what have I ever done to you?* That would have put the cat amongst the pigeons, or was I the pigeon here?

Maya's eyes had narrowed into spiteful slits. She walked over to where Janamma was standing, put her face close to the woman and gave her what sounded like a furious tongue-lashing.

'That *mundi*, don't bother with her. She is life dust,' she informed me at last. 'Not worth talking to.'

'Tell me what she said, Maya,' I said. 'Else I won't know, and my reports will be pointless.'

'Nothing to tell. She says she wants money for the days she has wasted here, and money for transport home. She's taking her friend with her; she says she has had a horrible time here also.'

So class dismissed. Five minutes or so later, on our way back to the wards, we both giggled nervously when Maya confessed, 'I wanted to strike her too. So rude, so ungrateful, plenty more to take her silly place.'

'But I can see her point, sort of,' I said. 'If a group of Indian doctors came to England and talked about sterilisation, it might cause a bit of a rumpus.'

Maya, like me, was bored with being fair. 'She is a rude woman,' she repeated. 'We should get *her* sterilised before she has rude children.'

Chapter 40

Anto felt grumpy when he got home from work. A long, fruitlessly busy day, trying to penetrate layer upon layer of government bureaucracy to get a simple answer about funding for his research. No time for lunch. Kit late home from the Moonstone. When he walked in, his mother-in-law leapt up, gave him a nautical salute and said in a silly drawl, 'Ah, sailor returns.' She was sitting in his favourite chair on the veranda.

When Raffie toddled in, gave a reckless gummy smile and ran into his arms, all Anto wanted to do was to lie on the floor with him and do the pretend wrestling the little boy loved, smell his sweet skin.

But for Glory, dressed up and lipsticked, this was, as she announced gaily, 'the *chota peg* moment'. A gin and it for her, and one for him. He'd tried gin once at Oxford, hated its taste of old perfume, but she insisted on it: 'I don't want to feel like some frightful old lush.'

While they were drinking, he looked at her closely. A stunning beauty she must have been in her day, but the prominent cheekbones were growing sharper; her eyes looked bruised.

'How are you feeling, Glory?' She'd insisted on being called by her first name, though he had slipped several times, calling her Mother. 'Did you have a good sleep today?'

'I'm absolutely fine.' She moved the ice around with her finger. 'I shan't hang around much longer.' She dipped her head, took a quick suck of her drink.

'What do you mean?' He was genuinely bewildered.

'I'll get out of your hair. Hotel, go home . . . something.'

'Glory,' he said gently, 'you're not in my hair. You are my mother now too, and always welcome. Though I'm thinking,' he went on quickly, because her chin was puckering violently and she was plucking at her skirt, 'you should definitely get your cough checked – an X-ray maybe.'

'You're terribly sweet.' She took another sip of her drink, recovered quickly and looked at him grandly. 'But you know, when you're old, you expect bits to drop off. So, tell me something funny about your day.'

Oh Lord, he thought, the English thing. His tutor used to call them 'the Western Orientals'. So exhausting sometimes, quenching the emotion, the tears. He understood it only too well – it was part of his own routine now – and while he racked his brains for a bit of light relief, she rattled on gaily about old people and their ailments and how extraordinarily boring they could be: Oscar Wilde, she said, only allowed self-pity between the hours of three thirty and four. He laughed politely and watched her. She'd come here to die, he knew that: her pallor was growing day by day, and at night there was that gravelly cough. A few nights ago, Kit had lain rigidly awake beside him, listening to her gasping and coughing. 'I can't go in, can I?' she'd said, her face white in the moonlight. 'She wants me to pretend I haven't heard.'

And the dying were entitled to their secrets, so pouring another gin, waving the Angostura bitters over the drink, just the way she liked, he told her about Arjunan Asan, an insufferable civil servant who'd dropped in to check on their department today and, puffed up with professional pride, told Anto that for the next few weeks, he would be so busy that he would only have time to say good morning to him; no other conversation would be tolerated.

This went down a treat. 'Oh, the pompous prat,' she laughed. 'That *ullu ka patta*' – son of an owl.

It was the first Indian expression she'd used in front of him, and she looked as surprised as he did. More than surprised. It was Raffie's look when he thought he'd done something very wicked, like being caught with a hand in the sweet tin.

Chapter 41

I got home late on the night of the next big drama. I was running across the small maidan at the end of our street, panicked at the thought of Mother and Raffie waiting for supper (Anto was away in Bombay), when a man ran up behind me, shouting.

'Madam! Stop!' It was Murali, the fruit seller.

He was usually a genial, smiling presence, waving to me or wrapping my fruit, but tonight, his eyes were bulging with fright, his shirt soaked with sweat, and I had the sudden terrible thought that a bad thing had happened to Raffie and he'd been sent to find me.

Instead he told me, between gulps of air, that his young wife Kamalakshi was in very great pain. She was in the seventh month of her pregnancy. She had lost two babies already.

'It will break our hearts to lose another.'

I knew Kamalakshi only as a pair of dark eyes peering above a veil from a shadowy room at the back of the shop. Whenever she saw me, she backed away, like a beetle disappearing into the cracks.

'Can you get her to the Matha Moonstone?' I said to him. 'I work there with the local doctors.'

He squeezed his eyes shut to stop the tears falling. 'Please, madam, help me take her there.' He clasped his hands together in prayer. 'My son has a rickshaw.'

In the heartbeat that followed, I thought of dinner going cold, Raffie bellowing for his goodnight kiss. I was longing for bed, and a million miles away from being the saint he imagined me to be.

'There's a doctor on duty there tonight, and good nurses. They'll look after you. Try not to worry too much.'

He tugged at my sleeve. 'Please.'

Kamalakshi was lying on a large pile of empty hessian sacks in the storeroom when we found her. She was shaking, crying, holding her stomach. At the back of the room, there was a lurid goddess statue, propped up by cans of cooking oil. When I asked if I could look at her, she wailed, but when Murali spoke crossly to her, she stared at him and moaned her assent. A few moments later, I got into the rickshaw with her, and with Murali behind, we sped off.

When we arrived at the Moonstone and bashed on the door, Parvati, one of the midwives, let us in.

In the surgery, Dr A, gloved, gowned, brisk and comfortingly bossy, did the preliminary investigations, removing the loincloth that women here used for their periods. With her hand on Kamalakshi's stomach she delivered the good news.

'Everything is fine, baby is still there. Find her a bed for the night. This baby is impatient to be born.'

Murali said he didn't want his wife to stay overnight, but Dr A, inflating like a puff adder, said it was not up for discussion; it was imperative. She herself would watch over her, and so would Parvati. Treatment could not be finer.

Murali gave in with the relief of a tired child ordered to bed. His gratitude poured out: 'Nunni valarey, valarey nunni' – thanks, much, much thanks. He insisted I take his rickshaw, but even so, it was well past midnight when I arrived home. Apart from a faint light coming from my mother's room, the house was cloaked in blue darkness. In the distance, I could hear the hoot of a steamship.

When I crept up the stairs into Raffie's room and stroked his hair, I felt puffs of air coming from his mouth on to my hand, and the simple fact of him being alive seemed in that moment to be the most stupendous gift. I kissed him, and adjusted his nightshirt, and he, involved in some lip-smacking dream, barely stirred, except to kick out one fat honey-coloured leg.

'I love you, Raffie,' I whispered. 'I love my boy.'

I went out like a light after that, until: 'Meesskeet! Meesskeet!' Coming up with the greatest reluctance through various levels of sleep, I thought at first I heard birds chirruping, and then realised it was my name being called. When I opened my eyes, the pre-dawn light was full of shadows. I heard a jumble of voices in the street, and the rickety sound Raffie made when he was woken suddenly.

'Miss Kit.' The voice outside was panicked and thin. When I ran to the window, Maya's grey face looked up at me.

'Hurry, Miss Kit, hurry,' she said. 'The home is on fire and I can't find Dr Annakutty.'

I felt blank with shock as I buttoned my dress and put on my shoes, as if everything around me would break if I didn't remain perfectly calm. I was calm too when I gave Kamalam instructions about Raffie and my mother's breakfast. During my training at St Andrew's, we'd had fire drills aplenty and lots of false alarms, but at the Moonstone, there had been no training and no warnings. I should have thought of that.

Outside on the street, Babu from the general store had arrived, unshaven, groggy with sleep and in his night lunghi. Maya crouched near the bushes, crying and pleading and speaking broken sentences that made no sense. She point-blank refused to get into Babu's rickshaw, so we raced hand in hand towards the home.

The street was shadowy and dark, the sky still full of pin-bright stars. When I caught my heel on a broken pavement and fell headlong, Maya jerked me up roughly. 'Hurry, madam, come.'

At the corner of Main and Tower Street, we came to a skidding halt. It was a terrible shock to see the Moonstone crackling and burning, the sky above it full of an unstable rosy glow in which black objects floated and swirled.

'Oh my God. Oh my God,' Maya wailed, clutching my arm. She'd tried to reassure me on the way that the fire engines would get there before we did.

I felt myself go cold. We'd tried, before the government inspection, to keep patient numbers down, so we could clean and whitewash the wards, but this was our worst nightmare. We had four patients inside: Murali's wife, possibly with a new baby, one other woman about to deliver, and two for observation, one very seriously ill with eclampsia.

At the gate, I was stopped by two young policemen with lathis in their hands. 'Don't go in there,' said one. 'You will burn to death.' They weren't exaggerating. From fifty yards away, I could feel the fire's tremendous heat. The flames surged and died and surged again, and the small crowd gathered by the gate oohed and aahed and shrank back, one or two of them even laughing as if this was a child's game.

'What are they doing? What are they doing?' I yelled. I could see three or four boys running from the building, putting tables, chairs, a filing cabinet on to a waiting bullock cart. Maya dashed towards them shrieking, and came back with her face black with soot.

'Where are the patients?' I asked.

'Two out, two still in there,' she replied. 'They're moving them now – the fire has not touched the back ward.' She sank to her knees and put her head in her hands.

'Where are the fire engines?' I shouted. 'Why aren't they here?'

Maya spat a black cinder into her hand and began to sob. 'They were here, they went away. They ran out of water. They said they would come back.'

The crowd near the gate was growing. They were watching smoke pouring from the roof and the porch. When Mr Namboothiri's lovely yellow, red and purple sign started to blister and run, someone in the crowd gave a small cheer, and I wanted to punch them.

It was getting lighter now, and the flowers, the geraniums we'd planted, stood out in a red haze, almost surreally bright in the half-light of dawn. Murali appeared, sobbing with relief. His wife had a three-hour-old baby boy, and they had been rescued. He was taking her home. Then Maya suddenly clapped her hand over her mouth.

'Oh my God,' she said. 'There's one more patient in the dispensary room. I don't know if the firemen got her out.'

'Where's the key?' I shouted.

'I have it here,' Maya said. 'We must go in.'

The policemen on the gate let us through, not eager to come with us. Through the smoke, I saw the main part of the roof collapse in a jumble of wooden struts that stood out like ribs against the pre-dawn light. I heard the murmur of the crowd behind us as Maya and I covered our faces with our shawls and ran down the path towards the dispensary.

The wind changed as we ran, and when the smoke moved towards us, we started to cough. My legs had turned to liquid and my head was shouting, *Don't make me do this! I don't want to die!* but I was moving forward. When I looked at Maya, she was praying.

'In quickly,' she shouted, waving the bunch of keys. 'Out quickly. We can do it.'

When we were less than twenty feet from the dispensary door, two local policemen appeared, one tall, one short, faces covered in the black slime of soot and sweat. At first, they tried to push us back. They snatched the keys from Maya. Then we all stopped. A baby was crying inside. A high-pitched wail. Maya started to scream and bang on the door.

The dispensary had been flung up as a temporary dwelling – tin roof, cheap door – to house a few patients while necessary repairs were done to the main house. Its door had swelled in the last monsoon, and now the tall man was having trouble with it, yelling and kicking and shoving the key fruitlessly from side to side.

Maya grabbed the keys back. Now we could hear a woman's voice, a squeal of fear, and the baby shrieking. Maya swore and wrestled and grunted, trying the key this way and that. No luck.

'You try.' She handed me the keys. My eyes were streaming; my fingers felt swollen and useless. I tried one key after another, sobbing, swearing: 'Come on, you bastard, do it! Do it.'

After a few seconds that seemed like a lifetime, I felt the lock swivel, click, give. A gigantic kick from Maya shattered the door, and in we went.

The smoke was so thick inside the room, we couldn't see anything at first; we could only blunder in the general direction of a screaming voice, a prolonged coughing fit. The baby had stopped crying. I paused for a moment, hearing the *boom crash* of the ceiling falling in another part of the building, and after a moment or two of stumbling around, I felt a hand clawing at me. A wild-eyed woman loomed into view, hair loose, face wet with sweat. She was clinging to the bed with one arm, and held the baby in the other, shouting over and over in a monotonous wail, '*Ayyoo daivamey ... Rekshikkaney*,' cries for help from God that I was familiar with by now.

The baby was screaming again. Maya wrapped her shawl around its purple face and tiny body, which now lashed out convulsively.

'Out!' she shouted.

The fire was still raging at the front of the dispensary. The policemen, who had hung back, pushed us through the door that led from the back, over a small strip of concrete, and towards the seven-foot wall that bounded the property. Glass and barbed wire had been put on top of the wall after the last break-in.

We stood for a moment, all of us, in the flickering light. Three women, one post-partum and bent double, two men, and the baby, its mouth a dark red hole of protest.

'We can't do it.' I looked up at the wall, the red sky above it, the dark ash spiralling up. 'We'll have to run back by the path.' I tried to take the baby, but the mother held it like a vice. Maya, shouting ferociously, wrenched the woman's arms apart, flung the baby into mine.

'Go first!' she screamed. 'Open the gate, take the baby. God bless you.'

And then the weight of the baby in my arms. So light, so easily disposed of. I remember closing my eyes, and the sensation of running. Speeding through my mind: Anto, Raffie, my mother. Amma. Finally, sitting on the ground, the feeling of grit and earth underneath me; pain flaring in my arm, and bells ringing before the lights went out.

Chapter 42

Burns, I knew from my training, don't hurt in the way you might imagine. First-degree burns can hurt like hell – they catch the top layer of nerve endings. The more serious second-degree burns are often less painful, because the damage is greater and the heat sears through the nerve and the sweat glands. Most serious of all, third-degree burns can send a patient's body into a state of shock that resembles coma.

The second-degree burns to my arms and lower legs felt like being stung by a thousand bees, but were not serious enough to keep me in the General Hospital Ernakulum for more than a couple of days. A much worse pain for me, as I lay in my room on the third floor, watching my skin turn chalky and white, was the knowledge that I'd been so stupid.

I kept imagining the conversation I might have with Daisy.

'So you were told by Neeta before the fire that funds were definitely being embezzled?' Yes.

'That the home had clear enemies?'
Yes.

'That some kind of attack had been threatened?'
Yes.

'And you decided to do nothing?'
Yes. Or was it no, or maybe?

The facts were so shot through with holes and uncertainties that my mind dashed around for excuses, like a bird trapped in a windowless room. I had definitely dropped hints, tried openings, made tentative suggestions to Dr A, and asked, many times, for the accounts. But I should have been clearer, braver, less anxious about being the know-all memsahib, and although nobody had been killed, the home was now a smouldering wreck, and that was partly my fault. I'd behaved like a coward.

*

On my third day in hospital, it was Glory who, to my horror and amazement, turned up to drive me home. Pale and thin in the blinding sunlight, she was wearing a green silk suit and white crocheted driving gloves, and when I saw her behind the wheel of Appan's car, I thought at first I was hallucinating.

'I didn't know you could do this,' I said nervously, as she threaded her way through a street market, hand on horn, shouting '*Kazhutha!*' – donkey – at a careless rickshaw driver.

'Well there's quite a lot you don't know about me,' she said with a pert look. 'I did this all the time when I worked in Ooty for Major General Willoughby and his wife.' Another employer floating up from the mists of her past. 'He loathed driving up hills, and rather liked me.'

I looked at her in amazement: a pale shadow of herself a few weeks ago, now double-declutching and flipping out her indicator at the crossroads. The mother I thought I'd imagined had flared into life again.

'D'you promise me Anto and Raffie are all right?' I said, when we stopped to let a bullock cart go by. I'd worried about them obsessively in hospital, but felt Raffie was too young to visit me. The burns unit was a frightening place.

'Fine and dandy.' She was checking her lipstick in the rear-view mirror. 'Raffie and I played trains yesterday. I think he quite likes his old grandma now.'

'Anto?' I gripped the handle on the side of the car.

'He phoned again yesterday from some godforsaken place. Typical man, never bloody well there when you need them,' she added, with a flash of her old bitterness.

She made me rest on the sofa all afternoon, joking that I was her 'little dolly' again. She played with Raffie, and bossed Kamalam about, telling her I was tired and to take him upstairs. She went off to find me a decent nightdress to wear. The one she brought down, cherished in tissue paper like some holy relic, was Christian Dior. A present from an admirer? Something she'd borrowed and forgotten to give back? Hard to tell. She said she'd never worn it, and was keeping it for her funeral.

As I lifted the tissue, the faint musky sweetness of dried lavender floated in the air.

'Wickam,' I said, hearing the click of Daisy's secateurs as we stripped the plants and poured the flowers into small muslin bags. I began to cry.

'Whatever's the matter?' my mother asked.

'The Moonstone,' I said. 'I've got to tell Daisy about it.'

'Well she won't blame you.'

'She should,' I gulped.

'That is absolute codswallop.' It was strange to feel her arms around me. 'How could it possibly be your fault? You didn't do it.' The mother tiger again, eyes blazing with indignation.

'I could have done more. I'd heard rumours from the moment I got there.'

'Oh stop that.' She adjusted the ribbon on my nightdress, and glared at me. 'Stop it immediately. There are always rumours. You can't spread panic. Besides, Indians love a drama.'

I let it pass. The days were long gone when she could kiss and make it better. 'Do you promise me that nobody died?' I asked for the umpteenth time that day.

'Nobody died.' She said this in a firm voice, then put one hand over her eye, which was never a good sign. 'And I actually meant to tell you this: I got a telegram from Daisy this morning. She knows, and she says the main thing is you're safe, and you're not to worry about a thing.'

'Honestly?'

'Honestly.'

'Can I see the telegram?'

She put her cup down and gave me her hurt look. The one I'd always dreaded. 'You never believe a word I say, do you?' she said. 'And that's quite upsetting, you know.'

I chose my words carefully, knowing the wrong ones would send us both tumbling into a dark and frightening place.

'I believe . . . I think you sometimes try to make the world seem nicer than it is.'

'Oh really?' Her eyes narrowed. 'Can you give me an example of that?'

I thought for a moment. 'Well, I seem to remember an incident when we saw a dead rabbit on the road, and when I asked what had happened to it, you said it was having a little sleep on its way to a party. That might be one example.'

It felt like a high-board moment, but Glory flung back her head and laughed, the first time I'd seen her do that in a long time.

'I do remember that. Flat as a pancake, and you crying your silly eyes out. We were off to Northumberland: that widower, ex-navy, who couldn't, in six months, ever quite get the hang of my name. Rude bugger. The car broke down twice. We had to walk the last mile or so with our suitcases.'

'I don't remember that bit,' I said.

'No,' she said quietly. 'Of course you don't.'

'It wasn't easy for you, Mum.' I broke the silence that followed. 'I can see that now.'

'My fault,' she said, almost brusquely. 'And please don't call me Mum, it's common.'

'Your fault how?' I said. She was clutching at her pearls, twisting them.

'I was feeble really.'

'Feeble! I'd never call you that!'

'I was.' She scratched her head. 'I've lived my whole life in a sort of dream. At least you were brave.'

Sweat broke out along my hairline and scalp. My mother making me into some sort of martyr felt completely unbearable.

'No.'

'Brave enough to make mistakes. I mean, to defy me.'

'Well, that.' We smiled in a wary way at each other. 'I suppose. Not often.'

Another long silence fell between us. 'Anto wasn't one of my mistakes, Mummy,' I said at the end of it. 'You do know that, don't you? I love him.'

She took off her pearls and examined their gold clasp. 'Oh love... we'll see,' she said, laying them down. 'I can certainly see the attraction. He's very good-looking.' Her smile was hard, defiant: her don't-think-you-invented-sex look.

I let it lie. We'd come as far as we could today without hurting each other. Now I hoped she'd go away and have a rest, and I could spend some time with Raffie, who I could hear upstairs playing with Kamalam, but instead, she kicked off her shoes and lay beside me.

'One more thing.' She sounded breathless again. 'You know that story I told at lunch about finding the extra room at Wickam? The one we didn't know about? I don't suppose you believed a word of that either.'

'It was a good story,' I said, meaning, I'm too tired, don't make me think about it. The frantic look in her eyes signalled more emotion than I could cope with.

'People dream about that,' she said. 'Don't they? Discovering a marvellous secret room – a place they knew nothing about before that makes everything feel more spacious.' Actually, I'd never heard of this, but I let it go.

'What was it like?' I asked, more out of politeness than anything. 'Daisy hasn't said anything about it.'

'It was horrible,' she said. 'There was a nest of squirrels in the ceiling, and their pee-pee had dripped through the floorboards, so it stank, and all we found at first were heaps of clothes, and a dead rat. But here's the thing.' She clutched my arm now. 'When my eyes had grown accustomed to the light, I could see that there were three pictures stacked against the wall. I actually joked to Daisy that if one of them was a Picasso, all our troubles would be over. And there it was, suddenly, this tiny canvas, with his signature on the corner. We took it towards the light to check we weren't going mad, and it really did crumble like sawdust in Daisy's hand, and I wanted to scream.' Glory shifted on the sofa, her sharp hip bone sticking into mine. 'I was livid with her for being so careless. I suppose her mind was on higher things, but what a fool.'

'She has an awful lot to think about,' I said woodenly. I couldn't bear hearing Daisy described like this.

'Clever women are often very stupid.' A favourite theme of my mother's. 'It would have paid for *everything*: the roof, the barn, the new fences, and of course she longs to come back to India.'

'Wickam felt like the only real home we ever had,' I said. 'You must have felt it too.'

'I know you like her better than me,' Glory said suddenly. 'I don't blame you; she's better than me.'

'Mummy, no!' We gazed miserably at each other.

'Anyway, that's not important now. Let me finish what I wanted to say.' She hauled herself up and clutched my hand again. 'Daisy gave me something else that day you might be interested in.' She got up from the sofa, sat down in a chair and faced me.

Dramatic pause.

'A box of letters.'

'Love letters, bills, what?' I was sticky and hot again, and weary of her.

'Not love letters, not bills.' Another pause, pregnant with meaning.

'Letters from your father.' She licked her lips and stared at me. 'Enclosing money for you.'

'Money for *me*?'

'Yes.' I could hardly hear her now. 'Ever since you were born, he sent money every three months: enough to keep you ticking over. I made Daisy swear never to tell you, so she gave it to me as wages.'

My mind went perfectly blank.

'Why couldn't Daisy let me know? And why wages? I don't understand.'

'Because your father was a shit.' She spat the word out. 'Oh, don't look at me like that. He let me down badly, so I sent him away. I told him—'

'No, don't tell me! Let me guess...' I still felt surprisingly calm. 'He was dead to you.'

When I tried to get up, pain flared in my hand, and I felt dizzy.

'Why tell me now?' I said after an incredulous pause. 'What in hell is the point of that? God, I wish Daisy had told me, or even shown me the letters.'

'I told her we'd leave if she did, but that's not the point. The point is this.' She raised her head and looked at me. 'He lives in Ooty,' she said in a flat voice. 'Not far from here. Have you heard of it?'

I had, of course. Everyone knew about Ootacamund – snooty Ooty – the butt of many jokes about gin fizzes, polo, brigadiers, retired box wallahs.

'Are you sure?' I stared at her, feeling nothing: not thrilled, not grateful, not relieved. A big blank nothing. 'I don't understand.'

'He stayed on – it's a long story – and he stopped sending money ages ago.' I could almost feel her deflating, regretting this already. 'Don't expect a fairy tale,' she continued, voice squeezed. 'He'll be old and tired like me. Daisy gets the odd note from him; she says he doesn't have a bean.'

'Well that's wonderful news.' I was angrier than I'd been in a long time. She might have been talking about a distant friend's lost dog. 'Anything else I should know? I don't know, a twin I haven't met or something?'

'Not a thing,' she said with a defiant look. 'And no need to take that tone with me. I'm going to go and have a zizz. I've had enough of today. I just thought you'd want to know,' she added in a huffy voice, as if I was the one who was being unreasonable.

After she left, I felt so unhinged I wanted to scream. Instead, I sat and stared wide-eyed at nothing, and then I put a cushion over my head and fell into a strange sleep that was like falling into a deep hole. There were no vivid dreams; just dread and shock and suspicion, and a sense of swooning shame before my mind shorted out.

The slam of a door woke me up. When Anto came into the room, I put my good hand over his mouth.

'Have you spoken to my mother?' I couldn't bring myself to tell him about my possible father, in case this proved another version of the dead rabbit story; I couldn't risk the pain.

'Haven't seen her.' His words tumbled out. 'I wanted to see you first. How is your hand? I'm so sorry I was away. I won't do that again.'

'I'm fine.' I lifted my bandaged left arm to show him. 'No infection, healed well. Oh Lord.' I squeezed my eyes shut, feeling that if I started crying, I would never stop. 'Please don't be nice to me. It's not as if I wasn't warned.'

He kicked off his shoes and sat beside me on the sofa. 'It's my fault.'

'For what?'

'For leaving you alone.' He threaded his fingers in my hair. 'I don't know what I've been thinking when I have a wife and child at home.'

'No,' I said. 'That's not right. You have to do your work, but I've been such an idiot. I should have talked to you ages ago. Have you seen the damage?'

He put his finger on my lips to shush me.

'I went on my way here.'

'And?'

'It's a mess. There were some locals there, some of them looting. The Moonstone was always going to be controversial after Independence. One way or another, it would have happened. But here's the thing, Kit.' He put his hand on the top of my head, and I heard him sigh. 'I spoke to Appan. There will be an inquiry, and I think you'll have to give evidence.'

'Me?'

'Yes, and the rest of the staff, but you've attracted some attention, naturally.'

My mind began racing. 'What if they find out I've been delivering babies and I'm not fully qualified?'

Anto stared at me, thinking hard.

'I didn't lie to Dr A,' I said. 'We just got so busy. She did say she would write and get me accredited. I've never asked her to show me the papers, and my guess is, she's done nothing, because if she had, she would have shown them to me.

'Kittykutty, you're not on trial to me, and the inquiry will be far more concerned with who started the fire.'

'I know, but I went ahead without those assurances, and that was stupid. I should have said no.'

'Well you didn't.' He stroked my hair. 'And if all the unqualified women in India who delivered babies were tried, the jails would be overflowing.'

'But in their eyes, I'm a foreigner. They might make an example of me.'

'They might,' Anto said calmly. 'And if they do, we'll ask Appan for advice. He'll know exactly what to do.'

'If he finds out I'm unlicensed, he'll hit the roof.'

'Appan is a realist; he'll do what's necessary. Now, stop talking and show me your arm.'

He unwrapped the bandages and looked closely at the blisters, already crusted and healing. He asked what ointment I was putting on it, applied some more Germolene, bandaged me up again neatly, and looking at his glossy head bent over my arm, I thought, What have I done to deserve you?

A couple of days later, Anto and I were strolling on the waterfront after supper. It had rained fiercely for an hour or two that afternoon, and the sky was misty and grey.

Anchored across the water was a rusty old cargo ship with Arabic lettering on it. We were trying to imagine what it carried when I blurted out, 'Anto, while you were away, my mother told me the oddest thing.' I tried for a lightness of tone I didn't feel, because even saying it out loud threatened me. I'm not sure what frightened me most, my longing or my anger, but my family background, whether false or true, seemed so shallow, so threadbare, compared to the clever, dignified, solidly rooted Thekkedens'.

When I'd finished talking, he sat down on a bench. I could see him thinking, and I thought, I've put him off me now. I'm not good enough, and never will be. It was a terrible moment of darkness and insecurity.

At last he said, 'Are you angry with Daisy for not telling you?'

'No. I think she knew Glory might leave and never come back, and that would have upset her. Daisy knew I adored her, and the feeling was mutual: she once told me I was the daughter she never had.'

'Well I think it was brave of your mother to tell you after all this time,' Anto said.

'Really?'

'Really. She had so much to lose, and nothing to gain.'

'Well, possibly.' I wasn't convinced. 'But you always stick up for her anyway.' It was a feeble joke, because I was still shivering and felt in danger.

'I believe in mothers,' he said. 'Even imperfect ones. Don't forget I was without one for many years.'

'But yours isn't a nutcase. Don't you think the timing was odd?' I still needed him to feel some indignation on my behalf. 'I've been nagging her to tell me for years, and she waits until the home burns down.'

'Not so odd. She knew you could have died in the fire. Hence the high-speed dash in Appan's car.' I'd made him laugh earlier describing the driving gloves, the double-declutching. 'I would say it was a moment of truth.'

'Not something she has many of.' I was still angry. 'And that's another thing: how in the world do I know it's true?'

He gave me a long, considering look, and in it I saw my own hurt and confusion reflected, and thought, that's what love looks like.

'What did you feel,' he said at last, 'when you first heard about even the possibility of him?'

'Nothing,' I said. 'Not a thing.'

He thought for a bit. 'I understand that,' he said. 'That day we arrived at Mangalath, I felt the same. Too much noise, too much attention on me. I thought I wouldn't mind if I never saw them again. I was so used to living without them.'

'But at least you knew them.'

'Kit.' He put his arm around me. 'What are you most frightened of?'

'Everything, really.'

'That he'll be an axe murderer, a hopeless drunk, a wog-hating tea planter?'

'All of the above.' My laugh was a croak.

'Ooty's not far. We could get there in a day. I'll come, or you can take your mother, if that's what she wants.'

I told him there were more important things to do. A note, signed by Dr A, had been dropped through our door by a rickshaw boy that morning. *Urgent staff meeting. Moonstone. Two o'clock Thursday* was its brief message, and because I felt well enough – I could move my arm freely now, and a shiny pinkish skin had appeared over the original burn – I badly wanted to go. I felt a survivor's need to talk about what had happened, and I wanted to confirm with Dr A that I was officially accredited. If there was to be a government inquiry, I needed to prepare for it.

'And then what?' He was quietly persistent. 'The meeting won't take long, and this will work away at you if you don't act.'

I told him not to push me. I told him I would have to think about it. I told him not to discuss it with my mother. The whole idea of meeting my father after all this time filled me with a kind of fizzing panic. I needed time to think.

It was a shock seeing the Moonstone again. Everything about it foretold its end. Its splendid purple, red and yellow sign was a charred mess; the main building, shrouded in tarpaulins, stank of charcoal; the old fish tank we'd converted to keep prem babies in lay smashed and useless, alongside upturned beds and broken Petri dishes. Dr A held the meeting in the only serviceable room: a tin hut where we once stored garden equipment. Maya, myself, and two nurses had been invited.

Dr A, at her most grand and imperturbable, chaired the meeting from a wonky garden chair. When we were settled, she opened a large leather-bound book with a torn cover and bleached bindings and said in a flat voice, 'Fortunately, our account book survived the blaze.'

This surprised me, given its elusive nature before.

'So,' mirthless smile, 'let's not waste time on spilt milk talk. Nobody died thanks to quick action by our staff, but we are facing a big crisis.' I couldn't tell if she was praying or counting as her lips moved and her finger slid down a column of figures.

'I estimate,' she said at last, 'that to restock the home – chairs,

beds, boiler, floor coverings – will alone cost us in the vicinity of ...'
her eyes went blank as she did some quick sums, 'six thousand
rupees.' She sighed heavily. 'Training equipment will cost approxim-
ately one thousand rupees. Rebuilding of the wards, God knows.
I am waiting for quotations from our builder. It won't be cheap.'

Maya gave a small groan.

'Replanting the garden, five hundred rupees. New sign,' her voice
had sunk to an almost inaudible whisper, 'fans, benches ... So actually,' she closed the book, 'we must face the facts: all our plans, all
our hopes are dashed. Our work of the last five years is over.' She
looked directly at me and administered the final kick. 'And there
were people who didn't like you here.'

There was a moment of terrible stillness and calm in the room.
Maya took off her glasses and rubbed her eyes. Dr A scrutinised
the book again, as if the money might be hiding somewhere in its
pages. The nurses bowed their heads and sighed. Sweat broke out
along my hairline and down my spine; it was hot in that shed, and
someone's armpits were giving out a fruity pungency.

'The government will not provide this money,' Dr A said, 'so
there is only one solution: we must turn to Miss Daisy Barker and
her committee again.' I heard Maya murmur her agreement.

I did a quick calculation in my head. Based on Daisy's original
sums, it would take about twenty-one thousand rupees to get the
Moonstone up and running again. That was roughly three thousand
pounds: an awful lot of pots of jam, pickled onions and jumble
sales.

'She hasn't got that much money,' I said at last. 'She's actually
quite poor.'

Maya spoke now, in a thin, sarcastic voice, one I'd never heard
before. 'When she was here, I saw a photo album picture of her
house and her car. I would like to be poor like that.'

'I'm not sure you would.' I was stung by her tone. 'That house is
an albatross around her neck: it leaks, it's freezing cold, there were
snowdrifts up to the windows last winter. When you wash in the
morning, you break the ice on the water *inside* the house. And the
car, by the way, is held together with sticking plaster.'

Dr A looked at me blankly.

'Won't your new government help at all?' I said. 'They gave us
a grant.'

'No.' She seemed very sure about this. 'They will blame us for the fire.'

'Why would they blame us for that?' I asked.

Dr A closed her eyes. When she opened them again, she flashed me a warning look. 'This is for the police to decide, not us. Meeting is over; you can stay behind,' she said to me.

The nurses had looked so funereal during the meeting that it surprised me to hear a sudden burst of laughter as they stepped into the flat, bright sunshine. It seemed to emphasise the sudden gulf between us. In their world, suffering, the chaotic nature of life, was accepted as normal, and while I admired their resilience and could see that passivity in these circumstances might be a strength, it infuriated me too. I was also hurt by Maya's flash of hostility; she'd barely met my eye during the meeting.

Back in the hut, Dr A gave me a frowning, considering look.

'I wanted to ask you something,' she said. 'But not in front of the others. The police found rags in the garden soaked with paraffin. One of the rags had been torn from a dress. The label in the collar of the dress said "Tuttles". Is that an English company?'

'Yes, it is.'

'Do you have any clothes from there?'

'Yes.' I could feel my mouth going dry. 'A blue dress. But I didn't do it, you must know that.'

'It doesn't matter what I think,' she snapped. 'And there is more. There was a note left near the fire, when it had burned out. It said, "The Englishwoman is a spy." Do you have enemies here?'

My head was scrambling. 'I don't know. I don't think so,' I said. 'But you can't possibly believe I did it. Why would I? It makes no sense.'

'The police will interview you soon, so you must get your story straight.' She put her chin in her hand and looked at me, and I saw that lines were being drawn and teams picked, and I was not on hers.

'Could we open the door, please?' I asked. The heat was intolerable, and I felt light-headed. The hut smelled of coconut oil and female sweat, petrol from the mowing machine.

'No. Others will come, this is private.' Sweat trickled down the side of her face. 'Is there nothing else you want to say?'

'This may or may not be relevant,' I said at last. 'But about eighteen months ago, a boy followed me home from the Moonstone. I was taking a short cut through what was the English club gardens. He tried to touch me. When I fought him off, he spoke angrily about our work.'

Dr A remained motionless. Her strangely prominent eyes bulged as she continued to look at me.

'What did he look like?'

I drew a line along my lip. 'Thin moustache, about eighteen, I would say. Very skinny.'

'What angry thing did he say?' She picked up a pen and began to make notes.

'Oh, the usual. That I was a foreign woman teaching Indians, no right to be here, and so forth.'

'Why didn't you tell us before?'

'I should have, but I didn't want my husband to know and stop me working here. I thought you might not care, might even...' I stopped myself from saying *think the same way yourself*.

'I do care,' she said drily, making more notes in her book. It raced through my mind that I should tell her now about my meeting with Neeta Chacko, but I was in a dilemma: Neeta had pleaded with me, with tears in her eyes, not to reveal her as a source of information; plus Dr A had forbidden me to talk about Neeta again. This could prove a mousetrap with no cheese.

'There is one more important question to address. When you came here, I was told you were a fully qualified English midwife. If you are interviewed, the police will want to see your qualification papers. Do you have them?'

I felt a flush of heat race through my body. 'You know I don't, Dr Annakutty. I am a fully qualified nurse, but two deliveries shy of the full midwifery qualifications. I told you that on the first day I was here. You told me that when the time came, you'd apply to the government for full accreditation. I should have asked for that. I didn't. But why, if I didn't have it, did you let me deliver babies?'

She gave me her basilisk stare. I might as well not have spoken.

'I have no record of it.' She opened the leather accounts book and shook her head regretfully. 'I took you on in good faith. I'm not saying they will check you, but they might: the gorement now are very fussy about the correct paperwork.'

'This is not fair,' I said, 'and you know it.'

'Which is why,' she sailed on, 'I tried to suggest earlier that money from Daisy Barker would be a better way than trying to get money out of a gorement already squeezed. Do you understand that?'

I did. Blackmail: ugly word, ugly feeling.

I was down by the harbour half an hour later, sitting on the sea wall by myself, absorbing the shock of all this, when Maya sat down beside me. She placed at her feet the small canvas bag that usually held her lunch tiffin, and gave me a sideways conciliatory look, as if she wanted to make up.

'What did she say?' she asked. Her eyes darted nervously over my shoulder.

'I think I'm in trouble, Maya,' I said. 'But I don't really want to talk about it.' I wanted to tell her about the scrap of blue dress and the petrol. I wanted to tell her about the boy in the park, but I didn't know who to trust now or what to say.

'Dr Annakutty doesn't always put things well into words,' she said at last. 'But she has no family supporting her, and no children. She's given up everything for this, and she is a fine doctor.'

'I know.' I was almost too low to speak.

'You should see the home she lives in.' Maya peered at me.

'I doubt I will.'

'I liked working with you,' she added softly. 'You were a good nurse. We learned a lot.' The past tense saddened me more than I could say.

'So you think it will close, too?'

'Yes.' She scrabbled in her bag. 'Sorry.' She dabbed her eyes with a handkerchief.

When I thought of what it had cost Maya to work at the Moonstone – she'd told me once about nights spent studying under street lamps in Madras, the cramped dormitories, the beatings from her husband – my right foot kicked out in frustration, and sent her bag flying. A roll of bandages unfurled and a jar of Germolene cream shattered in the dirt.

'Don't do that,' I said. She was kneeling, trying to scoop some of the cream on to a shard of glass. 'I've got some at home. I'll give you a new jar.'

'Don't worry, ma'am.' She carefully wrapped the piece of glass in her handkerchief. 'I can use this. It's for my aunt. She's hurt her foot.'

'I'll bring it tomorrow,' I said. 'Don't cut yourself.'

'I won't be here,' she said. 'I'm coming next week, for the clean-up.' This was something we'd all agreed to do before the meeting broke up.

'What will you do after that?' I asked.

'I don't know.' She glanced at me. 'Stay home with my husband,' came the bleak reply. 'He doesn't want me to work again. He'll be glad.'

As I watched her small, upright figure walk towards the ferry that would take her home, I wanted to scream. I couldn't presume to understand the thoughts in her head, but I knew they would run along the lines of all this being part of God's plan for her, her punishment, even, for getting above herself, or for sins committed in a past life.

I admired the stoicism. I hated it too: the meek surrender of all that training and hope and energy. She was a fine midwife; India needed her. Why did it have to be so hard?

Chapter 43

On the day of the clean-up, I kissed Raffie goodbye, and told Kamalam what to give him for his lunch. I was about to leave for the Moonstone when my mother said, after a prolonged bout of coughing and an 'Oh blast!', 'Have you thought any more about what I told you?'

'About what?'

'About Ooty.' She clung to the veranda railings and took several shuddering breaths. She had dizzy spells now.

'Oh, Mummy,' I said. 'Isn't it all too much?' The very thought made me go blank with terror.

'I just thought it might be a nice break for you, darling,' she said sunnily. 'You've had a perfectly horrid time here recently, and it's nice and cool up there.'

Later, pushing Raffie through the park in his pram, I had a bitter conversation with her in my head. Oh, a nice break indeed, meeting a father I had never seen, whom she'd successfully buried till now. A lovely little holiday tracking him down and filling the black hole of his absence with . . . what? Shock? Embarrassment? Remorse? Or something worse and more damaging: bitter, bilious rage at how he'd successfully ignored us for years and years and years?

But another part of me had also leapt into life at the thought of meeting him, and as I walked, I ran a film of him in my head. He was tall, distinguished, wearing a tweed jacket and a kind smile. He was my twin, only older and a man. He was hugging me, saying father things: *My God, my little girl. My darling, after all these years.* Crying at the waste of us; hugging Raffie too. The grandson he never knew he had.

When Raffie's bellows interrupted this train of thought, I took him out of his pram and cuddled him. He was teething again, and unusually miserable and demanding. Any normal grandfather would hand him right back. That was what I said to myself, trying to make things normal again. I put him on my knee, grateful for the solid reality of his plump little body, now patting me on the lips, then wriggling to be let go, and I thought, this is my life now, and if I met my father and it all went wrong, it would set the cap on one of the worst months of my life. And yet... and yet...

All these thoughts were spiralling and somersaulting in my head when someone ran up behind me and made me jump.

'Miss Kit. Miss Kit.' It was Neeta Chacko, breathless and agitated.

'Please, I beg you to help me. They have got my boy Pavitran. They have taken him to the police station and beaten him severely there, and now he is in the jail on Tower Street. They came to our house this morning.'

'Neeta!' She'd been so petrified the last time we'd met, I'd assumed her plan was to scuttle back into hiding. Now she was trembling, and grey with fear.

'What did he do?'

'They say he torched the home. I know he didn't. They are blaming him for things he didn't do.'

She looked on the point of collapse. I led her to a bench and we sat down together. Raffie, worn out with teething problems, fell asleep in his pram.

Neeta resumed her story. 'Husband says to leave my son there, but if we do, he will die. He is a harmless boy who loves his animals, his family.'

'Who says he did it?'

Neeta shook her head violently; she either couldn't or didn't want to say.

'I know he didn't do it, Miss Kit.'

She was crying properly now, and in between gasps and sighs, the whole story tumbled out. She explained that she knew he didn't do it because the boy had had one of his spells this week, and they always left him very weak.

'What do you mean by spells?' I asked her.

Glancing around her, she said the dread word 'epilepsy', a condition I knew from Maya was sometimes mistaken here for possession by evil spirits.

'My husband tied him to the bed afterwards. I didn't want him to do this, but he says we must, and I obeyed him.'

She looked at me then and put both hands together in prayer. 'Please help me, madam. I have no one else to go to, and I need

267

money to get him out of the prison. I'll pay you back. I'll go away again after that.'

I looked at her, and then at Raffie, who was stirring again. I opened my bag and collected the few rupees I had there.

'This is all I've got,' I said, handing them to her. 'I'll ask my husband later, when he comes home. We'll do what we can, but we're not rich people.'

She snatched at the handful of notes. 'I'm going there now,' she said. 'If you come with me, it would help. They will see an English-woman and be ashamed of their wickedness.'

I doubted this very much, and given that I was under suspicion, I didn't want to go. But despite my reservations, I dropped Raffie off at home, then tagged along with her.

The jail on Tower Street was a twenty-minute walk from our house, a crumbling grey two-storey building. Looking up from the rubbish-strewn garden in front of it, I saw the glint of eyes peering down from behind barred windows. The reception area, a dungeon of a room, was lit by a naked bulb. It was hot, and stank of urine.

A large, frowning man was sitting in a kind of cage to the left of the entrance. I saw Neeta disappear into the cage, heard her sobs and pleading. Five minutes or so later she came out again, ashen-faced but with a shaky smile.

'It's done,' she said. She patted her empty purse. 'It was mistaken identity.'

I heard footsteps disappear down a dark corridor, the clank of a door, a man shouting. When Pavitran came out, unshaven and blink-ing, he flung himself at his mother and hugged her hard, mumbling and crying. When he looked up, I saw he had a small cut over his swollen right eye, but otherwise he seemed fine. Neeta said he had fitted again in jail – his trousers were wet in front and he looked bewildered.

During the interminable paperwork and rubber-stamping that followed, the boy looked on placidly like a well-trained domestic animal and held his mother's hand. Two hours after we had arrived, we were in the street again, in the merciless flat light of midday. Neeta was beaming and telling me, 'God is good.' I was not so sure. She told me never to tell anyone what I had witnessed that morning in the jail.

*

But I did tell Anto that night about Neeta's son, and about my worries concerning Dr A and her vague threats to me. It did not go well.

'I want you to stay away from the place, at least for the moment,' he said. 'It's too dangerous, anything could happen. If you won't do it for me, do it for Raffie's sake.'

'I don't want to stay away,' I said. 'I can just see you abandoning your work at the first sign of trouble.'

'I'm not talking about me. You're my wife.'

He didn't even bother to keep his voice down, as on and on the argument raged, and we were back where we'd been at Trivandrum during the monsoon, like two angry strangers who had collided in a freak accident.

'Do one thing for me if not for you,' he said, holding my hand when we had both calmed down. 'Take a holiday with your mother. Go and see your father. You know that's what you want to do really, and if you don't, you may regret it for ever.'

'A holiday!' I said. 'Hardly.' His words had made me feel instantly tearful, and I didn't want to cry. 'You're right, I do think about him a lot.' I was childishly grateful for his hand in mine. 'But what if it's not true? What if he's not there?' Anto stroked my hair.

'I think it's genuine: Kamalam told me your mother had hysterics when you were taken to the hospital. She thought you'd died.'

'She didn't tell me that.'

'Well she wouldn't, would she?' he said. 'But what if she's changed? What if she really wants to do this for you?'

I looked at him in disbelief – wasn't it my job to protect her?

Chapter 44

I marked the date we left for Ooty in my diary – *27 September 1950* – thinking that if we did find him, I'd want to remember it, and then I wrote *fat hope* and underlined it twice, just to keep me straight.

'So, darling, off we go,' my mother said brightly, as we stood on the platform at Mettupalayam waiting for the 7.10 train. The same words she'd spoken with the same upward inflection at the beginning of so many trips, to so many jobs, when I was young, as if to light the touchpaper on some splendid adventure.

And there was the usual fudging about any difficulties involved, because Ootacamund turned out to be much further away from Cochin than Glory had said. It had begun with a bone-crunching, boiling eight-hour drive to Mettupalayam to catch the Nilgiri Blue Mountain train. When we got to the station, Glory, wheezing and pale, sat with her head in her hands in the ladies' waiting room, looking so ill my heart began to thump.

'Are you sure you want to do this?' I asked. 'We could just go home.'

'Don't be stupid.' She gave me one of her famously frosty looks. 'We've bought our tickets; we have to go.'

Our bright blue train was tiny and narrow, like a toy train, with uncomfortably upright seats, but as we rose higher and higher, often at an agonisingly slow crawl, my mother seemed to revive. When she began to gasp out facts and figures about the sixteen tunnels we'd pass through, the nineteen bridges, I remembered the endless games of I Spy we'd once played to distract me from friends I was leaving behind, or a cat I'd loved, a house, another fading scene.

It was stifling hot in our carriage; if you put your cheek against the window, it stuck and burned. When Glory stopped talking suddenly and fell asleep, the journey took on a nightmarish quality for me: the darkness of the tunnels, the heat, my mother's gargling cough, the screeching of the train, the lurching views into steep ravines. Everything was unstable and chaotic and hot as hell.

When we stopped for refreshments at a tiny hillside station, I had to wake her. I felt a clutch of my heart looking down at her; she looked so dangerously breakable, all sharp angles and delicate surfaces. Her hands clasped her handbag for dear life.

On a station platform almost buried in misty trees, we were served fruit cake and tea by a winsome turbaned man who called out to her, 'Hello, Mrs Shakespeare,' which made us laugh. I was hungry enough to eat one of the curries another merchant offered, but Glory begged me not to. 'They're riddled with germs.'

'I don't think they are, Mamji,' I said to her, my facetious name for her. 'I find that many Indians are fastidiously clean, far cleaner than the Brits.'

Back on the train again, she became more and more silent and more and more fidgety as the train rose higher and higher. She took her purse out of her bag and counted all the coins very slowly. She lit a cigarette and stubbed it out. She strained to look through the window out on to the hills, where a light rain was falling on a coffee plantation so green it looked as if it was underwater. She studied her shoes, examining them from several angles. After the silence had stretched to about an hour, I took her hand.

'All right, Mummy?'

'Fine,' she said, in an echo of her brave young voice. 'This is rather fun, isn't it?' I thought about this for a while, not daring to speak. Had she really said *fun*?

The train shrieked through another of the sixteen tunnels, and when it came out, I said, 'So . . . will you tell me more about him before I meet him?' as gently as I could. If there was to be an emotional outburst, I hoped for both our sakes it would be in private.

Another dark tunnel; my mother's face flickered, went out. 'You'll have to ask him yourself,' she said. 'It was such a very long time ago.'

I could feel my veins going watery with alarm. I should never have come.

More tea was served, this time on the train, delicious.

'Orange pekoe,' the chai seller told us proudly. 'Special from here.'

'Your scar has healed nicely, darling,' my mother said, looking at my arm. 'That was a very nasty do, wasn't it?'

She sipped her tea.

'You know, I've been thinking.' She placed her cup elegantly on her saucer. 'Forgive me, but if the subject of your job comes up between you and your father, it might be cleverer to say you don't work.'

'Cleverer?'

'Wiser. Better.' Her tone implied she was talking to a halfwit. 'Why?'

'Do I really have to spell it out? If he's got any money, he—'

'For God's sake, no!' I was angry again. 'Is that why we're here?'

'Shush.' She looked around the carriage. In her world, there were spies everywhere. The old man sleeping opposite did not stir, and our other companions, a peaceful-looking Indian family, carried on handing out oily snacks to each other.

'Don't be ridiculous,' she said. 'Of course that's not why we're here, but there's something else I must say too. Now don't get angry, but he will probably be put off by what you do. Birthing native women, it's all very new. I've had to . . .' she brushed a crumb off her chest, 'to like it or lump it, but other people,' she finished more firmly, 'might see it differently. It will come as a shock to him.'

So we start with a lie, I thought bitterly, but did not say it. Another suspicion had grown during her speech. Had she even told him I was coming?

'Absolutely,' she said when I asked her. 'All the arrangements have been made, so don't go on about it now, darling.' Her lip had started to tremble. 'This is not easy for me either, you know.'

We were nearly there. I hardly dared talk now, so full up was I with a feeling I could neither name nor understand. Fear and longing, fury, a kind of breathless anticipation, a homesickness for something I'd never had. Through the carriage window, I saw plumes of mist hugging the trees, peaceful green fields that shimmered and disappeared.

'Look.' My mother raised a feeble hand at the church spire that suddenly appeared, an artificial lake, a row of bungalows, all misted in a faint drizzle. 'Snooty Ooty,' Anto had joked, 'frightfully like parts of Surrey.'

A uniformed conductor ran through the train. 'Ootacamund, Ootacamund. Train stops here.'

'Don't rush off.' Glory closed her eyes and panted lightly. 'I'm a little bit breathless. I hope the old lungs can take this altitude.'

Chapter 45

The Hotel Victoria was a modest mock-Tudor house at the end of a steep drive. When we got there, I asked for separate rooms, and said I'd pay for them out of money I'd earned. An unpleasant dig, I suppose, at Glory's earlier idea of using me as a sort of bargaining chip, but the truth was, I didn't trust myself to share a room with her – we were too vulnerable, too combustible.

My room, small, whitewashed, clean, had a pretty mother-of-pearl chair and a plain white bed. Nothing fancy – we couldn't afford it – and not in what my mother said was the posh part of town.

When the rain stopped, I looked through my window at terraces of shabby little houses, cows, small gardens. The steep hills, the mist around the trees, gave me a strange feeling of vertigo, as if I was dangling between one life and another.

There was a Bible on my bedside table, a carafe of water, a copy of the membership rules of the Ooty golf club, left by a previous guest. I put a photo of Anto and Raffie on top of the Bible, stared at them for a while. They at least felt solid and real: not something that could be changed at a whim, not a destination, nor a hope, but a reality like my lungs or my breath.

I could hear my mother next door: the clink of her glass, the trickle of water from a tap, the twang of bedsprings as she sat down. Her cough. I knew her habits so well: the miniature storm of activity in which she laid out her clothes at night – 'Hang them quickly before they wrinkle, no matter how tired you are.' The splashing of her face, at least fifteen times, to remove every bit of dirt. The eye mask that never worked in the fight against insomnia. The All-Bran for breakfast, 'just a smidgen' of milk. Cries of 'Gin and it!' at six o'clock.

As I child, I'd watched these rituals with the deepest fascination. The way she put her earrings on, sliced her bacon, closed her hand-bag with her beautifully manicured nails. And still she exerted an electrical pull, deeper than words, the circuit fixed during hundreds and thousands of moments shared, habits observed; the kindnesses, cruelties, disappointments added up whether I wanted them to or not.

And tomorrow – my stomach clenched at the very thought of it – I'd meet my father. Or so she said.

'He *said* he'd be here at four,' my mother said before we went to bed, in the same offhand voice she might use to confirm, let's say, a hair appointment. She was sitting in the visitors' room of the Victoria, clutching the key to her room. 'Does that suit you? I've been casing the joint,' she added, without waiting for an answer. 'I think this will be the best room to meet him in.'

This damp parlour on the ground floor had, with its unlit fire and mismatched chairs, all the atmosphere of a dentist's waiting room. I'd imagined we'd be going to his house, and said so. I was frightened of making a fool of myself in a public place, but I didn't tell her this.

'Oh, we can't do that, he's married. Didn't I tell you? I'm sure I did,' my mother said, as if announcing some minor change of plan.

'No, you didn't, actually. That might have been a helpful little clue.' I was so angry I could have struck her. The careless way she flung information, and how I had to snatch and scrabble for these snippets, like a refugee with a food parcel.

'Look, Mummy, I think I'm going to turn in early,' I said. I didn't trust myself to stay. 'Big day tomorrow.'

'Kit!' A kind of wail. A plea for sympathy and understanding as we looked into each other's eyes. 'Don't.'

Meaning what? Don't fuss about minor details? Don't hate me? Don't spoil this perfectly ordinary day? A nicer daughter might have amended, *but I love her anyway*, before she turned her lights out, but on that night, I hated her: her muddles, her lies, her attempts to be grand, her refusal to ever be straight with me.

Cough, cough, clink, clink. Around 3 p.m. the next day, I could hear my mother putting her face on. The fierce stare in the mirror, then cream, powder, lipstick, scent, several changes of wardrobe, if she had the breath for it now.

My own legs felt weak as I put on my stockings, washed my face, combed my hair, buttoned my second-best green dress. From time to time, I stared through the crack in the curtains at the hills he'd be driving through now. A solid knot of fear grew in my stomach, and then – hard to describe it, since it had never happened to me before – the knot of fear started to uncoil like a living creature, and I only just made it to the sink, where I vomited. No doubt about it, I was terrified, and there was still an hour to wait.

It was cold in the visitors' room by the time I got down there. Cold enough for your breath to show, and damp – it had rained off and on all morning. There were not enough logs in the brass bucket to keep the fire burning once it had died.

When I walked in, my father, a gaunt, hunched figure, was sitting near the fire. When he saw me, he rose from his chair with a great deal of difficulty. I had imagined him as a much younger man, someone tall and handsome, let's say like Ronald Colman, with a moustache and a mellifluous speaking voice. This man looked old for his sixty-five years – age being the one bit of information my mother had vouchsafed. He was wearing a worn tweed jacket, a too-big shirt that made his throat look shrivelled and gizzardy. He had thick white hair, and greeny-brown eyes – the same colour as mine. So peculiar: my father in the same room as me, both of us staring and trembling, a little like dogs about to start a fight.

'Where's Glory?' he asked.

'I don't know,' I said, pretty sure she was lying down in her room. 'I'm Kit.' When I held out my hand, he shook it in an absent-minded sort of way, and blinked at me several times.

'Is it short for anything?' he said at last.

'Kathryn,' I said. 'No one calls me that.' Thinking, surely you know my name! Or was I just referred to as the baby, or the child?

'Will she be long?' He glanced towards the door.

'I don't know.' And when he looked back, there was such longing, such fear, in his eyes, I understood in a flash that I was not the person he most wanted to see.

We sat down on opposite sides of the feebly burning fire. Rain on the window pane. I kept my eyes on my hands, which were folded in my lap, because what I felt most was a flooding sense of shame, as if I had no right to be there.

He patted his top pocket, took out a pipe and laid it on the arm of the chair. 'Is this allowed?'

'I don't know.' I sprang up, grateful for an excuse to leave. 'I'll ask the landlady. You'll need an ashtray.'

'It's all right,' he said. 'Don't go. I don't need it.'

'What's your name?' I said, when the pipe had returned to his pocket again. 'Your whole name.'

He looked at me warily. 'It's William,' he said in a quavering voice. 'William Villiers. Major Villiers when I was in the regiment.'

Kit Villiers. Quite a nice name, all things considered, but I was still in a weird state of shock as I said it to myself. No joy, no relief, still this feeling of profound embarrassment, and something like disappointment, because he was so obviously not pleased to see me.

'Is Glory ill?' he asked anxiously. 'Will she come?'

'I don't know.' My voice sounded wooden and strange. 'Do you want me to . . . ?' I stood up.

'No, no, no,' he said, watery eyes still trained on the door. 'I was . . . only if she wants to.'

Which she self-evidently didn't. My mother had many faults, but unpunctuality wasn't one of them. There were no signs of life from upstairs.

And so we sat there in a trap of her making, the minutes ticking away, the fire gone out by now, until he said, in a small, meek voice:

'So, what do you want to know?'

Chapter 46

The task suddenly felt enormous. I looked out of the window, at the grey mist, the trees, and wished I was anywhere but here.

'I am going to have to smoke, you know,' he said. 'Do you mind?'

I watched in a kind of stupor as he fumbled for his pipe, his baccy pouch, his box of matches, all of which he managed to drop as he got them out.

'The thing is,' I said, 'I don't know anything about you.'

He tamped his pipe with one stained finger. 'She must have said something?' He actually looked hurt.

'No ... not really. She told me a couple of weeks ago that you'd sent money for me, that was all.'

'Not about the letters?' His finger stopped. 'I wrote lots of them.'

'To me?'

'Not to you, to *her*.' His fingers clutched at the pipe.

'She said there was money in the letters, that's all.'

'Well bless my soul.' He squeezed his eyes shut and shook his head. A servant came in with tea. He asked for his black, and reached for it with a shaking hand. After another long silence, he said: 'I thought she'd told you.'

I took a sip of my tea. I didn't want to bully him, but I had the sense he was fading fast and I must choose my questions well, before he got too agitated or exhausted to answer them.

'How did you meet her?' I said.

There was a long silence. The teacup rattled in his hand. He looked at me, his eyes bright with tears.

'D'you think she'll come down? Today, I mean. It took me ages to get here.'

'I have no idea,' I said, my heart starting to pound. I tried again. 'Where did you meet?'

He gathered himself with a shuddering sigh, and his eyelids came down, as if he was picturing the whole scene on the back of them. 'I was a cavalry officer. Third Regiment,' he began. 'Family from Somerset. I'd never been out of England before.' He stopped abruptly, and sank a little further down in his chair, his eyes still tight shut.

'Go on,' I said. 'Please don't go to sleep.'

'I'm not asleep.' He puffed vigorously on his pipe to prove it. 'I'm frightened.'

'Of what?'

'Of saying too much. It got me into awful trouble last time.'

'Please.'

'I had a training accident.' Another agonising silence. 'Fell off a horse, broke my leg.'

'Look, do you mind if I take notes?' I said. It felt easier to regard him as a case history, rather than face the rising distress – or was it anger? – inside me.

'We met in Bombay. Please could you stop that?' He glanced at my pencil. 'I want to look at you when I say this.'

'It's all right. I'll stop. I understand.' I put the pencil down.

'Must we do this all at once?' he suddenly pleaded. 'I hardly know you.'

'Yes, we must.' I felt icy cold. 'We leave tomorrow, and...' I might as well have added, *and you're going to die, and I have to go on living.* That was what I felt.

'You have to understand how it was then,' he mumbled, pulling his jacket around him. 'Lots and lots of girls came out from England, lots of parties, but she was...' His eyes filled with fresh tears. 'Beautiful. What's the word?' He tapped his pipe on the side of his head. 'Radiant: very black hair, those cat's eyes, and she was very warm.' He clutched his chin in his hand. 'Oh dear, shouldn't bang on like this, but I think of her every day.'

'So you met in Bombay?'

'The regiment had its HQ in Poona. There was a ball there. I was halfway up the stairs, and when I looked down and saw her...' He fumbled for his handkerchief; I gave him mine.

'Go on.'

'Oh God,' he said. 'This is why she brought you here.'

'I don't know what you mean.'

'I loved her.' He ended in a gasp, and looked at the door again. 'We had, let me see,' he counted it on his gnarled fingers, 'four, five, six months of complete happiness together. You're very pretty, by the way, you remind me of her. She was working for the resident, some sort of secretary. When my leg had mended, we rode out together in the mornings. Spins on my motorbike. Everyone was very keen on her, so it was quite a feather in my cap. I adored her. She didn't tell you the rest?' He looked at me anxiously.

'No!'

His eyes shot open. I hadn't meant to shout, but I was panicked in case he stopped.

'I shouldn't tell you this, but I proposed to her on a beach, north of Bombay. Knew I would never be this happy again. Don't tell my wife that.' He gave me an almost waggish look. 'No proper ring, so I put a piece of seaweed around her finger, and she kissed it.' He closed his eyes in a grimacing way.

Don't cry, I thought, amazed to hear my mother had ever been this romantic.

'You must have heard the rest,' he pleaded. 'It's horrible. Awful.'

'No! Keep going.' I knew I had to ride him hard or he would stop.

His hands fluttered to his face. 'If I tell you this, you must swear to God you will never tell my wife.'

'I won't say a word.' Hard not to look incredulous; I didn't even know the bloody woman.

'I hate to think of it.' His eyes fixed on the floor. 'It makes me sick. Glory was so excited – the dress, the reception, everything; she'd talked of nothing else for months. She'd told all her friends at the residency. She was very popular there, great fun; women loved her as much as men. We set the date, October the seventeenth, St George's Cathedral, told my colonel, got the banns read, she was excited...' He tailed off.

'Could you speak up?'

'Sorry,' in a squeak. More dabbing with the handkerchief. 'I can't... I'm not...'

'What happened?' Anyone with an ounce of humanity might have stopped there, but I couldn't; I knew I would probably never see him again.

'She arrived at the cathedral. Our friends were inside; my chums were there with their ceremonial swords all ready. The happy couple run through them afterwards, you know. We'd practised it together.' He stopped again, and seemed to have difficulty swallowing.

'Then what?'

'I didn't come.' His voice almost inaudible.

'What do you mean?'

'My colonel came. She was standing in the vestry, and he told her the wedding was off. Another chap in the regiment, who'd had his eye on her, had guessed what I didn't know: that she was a chi chi girl.'

'A what?'

'Half-caste. Her father was an English railway worker. Mother a local girl. Never guessed. The pale skin, with powder on, was deceptive. The colonel said that marriage to a native was out of the question. If I did it, other chaps would follow suit, and where would that leave us? I was stupid enough to go along with it. He'd already written to my parents and told them what would happen. He knew they'd agree, and they did.'

He looked at me like a whipped dog.

'Worst thing I ever did,' he mumbled. He looked up. 'You must have known.'

'Only bits,' I said. 'None of this.'

'Can I say hello?' he asked. 'Please. I want to say I'm sorry.'

'I don't know. I doubt it. She's stubborn.'

'I know.' A wincing smile.

'So when did you learn about me?' I asked.

'When you were two years old. Daisy wrote. Glory had pneumonia and was in a very bad way.'

'Were you horrified?'

William Villiers looked at me. Old, bewildered. He began to weep. 'What a waste. What a waste,' he said when he could speak. 'I'd like to have known you.'

'Do you have other children?' I said.

'My wife couldn't have them. Listen.' He stared in a dazed kind of way at his watch. 'I'd be so grateful to you if you'd go up and see if Glory would come down. I can't stay much longer.'

I stood and went to the door. 'She's locked us in,' I said when it wouldn't budge.

He got up too and tried the handle. 'How bloody typical,' he said, and we laughed identically, a sort of mirthless snort.

'She'll be down,' I said, knowing that with her theatrical flair, it would be in her own sweet time. We sat down on the faded chintz chairs, one on either side of the tiny fire.

'Is there anything you want to know about me?' I said at last. 'You haven't asked a thing, you know.'

'I'm sorry.' He blinked and looked at me. 'I've worked it out. You're thirty years old now, correct?'

'Yes.' I put my hands over my eyes.

'Married?'

'Yes. To an Indian doctor. I met him in England just after the war. He was a postgraduate student at Oxford.' I felt a glow of reflected pride. 'He has a good job here.'

'Do you love him?'

'Yes.' For that moment, it felt as simple as that.

'Children?'

'One. Raffael, seventeen months old.'

He thought about this, sighing and shaking his head. 'Was Glory horrified?' he asked at last, gazing down at his battered brogues. 'You marrying an Indian?'

'She was. What happened with you can't have helped.'

'Any pictures of your nipper?' he asked softly. I showed him one of Raffie lying beside me on a hammock, laughing his head off; he'd just stolen my beads and was wearing them around his neck. He looked at it for a long time.

'What a balls-up,' he said at last.

When the door rattled, we both jumped. The servant who unlocked it said, 'Madam will come down in one hour,' and padded away.

'It's getting dark.' William got up creakily from the chair, scattering pipe and matches. 'I can't stay that long. I'm sorry, I would like to have asked you more.'

I might have reassured him, but the shock of hearing about my mother was followed by a spurt of anger. 'Does your wife know you're here?' I said.

'She thinks I'm playing golf.'

I shrank from the hangdog look that followed this admission. In some secret, stupid part of myself, I still wanted the Ronald Colman father – strong, invincible, perhaps in uniform – rather than some weed pretending to be on a golf course because he was frightened of his wife.

'Does she know anything about us?'

'No. It would be the death of me if she found out.'

'D'you mean she'd kill you?' Hard to keep the contempt out of my voice.

'She's highly strung; older than me. I couldn't do it now,' he told the floor.

'Not much more to be said, then.' I was hoping to wind things up now.

'No.'

I took a mental snapshot of him, trying to strip away the frayed tweeds, the air of defeat, and to see him as my mother must have done, except there wasn't much left. I noticed that his hands, fumbling for the doorknob, were long-fingered, like mine. Before he left the room, he turned. 'Please try and get her to see me. I could come back tomorrow at two.'

I gave him the number of the hotel. 'I can't promise anything,' I said. 'But if you telephone tonight, I'll let you know.'

We didn't kiss. We didn't even shake hands. At the last moment, we seemed to calcify, like Pompeii statues, into stone.

'I was a nurse in the war,' I told him quickly, full of an anger I could not name. 'In case you're interested.'

'A nurse in the war,' he repeated. 'That must have been grim. A brave girl, then.'

'Not really,' I said. 'Not at all. I'm training to be a midwife now.'

His expression did not change. 'Well done,' he said, and there our conversation ended. He was busy looking for the taxi that would shortly take him away.

Chapter 47

He phoned that night, but Glory refused to answer. She breakfasted alone, and as our train chuntered back down through the hills, she pretended to be asleep.

When he'd phoned again shortly before we left, I was sent in to bat to tell him she was not available. After a number of wordless sighs and gasps, William (how could I call him my father?) said, 'I have a message for her, and it is this. She did nothing wrong. She was . . .' I heard him gasp, 'a fine person who was jilted by a weak and wicked man.'

But she hadn't asked me a thing, and I, in the midst of my own hurt and confusion, was afraid to broach anything. As the train moved south, what I felt, watching her sleeping beside me, was a complicated mixture of sorrow and hurt.

I pictured her innocent and full of hope, standing in the vestry, a bunch of canna lilies in her arms. When the colonel arrives, she bends her slender neck towards him. She is listening to the news. It was unbearable to think of her enduring so much pain, and it explained so much: her rootlessness, her prickliness, the important outer armour of good shoes and manicures. *You can always tell a lady by her hands.* Her fundamental inability to find a path in life that she could believe in wholeheartedly. She'd never felt truly safe, or at home anywhere, and now it was probably too late.

'So what did you think of him?' she said, as the train approached Coonor. 'He is a perfect shit, isn't he?' Only the second time, as far as I could remember, that she'd sworn in front of me.

'I'm glad I know,' was all I could come up with for now. And then, 'He was full of regrets. He said you were beautiful; that he was older than you, that he should have known better.'

She gasped, and pulled in her mouth like a person with no teeth. She always hated crying in front of me.

'He wanted to see you.' A tear cut a line through her powder.

'Well he can't,' she said, a picture of childlike defiance as she dabbed her eyes. 'Can he? He should have thought of that a long time ago.'

When she fell asleep again, hunched against the window, I imagined the waiting congregation, their shuffles and concerned murmurs, faces craning around to look for her as the minutes ticked by. Had she sped away in a taxi, I wondered, or been driven to the colonel's house to take her dress off and sit in her underwear on some strange bed, wondering about the rest of her life?

She woke with a cough, and I gave her some of her favourite Fox's glacier mints from my handbag. In general, she disapproved of eating in public, but now she sucked one quite happily. In my mind, I saw her in pigtails at the orphanage in Orissa for half-caste girls.

'We didn't do too badly on our own, did we?' she said after she'd swallowed her sweet discreetly.

'No,' I said, 'not badly at all.' And then, because I meant it, 'I'm so sorry about what happened. It was brave of you to let me know.' I wanted to hold her hand, but that would have felt false. 'He said . . .' I watched her face anxiously; this felt like inching along a precipice. 'He would really like . . .'

'Don't say anything else. Please.' She was interrupted by another coughing fit. 'I don't want to know,' she said when it was finished.

When our train arrived at Mettupalayam, Anto was waiting on the platform. Raffie was in his arms, smiling his reckless three-tooth smile, stretching his podgy arms towards me, giving his grandma a kiss. The kiss seemed to perk her up. In the car on the way to Mangalath, where there was a family party, Raffie sat in the back on my mother's lap. She gave him one of her mints and allowed him to rearrange all the things in that normally sacred place, her handbag; even seemed to enjoy it, though she looked worryingly tired.

Amma came down the path to meet us. She took my mother's hand and led her into the house. 'You look dead on your feet, Glory,' she said. 'Take forty winks before lunch.'

My mother turned around, shot me a look of wild accusation. 'Does she know?' she whispered.

I shook my head. Anto had been primed to tell her we were simply having a little holiday, but Lord, I was weary of all these secrets.

I was surprised this time how glad I was to be back at Mangalath. With its familiar smells – furniture polish, cardamom, lemon grass – it felt like a solidly comforting presence. It was not rented; it would not be snatched away, but would go on for generation after generation being tended to like a demanding but much-loved relative, a little faded maybe, but still beautiful.

In the upstairs room that was now known as 'The Glory Room', I helped my mother into bed and put the cough mixture that Amma had given me on the table beside her. As I straightened her sheet, I heard voices in the rooms below, and felt the unfathomable comfort of knowing there were other human creatures around me, and that they would help with sympathy and respect. For this family, hospitality was an opportunity to show love, whatever your private feelings or passing irritations might be. It went beyond good manners, or strict codes of conduct, and I appreciated it fully maybe for the first time.

'She's asleep,' I whispered when Anto walked in.

He wiped my eyes, and when he put his arms around me, it felt like a transfusion of blood. We looked down at her together. Her face was waxy; her breath came in uneven sips. We moved away from the bed.

'She's dying, isn't she?' I said it out loud for the first time.

'We'll take care of her,' he said. 'It could take months; she's a tough old girl.' He was crying too.

'I hope you missed me,' I said, when we'd both stopped.

'Like mad. Raffie's not as much fun as you are. We were like two crusty old bachelors.'

'I haven't been much fun recently,' I said.

'You've had your reasons.' He looked guarded.

'Talking of which, any news from the home while I was away? Did Dr A try and contact me?'

'Kittykutty,' he said. 'Let's think about one thing at a time today. Your mother isn't well. You've just got home. Come here instead.'

He led me into a dim and shuttered guest room at the other end of the hall. He locked the door, unbuttoned my blouse, and we lay down on the bed. It was done at a speed that made us both gasp. A moment of pure animal comfort, deeper than any words he could have said.

'That's the best thing that's happened to me for days,' I told him as I was buttoning up my blouse again. I was smelling him – oh, delicious! – cinnamon and sweat, all of it.

'So how was Ooty?' he asked, propped up on one arm, serious again.

'Necessary,' I said at last.

'That sounds bad.'

'Not all bad,' I said. 'I'll tell you about it when we get home. Unless Mother seems too ill to travel. In which case, I'll stay here for a few days.'

'Good plan,' he said. And then, in his Barkis-is-willing voice, to make me laugh, 'My life. My old darling.'

'Sorry I have to go back to work,' he continued, serious again. 'I have a paper to prepare before Wednesday. Dr Sastry wants funding for a larger programme on epidemics.'

'It's all right,' I whispered, and meant it. 'As long as I know you're here.'

Chapter 48

Lunch felt comfortingly normal. Ponnamma banging on in a loud voice about how it was impossible to make a proper pilau without dribbling saffron-soaked milk over the rice and then slow-cooking it. Amma snapping that this was plainly nonsense, since she herself had been serving chicken pilaus for years without saffron milk and no one had complained. Raffie was sitting on Mariamma's lap having his toes tickled. Appan, home from trying a homicide case in Bombay that had kept him up for three nights, looked done in.

Amma pushed bowls of salad, date chutney and pappadams towards me. 'Eat up.' When I'd finished, Appan asked me gently, 'How is your mummy faring?'

'Exhausted,' I said. 'It was a long journey.'

He blundered on. 'But a nice holiday, hey?'

Happy shrieks from Raffie interrupted our conversation. Mariamma was counting his toes: '*Onneh, randeh, mooneh, naaleh, unche.*'

When Raffie's head began to droop, I lifted him out of Mariamma's arms, and was about to take him upstairs when Amma stopped me. 'Walk with me in the garden,' she said. 'Your mummy's asleep. Mariamma will take care of Raffie.'

We went down the path towards the summer house, dry leaves rustling under our feet, a small lizard dashing for safety. 'That husband of mine never rests,' Amma said as we passed Appan's bent head in his office. 'All my boys work too hard. By the way, he needs to speak to you later in his office. Do you know why?'

'No.'

'Something to do with your work, I think. He wouldn't say.' She picked a dead insect off my blouse. 'Sometimes he fusses.' Her face was as impassive as a smooth pond.

To the right of us, two farmhands were cutting down a large bunch of small green bananas. They stopped working as we passed, heads bowed in respect. When we stopped at a raised bed of earth behind the summer house, Amma pointed to three shrivelled orchids, freshly planted in coconut shells.

'Appan brought me two new invalids from Delhi: the brassia and the cymbidium. He'd kept them in his suitcase for two days, completely forgot them. He is so absent-minded, but sweet of him to try,' she added hastily. Didn't do to criticise husband in front of daughter-in-law. 'Orchids aren't like other flowers.' She prodded the soil gently with her forefinger. 'They have both man and woman inside them and make their own babies, and they're all different.

'This one,' a pink and green specimen trembled like a butterfly at her approach, 'I spray twice a day, otherwise she faints like a lady in a crinoline. This one,' she picked up a gorgeous yellow flower stippled with pink, 'was withered and sad when it first arrived. Now look at it. They all have different natures, too. It took me a long time to understand that. This one likes the air, this one lots of feeding and the shade.'

'My mother's dying,' I said. 'And I don't know what to do.'

'I know.' Amma put down the orchid and looked at me. 'I'm sorry for this.'

'I'm frightened. I should be used to death, after the war and everything, but I'm not.'

'Nothing prepares you for this,' she said. 'But don't be frightened. We'll do everything we can to see Mummy goes quietly.'

I squeezed my eyes shut, and when I opened them again, I saw a large bumblebee fly into the mouth of the yellow orchid and forage busily there.

'I'm glad you went to Ooty,' Amma said.

I took a step back. I felt too raw to discuss it, particularly with Amma, who generally discouraged family holidays that weren't to do with visiting other Thekkedens.

'Why are you glad?' I said.

She looked up at me. 'It was my idea. I was watching your mummy from exactly this place a few weeks ago. She thought she was alone. She was walking like this.' Amma mimed someone hugging themselves. 'I said, "Come and talk to me." She was very sad. We had a talk. She said at the end of it, "How can I make friends with my daughter again?"'

'She did?' I was trying not to sound too amazed.

Amma's head nodded from side to side. 'She told me she'd been a hopeless mother. I told her we all felt like that sometimes, and that occasionally I came out here and wished I was her.'

'Really!'

'Yes. She seems so free. I'm stuck here, very invisible sometimes.'

'You, invisible?' I said. 'Never. You're home to a lot of people.'

Amma made the tsskkk sound she made when she was trying to be modest. 'So, I asked her for more information about you.' She prodded the soil around the cymbidium. 'Said you never talked about your family, or your father, or anything like that, and when she told me you knew nothing about him, I was shocked. When she told me he lived in Ooty, I felt worse. Family secrets are horrible.' She stopped prodding the plant and gave me a beady look.

'So, tell me. How was it there?'

'Awful,' I said. 'I've never felt so confused in my life.'

'But at least you've seen him. That's a good thing, no?' She was looking at me dubiously.

'I don't know. Was it? She wouldn't see him at all; that was sad.'

'Why not?' Amma was shocked.

'I should let her tell her story... it explains a lot.' I felt the old sense of shame when I said this, of being slightly substandard goods. Part of a scam.

Amma sighed deeply. Beyond her, a heron was dipping its beak into the water.

'I was hard on you when you first came.' She didn't say this in a conciliatory way – in fact, having been kind about my mother, the old thread of irritation had returned to her voice. 'There were many things I didn't understand, and I was so nervous about Anto coming home.'

'With an English mongrel – I don't blame you.' We both smiled uneasily. 'Plus our timing was not impeccable.'

'He was so like Raffie when he was young,' she said, both wistful and aggrieved.

'In what way?'

'He was jolly. He talked to me all the time.' She grimaced, then suddenly grabbed my wrist.

'Oh God. You're late for Appan. Run, run, don't upset him, and don't tell him we've had this conversation.'

Appan was sitting under his green lamp when I walked in, desk piled with manila folders. His high cheekbones popped out when he smiled at me, and he put a pair of gold-rimmed spectacles on his nose. 'Sit down,' he said. 'This won't take long.'

He began to speak in his usual soft and confiding purr. He was off the following day, he said, to represent a scoundrel in Bangalore who had been embezzling money from his employer. It was a complicated case, but the important principle was to marshal what facts you had at your disposal and compress them in the simplest way possible.

'But I have something here,' he pulled out a folder, 'that has caused me a few sleepless nights lately. It concerns you.'

I could feel my palms growing clammy and my heart thumping. A clock struck slowly at the end of the room.

'Such a noisy thing.' Appan waited patiently for the chimes to stop. 'I bought it in Hatton Garden years and years ago . . .'

He pushed at his glasses, took a sheet of paper from the folder and sighed.

'A letter came while you were away, from my old friend Chief Medical Officer Kunju. He was the one who interviewed Anto when you first got back. He is a bigwig now in the new government, a pompous fellow who is trying to make a name for himself. A stickler for detail also.

'He wants to know,' Appan's lips moved silently as his pen skimmed down the paper, 'one: under whose authority you were working at the Matha Maria Moonstone Home for Expectant Mothers. Two: who finances the home? Are you a member of the British government? And he would like, in triplicate, copies of your nursing certificate and subsequent midwifery certificate.

'Those things you can deal with easily, I'm sure.' His pen stayed on the letter while he stared at me. 'What follows is more serious. He says that you helped to deliver a baby to a Mrs Nair. The baby subsequently died, and the woman, who is a fully trained lawyer, a clever one at that, has launched a formal complaint with the government regarding . . .' Appan squinted to read the exact words, 'substandard treatment received at the home. Dr Kunju wants to know if it is correct that you were the midwife present and thus directly responsible.'

'Mrs Nair? But that was over two years ago. She and the baby were healthy when they left us. Are you sure it was her?'

'Why would I make it up?' He glared at me, and I could hear a strange shrilling in my ears.

'As a member of your family, naturally I can't represent you,' Appan's words rolled on, 'and it may be nothing more than a warning shot across the bows, but now I have my own concerns. You see, I have been kept in the dark about your real work at the home.' A note of steely authority entered his voice, and for the first time, he scowled. 'No one actually told me you were a midwife. Not you, not Anto, not Amma. She told me something about a charity, a nun, a survey you were doing on local midwives. Why has everyone said these things to me if they weren't true?'

I took a deep breath and looked at him. When you married an Indian, I'd been told countless times, you married a whole family, and it seemed I was about to disgrace them all.

'Where shall I start?'

'Wherever you like.' A flash of anger in his voice.

'I am a fully qualified nurse. I did three years' training at St Thomas's Hospital in London. I worked there during the war, and then I studied midwifery at St Andrew's, also in London.'

'I was told you did charitable work.'

'I was told you wouldn't approve. That in your mind it would be a job for a lower-caste woman.'

'So are you ashamed of it?'

'Not at all. I'm proud of it. I should have told you that right at the beginning.'

He closed his eyes, thought for a while. 'I knew about the nursing, but not the rest. Does Anto know you're a midwife?'

'Of course.'

'This is a most unusual job in our family.' He frowned at me. 'I've never heard of such a thing. But if you can give me the relevant certificates, that part of the investigation at least can be rubber-stamped and ended.' He began to rub his hair irritably.

'I can't,' I said, staring down at the desk. 'Not exactly. I can give you my nursing certificate, but I'm not a fully qualified midwife and never pretended to be. I had to leave shortly before the end of my training.'

'Why?' His voice was sharp as a whip. I closed my eyes, and felt my stomach fall away.

'A birth went badly wrong while I was training... I wasn't sure I could do it again. It happened in London, the hospital was being bombed. After the war, I wanted to finish the training, but it didn't work out, so... I went home.'

'So no chance to get back on the horse again, metaphorically speaking.' A faint smile. 'Until this chance to practise on Indian babies.'

'That's completely unfair. They were short-staffed at the Moonstone. I was asked to help, and bit by bit my responsibilities increased. Nothing was hidden from Dr Annakutty, the director of the home, but it's possible she'll deny it now.'

Appan was writing busily. 'And so you performed a delivery on Mrs Nair, in spite of not being fully qualified.'

'She asked for me particularly. Dr Annakutty was in the building at the time.'

'Did it not occur to you that Dr Annakutty knew the dangers of helping such a woman if things should go wrong? A lawyer closely connected to the new government.'

'She is a fine and experienced obstetrician.'

'Yet she let you do it.' His expression was half crazed, astounded by my naivety. 'Because these facts, twisted, will sound like a classic case of colonial overconfidence.'

'Appan,' I appealed to him. 'What do you think will happen?'

'I can't predict.' He closed the folder and looked at me. 'Too much is changing at the moment, and I'm worried. I've met this woman once or twice in court; she is very sharp. My short-term plan is to telephone an old friend of mine, Suresh Patel, and see if he can represent you. He's a fairly decent lawyer. I must also forbid you to discuss all this with anyone else in this house: not Amma, not your mother, not Mariamma. They don't need to know.

'As for you,' his expression softened a little, 'we must wait and pray.'

Chapter 49

I hardly slept for the next two nights thinking of the jail in Cochin – the broken lights, the cracked concrete walls stinking of pee and Dettol.

If Appan was right and they made an example of me, I would lose everything: my work, my reputation, Anto, Raffie, the honour of the family.

I was also baffled and horrified to think that Mrs Nair's baby had died, when it had left us so bonny and thriving, and her so happy. And these clammy, sleepless nights brought me face to face with every bad thing about me: my arrogance, my stupidity, my cowardice in baling out of the midwifery course.

A judge and jury would want clear facts about the home – figures, accounts books, official approvals – and mine were shot through with holes and inconsistencies. Straining to remember conversations Daisy and I had had at Wickam Farm, my brain felt too numbed to recall them with any confidence. The home had been set up in pre-Independence days, a time when proof of Englishness was pretty much all you needed to be a do-gooder in this country and be applauded for it. Now, the law would see me as a half-qualified incompetent busybody, and the fire would further complicate things.

I poured my heart out to Anto. We were back in Fort Cochin, and sat up late on the veranda talking long after Raffie had gone to bed. I reminded him of his warning during that awful row in Trivandrum: 'Kill one baby and they'll kill you.'

'Let's hope you weren't right,' I said. 'But you know, I didn't lie about my qualifications. I thought I'd never have the guts to do another delivery again.' He tightened his clasp on my hand, and waited a while in case there was more I wanted to say.

'Do you know something?' He shifted on the swing and sat closer. 'You've never really told me what happened that night.'

'I don't know if I can.'

'You don't have to.' After a long silence, he peeled my hands away from my face and looked at me dubiously, not sure he wanted to hear this either.

I started slowly, with a feeling of creeping shame, but then it all came out in a rush, because it was, I suppose, the confession I needed.

'It was a September evening. My first attempt at the training and I was happy as a clam: the last part of our exams was over and I'd done well, and I was one month shy of being fully qualified. I had no one apart from Daisy to tell the good news to, because, well, you know my mother would hardly be throwing her hat in the air. So I was cycling over Westminster Bridge with a bottle of gin in my basket, and a cake, so I could celebrate with Josie, who was working at Thomas's.

'Josie sneaked me into her room. She'd been on duty for hours. I was pooped too, so we lay on her bed and drank some gin – not a lot, a glass or two – and were just going off to sleep when there was an air raid, and the hospital was full of casualties, and then...'

'Kitty, you're shaking.' Anto put his arm more tightly around me.

'About midnight, there was a pounding on the door. A young girl had been found in a bus shelter on Lambeth Road, just behind the hospital. She'd gone into labour and was petrified, what with the bomb and the fires, so they'd brought her in. There was no room for her, so they made up a bed in the corridor. A friend of Josie's who knew I was studying midwifery asked me to help out. All the other nurses were busy; no one questioned it. They just told me to get on with it. It was the war: policemen, firemen were delivering babies. So I did. It was very frightening, with the roof shaking and the lights going out, but it was a fairly straightforward delivery, and I was pretty pleased with myself.

'We put the baby, it was a boy, in an air raid helmet in case the roof fell on his head, but then... I don't know what happened, honestly I don't.' I'd started to sweat just thinking of it. 'The baby made this awful sound, like a crow or something, and then it began to fit, and I didn't know what to do. The thing about being a good midwife is being able to react to change very quickly, but also to keep calm, and I just didn't.

'I'll never know exactly what I did wrong: maybe I didn't clear his lungs properly, or perhaps if I hadn't had the gin I would have been more alert, but he was frothing at the mouth, and then he started choking on his tongue, and the mother was shouting: "Do something! Do something!" She was completely mad with panic. And I didn't, or at least I tried, but not the right thing. I ran to find someone and got lost in the corridors looking for help. When I came back, the baby was dead.' I had the usual clear memory, as I said this: the mother howling, the baby in the tin helmet in her arms, its lips turning blue.

'Oh Kittykutty,' Anto said when I had finished. 'Why didn't you tell me before?' He stroked my hair. 'Why are you so sure it was your fault? It could have been a congenital heart problem, all kinds of things.'

'I couldn't bear to; I felt so disgustingly stupid. I've never properly forgiven myself for going to a party and ending up killing a baby. Don't tell me it wasn't my fault. I was there, and I panicked, and maybe if I hadn't had the gin ... and I've only just thought of this, but although I'd delivered lots of babies by then, it was always under supervision. I was no good in an emergency – knowledge but no experience, the very opposite of the midwives we're training. Any one of them would probably have known what to do.'

It was all back in my mind now: the wash of green light; the blackout curtain, the smothered cry the girl had made as she'd tried herself to bring the baby back to life.

'And now I've done it again,' I told him. 'Appan said the lawyer's baby died. It's hard to believe because it was such a good delivery for us both, but maybe I did do something wrong.'

'Kitty.' He took both my hands in his. 'The first thing to do is to go and talk to Dr Annakutty. Thanks to your work, they will have the proper records now.'

'No we don't! That's the point. The records were burned in the fire.'

He bit his lip. 'Well, Dr A is a well-respected woman. She'll vouch for you.'

'That's the other thing.' I stared at him. 'The last time I spoke to her, she swore she had no idea I wasn't qualified.'

'What!' Anto's grip on my hand tightened. 'She can't do that.'

'You don't know her, Anto. She can be a number one bitch. If it goes to court, she's quite likely to use me as a scapegoat: a baby has died, the mother's a lawyer. I didn't have the right qualifications. I'm her perfect get-out-of-jail card.'

'The other nurses?'

'I can't count on it. They're all too new, and terrified of her.'

'Maya?'

'No, she's a straw in the wind whenever Dr A's around, not that I blame her for that.'

'We'll think of something.' He was sounding a little desperate himself.

There was a long and thoughtful pause.

'Going back to what you said earlier. Do you imagine that there is a single nurse or doctor in the world who doesn't feel they have blood on their hands? We're human, we make mistakes. You did the best you could. The alternative that night was what? To say to that girl in labour: "Sorry, love, can't help: I'm not fully qualified, deliver your own baby." Conscience absolved, girl left screaming. That, in my opinion, would have been the greater sin.'

'Ah, sin,' I said. They'd wrapped the baby in a towel and taken it away. 'I wish I were a Catholic sometimes, and could just empty it all away.' Like the rubbish on a Monday, I thought.

'It doesn't work like that,' he said. 'I wish it did.'

Then Raffie woke up crying. He was always unsettled when he came home from Mangalath, his favourite place in the world. Anto ran upstairs and brought him down. Raffie sat on his lap, rubbing his fists in his eyes and looking blearily around.

'Oh, Anto.' The two of them seemed suddenly inexpressibly dear. 'What if I do go to jail?'

'You won't,' he said, but I saw the strain on his face. 'Take your little worry bead and give him a hug.' He handed Raffie over. I tried not to squeeze him too hard, as I prayed to a God I wasn't sure I believed in.

Chapter 50

When the monsoon came the following week, it was almost a relief to be imprisoned inside the house. But when the rains stopped, I couldn't sit still. I left Raffie with Kamalam, took a taxi to Allappuzha and boarded the backwater ferry to Champakulam, Maya's village, the place I'd set out to with such excitement over two years ago.

If it hadn't been for the giant knot in my stomach, it would have been a lovely trip. An earlier shower of rain had left a fine net of diamonds on the hibiscus and palm trees; the rice paddies on either side of our boat were intensely green.

When we arrived at the village, I went to St Mary's, the Christian church where we'd done the first midwife class. The streets leading there were puddled and potholed, and the whole place looked even scruffier than I remembered it, with debris from the monsoon washed up on its shores.

The church was empty. I sat near a statue of the Virgin Mary. The wooden snake wound around it had a malevolent look, as if to say: *I could strike you at any time, and you would never know.* I didn't pray to God. I prayed to Dr A, and to Maya. Please help me. You're my only chance.

An old man was sweeping up leaves outside the church. I showed him a piece of paper with Maya's name and address on it. He put down his brush, and pointed very precisely left and right in the direction of a scattering of small houses. I thought I'd followed his directions accurately, but the alleyways got narrower and narrower, and one dusty lane hung with washing looked pretty much like another. I was sweating and flustered by the time I reached a bicycle shop and showed my piece of paper again. A man covered in axle grease led me to a flimsy door, which opened when I knocked on it.

If it hadn't been for her familiar gap-toothed smile, I wouldn't have recognised her, she looked so small and squashed.

'Maya,' I said. 'I'm sorry to bother you at home, but I'm in trouble. I need your help.'

'You mustn't stay, ma'am,' she said with a panicked glance over my shoulder. 'My husband will be back soon; he's at the toddy shop.'

But she let me in anyway. I was shocked at how small and squalid the house was when Maya was so meticulous at work. The sitting room, with its broken chair and two stained beds in the corner, was so low-ceilinged, I could barely stand up. It stank of curry.

'My son is here,' Maya said, looking anxiously at me.

The grim-faced boy who used to deliver her to the home got up from a charpoi in a dark corner of the room. There was a large gauze bandage on his left arm. He snarled something to Maya and shot out the back.

'He is shy with visitors,' Maya said, looking crushed and ashamed.

'I won't stay long,' I assured her. 'But Maya, please listen.' I told her in a rush about the lawyer, the possible tribunal. I could hear her breathing heavily while I spoke. Twice she went to the door and peered out into the street.

'What can I do?' she asked when I had finished. It wasn't an offer of help; more a passive acknowledgement that the universe was not designed to give us what we wanted. 'I have no job now. Everything has ended for me also.'

'Do you miss it?' I said.

'No.' The eyes turned towards me were bruised and weary. 'It's too hard. My husband and son don't like it.' I heard, out in the street, a shout, the whirr of a bicycle wheel going by. She jumped up and stood at the door, desperate for me to leave. 'Sorry, Miss Kit.'

I stood up to reassure her.

'Maya,' I said, 'if there's a tribunal, will you speak up for me?'

'What is a tribunal, ma'am?'

'Three government men will ask us questions about the home and the work we did there. You won't have to say anything that isn't true.' Maya looked dubious. 'Our aim was to make things better, you said that yourself.' I didn't like the note of whiny self-justification in my voice, but what could I do?

She shook her head, twisted her hands. The boy began calling from the back of the house, a monotonous roar like a trapped calf, with a hint of threat in it. A scum of rice had boiled over on the stove and was dripping down the side of the saucepan.

'Sorry, madam.' Maya could no longer disguise her panic. 'I can't help.'

Before she closed the door behind me, she gave a small, sad wave. It felt like the final goodbye to the joyful, practical, funny colleague she'd grown into at the Moonstone. I feared for her, and I feared for myself. I'd lost my first ally.

I went to the library on Lily Street to see if I could find any legal books on the minimum statutory requirements for a midwife in India. I also wanted to check if there was anything in writing about the origins of the Moonstone, hoping it might mention the collaboration with Daisy Barker, the Oxford charity and the Indian midwives they'd worked with.

In a mood of increasing despair, I read through back issues of *The Hindu* in the hope of seeing some stray announcement, but all I found in the social columns were memsahibs cutting tapes or opening flower shows, long-gone polo and cricket matches. The library, like so many Indian institutions, was in a state of hectic renewal.

Next, I plucked up courage to go and see Dr Annakutty. It was three weeks since our last meeting, and she already had a new job as a locum at a small government-sponsored clinic on the edge of town. As grand and impersonal as ever, she ushered me into a sparsely furnished cubicle on the first floor of a flat-roofed modern-looking building. She told me that this new job of hers was a logical progression from the home. In the past, she'd stressed that Indian women liked female midwives because their husbands didn't want another man looking at them; now she sang a different tune: 'We have twenty-five beds here, solely for the women, and we have gorement funding to pay them a little reward when they use our facilities. The doctors here are very kind to the women; they don't want them to be frightened of them. It's important for us to wean ourselves from US and English medics.'

When I told her my problem, she said immediately, 'Sorry, can't help. I thought from Miss Barker you were qualified, and we're busy here now.' She couldn't wait to get rid of me; every fibre of every nerve ending in her face and posture said *case closed*, and there was nothing I could do.

Struggling through the heat on the way home, trying to put the pieces of this puzzle together, I realised that deep down, I didn't blame either of them particularly. Maya was poor and desperate:

why put her life on the line for an Englishwoman who must seem to her to have been already magnificently rewarded by the world?

As for Dr A, she was ambitious, and had already paid a high price for her right to work. Why risk that for a half-qualified foreigner?

To cheer myself up, I bought treats from the *barfi* man near the beach by the fish market. A twist of brightly coloured sweets for Raffie, a sesame ball for me.

I walked the last few blocks home slowly. I put the sweets in my left hand and opened the door.

'Anto,' I said, seeing him there. 'You're home early.'

'Yes.' He was trying to smile.

He had a manila envelope in his hand with a government stamp in the corner. 'This came for you,' he said. His voice sounded unusually trembly. 'I opened it. They've set the date.'

The one relief on the morning of the tribunal was that Glory was still convalescing at Mangalath. With any luck, she need never know about this, and neither did Amma and the rest of the family.

I woke with a sense of dread so strong I could not eat, and took a walk to the home. Most of the old building had been pulled down, and the trees were still blackened. I tried to summon up the good times – the prayers and dancing in the mornings; the gales of laughter as Rosamma produced the plastic baby from her sari; the cries of the newborns from the ward – but standing in the ruined garden, my mood was bleak.

I was about to leave when I heard a sound from the direction of the tin hut, a soft scraping, a murmur of voices. Behind the hibiscus bush I saw two local women sitting on their haunches tending a row of dusty geraniums that had somehow escaped the fire.

One of them I recognised from the clinic: a victim of violent intercourse that had left her bleeding. I'd stitched her up as tidily and gently as I could during a long and tearful session that had lasted an hour. Nurses had brought her chai and a meal. She looked shy when she saw me now, and covered her face with the end of her sari. At her feet was a jam jar of water. Her friend had brought a rusty trowel. To the right of the hibiscus, they'd erected a tiny shrine with bricks scavenged from the ruined building, a plastic goddess inside. The woman we'd treated sprang to her feet, about to run, before her friend stopped her.

'We are here to keep the garden going,' she announced boldly. 'This is a nice place.'

That was all, but it meant a lot on a morning full of dread for me.

Anto was pale, and we barely spoke as he drove me to the government hospital on Fort Street. When we parted, he told me not to worry – whatever happened today, the tribunal would almost certainly only be sabre-rattling, and I was not alone. I hardly heard a word, I was so nervous. Inside the hospital, I was taken in a clanking lift up to a sterile room on the fourth floor.

Three frowning men looked up as I entered. They sat behind a long table in the middle of the room. The empty chair facing them was mine. A youngish man wearing a turban and a dark Western suit stood up. His eyes were watchful, hard.

'Madam,' he said, 'we are convened today by the Medical Council of India to enquire into the specific matter of the Matha Maria Moonstone Home for Expectant Mothers and your role in it. My name is Dr Diwan; these are your other interlocutors. To my right' – a busily scribbling man looked up – 'Dr Vijay Masudi. To my left, Dr Mohanty. All of us are elected officials of the new Indian government. We have a high level of expertise and experience.'

The fluorescent light above my head was so bright, his face became a blur.

Dr Diwan opened a bulging green file with a fresh piece of paper on top.

'Your first birth name, please.'

'Kathryn.' Kathryn, my punishment name, only used, by my mother or a headmistress, in times of trouble.

'Surname?' The pen scratched on.

'Smallwood.' Safer to give my maiden name.

'From what country you are hailing?'

'England.'

'Address?'

Wickam Farm seemed the logical choice for this; I could barely remember any other.

'Can we see your certification to practise medicine?'

'Here.' I tried to smile confidently as I handed it over, but there was a strange wobble in my lip and my mouth was dry. Dr Diwan took the certificate, read it with forensic concentration, held it up to the light as if it were a dud pound note, passed it to his colleagues, then handed it back to me.

'Midwifery certificate?' His expression did not change.

'I don't have one.'

He narrowed his eyes, poked his tongue into his cheek.

'You don't have one? How is this possible?' Concerned glances at his colleagues. He went through his papers again. 'You see,' he scratched his forehead, 'it is written here that you have been delivering babies at the Matha Maria Moonstone Home for Expectant Mothers.'

'I was.'

'Under supervision?'

'Almost always.' I heard the rumble of trolley wheels above my head, somebody crying. I took a deep breath. 'There were one or two occasions, when we got very busy, when I was the person in charge.'

'Dr Annakutty was the head of your home.' Dr Diwan brandished a letter in her handwriting. 'Was she aware of your lack of qualifications?' He did not wait for my reply, but read from the letter in a voice that drilled through my eardrums.

'"All I was told by Miss Daisy Barker, one of the trustees of the charitable trust operating from Oxfordshire, was that she was sending a high-quality nurse to us. I worked with her in good faith. At no time did I check her qualifications, because I was assured that the British government had done so."' It was hardly a rousing endorsement.

'So here we get to the nub of the thing.' Dr Diwan's eyelids drooped. He knotted his fingers and stared at me directly. 'Who runs this charity, and under what authority? We have no proper record of it on our books. We have correct permissions for a number of charities from overseas, but you're not here.'

I kept my voice as steady as I could. 'Are you sure there is no record? Our founder, Daisy Barker, worked in India for years before Independence: first in a Bombay orphanage, then setting up this home.'

He opened his hands wider. 'Miss Smallwood, I can't conjure facts from nowhere. Was this Miss Barker a qualified doctor?'

I stared at him. 'No.'

'Under whose authority was she here?'

'I don't know.'

The three men exchanged incredulous looks. Dr Masudi shook his head and sucked his teeth.

'Madam,' Dr Diwan said at last, 'do you not think it an act of extreme presumption for two Englishwomen to come to our country with no clear understanding of our religion, or proper medical qualifications, and instruct our women in childbirth? How would you feel if the situation was reversed?'

'It wasn't like that.' A mouse squeak of desperation in my voice. 'Our aim was to work alongside Indian midwives to learn from them too.'

'And were the midwives glad for this?' rumbled Dr Mohanty.

'Some were,' I said. 'Some wanted the old ways.'

'Who started the fire?' asked the hitherto silent Dr Masudi with a penetrating look.

'I don't know,' I said, startled by this sudden detour.

'But you were there first.' He cleared his throat noisily.

'Was I? I honestly don't know.'

'One of the nurses said you had the key. Is that true?'

'No.'

When he ignored this, I saw in his eye the frozen look of a cat about to pounce. 'What was the purpose of the fire?' he asked softly.

'I don't understand the question.'

'For money? To cover up false records and end an already hot potato: the death of Mrs Nair's baby?'

'This is madness. It makes no sense.'

'Like much of what you've said to us today.' Dr Diwan blew his nose loudly.

'Don't bully me.' I was suddenly furious with the frowning men. 'Many women here die horrible deaths because nobody gives a damn about them.'

'Watch your tongue, madam,' Dr Diwan almost shouted. 'Don't you point your finger at me.'

'It was your midwives who told us about women with sticks in their cervixes trying to abort babies; about thirteen-year-old girls ripped apart in childbirth. I didn't make this up.'

I was determined not to cry. 'So we tried to discover the best in each other, and now it's gone.'

Silence in the room. I've done it now, I thought. They'll lock me up – the madwoman in contempt of court. Instead, Dr Diwan suddenly looked intensely bored. He licked his finger, rustled through his papers, then gave a deep sigh.

'Midwife certificate is not here,' he repeated like an automaton. 'So don't make any arrangements to leave the country. We know where you live, and we know your husband's family. If you thought you could hide that, you were wrong.'

'I won't be leaving. I love this country.'

He gave another snort sniff; he was not impressed.

'All I can repeat is not to leave until we have decided. In the meantime, my strong view is that the home must be permanently closed.'

Chapter 51

'You said *what*?' I was sitting on the floor in front of Anto, who was stroking the nape of my neck where the muscles stood out like organ stops.

'I was stupid. I got angry – the stupidest thing possible.' I moved his hand to the worst spot. 'God knows what will happen now.'

'I think they are trying to bully and intimidate you. Some other drama will soon obsess them. A bribe may settle it.'

'Anto, I can't believe you said that.'

'Your greatest danger is the woman lawyer.' He was thinking hard. 'If she decides to take you to court, the newspapers will hear about it, and then they'll have to do something.'

He was right, of course. She was highly trained, she was angry and hurt; she could put me in jail. What kept me awake for the next two nights was the thought that if I put my hand directly into this wasps' nest, I might make everything worse and seal my fate. But if I'd messed this one up, and the baby's death was my fault, maybe my career as a midwife should end anyway: the final proof that I wasn't up to it.

It wasn't hard to track her down, there not being many female lawyers in Fort Cochin. She lived in Quiros Street, a few blocks away from us. Her ground-floor flat, one of three in the house, was so small, the veranda was piled high with cooking pots and suitcases, a cot and a baby bath.

If she was surprised to see me at the door, she didn't show it. She stood there, very tiny, very poised, very neat, with oiled black hair and wearing a blue salwar kameez.

'I'm so sorry, Mrs Nair,' I said. 'I would have come earlier, but I've only just heard.'

'So you haven't forgotten me?' she asked when she could speak.

'Of course not.'

She beckoned me inside a tiny, dimly lit sitting room that looked like an office, with a large typewriter on the desk and bookshelves piled high with legal books.

'Sit down, please.' She moved a manila folder from the battered sofa. 'I'm surprised to see you.'

'I came because I heard about your baby. Do you mind talking about him?' I said, very tentatively.

'No,' Mrs Nair said. 'And please call me Saraswati.' She leaned forward, her brow creased with concentration. 'I wanted to see you,' she said faintly at last. 'To talk about Sanje.'

'He was beautiful,' I said, remembering his black hair, his little fists punching the air. I watched her anxiously. How much could she take?

'Nobody really knew him but you and my husband,' she said. 'And now my husband has gone too.' Close up, I saw that she'd been crying before I came.

'Your husband's gone?' Still feeling my way gingerly, sure that the anger would come soon.

'To my mother-in-law's house.'

'Will he come back?'

'No. Can I tell you the story?' She said this eagerly, hopefully, as if she'd been waiting for me to come.

'Of course.'

'Well...' She swallowed hard. 'We tried for a very long time for this baby. I had my daughter, twenty years ago, and then nothing. Everyone was so happy when we got Sanje, but now his family blame me for being too old and for working too hard before the delivery.' She shot me a look of wild distress and clutched her handkerchief. 'There was so much work after Independence, and I did work extra hours, but tell me honestly, was it my fault?'

'That's extremely unlikely,' I said as gently as I could. 'We have women coming in after working incredible hours in the paddy fields, or hauling bricks. Tell me what you think happened.'

She took a deep, jagged breath.

'I was frightened when I came to you, but the Moonstone had a good reputation and I knew English doctors were there.' I winced at this. 'You were all kind to me and I thought my delivery was good.'

'It was,' I said. 'You were calm, you were ...' 'excited' seemed too cruel, 'well prepared, your body strong. You didn't seem in the least tired. Most of the women we see are exhausted; some are very ill-nourished too.'

She grabbed my hand. I kept going.

'I can see Sanje's head, his beautiful black hair, and you held him in your arms. You were so happy.' I couldn't go on. There were no words of consolation to cover this loss.

'He died two weeks after I brought him home,' she whispered, glancing towards the veranda, as if he might suddenly and miraculously appear. 'He was feeding well, all lovely and fine at night when I put him to bed, and then gone.' She opened her arms wide. 'White like this,' pointing to the tablecloth under the typewriter. 'Cold.' The word reverberated like a clanging of a bell. 'Mother-in-law says it's God's punishment to me.'

'Why on earth would God punish you for that?'

'She is a very strict Brahmin. When we first met, I tried to follow all the rules for women, but I found them too constricting.' She waved a weary arm at the books, the typewriter. She bowed her head, then looked at me directly. 'My husband and I were becoming more isolated from religion, both trying to hide it. I loved my job. I loved my freedoms. But I must have done something wrong.'

'Nothing,' I said, leaning towards her. 'Nothing.' I only had words, and the wrong ones could wound her for the rest of her life. 'Babies and small children are always vulnerable. Particularly in the first few weeks after birth. We don't want them to be, but they are. It's hard to live independently.'

'Yes.' She was wiping her eyes discreetly, her mouth working violently. 'But they don't die like that in your country,' she said angrily.

'Yes they do. It happens many times in our country, to women who are strong and healthy, and to the weak. No one really knows why: it's one of those horrible mysteries.'

Beyond her sigh, I heard the Angelus bell chime from the church. I was going to be late home. A home where my live boy was waiting for me.

'Saraswati,' I said urgently, 'I'm so, so sorry, but I have to go now. If you like, I'll come back, but I have one important thing to ask you before I go: do you blame me for Sanje dying?'

She lifted her head. 'No.' She looked bewildered. 'Why?'

'Last week I had to go before a medical tribunal. I was told before I went that you had something to do with it.'

'*Me?*'

'That you were unhappy with your treatment at the home, and thought it had led to Sanje's death.'

'Who said this?' She looked flabbergasted now.

'I don't know.' I believed her instantly; the best actress in the world couldn't put on that show.

'Saraswati,' I said, 'what happened after you found Sanje in his cot?'

'My husband called a doctor from the local hospital, an old family friend. It was six thirty in the morning. He examined Sanje, confirmed what we knew. Later, he was the one who told my mother-in-law that I'd been working too hard, that my milk was thin. But this man is very traditional, doesn't like me, doesn't approve of working women.' Her face darkened when she said this.

'Did he have any idea where you'd had the baby delivered?'

'Yes,' she said, as we shared the same thought. 'He told me not to go there.'

Her eyes were wide open now, thinking. She stayed like this for a while.

'So, the home burned down,' she said at last in a faraway voice. 'I read about it in the papers. That was a terrible thing.'

'It was awful.' I felt it in my gut again. 'The worst feeling in the world. I think someone put a match to it.'

She gave me a sightless look, did some more staring and thinking. She tapped her fingernail on her front tooth. 'Don't forget that I am a lawyer,' she said at last. 'I have a first-class honours degree. If I can help, I will.'

Three weeks later, on a wet November afternoon, she turned up on my doorstep – thinner, taller-looking, her hair bobbed and shining, and wearing a raincoat over a chic salwar kameez. If she hadn't said her name, I wouldn't have recognised her. It was a Friday, and I was packing for Raffie and me to go down to Mangalath and see Glory, who still wasn't well enough to travel.

Saraswati asked if I'd had any news from the tribunal. 'Nothing' I told her, but that I worried about it constantly.

'We must wait and pray,' she said. 'Don't forget you have a friend in me now.'

We sat on the veranda, drinking tea, and talked for ages.

'There were things I couldn't tell you last time,' she said, 'but I'm ready to now.' Turned out that her husband had another woman in

Delhi. 'She is ten years younger than I am,' she said. 'More suitable, more traditional. He'd fallen for her even before Sanje was born. I cried for many days when I heard, but now that I've dried my tears, I'm ready to work again. I am at your disposal.' Her smile wobbled. 'It's a good decision. We were never really friends.'

I could hear Raffie laughing in the next room. His scampering footsteps. Anto had brought him a new wooden train; he was obsessed with it, talked to it, took it to bed with him at night. When Saraswati saw my anxious look, she shook her head as if to say, don't worry.

'I have my own flat now,' she continued. 'I'm earning my own money again.' (A sore point for me, this: my last Bank of India statement showed the sum of £21.50 in my account; soon I'd be completely dependent on Anto.) She put on a pair of horn-rimmed glasses that made her look about ten years older, and delved inside the large and impressive-looking briefcase she'd brought with her. She put pens and a large notebook on the table, talking all the while. She said that after the shock of her husband's defection had died down, she'd been surprised by a sense of soaring liberation. With no husband and no mother-in-law to placate, no family to impress with her modesty, or her cooking, no rumpy-thump, as she quaintly termed it, in the bedroom, she was free to play a proper role in India's Independence, and why hadn't she thought of this before? The Matha Maria Moonstone Home would be a perfect first project.

'With the tribunal breathing down your neck, I know you are unable to help properly,' she said. 'But I can make enquiries on that score.'

'I can help behind the scenes.' I felt happier than I had in ages.

'Let's begin, then.' She handed me an empty notebook and a pencil. 'I will need a full list of everyone who ever worked at the home: their addresses and, if possible, their castes. Include all the trainee midwives. If we are going to get the home out of the ashes, we must rescue its reputation first.'

Addresses for some of the village midwives would be difficult, I told her: some lived in shacks, others were secretive about where they lived, in case their customers had complaints.

'As many as you can, then,' she said. 'We must rule out nothing and nobody.'

Raffie wandered in then, his train on a string. He was tired from his play and slid on to my lap, his head on my chest, murmuring sleepily.

'You're a beautiful boy.' Saraswati pulled one of his toes gently, and watched him fall asleep.

'D'you mind him being here?'

'No,' she said indignantly. 'I like it.' She kept her hand on his foot. 'You know, I've been thinking about it a lot, and it may sound funny, but being in labour with Sanje reminded me of what it feels like to use every ounce of physical and emotional energy in my body. Now that I know this energy is there,' she gazed at me through her formidable glasses, 'I will dedicate it to the job at hand.' It felt like a little speech she had rehearsed for herself and for me, but no less brave for it.

Saraswati came over almost every morning, and was nothing short of magnificent. I'd thought it might take months for us to get the information we needed. I hadn't reckoned on a whirlwind.

Our first task, she said, was to hire a rickshaw and call on local women so they could write or dictate testimonials about their experience of the Moonstone. The rains had stopped, the air was warmer, drier. I set up a desk at the end of the veranda, the coolest place in the house, with its soft sea breezes, and when the testimonials came in, typed them up in triplicate: one for officialdom, one for our files, one for Daisy. It did my battered heart good to read them.

Husband never let me go to a hospital before, so was very frightened, wrote Bachi from a local slum. *But the ladies at the home were kind to me and very gentle, I would go again if I could.*

I liked this place: nice food, and very clean was another typical response from Parvati.

Not everyone was so rapturous, though. *They are all government spies there, so good it burned* came from A. Frend (*sic*).

Next, Saraswati had a breakthrough with Cyclops, the battered old truck that Mr Namboothiri had loaned us. On its first outing since the fire, it belched blue smoke, spluttered and died, so Saraswati persuaded a cousin who was 'a mechanical' to look at it. The cousin returned it oiled, tyres pumped, bodywork polished, and with a wreath of marigolds and Hanuman, the monkey god, hanging from its rear-view mirror. A few days later, he drove us to the village of Nilamperur to see Subadra, one of our first trainees.

Subadra, more stooped than ever, yelped with joy at the sight of us. She took us into her hut, where she plied us with tea and sticky pastries and some livid pink *barfi* the colour of calamine lotion.

The pride with which she produced her certificate from the Moonstone was touching. When Saraswati got out her notebook and started to question her, Subadra said, 'I've delivered more than twenty babies since the Moonstone training, and have definitely changed in my practice. I follow the hygienic wash between the babies, and I use sterile equipment to cut the cord.'

The scissors, swabs and needles we'd given her were kept in a jam jar on the shelf and were obviously unused.

'We want you to use them all the time,' I told her. 'If they get old, we will try and find some more.' She looked at me dubiously, as if I might snatch them away. 'I like them new,' she said.

'So what are you using instead?'

She produced a battered knife, a pair of scissors, a pot of herbs. 'But I boil everything in water now to keep them sweet and clean.'

At the end of our visit, Subadra said: 'It was good, our time with you. We still talk about it. We taught you our ways, but we learned too.' Her words reminded me of the basic goodness in so many of the women we'd met – it lay underneath like an underground river, deeper than race or nationality.

I didn't bother sharing this thought with Saraswati the realist: she might have teased me, and anyway, as Cyclops lurched along the track going home, she was complaining: 'Some of these women will go on exactly as they always did, with the rusty knife and all the ignorance of poverty. They shut their minds.' But she did concede that Subadra was at least boiling water now, and very disapproving of another midwife who made girls lie in their own filth for days.

Our truck was passing through a small village, where four half-naked boys were washing at the village pump. They ran alongside us, shouting and laughing, then jumped on the running board and waved vigorously through the window.

I saw Saraswati flinch as she looked at them, and then she waved back. 'Silly boys,' she said softly, and closed her eyes.

Chapter 52

'Don't take this cancer lark too seriously,' was Mother's breezy message to me when she broke the news. The doctor had confirmed lung cancer, but she was desperately keen for me to see it as a temporary irritation: another rabbit on the road. But a childlike terror, a darkness was rushing down the track towards me, and I was no good at this game any more. *Don't leave me*, I wanted to say to her. *Not now. Stay with me.* How powerless we all are in the end.

Since Glory was so ill, Amma had suggested I come to Mangalath for a few weeks to be with her. On my first afternoon there, my mother and I lay on either side of her bed in the cool, restful, high-ceilinged room that she liked so much. We watched a small lizard dart across the ceiling. 'Sweet little fellow,' she murmured.

Her face was all bones and eyes now, and deathly pale. I wanted to hold it in my mind for ever. Her teeth looked larger in her head. But there was beauty there, and nobility, and a kind of grace under pressure, which I admired, and when my fear subsided, I had odd moments of seeing what was so obvious in the end: I loved her, and always would.

'When did you know she was this ill?' I asked Amma one afternoon when my mother was asleep. Amma put a plate of perfectly sliced mango on the bedside table.

'We were out in the garden walking,' she told me in a breathless whisper. 'Glory refused the walking stick that made her look like an old granny. I was looking for one of my chickens. When I turned back, she was in a heap underneath the flame of the forest tree. When she woke up, she said, "I'm a clumsy clot, and a damned nuisance." Then she said, "Don't tell Kit." I said, "Why not, she is your daughter. It's her duty to help and she will be happy to do so."' She touched my hand but I still heard a hint of challenge.

I could see that Amma was upset, too. It seemed to me she'd grown fond of Glory in the way of two horses put in a field together, who would either kick each other to smithereens, or eventually sniff and accept each other and become glad of the company. I'd eavesdropped on their minor skirmishes on the best way to clean a Persian rug, or where scent should be placed (Glory: the pulse of your wrist; Amma: the folds of your clothes). They appreciated each other's high standards, the many small and unremarked acts it took to create a house of real beauty for other people to carelessly enjoy.

'Your mother and I are both at the lonely end of life,' Amma told me now. 'Children mostly gone, husbands busy or dead. It's easy to think, what am I for?'

I was about to protest, but she added quickly, 'Don't say anything. I'll always love my boy, but I don't know him any more. He's very Western.'

My mother hovered between life and death for five days. On the fourth day, when I set her special cup on the bedside table, she opened her eyes and said, 'Oh, you angel. Nothing nicer than the smell of coffee in the morning.'

I watched her take a sip, saw the almost transparent thinness of her hands, the blue and white veins that stood out like a medical drawing. At night, her cough rattled the house.

'It's nearly night-time, Ma,' I whispered. Through a gap in the shutters, the sky was streaked with turquoise and pink stripes; a cockerel was crowing.

She drained the cup, dabbed her lips delicately with a white napkin, and fell abruptly asleep. Her breathing, irregular and hoarse, was a tremendous effort now.

'Lie beside me,' she patted the empty space beside her. While she slept, I thought of all the things I'd found to criticise her for: my lack of a father; the way she'd despised my job; the constant moving; the advice, which had increasingly seemed so trivial, about keeping men happy, or looking smart, or being posh.

I understood better now that the clothes, the right notepaper, the jokes had been her weapons in a world that had treated her badly. I could see her life distinct and separate from mine. I pictured the high-spirited misfit she must have been at the orphanage, and later, the glamour puss at some government ball: coiffed, amusing, a little bit acid, a challenge. Or later still, when life had really left its mark on her, on her own, in a café in London, husbandless, penniless, scanning the Situations Vacant. Me beside her. With no family and no home, no wonder she'd needed, or felt she needed, every mask she could find in order to survive, and I'd despised her for it.

'A rupee for your thoughts, darling,' came a faint voice from the pillow. She'd been watching me, as she had for years, anxiously gauging my state of mind.

'Not worth it,' I said. Pity was the last thing she would want now. 'Only that I . . .' But she was back, as she would put it, in the arms of Morpheus, and while she slept, I longed for her forgiveness.

The next day, she took a turn for the worse. Breath laboured and harsh; narrow ribs jerking when she coughed; red toenails clenching, unclenching. Conscious, she grimaced, sweated, sometimes roared with pain, or maybe frustration, but my God, she clung on.

At sundown, the family priest, Father Christopher, came and read a prayer: 'Dear God, You love me too much to let me suffer unless it be for my good. Therefore, oh Lord, I trust myself to You; do with me as You please. In sickness and in health, I wish to love You always.'

I watched Glory's face while he read this, half expecting a sceptical eye to open and for her to say, 'If this is Your idea of love, God, forget it.' But she was too ill for quips.

She was never alone. The doctor came with medicines, and we sat beside her hour after hour: Anto and Mariamma and Amma, and Appan when he was at home; even Ponnamma took her turn, bringing some wobbly sewing with her and saying with the cheerful heartlessness of the old, 'How long can she go on for now? Taking her time, isn't she?' Glory enjoyed this sort of tactlessness; laughed about it with me when she had the breath.

Raffie ran in from time to time to show her things: his train, a teddy bear. He told her what he was doing. He wasn't scared, or didn't seem to be. But that day, she was coughing fit to bust as we left the room, and he held my hand as we walked downstairs, and explained to me in his sensible voice, 'Grandma Glory is very old now,' and glanced at me anxiously, just as she did, to see if I understood, and if I minded.

And then – it was a Sunday morning – she suddenly said, without opening her eyes, 'There's no one there,' with a note of horror in her voice, as if she'd already been to the other side and found it not her cup of tea at all. I missed not being able to laugh about this.

Around four, I heard the crunch of a car drawing up on the gravel outside, the squeak of brakes. I went to the window, looked out, and froze. It was my father. He was walking slowly towards the house with Amma by his side.

It's too late, I thought, watching his pottery gait up the path. And you're too old. That was all I felt: not glad, not relieved. I was guarding her now as fiercely as a mother guarded a baby, worried that the shock of seeing him might finish her off.

When he came in, he went straight to the bed, put a gnarled hand on her forehead and gave a queer sound somewhere between a sob and a groan. It was awful.

'Glory,' he said. 'It's me. It's William,' and then, in the same cracked voice, 'I love you, Glory, that's what I've come to say. I love you, and I'm so terribly sorry.'

His eyes were streaming, so I gave him my handkerchief. Amma turned away from him; she was praying.

'I'll leave you to it,' she said, and squeezed my hand. 'I'll explain later.'

When she was gone, I said, 'What are you doing here? Please don't do that.' He was making a bubbling sound.

'I'm sorry... I'm so sorry.' His eyes were trained on her. 'I couldn't not... you see...' His mouth kept opening and shutting without any sound coming out, and when he held her hand, it took all my willpower not to snatch it away. 'She wrote to me. She asked me to come. I couldn't let her down again.'

He sat beside her on the bed, and put his head against hers, two shrunken and collapsed puppets almost unbearable to look at.

'She can hear me,' he said. 'She squeezed my hand.' I looked at him. I looked at her.

'Never turn strangers away from the door, lest you turn away angels.' It was one of Amma's frequent expressions. Well, he was no angel, God knows, and there had been times since I met him when I wished him to rot in hell, but even I had to admit that though my mother's eyes were still shut, she had a strange inward look on her face that was different. I saw her fingers bend around his, the tense lines of her face relax into a look of safety, even contentment, as if she'd been returned to a time when his presence meant happiness.

When evening fell, the light through the window deepened to a purplish black. Pathrose came in, 'to freshen up water for Mummy' and light the oil lamps. He left a whisky and soda for us both, and some sandwiches, biscuits and cheese for the English visitor. We ate and drank in silence, the pop of the lamp, her breathing between us. And this was strange too, and still painful to write: for the three hours we sat there, we were, for the first and last time, a family.

'Anto,' I said, when he walked in at 3 a.m., 'this is my father.' William struggled to his feet, crumpled and red-eyed, trying to straighten his spine into what I can only assume was some remnant of military bearing. Anto smiled at him.

'I'm very glad to meet you, sir, but sorry it is under these circumstances. Glory,' he knelt down beside her, 'it's Anto. I want to see how you are.' He turned her thin wrist, took her pulse, rested his hand on her forehead. 'I hope you don't mind stepping outside for a moment.' His gaze came to rest on William, and then on me. 'I need to do a further examination.'

I was about to write that the performance was vintage Anto, but this is the important point. It was not a performance, but a demonstration of everything I valued in my husband now: the kindness, the undramatic goodness, the competence. It would have been against his nature to hurt the feelings of this unexpected guest.

My mother died on the wave of one last spluttering sigh. No death rattle, and absurdly, I was glad about this; she would have hated one. So unladylike!

Amma and Mariamma came in with water and cloths and clean white burial clothes. They tied her jaw. When we washed her, I was shocked at how thin she'd become, her veins a road map inside her. We dressed her in the Christian Dior nightie, and followed the Nasrani custom of placing her dead body with her head pointing towards the east and her feet towards the west, although Glory, I think, would have preferred it the other way around.

We lit a row of candles beside the cot, where I imagined dozens of Thekkedens must have been laid out. It's a funny word to use, but I felt at that moment almost euphoric with relief and gratitude. It was done so quietly, so kindly, so naturally, with all the dignity that ritual bestowed. No high-speed hospital dash, no drama, just this quiet slipping-away in a place where she'd been loved.

As for my father, when the shock receded, I was so angry, I could have kicked him. *See, she survived*, I wanted to tell him. *She got over you. She lived her life. We didn't need you.* But he'd already scuttled away.

Chapter 53

When it was done, Amma took a pail of hot water into the bath house, and spent forty minutes scrubbing herself from head to foot. Hair first, with the coconut oil soap she made herself, face, nails, legs, arms, with a soft brush. She cleaned her teeth with a twig, dressed herself in a clean *chatta* and *mundu*, and when she emerged, glowing and oiled, she rattled off a list of instructions to Pathrose on the removal of the bed and mattress, and the purification of the house, which would take several days. Father Christopher would come that night to bless the house and sanctify it.

As she walked towards the summer house, she was hollow-legged with tiredness. The family had sat with Glory all night, saying the rosary and singing hymns. There had been endless cups of black coffee and tea. Now, the Christian part of her brain muttered prayers for Glory's safe departure, while the pagan part rejoiced to be free of the heavy fug of the invalid rooms, the blanket bath, the bedpans, until the next time, which would probably be Ponnamma.

Ten days is a long time to hang on, she murmured to the deceased. The arrival of the sad old man had put them all under extra strain.

It was lovely out. An early shower of rain had scattered the path with the scented golden flowers of the champa tree, and death had charged the evening with significance. Tucking a flower in her hair, Amma wondered how many more years she herself had left. Her eyes misted as she imagined sobbing grandchildren, an inconsolable Mariamma and Appan – then the fantasy dissolved into darting concerns about food for Glory's funeral. The traditional meal – vegetables, rice gruel, a buttermilk curry, pappadams – was easy to make, but how many to ask? Who would be staying?

She stopped and deliberately emptied her mind. 'Take a breath,' her father used to tell her when she got too whizzy. 'Chew some air.'

She looked around her slowly. The garden was always at its most

318

beautiful before the sunset: an intense, luminous underwater light that illuminated the jagged fringe of palm trees, the flowers, the silver flash of the cove, deepening and fading before darkness descended. She bent down to the dancing girl orchid, touched its leaves. The sprinkle of purple spots at its tip were as sweet and delicate as the freckles on a child's nose. She was prodding the soil around it, at peace for the first time that day, when she heard a low rasping sound coming from the summer house, and then a long-drawn-out howl. She picked up a spade, ready to throw it at the pie-dogs who came regularly to scavenge, but when she peered through the window, she saw William Villiers sitting on the bench, his arms clasped tightly around him. He was rocking and sobbing with the abandon of a child.

She stood frozen for a few moments, spade in hand. For a man like this, to be caught crying would be worse than being seen on the potty. Appan, who'd spent years observing the English, with the kind of anxious love a collie felt for its master, had told her once about stiff upper lips, and she'd laughed, thinking it was a phrase he'd made up. She took another step forward, touched the pane of glass with her hand and listened intently. When the sobs dwindled into an 'oooohhhhh' of despair, she gave a sigh, straightened her shoulders and pushed the door open.

'Mr Villiers. I'm here also.' She put down the spade, as if a bit of shed tidying was all she planned to do.

'Oh Lord!' He glanced up, dotty-looking in his surprise, and his mouth began to work violently. 'Oh God.' He pulled a spotted handkerchief out of his pocket, buried his face in it. 'Sorry,' he said in a muffled voice. 'Can't go home like this.'

She touched his arm. 'Don't dash off,' she said quietly. 'Take your time. We'll be saying prayers for her soul tonight.'

'I shouldn't have come,' he said. 'It's made everything worse.'

'It was what Glory wanted,' Amma said.

'For herself? For the girl?'

'I don't know.'

This was true. During the long night when Glory had raged incoherently about this man, she had told Amma that he should come, that she needed to tell him things, and Amma had indulged her. As for Kit? God knows: she'd played her cards very close to her chest regarding this father of hers.

'This was Glory's gin and tonic spot.' She pointed to a bench overlooking the water. 'She liked looking at the water and the trees.'

He stood up, shifting the ripe smell of distress and pipe tobacco towards her.

'Such a shock, you know.' He fumbled the handkerchief into his pocket. 'Didn't see her for years, decades, and then all this.'

'I understand,' she said, although the messiness of it appalled her. To give him time to start breathing normally again, she offered to show him her orchid garden.

'These are my invalids.' She led him to the row of coconut shells. 'My husband brings them from all over India. They take a while to find their feet. This one,' she pointed to the orchid tree, glowing against the darkening sky, 'is a miracle worker. The stems are used for leprosy, or ulcers. Paste from leaves, for headaches. You can also eat it as a vegetable.

'And this is my dancing girl,' she said at the next plant. 'Glory loved her. She was a wreck when she came from Bangalore. Now look – eight new buds on the stem.'

William knelt down obediently, with a great cracking of knees, and touched the flower. As he did so, his regimental signet ring flashed and fell into the earth. 'Damn thing doesn't fit me,' he said as she passed it back. 'I'm bound to lose it one day.' He shoved it in his pocket and sat back on his heels, looking at the garden with a bemused expression. 'I never thought she'd come back,' he said.

'No way of contacting her?' Amma said with a lemony look; this was going too far.

'I tried. Wrote for years. Never got a reply. Only from her friend, Miss Barker.'

She heard the clicking in his throat.

'Sorry,' he wheezed at last. He was at it again, an unstoppered tide of grief he seemed unable to control. 'Sorry.'

She waited until he could talk again.

'What would you like to do now?' she said gently.

'I want to go home,' he said. 'My driver's waiting in the village.'

'Will you come back?'

'I don't think so.' He looked down at his brogues; they were covered in dust. 'There are a few... complications.'

'I know.' Glory had told her about the wife in Ooty. 'But not even to see Kit?' She looked at him directly. 'Your grandchild?'

'I don't know.' There was a question in his eyes, and an apology. 'Do you think I should?'

'That's for you to decide.' She smiled her practised smile, thinking, what an absolute bloody fool – another phrase that Appan had taught her – be a man, find out for yourself.

Chapter 54

I spent yesterday at Mangalath with Amma who was sorting out her linen cupboard and wanted to give me some new sheets and tablecloths, and, hint, hint, some baby clothes that might be useful to me in the future. It was exactly the sort of task Glory would have enjoyed – the folding, the scenting, the doing something undemanding but practical with me – and the thought of how, in the last few years, I'd denied her these small pleasures was like a knife in my heart.

Saraswati's arrival later in the day cheered me up, though Amma was clearly annoyed. The Nasrani custom, she reminded me in a tight voice, was to mourn the dead for nine days, during which time no one came to the house. 'This is not normal.'

Well, Saraswati was not normal. With her charming and brilliant smile, she apologised to Amma, put a bulging briefcase down on the floor, and, as soon as Amma had left the room, exploded with plans.

'I'm twisting the arms of more local businessmen. My sales pitch is straightforward: "Wake up. See the situation plainly," she declared, eyes flashing. "Too many babies are dying all over India; share the knowledge we have gained in our training centres." Only one or two have given me some stick. "Why change the old ways?" they say, or "Are you a man-hating feminist?" "Man-hater?" I say. "We're here to protect your male babies too, by the way. Your indifference will kill them."'

Her next rabbit from the hat was a set of plans donated by an architect she knew. The drawings showed a fifteen-bedroom unit to be built in breeze block with a properly tiled roof, and enough space for three consulting rooms, a dispensary, a reception area and a large veranda.

To ensure that there was no jiggery-pokery about the Moonstone's ownership of the two acres of land it stood on, she'd also undertaken a search at the local Land Registry office. She was pretty sure the actual deeds had been lost in the fire, but she also asked me to write to Daisy in case they were at Wickam Farm. The thought of the chaotic attic there made me shudder.

The dark rings under her eyes had grown. When I asked if she was getting enough sleep, she reminded me that with her husband gone, and no mother-in-law to please, 'I have plenty more hours in the day, and I'm using them.'

But the biggest fly in the custard, the one we avoided discussing until the last possible moment, was the fact that we were practically broke. Saraswati estimated that the new home, plus fixtures, fittings and restocking the pharmacy, would cost in the region of one hundred and thirty thousand rupees, the equivalent of ten thousand pounds in English money. An impossible amount, a pipe dream.

As she was busily scribbling the sums down, she saw my expression, put her pencil down and stuck her finger in the air.

'First it was impossible. Then it was difficult. Then it was done,' adding, without a glimmer of a smile and with an intensity that frightened me: 'It has to work, else I'll throw myself on the funeral pyre.'

Four months after my mother's funeral, I got a big scare when a khaki-coloured official-looking envelope arrived covered in unfamiliar handwriting. Saraswati had told me not to worry too much about the medical tribunal, telling me they were months behind with cases and would probably forget me. But in that panicked moment, I pictured jail or deportation, or at the very least, a fine we couldn't possibly afford.

It turned out to be a brief note from my father. The spidery hand informed me that he was back in Ooty, and wanted to give me 'one or two things of Glory's that you might like. Nothing precious, mementoes.' I was to write back to Box Number 36, the Ootacamund Club.

When I read the letter, anger flared up inside me, and I thought, stay where you are, you slippery old fraud, with your aliases and your box numbers. I didn't want my phantom father breezing in again and stirring things up.

When Anto read it, I watched his expression change from frowning concentration to sympathy.

'Poor old man,' he said. 'Let him send whatever it is. This could be the Hope diamond.'

'Poor old man!' I exclaimed. 'That envelope scared me to death, and anyway, what about poor Glory, poor me? He behaved appallingly.'

'You asked me what I thought.' Anto trained his green eyes on me. 'I am saying what I think.'

'I'm fed up with you being nicer than me,' I said after a while.

'Me too,' he said. 'It's a burden I bear.'

I was pulling his hair. 'Grey ones, please!' he said as he held me close. 'When are we going to have another baby?' he whispered.

'Soon,' I said, ruffling his hair. 'And you really won't mind if it's a girl?'

'No.' He looked hurt, because I still kept getting this wrong sometimes, assuming things about him that were crude approximations based on what I thought I knew about Indian men. These were the moments when we made each other foreign, and I deeply regretted them.

'I'd like one too,' I whispered, as he stroked my stomach. 'I love my silly old man,' and then he looked around like a guilty schoolboy, because we were in his mother's house.

'Anto,' I teased him, stroking his hair, 'how old are you?' He knew exactly what I meant. 'Six years old when I am here,' he said.

The next job was to sort through the sea trunk Glory had left in the spare room at Mangalath. As we opened the lid, the rush of something both spicy and sweet came from a half-finished bottle of Shalimar, one of her little extravagances during the grim years. The kind of thing (the baccarat-cut glass bottle, the little velvet ribbon, her snooty expression as she dabbed it here and there) that had once made her seem, to me, so impossibly glamorous.

Her possessions made a pathetically small pile in the end. Two tweed skirts (Donegal tweed, as she'd been fond of pointing out, donated, or maybe not, by the vicar's wife in Durham), the dull cardigans and liberty bodices worn at Daisy's to stop her freezing to death. A few light cotton dresses, and underneath them, wrapped carefully in layers of scented tissue, the remnants of a life lived for one shining hour, and never again.

Amma and I laid them out on the bed: a slippery green satin dress, a silk suit with a Swan and Edgar label, a shagreen brush and comb set with a chipped handle, lipstick samples, a pair of jodhpurs, an Aertex shirt, a tin of Coty talcum powder with a carefree, brilliantly laughing woman on it, a pair of beautiful gold leather sandals (Charles of Lewes), still in their original box, an invitation for a free facial at the Belle Rose beauty parlour in Chelmsford.

The green satin dress had tiny heart-shaped mother-of-pearl buttons stitched on its waistband. I imagined her wearing it at a garrison party, and the hectic preparations beforehand. Her weapons: the tweezers, the comb, the wax strip. It mattered, really mattered, getting it right.

Inside a faded floral box, I found her wedding veil, wrapped in pink tissue. Its brittle fabric, edged with crumbling dried flowers shaped like violets, the final symbol of her humiliation.

I wondered where she'd gone after the colonel had driven her away from the church. At what point in this whole horrible shambles had she learned that I was on the way? I ached to find out more, and now I never would.

'Shall I throw these away?'

Amma held out a few faded invitations: a pantomime in Braintree; a garden party at Major someone or other's – the name was past reading – house, The Palms, in Malabar Hills on 7 June, on the occasion of his return to England; a ladies' coffee morning at the Bombay Yacht Club.

What a meaty bone of gossip Glory must have thrown to the ladies at the club to gnaw on: 'A chi chi girl, can you imagine, darling?' 'The poor man had absolutely no idea whatsoever; she does look very pale.' I hated them all.

At the bottom of the trunk there was a book, *The Good Soldier*, by Ford Madox Ford. The inscription on the flyleaf read, *To my darling fiancée Glory, with grateful thanks for her eternal light-heartedness. Love, William.*

Bits of me, too: a smocked pink romper suit, a rattle shaped like a horse, a letter with a wonky drawing: *When you die Mummy I will die wiv you* – dramatic child! – and finally, right at the very bottom, a picture of me in my nursing uniform, aged nineteen, on the day I got my certificate. The photo was half hidden under the lining. It was not her dream for me, and never would be.

My father turned up at Mangalath later that week, unannounced, uninvited, and on the flimsiest of pretexts. He said he'd brought a box of tea from a planter friend who happened to be driving by, and wanted to give it to Amma, who had been so kind. He'd smartened himself up for this outing: polished brogues, a worn but clean suit, a paisley tie. When he held out the box to Amma, he shot me a quick hangdog look, and I could barely glance at him. It was Amma who offered him refreshments, a chair, a bed for the night. I would have shown him the door.

After he'd drunk his tea, I asked if he would like to see my mother's things. I don't think I was being deliberately cruel, but my ears buzzed with anger as I took him upstairs. I wanted him to see how little she'd ended up with; that there had been consequences.

In the spare room, he looked at her dresses, shoes and knick-knacks in silence for a while. He picked up the jodhpurs.

'I taught her to ride,' he said. 'She was getting rather good at it.' When he started to paw the green dress, I wanted to scream and snatch it from him.

'I've got a lot to do today,' I said.

He was sniffling again, and blinked at me like some sort of woodland animal coming out of a hole. 'I'm so sorry,' he said. 'I must let you get on. I've been meaning to ask you, do you have any other children?'

'No, but we will.' He'd asked me this before, so now I wanted to hurt him too. 'And when we do have girls,' I said, 'we'll send them to the best school we can afford.' The words were bursting out of me like hot water from a geyser.

'Good idea,' he said. He folded her Aertex shirt, pressed it to his face.

'I want them to have good jobs. Something solid and clean. Being defenceless is for the birds.'

He looked at me warily. 'I thought Glory got rather good jobs. Friends were always very kind and so forth.'

'Oh God.' That was when I really wanted to strike him. I could feel the blow running like an electrical current through my hands. But he wasn't listening. The tips of his fingers were running over her green dress, a dreamy expression on his face.

Why did you dump her, if you felt like that? I almost said, but my anger was frightening me, so instead I took a deep breath, said I was tired and wanted to eat. That he should take a memento if he wanted it. The rest I'd give to charity or chuck away. He winced at that; I wanted him to.

He picked up *The Good Soldier*.

'I'd like this,' he said. He was breathing strangely, and I thought:

for God's sake don't have a heart attack here, and how if he did, I'd have to tell his wife, and cart him out, and all manner of hard thoughts, because I didn't want him in my life. Not now. 'It was the first present I ever gave her.'

'I read what you wrote inside,' I said. 'Sweet.' I was breathing heavily now too.

He touched the dress again.

'She wore this to the Mess ball. Turned a lot of heads, I can tell you.'

And a fat lot of good that did her.

'*This is the saddest story ever told*,' he said in a faraway voice. 'The first line in the book. I only read the thing last year. I gave it to her to impress her. Turns out it wasn't about a soldier at all.'

'I know,' I said. 'It's about betrayal.'

In the silence that grew between us, I heard the clink of pots from the kitchen. He'll be gone soon, I thought, and you won't have to think about him ever again, because he doesn't want to know you, not really.

Before he left, he took a small box out of his pocket. 'I've brought you some things of hers.'

His shaky fingers struggled with the catch, and then he held up a nondescript gold ring with tiny pearls in it, and a few chips of what looked like garnet. It was dented on one side.

'It was all I could afford on a captain's pay. One of the stones is loose, and one is gone,' he said. 'I think she bashed it before she sent it back.' The hangdog look again. 'And this.' He pulled out a silver chain with a milky-coloured stone at the end of it, the size of my little thumbnail. 'It's a moonstone. Common as muck over here, but very pretty.'

'They're supposed to be lucky,' I said.

'You won't get rich on it.' He dropped it into the palm of my hand. 'But you might give it to your daughter.'

'I'm not sure I can keep them if she sent them back.'

'Please have them,' he said in a low voice.

Part of me felt like a traitor as I put them in my pocket. I couldn't bring myself to thank him. They felt like such paltry gifts, when we could have had a life together.

Chapter 55

And then I was arrested. At the time, it felt as sudden and jarring as that. I was sitting on the veranda at Rose Street, catching up on some paperwork, when out of the corner of my eye I saw a dusty black car draw up outside the house. Two men got out, cocky, self-assured. It took me a while to see they were wearing policemen's uniforms, and had lathis stuck in their belts. They were walking towards my house.

And even then I wasn't too concerned. There had been a spate of robberies in the street, and they were smiling at me in a friendly way, so I assumed they were doing house-to-house enquiries.

The taller policeman took a piece of paper from his pocket.

'Your name is Miss Kit Smallwood?'

'Yes.' I felt my mouth go dry.

'We are here with a warrant for your arrest. We will take you down to the Cochin police station for questioning. We must warn you that anything you say will be taken down and used in evidence. It is advisable to bring a suitcase with you.'

'A suitcase!' I was shocked. 'Why?'

'You may stay down there.'

'I can't! I have a child here.' Except by horrible timing, he wasn't here. The previous afternoon, clutching his teddy and a small bag, Raffie had walked with me in a state of high excitement and a few nerves to stay at his cousin's house a few streets away. His first night ever away from me. The cousins had said they'd drop him back this morning, and now I imagined him racing up the front steps, bursting with news about his important adventure, and I wouldn't be there.

Anto was also away: he was giving a paper at a conference in Quilon. It was an important step professionally for him, and the thought of him coming home and finding me gone was horrible too.

'Can't I wait until my husband gets home?' I said. The small policeman leaned close enough for me to see mean, dark crevices from his lip to his chin.

'You have servants here?'

'Yes, two.' I'd just seen Kamalam's frightened eyes peering around the door.

'So let them see to your child, and they can tell your husband where you are,' he told me. 'There is a room waiting for you.' I shuddered, thinking of the dark, pee-smelling jail I'd been to with Neeta.

I gave rapid instructions to Kamalam. She must feed Raffie, and reassure him that I would be back soon. I'd bought his favourite cashew *barfi* to celebrate his return; she must make sure he got it, and tell him that Mummy loved him. She was not to worry, I would be back soon.

In the back of the car, the small policeman took a pair of hand-cuffs from his pocket. He locked one around my left wrist, and one round his right.

I was driven to a small police station near the docks, and locked into an interrogation cell – a high-walled room with a small window close to the roof that showed about one square foot of sky. A chair, a potty: that was it. I listened to their footsteps echoing away; someone in a nearby cell was shouting and crying.

After hours of waiting, I fell into a clammy sleep, and woke to hear evening sounds outside: the market men putting up their stalls, the shouts of the rickshaw men. Suddenly a policeman appeared in my cell – youngish, with a gap-toothed smile. He was wearing a cheap gold wedding ring and carrying a manila folder. He placed a chair a couple of feet away from me and sat down with an amiable grunt.

'Sorry for all the noise earlier.' He fixed me with large, sad eyes. 'We had a man in too much for the toddy. He was calling for his mother.'

I tried to smile; I desperately needed him on my side.

'So.' The wedding ring flashed as he opened the folder. 'My name is Inspector Pillay. You are Miss Kit Smallwood, from the Moonstone Clinic, Fort Cochin?'

'Correct.' You bloody idiot, I thought. It was clear from the thick-ness of the file that they'd had their eye on me for months, maybe from the moment I'd arrived.

'And you are married to Dr Anto Thekkeden.' So much for protecting the family name.

'Can I speak to my lawyer?' How corny this sounded; I was in a bad play, one that made my voice tremble and my limbs turn watery.

'Name of lawyer?' I'd been thinking about this earlier, stubbing my toe on the same door. Saraswati wouldn't do. When I'd asked her, in the early days, whether if the case ever went to court she'd represent me, she'd said it was impossible. 'Because they'll call me as a witness, and the law is you cannot be both witness and lawyer.' Our only slender hope was that the medical authorities wouldn't call her as a witness because they'd lied about her accusing me, and they wouldn't want that can of worms opened. Appan, as my father-in-law, was no good either.

I had a vague memory of Appan mentioning another lawyer who might help, but I'd forgotten his name, and Pillay was saying impatiently, 'So you don't seem to have a lawyer, and anyway, that would delay our proceedings tonight, and you have a child to attend to at home.' The sweet smile had turned sour and faintly incredulous. 'Isn't that what you think of first?'

It was growing dark outside, although I couldn't see it. Cell doors slamming, shouting, a subdued whimpering, and then a dead silence. An old woman in a sari came in; she gave me a bowl of water, a square of cotton to wash myself with.

Don't you dare panic, I told myself. You don't ever, ever have to tell anyone about this. Anto will come soon, Appan's fine legal brain will think of something, and then you'll be home. You'll bath Raffie, tuck him into the new big-boy bed he's so proud of, smell his hair, kiss him, *night night, sleep tight, hope the fleas don't bite*, a whisky and soda on the veranda with Anto, try and laugh about what a close shave this has been.

When night fell, the lights went out. A leaking tap in the slop room next door went *drip, drop, flop*. The sounds swelled and magnified and became the nightmare accompaniment to a night when I hated myself intensely. I could practically see the lurid headlines already: *Unqualified English midwife kills Indian babies.* Anto could lose his job as a result of the fallout. My fault: my laziness, my pride, my condescension, *drip, drop, flop*, and worst of all, I was bringing fear and misery to a child who was too young to understand.

When morning came, the old woman reappeared. She put a flat bread on the stool, and a small bowl of rice.

Two hours later, Anto arrived, pale and huge-eyed with shock. I saw him in the visitors' room, a bare space with spittoons in the corner full of sand. When I asked him how Raffie was, he said, 'I was hoping they might release you today, so I wouldn't have to tell him.'

There was a long, tense silence.

'I'll tell him tonight.' His expression made me think I had pushed him over the line that separated love and support from complete exasperation, contempt even.

'Are you angry?' I asked him.

'No,' he said eventually with the yes-no gesture. 'Only with myself.'

'It wasn't your fault.'

He didn't answer.

'Haven't they said anything?'

'Nothing. Only that it will go to trial. I'm worried they're going to make an example of you.' He put his head in his hands.

'Anto,' I said, 'if it does go to trial, you must tell Amma.' I winced with shame at the thought of it. 'She'll help with Raffie.'

'I can't. I've already spoken to Appan. He doesn't want her to know.'

'That makes no sense – she's bound to find out.'

The muscle in Anto's jaw was twitching, never a good sign.

'He's adamant, but as soon as I leave here, I'm going to talk to him again. And if he won't help, I'm going to borrow Saraswati's law books and work through every precedent for voluntary and involuntary manslaughter, which is what Saraswati says they will charge you with if they charge you at all. She's confident this is just a sabre-rattling exercise. The case is so full of holes, it's a farce.' His smile didn't make it to his eyes, which were red-rimmed, as if he hadn't slept all night.

'How was the conference?' I asked shortly before he left. 'Did the paper go well?'

'I didn't give it. I came home when I heard.'

'I'm so sorry.' He'd spent months writing his paper on the management of epidemics with particular reference to African sleeping sickness. We'd rehearsed it together.

He looked away. 'Forget it, but if you do have to stay, I can't just stop work.'

We stared at each other.

'Let's wait,' I said. 'The whole situation might resolve itself quickly.' Though I knew from Saraswati that the legal system was clogged with cases. 'What about Raffie? Should he go to Mangalath?'

'Appan's taking Amma away as soon as possible in case the newspapers get on to it.'

'I thought they were strapped for cash at the moment?'

'They are – he's not happy about it.'

'Will they be bad? The papers, I mean.'

'Sticks and stones,' he said wearily. 'Who cares?'

'Anto, I'm so sorry. I should have listened.'

'Don't keep saying that,' he said with a twisted smile. 'And try not to worry too much. I'm going to get you out if it kills me.'

Chapter 56

The newspapers had pounced on the story with the speed of a dog spying a fillet steak.

English midwife may be held responsible for new baby deaths was front-page news in the daily newspaper, *The Malayala Manorama*. *The Hindu* led with a picture of the charred remains of the Moonstone. *First arson, now baby slaughter. What next?* was the caption.

When Anto went to work the following day, his boss's expression was grim. The conference organisers were furious that he hadn't presented his paper. Their research team would never be asked again. 'This won't help matters.' Dr Sastry stabbed at his copy of *The Hindu*. 'Soon her name will be connected with yours. How many English midwives are there in Fort Cochin?' The same Dr Sastry who had been so genuinely kind and welcoming was clearly frightened of contagion, and Anto understood why: research grants could be slashed overnight in the new India.

When Anto asked for three days off, Dr Sastry agreed with bad grace, slamming the door behind him. Anto took a taxi and went at breakneck speed to Mangalath. As the car turned into the drive, he saw a pall of black smoke rising above the house, messing up the clear blue sky with cinders and soot.

'I got up early and burned all the newspapers I could find,' Appan told him in a furious whisper in his study, where the windows were shut. 'If your mother sees them, she will die of shame.'

'Those are lies, Appan! Do I really have to convince you of that?' Anto said. 'The important thing now is to get her out of jail.'

'All I know,' his father was pale with rage, 'is that up until recently, I have been systematically lied to about the true facts of your wife's occupation, and I find it hard not to blame you for not controlling her better.'

Anto said nothing, just stared at his father and shook his head. The final betrayal.

'Are you saying you won't help?' he said at last.

Appan heaved an enormous sigh. 'Here are the two possibilities: she could be tried for involuntary manslaughter, which is a serious offence.'

'I've looked it up,' Anto said. 'But it doesn't apply: involuntary manslaughter means you have shown a callous disregard for human life, the same thing you might be charged with if you drove a motor car while drunk, or left someone old with a mad dog.'

'So you're a lawyer now too, are you?' Appan's voice was a slap. 'Some midwives are charged with this when things go wrong, but the other possibility is a charge of manslaughter and gross negligence. This could bring up to ten years in jail, if your wife had no licence to practise. What was she thinking of?' His eyes bulged with disbelief.

Anto bowed his head.

'So reckless conduct is there too.' Appan continued tapping one hand impatiently on the desk. 'And you want me to put my whole career on the line for this? Well I won't. All I can do is thank God her name is listed in the papers as Smallwood rather than Thekkeden.'

'Well what a wonderful relief!' Anto sprang to his feet. 'As long as *we're* all right.'

'Who do you think you're talking to?' Anto saw two blue veins bulging in Appan's forehead, a glimpse of back teeth, a sure sign his father was losing his temper, but he no longer cared. Let the old bully boy rot in hell.

'I'm talking to you, Appan,' Anto said. 'And what I have to say is this: my wife is innocent, but you don't give a damn about that. Let's just worry about your reputation, and the noble Thekkeden name.' A drop of his sweat fell on his father's blotting paper.

'Leave my house,' Appan said eventually, in a quiet voice. 'And don't come back if this is how you're going to be. I've spent my whole life in the service of the law. I won't throw it away.' He took a handkerchief from the drawer and mopped his face.

'She's innocent. She was asked to help.'

'Her innocence was dangerous and naive. How many warnings did you need?'

Anto picked up his coat. 'I think we should end this conversation here. I won't come back until she's free.'

'Do what you want.' Appan shrugged. 'Your mother is my main concern now. She's coming away with me to avoid the scandal. If your wife is charged, I'll tell the family she's gone away to do more studying. That way, we won't have to talk about it.'

'If that's what you want.'

'It's what I want,' his father said, his eyes straight ahead.

Anto closed the door behind him and walked away.

Chapter 57

I was tried at the High Court of Travancore-Cochin at Ernakulum at 11 o'clock on the morning of Friday 5 May 1951. The date and the time were engraved on my mind. My crime: manslaughter and gross professional misconduct. Saraswati, who had expected right up until the last moment to be called as a witness, was not called. The sentence: three months at the women's correctional facility at Viyyur, seventy-four miles north of Fort Cochin. The judge said I was lucky to get off so lightly; that these were very serious crimes.

Six inches of rain fell on the day my case was heard. From the dock, the whoosh of bicycles going through puddles, windows rattling; puddles forming from dozens of sopping umbrellas near the door; steaming bodies. I remember those details, but surprisingly little of what was said. Just a blue ceiling in the court; wicker chairs, where Anto sat staring at me, trying to look encouraging, looking desperate, Saraswati Nair beside him, concentrating fiercely, wincing at the shortcomings of the only lawyer we'd been able to find at such short notice, a Mr Kurup, a cold-eyed man in a badly fitting shiny suit, who mispronounced my name and spoke so fast I could barely understand a word.

Long before the judge – an old foe of Appan's – sentenced me, I had a swooping feeling that I'd started down the path of my own destruction. When the sentence was read out, I felt light-headed: this was happening to someone else.

When Anto came to see me afterwards in my cell, we agreed that he should tell Raffie that night.

'But I'm not going to tell him for how long.' He tried to smile, 'Saraswati says it could be much shorter than that. She says it's a slap on the wrist.' The smile even less successful this time.

Before he left, I said, 'Can you bring Raffie to see me?'

He replied, almost curtly, that he'd see what he could do. 'It may upset him more.' And that was it. I longed for him to touch me, to

336

say something, but this unbelievable thing had left us both stunned and disconnected.

'So, I'd better go home now,' he said, even though the guard hadn't asked him to.

'Yes, go,' I said. 'Give Raffie a kiss from me. Tell him I love him.'

He tried to give me strength then: to tell me he was starting to understand the laws of manslaughter as well as any professional lawyer. That a retrial was inevitable, that it might only be a matter of days and weeks before I was set free. I heard these words as if through a thick pane of glass. He was surely talking about someone else.

And then he did kiss me: our arms and heads in a desperate tangle of love and sorrow.

'I'll be back tomorrow,' he said.

I was taken in a prison van to Viyyur, a drive of roughly three hours from Fort Cochin, still too shocked to think straight. Before, I'd imagined that Appan, with all his powerful friends, would pay some fine, pull some string, or that Saraswati, with her administrative genius, would do something, or even, in my wildest dreams, that Dr Annakutty would appear and admit that she had asked me to do the deliveries, and we had done them well. Now I felt like the most credulous idiot alive.

I thought about all the unremarkable things I normally did as part of a day's work. Getting up, getting washed, playing with Raffie, housework, the meals, the letter-writing, the walks with Anto, all the seemingly unimportant acts that made up a life. All shut down. The Department for Correction owned me now – my body and my time. A terrible thought.

When we stopped south of Viyyur for petrol, the guard in the van put his hand on the diary I kept from time to time. 'What are you writing?'

'Nothing,' I said. 'A journal.' And then, with as winning a smile as I could muster, 'You can read it if you like.'

For the few seconds his hand hovered over the pages, I almost stopped breathing; then he sniffed, his face contemptuous, and turned away. Why would an important man like him want to read a stupid diary?

'They may take it away in prison,' he warned when the van had coughed into life and we were moving again. I decided then and there I had to hide it, and hide it carefully. I needed an outlet, and for the time being, this would have to be it.

First sight of the Central Prison in Viyyur: worn earth, tired buildings, barbed wire, birds, blue sky, only the tips of trees.

As we drove down its long central road, the guard threw me a few scraps of information. This was mostly a prison for long-term male prisoners locked up for murder, for robbery, for theft. The women's prison was contained in two blocks: F and E, in the centre of the jail. There were two factory buildings where the women made baskets and clothes for a small wage every week; there was a prison garden.

When the van stopped, I was led down a corridor into a tiny windowless room lit by one naked bulb. The cell had a charpoi, a thin pillow like a bolster, a regulation grey blanket with *Property of Travancore Prison* on it. A bucket in the corner of the room.

An older man wearing stained overalls appeared with a bowl of water and a cloth. He told me to take my clothes off. He turned off the overhead light and locked the door. When I told him a woman should do this, he shook his head as if he didn't understand me. He didn't look at me as he ran his hands over my thighs, my stomach, my breasts, and finally between my legs. It was very mechanical, thank God; in fact, he treated me with some distaste: a contaminating white woman. When he saw my diary, tucked inside my dress, he rustled officiously through its pages, then sniffed and, to my surprise, handed it back to me.

He took away my clothes and my shoes, and gave me a coarse white sari and a loose white blouse to wear.

He looked at the wall while I was changing, then told me in a high staccato voice that I would stay in this cell for one or two nights and then I would be moved. He told me the cell was the regulation size, 'with sufficient breathing air'. The very idea of there being an officially recommended amount of air to breathe made the blood fizz in my veins.

The next day, a new guard, young, and with smallpox scars on his face, handcuffed me and led me down the corridor and across a square to the women's prison on F block. I stood at the door, blinking and very frightened, as another man drew aside a series of bolts and led me into a large communal cell, about twenty feet square, coir matting on the floor, high stained walls. A gravy-coloured light came from four or five smeared windows set in the roof.

When my eyes adjusted, I saw fifty or so women, some sitting on the floor, one or two staring vacantly, others asleep on thin mattresses. Most, I found out later, were here for long-term offences: illegal alcohol-making, vagrancy, prostitution, murder. There were three small babies in the room, and five girls under ten.

The guard said something about me that I didn't understand but which caused some of the women to mutter and look suspiciously at me, and made me even more nervous of the night ahead.

When he left, a woman with a lopsided gait and her hair cut as short as a GI's sat down on a mattress opposite me and sneered. I discovered later that this ex-schoolteacher had been one of a group of women rounded up during the riots and raped repeatedly. The shame of being raped, and subsequently disowned by her family, had driven her mad. She should never have been here.

As soon as the guard left, the air was full of noise, a parakeet shrieking that shredded the nerves. None of the women spoke English, or if they did, not to me.

It was hot in the room, and thick with smells. The madwoman sat staring at me until an older woman with an air of authority touched my arm and led me to a bed on the other side of the room. She held up her finger – wait! – and a few moments later came back with a cup of water. She didn't smile when I tried to thank her, but I was grateful nonetheless.

I was hungry, having had almost nothing to eat the day before, but when the prison breakfast arrived – a large round dumpling made of a gritty kind of wheat that smelled old – I couldn't eat it. I'd imagined, hoped, that after breakfast we'd be given a job to do – factory work, basket-weaving – but we all sat for the next two hours, the air soupy and hot. It was impossible to sleep to pass the time, but I lay down on my bed anyway, worried that in this thick fug of perspiring, leaking, coughing bodies, I would catch something and die and never see Anto or Raffie again.

On my third day there, after breakfast of a kind of rice gruel made from *chaakkari*, the lowest-quality rice available, we were lined up and made to march across a concrete yard to a room stacked with baskets. A thin woman with a hard, weary face and few teeth gave me a bundle of prickly reeds and machine-gunned instructions to me in Malayalam. I felt as gormless as some of the Moonstone midwives must have felt listening to me. I did my best, but three hours of sitting cross-legged on the floor made my back and hopelessly slow fingers tremble with tiredness. When the toothless one saw my horribly made basket, she held it up and jeered at it, and made the other women cackle.

I made baskets for six days, and when, on the seventh, a guard suddenly appeared saying, 'Husband is here,' I didn't know whether to cheer or weep. I hadn't slept and had a permanent crick in my back. I felt dirty, too. When I asked the guard if I could wash myself first, he snapped: 'Full female ablutions are on Friday.' But then he relented and brought me a basin of water and a small pot of sticky black soap.

Anto was sitting in the visitors' room when I walked in, very pale and still. Raffie was there too – a huge mistake. He leapt at me and covered my face in kisses, then lay on the floor and sobbed so hysterically that the guard warned us he would have to leave if he couldn't stop. Anto knelt down beside him.

'The man says we'll have to go if you cry,' he warned. He cradled him in his arms, but the sight of Raffie's brave little face struggling for control broke my heart.

'Mummy smells funny,' Raffie said when he could speak. When he took his thumb from his mouth and touched the ends of my hair, I could feel his heart jumping in his chest.

Anto, watching us, said, 'How on earth did we get here?'

'I don't know,' I replied. What I wanted to say was: I love you, I miss you, I'll be home soon, but I felt so degraded and ashamed, the words wouldn't come out right. Instead I told him he shouldn't have brought Raffie.

'You're not living with him,' he hissed in a low voice.

Raffie wriggled off my lap and sat on the floor in the gloomy light.

'You're a very good boy, darling,' I said. 'I'll be home as soon as I can.' He started to cry again.

Anto said I looked pale and had lost weight. He was worried about me. I told him about the basket-weaving, trying to make him smile, then I asked him to bring a Malayalam dictionary the next time he came.

'It won't be for much longer, you do know that?' He cupped my face in his hands.

I looked at him properly for the first time since his arrival. 'I'm sorry I told you off about Raffie,' I whispered. 'Is he sleeping?'

'Not much... not really. Don't worry,' he said, then, after a pause, 'He misses you.'

'Can't Amma have him for a day or two?'

'No, she's... Appan's taken her on a holiday.'

'So she really did go?' I'd been almost certain she'd refuse to, Amma seemed such a fixture at Mangalath, but there was no time to explain, and not much else to say that didn't feel either trivial or wearisome or freighted with unsaid things. The rhythm of our lives together had changed already: no more laughs, no long conversations, no tasks to do together, no teasing; just this shared humiliation.

'Saraswati and I are sure we can get you out soon,' he said before he left. 'I'll tell you more next time.' He stared at me intently. 'You're not alone,' he said. 'You're not alone. Do you believe that?'

I nodded numbly. When he hugged me, I wanted to imprint every part of him on me: his chest, his arms, the lemony, woody smell of him, but later that night, sleepless and boiling hot on my mattress, I felt a desert growing inside me. We had very little money left after the bad lawyer, and little support, I suspected, inside the prison, so what realistically could he do?

Chapter 58

At the end of my second week, I woke to find the ex-schoolteacher with the grey crew cut rhythmically pummelling my face, her yellow teeth bared. It was early morning; I was half asleep. Two guards, hearing my yells, rushed in and dragged her away, but not before she'd kicked me hard in the head.

When I woke, I was lying in the prison hospital, a large Nissen hut on the edge of the exercise yard. There was a nauseous pain in my temple, and my mouth and right cheek felt bruised. Coming round was like swimming to the surface of a scummy lake, full of the dirty rubbish in my head. When I looked up, Saraswati Nair was staring down at me. For a few weird moments, she became part of my dream, like déjà vu in reverse. Her face was still and unsmiling.

'Is Raffie all right?' I said. My spit tasted of copper.

'Don't worry.' She knelt down beside me. 'Kamalam and Anto are taking good care of him. Now listen carefully.' Her glasses were painfully bright. 'I have only ten minutes to talk to you; this is important.'

She brought her face close to mine and spoke slowly and distinctly. 'There will be a retrial. I have more than one hundred and eighty-three signatures on a petition from Moonstone patients. I am visiting government offices, twisting arms. I am insisting they call me as a witness next time; it was a grave miscarriage of justice. Are you listening to me?'

'Thank you, Saraswati,' I said feebly, sure she was making it up.

'What kind of talk is thank you?' she said fiercely.

'I shouldn't have done it . . .' I wanted her to stop my head banging, to take her bright glasses away.

'Listen,' she hissed, moving her face an inch or so closer. 'You have your husband on the warpath, also the many lion-hearted women in our community, and I am roaring with them. Don't forget this either: you never lied to Dr Annakutty about your qualifications.

She passed you as competent, but don't waste your breath on that. What we need now is money.'

'We don't have any,' I told her. 'Anto spent our savings on the lawyer, for all the good he did us. I wish I could have had you, Saraswati.'

'I would have blown the case to smithereens,' she admitted modestly. 'But back to the money: your family is wealthy, let them pay.'

'They won't pay.'

'Won't pay?' She could hardly contain her frustration.

'Won't bribe – not all Indians are corruptible, you know.'

Ignoring this she jerked back her cuff and looked at the man's wristwatch she wore.

'I have five minutes left, and it's important you understand this is not a good time to be an Englishwoman in prison: that madwoman may strike again.' She broke off suddenly. 'What's this?' She grabbed my right hand and stared at it in horror. It was criss-crossed with small cuts.

'It's the reeds.' I felt ashamed. 'We do basket-weaving, for the magnificent sum of one rupee a week.'

'Those stupids. What a waste!' Saraswati smacked the side of her head, looked around her. 'I'm going to talk to the doctor in charge.'

She flounced out of the room, coming back a few minutes later with a middle-aged man with a set smile, baggy, exhausted eyes, and a stethoscope around his neck.

'Dr Zaheer,' she said, 'is the chief physician here.' They talked over my head for a while, Saraswati translating. 'He says the prison and the hospital are overflowing. He's never known it so busy. They have a tent in the garden to deal with the extra patients; medical supplies are running out.' She broke off for another fusillade of words.

'Show him your hands. I'm asking him if that is any way to treat a state-registered nurse ... Where did you train? St Thomas's, where Florence Nightingale worked, am I mistaken? No. One of the finest hospitals in England. Correct?'

'It's certainly—'

'Now I'm telling him that you have safely delivered many children.' I was shaking my head before she finished.

'Saraswati, stop! Stop! Stop! Please! Tell him exactly why I'm here.' My lip still felt enormous, like talking through an inner tube. 'No false pretences.'

As she jabbered away for a while more, I saw a faint light dawn in the doctor's tired eyes. He ran his hand over a bristling chin, and spoke without drawing breath for several minutes.

'So here's the thing,' Saraswati said. 'He wants you to understand that this facility once had a very high reputation; he wants it to be like that again. I told him that was exactly how we felt about the Moonstone, that we were very proud of it, that we were doing everything we could to make it work. Sometimes we cut corners, not because we were stupid or cruel, but because we'd had to, and this time, we paid the price. You in particular.'

'That's nice,' I said wearily, not feeling anything but pain in my head, my mouth. When I woke up again, she was gone.

It turned out that Dr Zaheer spoke excellent English.

'Miss Smallwood,' he asked me four days later, with the same slightly unnerving set smile, 'do you have a certificate of nursing qualifications? Yes or no?'

'Yes, from St Thomas's, it was just the midwifery I hadn't quite—'

'That's all I need to know.' He got out a pad and started to write busily. 'I'm signing you off for three days' convalescence; after that, I want you to report here every morning at six thirty. We are badly in need of help with the women's clinic – general gynaecological problems, plus several deliveries a month. I will clear it with the governor. Your basket-making days are over.' This time the smile made it to his eyes, and I tried to smile, but it hurt too much, and anyway, I saw that if I proved too useful, I could just possibly get stuck in another kind of trap.

Chapter 59

Clinic hours at the prison hospital were from eight to twelve in the morning. Nobody stuck to them. A stream of patients came with every imaginable complaint, from boils to stomach upsets to secondary syphilis to broken bones. On my first week there, I treated one woman for vaginal tears, the result of a violent rape. Dr Zaheer told me pointedly that she had been assaulted twice: this time by a prison guard, who had been severely punished; the time before that by a British soldier the week before Independence. Was this true? No idea.

Dr Zaheer, whose mirthless smile looked more like a death's-head grimace every day, said the facility was close to collapse. Our main ward held twenty people comfortably, but we often had twice that number, making it hard to move between the beds.

But I respected this conscientious man, doing his best in difficult conditions. He was nice enough to me – even complimenting me on my stitching of the vaginal tear, an hour-long job – but he made it crystal clear I had no choice about being here, particularly as two local nurses were off sick. He also insisted I spoke to the patients in Malayalam. 'That's our state language, is it not?' he asked me sarcastically.

After a month, I could speak whole sentences without having to think about them; not necessarily phrases you might use in polite society – 'Have you tried to strangle yourself before?' 'How many men have you lain with?' – but it pleased me to be able to speak more fluently.

The ward nurse, a good-looking, hard-faced woman called Alka, was, I was pretty sure, sleeping with Dr Zaheer, a kind of *droit de seigneur* arrangement that was not uncommon in Indian hospitals; another reason, I imagined, why the Thekkedens found my profession so distasteful.

When I stumbled on them once in the dispensary, they sprang

apart, and afterwards, when I didn't understand her instructions, she widened her eyes in fury, like the wicked witch in a panto.

In my third week at the hospital, when one of the new prisoners arrived almost fully dilated, I was ordered to help a local midwife, Champa, who came to the prison whenever she was needed. With no time for formal introductions, we rushed the shrieking woman into a side ward, and performed what Sister Tutor would have called a textbook vaginal delivery together. Thanks to the Moonstone, I understood all the words, and we were a good team, and when the baby shot out, Champa gave me a sort of thumbs-up look that meant 'good, competent'. That poor baby would spend most of its life in captivity, as the mother was in for the murder of a bullying mother-in-law and had been lucky, Dr Zaheer told me, to avoid being lynched in her village.

By the time I got back to F block, I'd been gone for almost ten hours and was dizzy with exhaustion. When the guard appeared and told me I had a visitor in the reception area, I felt nothing but frustration.

Anto couldn't hide his shock when he saw me.

'Are you eating?' He grabbed my hand. 'You've lost so much weight. What are they giving you to eat?'

I told him that the nursing food was miles better than the ordinary prisoners' diet. That there were dosas, and fresh fruit, but I was never very hungry in the morning.

'Kit.' When Anto ran his thumb gently along my hand, a guard leapt forward – they were always on red alert for 'immoral acts' during visiting hours. 'Please eat breakfast.'

I didn't answer. I was trying to work out whether I should tell him then and there my suspicions about other possible reasons for my paleness. In the days leading up to my sentencing, we'd made love several times with the kind of desperate intensity that reminded me of our nights at Wickam Farm, and now I'd been sick for two mornings in a row and my breasts were tender. I'd put my three-week-late period down to anxiety; I couldn't think of a worse time or place to celebrate a possible new life. I didn't want to raise his hopes either, so instead I asked for news of Raffie.

'Sad,' said Anto at last. I could see him processing this thought, trying to find an honest way of answering without lying to me, which was the thing I always loved about him: how he tried to tell me the truth, however hard it was. 'He misses you.'

'Still not sleeping?'

'Not brilliantly.' Anto gave a long, shuddering sigh.

'Any help from Amma?'

'Not yet.' When he looked up, I saw purplish-black circles under his eyes. 'She's still away with Appan, but don't worry, Saraswati and I are full steam ahead. It won't be long, I promise you that.'

'What frightens me now,' I said, 'is that I may have become too useful – they're desperately short of staff.'

I blurted this out without thinking, my mind on the pregnancy test I would insist on tomorrow. When I saw the look of anguish in his eyes, I wanted to grab the useless woman I'd become by the shoulders and shout: Don't say those things to him! Don't add to the misery of the one person in the world who really needs your support.

A long silence fell between us, Anto with his head resting in his hands.

'How is your work going?' I asked him. An inane question.

'Not bad,' he said. 'I got my paper in.'

'Any news about the promotion?'

He looked up. 'Didn't get it.'

This was definitely my fault; before my conviction, Dr Sastry had told him it was a certainty.

'Any point in saying I'm sorry?'

'No, there's always another train.'

'You don't need another train, you need another wife.'

He tried a grimacing smile. His dark hair flopped over his forehead. I pushed it back.

To fill another silence, I told him about the delivery I'd helped with that morning.

'Good for your confidence, but do you trust them?' he said.

'Yes . . . no . . . I don't know. Dr Zaheer is a good man, I don't think he'll twist it. I've asked him if these deliveries can be used for me to get my final certificate.'

'But you're still not covered.'

'I am. I've insisted they put it in writing that I wasn't the principal midwife. He's told me he'll write to the Royal College of Midwives and get them to rubber-stamp it.'

Anto didn't look convinced, and neither was I entirely, but I knew

I had to trust Dr Zaheer or go mad with anxiety. Anto had opened his mouth to say something else when the bell rang, heart-attack loud; keys were officiously rattled, guards shouted. Visiting hour was over.

'The best thing about being married,' he'd once told me, 'is you don't have to finish conversations on street corners.' Now we did, and when I tried to piece our words together later, they seemed fragile, and badly made, and slippery. I wished in a way I'd told him about our possible baby, the promise of something new, because when he stood up, I saw I'd aged him. He looked stiff; there was a sprinkling of grey hairs I hadn't noticed before. He touched the side of my face very gently.

'I love you,' he said. 'Don't forget that ever.' I reminded myself to smile, feeling as empty as the sky.

Chapter 60

He'd had enough, Anto decided, as he exited through the prison gates. Two days later, after a quick trip to Mangalath, and some detective work with the servants, he arrived, shortly before lunch, at the Crown Hotel in Madras. His father was attending a conference there on the new constitution. At the gate, guarded by two uniformed lackeys, he stopped, confused: the hotel – dusky pink walls, tiled courtyards, blossom-scented gardens – was an unusually lavish choice for his normally frugal father.

He was shown to a room overlooking the garden, where he took a bath, and dressed himself carefully and slowly for the showdown he knew must follow. At the front desk, the clerk, a smiling, obsequious fellow in a cherry-red uniform with braided shoulders, told him that Mr Thekkeden, 'a very great man', was out every day, but he would almost certainly find Mrs Thekkeden in the garden, where she usually sat in the afternoon.

When he saw his mother from a distance, his heart clenched. She was sitting under a mimosa tree on a green bench, a small and lonely-looking speck, so deep in thought she didn't look up until he sat down beside her.

'What are you doing here?' She sprang to her feet when she saw him. 'What's wrong?'

'Amma.' He knelt beside her, took both of her hands in his. 'I need to talk to you.'

'Are you sick?'

He'd hoped for a grace period to ease her into this – an exchange of pleasantries, a mental taking of her pulse – but she had led him immediately to the point of no return, and he told her fast.

'Amma, we've been lying to you for months and months and months, and I can't do it any more. Kit's not studying; she's been in Viyyur jail for nearly six weeks now.'

Her brown eyes widened. 'Is this a joke?'

'No.' Telling brought no relief, only the shock of it again.

'For what?'

'Manslaughter. A trumped-up charge, for the delivery of a baby that died.' No point in fudging it now. 'The full details I can tell you later.'

'Oh my God! Don't tell me the details!' Her face wrinkled with disgust. 'I knew this would happen.'

He looked at her and shook his head. 'If you could see your face now, you would know why we lied to you.'

She jerked as if he'd slapped her. 'Who has lied to me?' she almost shouted. 'Who else knows?'

'It's been in the papers.'

'What papers?'

'You didn't see them – Appan's orders – but I'm telling you now because you're the one person who can really help me with Raffie. He's having a horrible time.'

'I knew something was wrong,' she said angrily. 'I tried to discuss it many times with Appan. I said, "I think his marriage is on the rocks." He said, "How many times must I repeat this: she's away studying. They are a modern couple doing things the modern way." Nice to know everyone was laughing at me.'

'My marriage isn't on the rocks,' he said, staring vacantly at the perfectly manicured terraces around him: the orange trees, the mimosa, the rioting bougainvillea, underneath which, with the precision of artists, gardeners had placed dollops of horse manure. 'But I need your help.' He pushed a mimosa blossom with his foot.

She shielded her face against the sun, stared at him. 'Isn't Appan helping?'

'He can't or won't, and this is the point of no return for me, because I'm sick of protecting the family name at all costs.'

'Antokutty,' her eyes pleading, 'don't say these things to me. It breaks my heart. I nearly died the day they sent you away.'

'I'm not talking about us, Amma. I'm talking about my wife, my family.'

'When you were little, we spent every moment we could together. I've never loved another person as much.'

'I'm a grown-up, Ma. I spent a lot of time alone.'

'So what can I do now?'

'I need help with Raffie. He's all over the place. I need money for a decent lawyer... Oh God, I hate this...'

'So give me time!' She put her hand on his arm. 'I will think of something. I don't want to lose you again.'

Chapter 61

When Anto left, Amma went upstairs, locked the bedroom door and, in a moment of pure rage kicked Appan's brown leather suitcase – a present from Hugo Bateman – as hard as she could. Then she closed the shutter and, hugging herself tightly, paced about the room, crying and shouting.

This was the worst public disgrace the family had ever faced, and what hurt most was that everyone had known but her, as if she was too feeble-minded, too conventional, too utterly and completely retarded to be told a thing.

Another source of humiliation was that, freed from family responsibilities, this unexpected holiday with Mathu had, after many years of drought, led to something surprising: they'd started to make love again.

'I'm too old,' she wanted to tell him, on that first night at the Crown, 'and it's too late.' Nothing but embarrassment at first, but then, her legs softening, her breath quickening, she'd felt something like an ice floe melting inside her. 'Don't cry, silly woman,' Mathu said fondly when she was lying in his arms.

'I'm sorry,' she'd said. 'I'm happy.'

Now she felt duped, and stupid, and sordid, and during the two sleepless nights that followed, her mind lunged back and forth between disgust at the girl, love for her son, loyalty to Appan and ice-cold fury at him for making her so stupid, such a nothing in the general scheme of things.

On the third day, she sat down on the bed, and forced herself to be calm. The time for weeping and wailing had passed; she had made up her mind: she had a plan.

She pulled Appan's suitcase on to the bed and, after forcing the lock with her manicure scissors, fumbled in the pocket of the silk lining for the envelope where she knew he kept his money. Her mood was so savagely vindictive that she was half hoping as she went methodically through every scrap of paper to find further evidence of wickedness – a failed business deal, a mistress she didn't know about.

She took a bundle of rupees from the envelope and put it in her pocket. Downstairs, she asked the swanky-looking desk clerk for train times to Cochin. She wrote the times down carefully, and left a note for Appan on the bed: *I've taken money from your case. I'm going home to take care of the children. I know about Kit.*

Her rage frightened her, and she wondered, as she folded the note carefully, if she would ever be able to forgive him. All the coochy-coo second honeymoon stuff had been a lie, and she, credulous fool, had lain there as panting and grateful as a starving dog.

She packed the brand-new suitcase she'd been so proud of, and then, from force of long habit, smoothed down the bedspread before closing the door. She was leaving. She was gone.

Calm yourself, woman, Kunjamma Thekkeden warned herself as she walked down the railway platform at 9.50 that morning. Her first trip alone on a train would take all her courage, and all her strength.

She fell asleep in the women's carriage with her face pressed against the window, and woke raging at Kit as the countryside sped by. Everyone knew that nurses had weak morals. Anto, thousands of miles from home, must have been a sitting duck. So fine, sleep with him, be immoral, but don't come home with him, bringing nothing but trouble and distress.

She closed her eyes tightly. What torture to think of all their friends reading the newspapers, gossiping and giggling about how the mighty Thekkedens had fallen, and in the most sordid and public way possible.

'Are you all right, madam?' the young woman next to her asked when she groaned out loud.

'Perfectly fine, thank you.' Amma peered through the window at a rubbish-strewn culvert. 'Thank you,' she said again, just to be clear.

Her words left an acid taste in her mouth. Was this what life was really like, lie upon lie upon lie? She recalled how she'd walked towards Kit that first day, hand outstretched, smiling, exclaiming; and later, welcoming the unstable Glory into the fold; sitting in the summer house while the ancient lover soggied up his handkerchief. All this suavity, this politeness, and look where it had landed her now that the big cat had pounced.

By the time the train had come to its screeching halt, she felt a tremendous weariness creep over her. What Anto was asking of her was not as simple as a change of mind, but a change of beliefs she'd led her life by.

'Why must I do this?' she muttered to herself as she pulled down her suitcase. Her plan now was to hail a taxi and go straight to Saraswati Nair's office in Fort Cochin. 'If your friends ever need legal advice,' Mrs Nair had said months ago, handing her a business card, 'you know where to find me.' Pushy, Amma had thought at the time, and disrespectful, when she had a first-class legal brain living under her own roof.

A stony-faced Anto waited for her on the platform.

'Why are you here?' she said.

'Appan sent me. The hotel manager told him what train you were on. He phoned the hospital. He's horrified.'

A spurt of anger invigorated her. 'He has no right to be horrified. He travels all the time.'

'He thought you'd left him – he's in an awful state.'

'I don't care,' she said. 'I have no time to waste. What I want to do now is to go to the place where Kit worked. I want to see everything.'

At the Moonstone, she told him to pick her up in an hour. She needed to talk to Saraswati Nair on her own. A few moments later, she faced the lawyer in her office – a converted Nissen hut under the stump of a charred tree.

'I know about Kit,' she said. 'I know about the prison. I'm saying this to save your breath, because I have my own questions now.'

'Take a seat, please, Mrs Thekkeden,' Saraswati said when Amma's fury had spent itself. 'I have a client coming soon, but I am able to talk for...' she consulted her watch, 'twenty minutes. Why are you here?'

'I'm here because my family have told me many lies.' It grieved her deeply to say this, but it was true. 'I don't trust them any more.'

'But you care for them?' Saraswati gave her a level look.

'I don't know.' Amma took a sharp breath. 'They have driven me to the point of madness.'

'I understand,' Saraswati said with a deep sigh. 'But as a professional person and as a friend, I am in a dilemma – I've been told not to tell you anything.'

'No line has been crossed,' Amma said. 'I came to you knowing the truth.'

Saraswati snapped the elastic band on a folder and stared at her.

'All right,' she said eventually. 'But we're going to do this my way, because you seem to be on the warpath, and that won't work.'

'Are you surprised? This girl has brought nothing but disgrace to our family.'

Saraswati shut the folder.

'So, I must stop you there. My time is precious, I won't have it wasted. There's too much to do.'

Amma pressed her lips together. 'Start again.' She folded her hands in her lap, trained her eyes on Saraswati. 'Sorry ... please ...'

'To go any further,' Saraswati continued in the same colourless lawyer voice, 'you need to understand some things. Put these on.' She handed Kunjamma a pair of galoshes. 'Come outside.'

They stepped from the hut. 'This way.'

Outside, a dazzling sun shone mercilessly on the charred beams, the smashed bricks.

'The Moonstone is not at its best at the moment,' Saraswati conceded, as they skirted around the stump of the neem tree. 'You must imagine it before they burned it down: a beautiful place full of hope. That,' she pointed towards a broken fish tank, 'held our prem babies.

'Maternity ward was there.' She pointed towards burned wire, and a sodden sofa. 'Reception there. There was the mango tree. But most of all' – she stopped and faced Amma – 'it was the people who made it. They were good people. Not just Kit, but the other midwife, Maya, the nurses. They were gentle, kind. *Kind*,' Saraswati repeated, angrily. 'It's so underrated, particularly by very traditional people.

'When I came here,' she continued as they crunched over some broken floor tiles, 'I was full of fear. I had fallen out with my family, who disliked me practising law. My labour was hard: fourteen hours, but nothing but kindness from Kit. Everything very sweet and clean here. I had a boy, and when she stitched me up afterwards, she was so gentle, I didn't feel a thing.'

'She stitched you up!' Amma's hand flew to her mouth.

'If you make that face again, I'll stop. She's a midwife, that's what they do when people bleed: you either take responsibility or you fail to, it's very simple.' Saraswati was glaring.

'I'm sorry. Carry on... you're right, that's what they do.' Amma made a visible effort to control herself. Her mind tripped back to the awful medical drawings she had seen in Kit's wardrobe: bare women with their bottoms in the air; varicose veins of the vulva.

'So.' Saraswati took a shuddering breath. 'My baby was born, over there actually.' She gestured towards a pile of broken glass, and burned timber struts. 'And then a few weeks after that,' her voice steadied and rose, 'he died. It was a cot death. Had nothing to do with the hospital. No infection was there, no injury at all. But this was the single thing that started the witch hunt. They said I would be called as a witness, but I was never called, and this is why I will stay and fight for this place, and for your daughter-in-law, with my last breath, and why your son and I are working around the clock to set her free.'

'I'm not a lawyer,' Amma said in a low voice. 'My husband is.'

'Your boy has a good brain, he could probably pass his bar exams now, but he's on his knees with exhaustion. We've been canvassing local women for their support. Two hundred and sixty-five signatures on our petition now.'

Amma sat on a bench, and put her head in her hands.

'I'm sorry about your son,' she said quietly at last. 'I had a miscarriage once; it would have been another boy.' She looked down at the ground. That memory had been buried so successfully – the pain, the total desert of the days that followed – that she had never spoken about it to anyone ever again.

'Well, you're lucky,' Saraswati said at last. 'You have a live son, but you will lose him if you cannot accept his wife. He adores her, and he is in hell right now.'

Amma put her hand to her mouth.

'I'll talk to him,' she mumbled at last.

'Not like this. It won't work.'

'No?' Amma looked up, her eyes full of pain and distress.

Saraswati put on her glasses and sighed. 'Spout your prejudices and things will get worse.'

'What then?' Amma was barely audible.

'Come.'

Taking her arm, Saraswati helped her over a small pile of charred rubble. To the right of it, the beginnings of a bonfire, with a couple of doors and a wooden doll on top.

'Look.' Saraswati pointed. Beyond the bonfire, a large rectangle of earth had been neatly raked and pegged out with lines of string. 'One day this will be our new clinic. We've already painted the sign to cheer us on. Some local women come every day to pray. They planted those,' a nod towards a row of marigolds near a fierce plaster goddess brandishing her sword.

'Mrs Thekkeden?' Saraswati saw her stumble, and took her arm. 'Are you tired?'

'Facts I need.' Light-headed from lack of food, Amma heard her own voice slur.

'So facts are these. We treat our village midwives like the lowest of the low. If men did this job, it would be seen as the supreme act of courage.'

'Don't point at me,' said Amma. 'I never treated my midwife like that. She is properly trained, she is clean.'

'You're rich, you have influence. A different story for poor women.' Saraswati's voice rose. 'Their lives are often destroyed by childbirth.'

Amma's eyes floated up in her head. 'I am tired,' she said. 'I need to think, but one thing I would say is, don't mistake me for a stupid or a cruel woman.'

'I don't,' Saraswati said softly. 'Kit has told me of your kindness to her family. But seriously, would you have the guts to be a midwife? No! Nor would I. Thank God someone does.'

Before she left, Amma told Saraswati she wanted to read the newspaper reports.

She opened the *Vantage* first, a local broadsheet. She smoothed it out, read it with her face going from white to red and back to white again.

'They haven't given her our name,' she said after a long silence. 'That's something, although the gossips will have spread the word by now.' She read on.

'These are disgusting,' she said at last. 'Poor Anto.'

'Poor Anto!' Saraswati barked incredulously. 'What about Kit? Now read these.' She pushed a red file towards her. 'This is what the local women said about her. Make up your own mind.'

Chapter 62

Two days after Anto's visit, Champa examined me and told me what I already knew: I was pregnant. I was almost sure I knew the night it had happened, a night of high moon and high heat, and desperate last-minute clinging that felt now like a lifetime ago. After she left the cubicle, I lay for a while wondering what this would mean now. Pregnancy in this place was not a get-out-of-jail card: babies were born and raised here quite routinely. My greatest worry was that I'd become indispensable to the crazily overworked Dr Zaheer, even more so now that my Malayalam had improved. When I'd warned him that afternoon that I only had six weeks of my sentence to run, he'd snapped, 'That's not correct. You must talk to the governor.'

Panicked, I wrote a letter to the governor asking for confirmation of my release date, but knowing the cumbersome bureaucracy of the prison, I did not expect a speedy reply.

A few days later, still suffering from morning sickness, I felt too ill to work and asked for an hour off. Dr Zaheer barked, 'Request refused,' but that night I was moved from the women's dormitory into a small cell of my own. A big relief. I longed for sleep with the intensity of a drug fiend, and when it didn't come, or I woke in the small hours, I felt I was in hell, and sometimes wept without sound, a clown's crying. It was one thing to lead myself down the path of destruction, quite another to be pregnant here. No one had said a word yet about my release.

The more tired I got, the more frightened I felt, a frayed cloth that grew thinner every day. Rumours flew about gangs of men and women who'd stockpiled weapons and were ready to riot; about guards who gagged and raped.

One night in mid July, I was escorted back to my cell after work, my feet aching from ten hours on the ward, my head blurry with tiredness. When I walked in, I saw the silhouette of a veiled woman sitting, very still, in the corner of the room. I thought at first it was Govinda, the sweet-faced nurse who sometimes helped me on the wards. The light in the cell came from a weak bulb high in the ceiling, so it was hard to see, but when I moved closer and saw it wasn't her, I remembered my attacker and froze.

'*Nee endha cheyyanae?* What are you doing?' I said. 'Who are you?' The dark shape stood up, laid aside her shawl and faced me. It was Amma.

She looked so pale, I didn't recognise her at first. Her eyes were staring dark hollows between the folds of her veil. When I looked around the room, I saw it through her fastidious eyes – the high scummy window, the potty, the iron bed, the grey blanket – and it made me want to die of shame.

'Why are you here?' I said when the guard had locked the door behind us. Something terrifying had occurred to me. 'Has there been an accident at home?'

'No, no, no, no.' Her expression softened a little. 'Nothing's happened,' she said. 'I'm here because I wanted to see you. You've lost a lot of weight.'

'There's been a tummy bug.' I backed away from her. 'I don't want you to catch it.'

'I'm glad to be here.'

I didn't believe her, of course. I'd seen her immaculately ordered house: the polished floors, the tidy medicine cabinet with labels lined up, even the bloody orchid hospital, for God's sake.

It was only when the light in the cell surged that I saw how much weight she'd lost too. Her skin, once plump and shiny like a ripe conker, looked as papery as autumn leaves.

'Amma,' I said, not even sure I could call her that now, 'I'm so sorry... I've made such a mess of things.'

She turned away, her lips working violently.

'... a big shock,' she managed eventually. 'Everyone knew but me.' I heard her gasp. 'And when you don't have the facts, your mind goes mad.'

'I know.'

'You shouldn't have left me in the dark.' She wiped her eyes on the corner of her shawl. 'You of all people should have let me know. You saw what lies did in your own family. Nothing but pain. But you didn't trust me either.'

I thought of Glory then. How I'd clung to her the night before she died and the lifeboat broke up into little pieces.

'I wasn't sure I could,' I said. 'I wasn't exactly your dream of a daughter-in-law.'

A look of wry amusement passed between us. There it was, out, like the head of a boil.

She closed her eyes. 'Well...'

'And this makes it so much worse.'

'That we cannot change, but listen, please, we don't have much time.' Her face was set and unsmiling. 'Anto and Saraswati want me to change overnight. I can't – that would be another lie – but Saraswati showed me the Moonstone. She says if they can raise the money, it will be built again. A long way to go.' She sounded resigned, and far from happy, and I felt the same: for me, the whole place felt freighted with failure now.

'Did Appan ask you to come here?' I asked in the silence that followed.

'No.' She stared into her lap. 'He's not talking to me. I stole money from him to pay the bribe.'

'The bribe?'

'How else am I sitting here?'

I was astounded. 'Who did you pay?'

'I'm not going to say,' she pressed her lips together.

'Oh God.' The damage was spreading and I was responsible.

'Amma, I'm so sorry,' I said. She looked so crushed, so old. 'I never wanted you to fall out with Appan.'

'A shake-up was needed,' she said. 'He'll be back.'

'Have you spoken to Anto?'

'A few nights ago,' Amma said tonelessly. 'We stayed up late unknotting things between us. He asked me a question: "Do you remember the parable of the Good Samaritan?" I said of course I did, everyone did.

' "Is it true or is it a lie?" he said.

' "Don't come to me with your clever Downside talk," I told him. "I'm a Christian, I know what it means."

' "OK," he said. "Let me put it another way. Tonight, when you leave me, you see a child bleeding to death beside the road. Do you cross the road to avoid the mess of it? Do you say to yourself, I'm not qualified, I won't look, or do you see the supreme value of a human life, and do what you can?"

' "I'm not stupid," I said. I knew where this was leading. "There are laws, and your wife broke one. Jail was the next step."

'He was stern with me. "Listen," he said. "I've spent months now looking at the legalities of manslaughter and criminal negligence, and they're muddled and unclear, all lawyers know this. For example, if I was a captain on a ship, and one of my crew got ill, I could be prosecuted for not doing anything. The law calls this failure to assist. New health system, new country, new laws: we're all at sea," he said.'

Amma raised her eyes and looked at me. She wasn't enjoying this one bit. 'He said you chose to help in a difficult situation, that you might have been foolish in your innocence and optimism, but you were at least brave, and that you paid a high price for it.'

'He did?' I could hardly speak.

'He said all this.' Her voice was low.

'You don't agree, though, do you?'

'I don't know.' She looked at me again. 'I'm never going to like you doing this.'

We smiled the same wry smile. She was, at least, honest.

'Anto says that you'll complete the medical requirement as soon as you get out.'

'I'm almost there,' I said. 'That's the irony. All I need is two more supervised deliveries. I should have organised them at the Moonstone, but we were always too busy.'

'So, what next?' She was watching me like a hawk.

'I don't know … Get my certificate, go back to the Moonstone – if they'll have me, and if the money gets raised to build it again. I'm not looking forward to it, but I can't seem to let it go. That's not what you want to hear.'

'No, it's not.' She looked miserable. 'But it's your life.'

We had come to the end of what was possible for now, and hearing the guard's feet again, the rattle of keys, I felt an incredible weariness: the heat pressing down on me like a wet blanket, the long night ahead.

'Look, Amma,' I said, 'I am not in control any more … I try not to make plans.'

She brought her face close to mine, and I thought for one strange moment that she was going to kiss me. Instead she whispered, 'You're wrong. It will happen, and it will be soon. Wait and see.'

Chapter 63

My knight in shining Amma, I thought unkindly after she'd left and darkness had fallen. She looked too old and frail to have any kind of currency in a place like Viyyur.

But a week later, shortly after breakfast, a package appeared in my cell. Inside it was the blue dress I'd arrived in eight weeks ago, nicely washed and ironed by the prison laundry, a pair of stockings and my shoes, lying there like messages from another life: both wonderfully familiar, and awfully strange.

The guard took me to a concrete room across the F block square with a sign on the door saying *Female Ablutions*. He gave me a pot of sticky black soap and a strip of cotton fabric to dry myself with. I filled the copper bucket and washed myself from head to toe.

My heart was crashing in my chest as I dressed, combed my hair and made my way to Dr Zaheer's cramped office on the side of the main ward. This is a trick, I thought, listening to the birds piping in the trees outside. It won't happen.

But then Dr Zaheer – grimy lab coat, bruised eyes – addressed me in his I'm-speaking-to-you-from-the-grave voice.

'You're leaving today. Not my choice.' No smile now. The look of a man betrayed.

There were, he added, a couple of important strings attached: I was to come back to the hospital and work two days a week at the clinic for the next six months. Part of this arrangement involved helping the resident midwife.

'Will I definitely get official accreditation?'

I watched his eyes flicker thoughtfully while I waited for this penny to drop, then he said in a barking voice, 'Prisoner rehabilitation is at the heart of what we do. We have a prison library here; I will order any books. You can be our first midwife graduate.'

*

When I saw Anto waiting for me outside the prison walls, I could not speak at first. When I got into the car, we clung to each other.

'Stop it!' Anto said, wiping his tears with his sleeve. 'We're bloody idiots! You're free.'

And then I told him about our new baby, and we started sobbing again, and laughing, and clutching each other for dear life.

'Actually, I'm not quite free,' I said. As we drove away, I told him about the agreement I'd made with Dr Zaheer.

'Do you mind?' He glanced at me and took my hand.

'No,' I said, and then, to show off my Malayalam, '*Athu nalla kachavadam tannae.*' It seems like a fair exchange. Which in a queer sort of way it did.

It took a while for things to feel right again. On my first morning home, the beautifully sliced ripe Alphonso mango laid out on my breakfast plate, the cup of freshly brewed coffee, they looked as if they had arrived from another planet. There was a note from Anto: *Morning, wife. I hope you slept well.*

The house had rearranged itself in my absence. Raffie kept asking if he could sleep in Kamalam's bed. We let him for a while, in order to avoid the explosion of tears detonated on the first night at the thought of going back to his old room.

At the end of my first week back, I sat with him on the veranda, where he was playing listlessly, jumping in and out of a cardboard box. When I tried to join in, he stood in front of the box and folded his arms like a sentry. 'I only play this with Kamalam,' he said.

'Give him time,' Anto said, when I told him later. Anto, who was wearing glasses for the first time, had lost weight and was starting to look like Appan. In my absence, our bedroom had been converted into an untidy study covered in papers and legal books. I wanted him to take those bad memories away, but didn't dare ask until I felt less of a stranger here.

I knew everything would start to get better when I slept, but I'd been running on adrenalin for so long, my motor wouldn't stop, and one night when I woke and felt Anto's hand on my head, I yelled so loudly I woke Raffie up. 'I'm sorry,' I said. 'I'm sorry . . .'

One evening, when Anto came home from work, he put me to bed. When he took off his new wire glasses, I was aware again of the beauty of his eyes, how they opened up in a seam of tortoiseshell and green. He needed a haircut; his hair was soft and silky when

I touched it. He brought me fresh lemon juice in a tall glass, and asked me if I would like to go with him and spend a few days at Mangalath. No, I told him, not ready to face the relatives. Their displeasure, their polite smiles. Not yet.

I didn't want to see anyone for a while, but Saraswati came anyway. Said she'd hired a special rickshaw to take me down to the Moonstone. It was a huge shock to see it again: the soil all churned up, the foundations dug in, but nothing else except broken glass and charred beams. She took my arm to help me over a pile of broken bricks. She wanted to show me the new Durga statue in the one patch of vegetation that had survived. This Durga, huge and pink, had been paid for out of donations by the ever-generous Mr Namboothiri. She was sitting on a lion, and to me seemed a fanciful waste of what little money we had left.

'Do you know what she stands for?' Saraswati asked.

'No.' I closed my eyes and thought, here we go.

'She has three eyes,' Saraswati said with the gusto of someone describing a marvellous friend. 'Her left eye is for the moon, or desire; the right eye, the sun, stands for action; the central eye is knowledge. And the lion,' she ended with a flourish, 'is determination. Willpower.'

'I had some of that once,' I joked.

'You still do,' said Saraswati. 'Shock will go and you'll be back. The three weapons in Durga's hand are a thunderbolt, a sword and – your mother-in-law's favourite – a lotus, in bud but not fully bloomed. That symbolises certainty of success but not finality.' While she was talking, I saw two huge rats move over the ground.

'I need some of your strength,' I told her.

'Give it time,' she said.

Mariamma came next, unannounced and unexpected, with a bag of fresh pastries in her hand. She stood at the door, framed in sunlight, motionless for a moment, as if taking the temperature of the room, then came towards me and, sinking to her knees, put her arms around me.

'Welcome home, sister,' she said. 'I'm so happy to see you. I know where you've been, Appan told me. We don't need to talk about it now.'

She stayed for lunch, and in the afternoon, she washed and

braided my hair. The beautiful smell of coconut oil. When I told her I was expecting a baby, her eyes filled with tears, and she hugged me. 'You're the first person to know,' I said. 'And don't tell anyone else, it's too early.' As a midwife, I was extra superstitious about that.

'I'm so happy for Raffie, too.' She dabbed at her eyes. 'He was miserable when you were gone.'

We caught up with the family gossip that Mariamma called *vayadi*, literally 'flapping mouth'. Theresa, she said, had graduated top of her class and was becoming a right little madam. Ponnamma was growing more and more nutty. Recently she had bellowed across the table at Amma, 'Do you miss sex, daughter? I do!' which had caused Appan to choke on his thoran. 'You know what she's like,' Mariamma continued, enjoying my laughter. 'She says, "Now I am old, I never apologise for being a nuisance, I *am* a nuisance!"'

I wanted to ask her about Appan, and whether he was still angry, but couldn't find the words yet, and was grateful to her for keeping things light.

That night, there was a flamboyant sunset, peach and vermilion flames in the sky, and I sat in the courtyard – I never used the veranda any more – and watched it dumbfounded, thinking of all the things I'd taken for granted. When Anto came home, I made him a gin and tonic the way he liked it, with a slice of lime.

After Kamalam had bathed Raffie, he came to me and of his own accord sat on my knee. His skin was warm, his hair damp. He said, 'You were a bad girl, Mummy, for being away for so long.'

He slept in my arms.

Mariamma came again a couple of days later. She slid her feet out of her slippers and sat next to me, and we chatted about normal things.

She was up to her neck in preparations for the festival of Onam, the biggest feast of the year in south India. I'd enjoyed it last year at Mangalath, but this year, with forty-four close relatives invited, I wanted to run for the hills.

'Oh my God, look at all these things I must do now.' Mariamma, indignant and happy, pulled the master list from her handbag. 'Banana leaves, chickens, fifty coconuts, rice, pearl fish, yoghurt, lentils. New cricket and ping pong bats for the children, new pillow-cases, new glasses. Such a carry-on.'

Raffie, who was leaning against my knee, sucking his thumb, was already excited about Onam. When Anto got home from work, they burbled on about playing cricket with his cousins, dressing up as tigers, the usual family boat race.

'Do you think you can make it?' Anto asked me gently.

'Not sure,' I said. 'I'll think about it, but you must go.' Manufacturing a smile when I was still frightened of every knock on the door.

'Do you know why we celebrate Onam every year?' Anto asked. Raffie was sitting on his knee now. 'It marks the ancient King Mahabali's return from Patala, the underworld. The story goes that he loved Cochin so much, he had to come back.'

Raffie took his thumb out of his mouth. 'I'm going to be a tiger!' He bared his pearly teeth.

'Noooo!' Anto shrank back in mock terror, then pulled him back on to his knee. 'But do you know why we're really going to Mangalath?'

'Sweets!' shouted Raffie. 'Cricket?'

'Harvest, home, family ties.' Anto flicked his eyes towards me.

'Here endeth the lesson,' I said, and even to me, my voice sounded bitchy. I walked out of the room, and sat on a bench in the courtyard, trying not to cry.

'Appan and Amma had a wee ding-dong about the Onam food last week.' Mariamma was back again with more Mangalath snippets. 'As you know, the veggie dish is traditional, but Appan wants to offer chicken and prawns as well. "Come on, woman!" Mariamma's voice deepened. "Times change, guests don't want to eat food like cattle."

'Amma got very huffy,' Mariamma continued in the same semi-delighted whisper. ' "*Mundi!*" she said, quite audibly. Appan rushed out of his study. "Sorry, did you say something?" Amma smiled like this.' Mariamma did her rictus smile. ' "No, husband, nothing at all." She said she would be going into the garden, and might be gone for some time.'

Mariamma took a bite of her pastry, still chuckling. I said, 'It's been kind of you to come every day like this.'

'You are my sister.' She brushed the crumbs from her skirt. 'I missed you badly while you were away. I thought about you every single day; my heart was breaking.'

She got down on her knees and clasped both her hands around my knees.

'Come back for the feast. Please. Appan and Amma really want it.'

'They do?' I could hardly hide my surprise. 'I thought it would be less awkward if I stayed here.'

I thought I'd become Amma's guilty secret. Before she'd left the prison that night, Amma had stabbed her finger in my direction and said, with her fiercest look, 'You must never tell anyone about this!' meaning the bribe, meaning her intervention. I didn't think I'd ever be forgiven.

'No!' Mariamma said vigorously, her big brown eyes trained on mine. 'They want you home.'

She dropped a parcel into my lap.

'You may wear it, if you decide to come,' she wheedled, her head on one side.

Later, I opened the parcel. Inside was a brand-new beautiful white and gold sari. The perfect symbol of a spotless Indian wife. I gazed at it not knowing whether to laugh or cry.

Chapter 64

In the end I went, reluctantly and mostly to please Anto, dreading the ten days of enforced jollity ahead. After a few attempts, and some help from Kamalam, I managed to put on the new sari Mariamma had so thoughtfully provided, while feeling that sackcloth and ashes might be more the ticket.

Mangalath was in its party clothes when we arrived: the sky almost artificially blue, the courtyard covered in the *pookalum*: a riotous carpet of fresh roses and marigolds, orchids and lotus blossoms, bursting with colour and light – the everyday miracles I was still too battered to appreciate.

When he saw the flowers, Raffie shouted, 'Zippitydoodah!' his favourite new word. He struggled to get out of the car, raced towards the house.

'Are you all right?' Anto touched my hand.

'Fine,' I said, taking a deep breath. 'The jailbird returns.'

'Stop it.' He tucked a strand of hair behind my ear. 'Half of them won't know; the other half will, in great Anglophile tradition, never mention it again, so stick with me, kid. You look beautiful, by the way. Really beautiful. How do you feel?'

'Physically fine,' I said. In the past few weeks, I'd felt that mid-term-pregnancy energy starting to flow into my bones, my hair, my skin, which had lost its pallor. 'Mentally, a bit like the wrong sort of prodigal daughter.'

'You'll be fine,' he whispered. 'It's our baby's first party.'

Amma was standing in almost the exact same spot she'd been in on the first day I met her, between the gold lions, wearing an almost identical white and gold sari. My heart began to thump. Given all that we knew about each other now, it felt presumptuous to be wearing the same uniform. She took both my hands in hers, looked at me for several fraught seconds, and then talked over my head to Anto, as she probably always would.

'I'm very glad you came,' she said. 'We were worried you wouldn't.' As we walked up the petal-strewn path towards the house, she put her hand on the small of my back.

'Should I speak to Appan before joining in?' I said. A trip to the headmaster's study felt like the least I could do.

'Only if he wants to speak to you,' she whispered quickly. An army of small children were racing down the steps to claim their youngest cousin. 'And don't worry too much. He's forgiven me for taking the money. A beautiful bunch of orchids came today.' She squeezed my arm. 'We did what was necessary; it's over now.'

Anto was right: no one said a word about prison on that first day, although I held myself in readiness, and felt stiff with nervous tension at the end of it. I was very much aware of Appan: elegant, gracious, commanding; circulating, checking drinks, patting children's heads, roaring with laughter at jokes. When he saw me, he dipped his head in my direction and said, 'Welcome.'

On our fourth day there, I was up in the middle of the night, jangled and unhappy and unable to sleep. I didn't want to wake Anto so I walked downstairs barefoot. I went into the family prayer room. A candle, burning in a rose-coloured glass jar, shed a dim, warm light over the Virgin Mary. When my eyes had adjusted, I saw a man huddled in the corner of the room. He was wearing loose pyjamas and was praying.

'Appan.' I started to back away. 'I'm so sorry ... I ...'

'Kit.' He looked at me. 'Are you all right?'

'I didn't mean to disturb you; I'm going back to bed.'

'Don't go.' He hauled himself with some difficulty on to the pew. 'I've been thinking about you all day.'

'You have?' I sat tensely at the end of the bench, waiting for the recitation of my sins I was sure would follow. He was staring at me.

'You were brave to come back like this. I mean to Mangalath, with the whole tribe here.'

I told him it had been Anto's idea.

'And do you always do everything your husband wants?'

'In this instance, yes. He's been amazing.'

I heard a sad snort.

369

'In what way?' He shifted on the pew, making it creak like a ship's bows.

'Loyal,' I said at last. 'Kind. I feel like the truest version of myself with him.'

I saw his head bow.

'I let him down,' he muttered. He glanced at me quickly. 'Do you think he will ever forgive me?'

It was quiet enough in the chapel to hear the faint sizzle of the candle burning; his bare feet brushing against stone.

'He loves his family,' I stalled, reluctant to speak for Anto. 'And,' after a long pause, 'I think we all get it wrong in our own ways. Look at me.'

He gave me a strained, considering look. The look I imagined had terrorised many prisoners in the dock.

'You erred on the side of wanting to help,' he said at last. 'Amma has explained your work to me. The good things your patients said about you. She says that you're going to finish your qualification. When you do, I will send some money to the home. A penance, maybe.'

'A penance!' I gaped at him and shook my head. 'I wasn't even sure I could come back here.'

'You were punished harshly,' he said. 'I knew that all along. All I'm giving is a few rupees – too late, probably. If I'd been another kind of lawyer, I would have got you off, but I couldn't. I've lived my whole life with certain rules, and I found I couldn't break them, so what I've decided to do is donate the same money as the bribe, and then we must never talk about it again.'

He shivered, as if he had reached the end of some long ordeal, and then looked up at the window.

'This is a creepy time of night, no?' He wrapped his shawl around himself. 'The veils are at their thinnest. I can almost imagine King Mahabali creeping back from the underworld.'

It took a while for his words to sink in. I was still experiencing a kind of flooding relief.

'What a discovery the world must have been.' I followed his gaze towards the window. The candle had gone out, but a soft streak of light was brightening the stained glass; I could hear the clucking of birds.

'Thank you for talking to me,' I said. 'I was so frightened of coming back.'

'Families are frightening. They mean too much. You look tired, daughter. You need rest.'

'I'm going to go and get some sleep,' I said.

I slept for twelve hours straight. It was like a tight hat coming off my head. And later, when night was falling and the prawns and the chicken were sending out tantalising messages from the kitchen, forty-three members of the Thekkeden family played cricket on the lawn behind the house. I could hear Raffie's excited voice breaking through the hubble-bubble of sound. When it got too dark to see, the batsmen played with Davy lamps on their heads. Fireflies flitting in the dark, shouts and laughter. Appan (two whiskies to the wind) was an erratic fielder, his Tibetan mastiff barking and leaping for stray balls. Mariamma running stoutly between the trees. Anto batting athletically, doing his Sunil Gavaskar impersonation. I stayed on the dark fringes of the fielding, where the lawn dissolved into darkening trees, and beyond birds skimming down across the silver backwater.

Amma, proud and mocking, stood framed in light on the veranda, watching. When it got too dark to play, she rang the bell.

'Dinner, everyone. Don't let it get cold!'

After dinner, the youngest cousins got into their night clothes and lay in piles on charpois on the veranda. Boxes of old cinema film were unpacked. Mariamma, the bossy older sister, told Anto to help put up the screen. 'Not there! There, higher! No, lower than that.' It was time, she said in a bad attempt at a Barnum & Bailey accent, for 'The Thekkeden Motion Picture Showee'.

The film began with a few Mangalath babies toddling drunkenly on to the screen, herded by a very jolly-looking mother, who waved at the camera.

'That's me!' shouted Ponnamma, who had drunk more than her fair share of ginger wine. 'What a minx I was!'

Then Appan, moustached and dapper in his plus fours, and Amma, his radiant bride, on a honeymoon holiday in Madras.

'Don't you dare go to sleep.' Mariamma shook Raffie awake. 'Wait for your daddy.'

Raffie's hair was still damp from his bath. He put my arm around him.

Anto, who'd disappeared into the kitchen, came back and sat

beside me. He was barefoot and carrying a bowl of golden banana chips. He handed me a weak whisky and soda.

A few seconds later, a jerky black-and-white image of him bloomed into life on the screen. He looked about twelve messing around doing pretend cricket shots for the camera. In the next frame, he was wearing a tweed jacket several sizes too big for him, with leather patches on the elbows, and he looked so young and sweet and skinny, my heart leapt with sorrow for him. Behind him was the ocean liner that would shortly take him away from all this, the whole of the wild sea ahead.

There were wolf whistles, catcalls. Ponnamma pinched him. 'Handsome devil!'

'Spiffing suit, what, Uncle Anto?' said Thaddeus, one of the younger cousins. 'The playboy of the Western world.'

I was thinking as I joined in the laughter what a lot he had made of his life: how resilient he'd been, brave too. I felt the blaze of the new baby inside me. I'd started to talk to it now, to feel sure of its small heart beating. I made up my mind to tell Amma tomorrow, which of course meant telling everyone – assuming Mariamma hadn't done so already, 'In the strictest confidence, of course!'

Appan, staring at his son, now on the deck, waving goodbye, groaned and sank down in his chair. Amma patted his hand. And then, to my surprise, there was me. I hadn't been aware of being filmed at the time. I was wearing the blue dress, smiling and shaking Amma's hand, looking scared out of my wits, as well I might, faced with the great roiling mass of contradictions, horrors and wonders ahead.

After the film show, Mariamma and I pushed the sleepy children upstairs. One of the toddlers was sparked out, draped like a shawl over Mariamma's shoulder. Raffie said he wanted to sleep in the cousins' room, otherwise he would dream about black spiders.

It was late by the time we'd left them all in a murmuring bundle in the spare room. Anto said, 'Let's go for a walk in the garden.'

We went down the steps towards the summer house, and sat on a bench overlooking the water. The air was warm on my face, spicy and sweet from the flowers. I told him about my conversation with Appan, and as I watched his expression change and grow hopeful as he absorbed the news, I felt the pure flame of my love for him again.

The water, black and crinkly, was lightly touched with gold from an almost full moon. From the temple across the lake we could hear the pulsing of drums. Onam was being celebrated there too, and in dozens of villages for miles around. The priests had lit a bonfire; its flames rose and dissolved in a million sparks in the sky, an all-night *puja* for the crops that didn't fail, and the returning king.

Acknowledgements

First I must thank Rema Tharakan for her constant stream of emails and her advice and encouragement with this book. Rema, and her husband Anthony were fantastic hosts and guides during my research trip to Kerala.

Midwife, Rachel Walker, and her obstetrician husband, Dr David Walker, gave generous guidance on midwifery matters, as did Jane Ash, Dr Suhas Choudhari and Gabrielle Allen from Guys and St Thomas' Charity. Any mistakes are mine.

I'm indebted to numerous books on Indian history, Nasrani customs and climate, particularly Diane Smith's fascinating *Birthing with Dignity*, and Alexander Frater's *Chasing the Monsoon*. Emma Jolly, from Genealogic, also dug out some fascinating facts.

Especial thanks to Delia and Caroline for their inspiration and support, to my editor Kate Mills, and to Clare Alexander, for being the best.

Finally, more thanks than I can express to Richard, for his advice, his generosity and good humour during many readings of this book.

MONSOON
SUMMER

Reading Group Notes

In conversation with Julia Gregson

When did you get the original idea for the book?

I've been obsessed with India since I was a small child, so when I sat next to this English woman at a dinner party in London, and she told me she had married an Indian doctor, and now lived in a small village in Northern India, my ears pricked up. I tried not to pepper her with questions (a family failing), but she seemed happy to talk.

Her story was this: she'd fallen in love with an Indian doctor while they were both students at Cambridge. He was handsome, irreverent, drank, smoked and they'd quickly become lovers, and a few months later, married.

Shortly after this, they'd gone back to live in a small village in North India, where something like thirty of his relatives lived, and where he was to be the village doctor.

The change in him, and in her circumstances, had been sudden and shocking. In India, she ate mostly with the women in his extended family, and was disliked and bullied by her mother- in- law. She was expected to treat her husband as a kind of God.

This woman, I can't even remember her name, left a deep impression on me. On this night, and on this brief trip 'home', and with her husband back in India, she seemed to be discovering everything she'd left behind. Several times she mentioned how much she missed this kind of banter and easy conversation, and yet, I sensed she still loved and admired her husband. Had the price been too high? Could I do that? All these thoughts later, got me thinking.

Why did midwives in India intrigue you?

I think of midwifery as being one of the most powerful and the most frightening jobs you could possibly do. You're meeting a woman at one of the most vulnerable moments of their lives. Such hope, such joy when things go smoothly, such devastation and distress if you get it wrong. Then I read about The Countess of Dufferin's fund, set up in 1885 and funded by Queen Victoria. She sent out teams of trained English midwives to India to work with the Indian Dais, otherwise known as TBA's (Traditional Birth Assistants). This struck me as adding on another layer of terror to an already difficult job. How could these midwives possibly understand the layer upon layer of caste complexity in India? Or the huge differences in birthing traditions within the country. So many ways of getting it wrong, particularly when I decided to set my book in 1948, a year after Indian Independence, when Indians would be particularly ill-disposed towards the British.

Has anything interesting happened as a result of writing this book?

One of the best things about researching the kind of books I write is getting to meet experts in the field. One such was an extraordinary young midwife called Anna Kent Alam.

In her early thirties, she's delivered babies by a head torch in Sudan, triplets in earthquakes, trained thousands of midwives in Bangladesh.

Co-incidentally, she has also married an Indian man, a champion surfer, they now live part of the time in Bangladesh where he is part of a huge extended family, and part of the time in Nottingham, England on a narrow boat.

How did you go about you research?

Lots of trips to libraries, lots of reading of midwife journals, and discussions with modern midwives, plus a wonderful research trip to South India. There I stayed in Fort Cochin, at the hotel where Anto and Kit stay on their first day, then I stayed at a Homestay with a Nasrani family, who had a beautiful house on the backwater. They were amazingly kind and helpful to me: showed me how to eat and prepare their food, how to tie a sari, how they did their hair, how they washed, when they prayed, all the intimate details that make a story come alive. I then spent three of the happiest days of my life alone, on a rice boat, observing the life around me and making lots of notes. I also went to the Royal College of Obstetricians and Gynaecologists to read accounts of midwives in the field then – all very interesting.

What other books or other writing have you done?

This is my fourth novel. The first *Band of Angels* was set in Wales and Turkey; the second, *East of the Sun*, in England and India; the third *Jasmine Nights*, in Cardiff and Cairo and Turkey, and now *Monsoon Summer* in what is now called Kerala. I rarely set a book in England, and I have no proper idea why, except I had, with an Air Force father, such a travelling childhood and still love to travel.

What are you currently working on?

I am really superstitious about talking too much about works in progress, but it's set in London, Paris, New York and Las Vegas, and I'm reading like crazy at the moment, and planning a trip to the Folies Bergère in Paris.

The Inspiration Behind Monsoon Summer

In my new book, '*Monsoon Summer*,' an inexperienced midwife, steps into a human land-mine, when she travels to India in 1948 to teach the local midwives Western ways. I based part of my story on the English midwives who travelled to India as part of the Dufferin Fund, set up in the 19th Century, by the Countess of Dufferin.

After I'd written the book, and keen to find out if there were any modern counterparts, I discovered a story as inspiring, and at times as heart-breaking as any I've ever written.

Enter, Anna Kent Alam, a slender, youthful looking 35 year-old specialist midwife from Nottingham, who looks remarkably untroubled by the extraordinary and gruelling life she has led. In her time she's delivered a baby by head torch in South Sudan in the middle of a tropical storm; triplets without back up, in a mud hut in the same country, and in Haiti, where she travelled after the earthquake; brought babies into the world from mothers desperately ill with cholera.

In South Sudan, where she worked for Medicin san Frontier, (MSF) and where the temperature was often over 50 c in the middle of the day, she lived in a one-man tent for a year, without running water or electricity. 'The clinic,' she explains, 'was four mud huts which I managed with one other expat nurse and ten national staff. We saw about 1,000 patients a month. Everything came to us: landmine victims, malaria, malnutrition, cholera, gun-shot wounds, obstructed labour. There was no other health facility, and sometimes people would walk across the swamp and sand for over nine days to get to us. If we needed to get a patient to surgery we had to call a flight, the roads were too dangerous with the fighting.'

Remarkably, they managed to save 'most of the lives of the people who came to us.'

'We' in this context means local nurses and doctors and this passionate and modest young woman asked me several times during the interview, not to put the spotlight on her, but on the mothers she helps, and the local midwives in Bangladesh and in Sudan she has helped to train.

She remembers exactly the moment she found her vocation. 'I was a very small girl, at home, watching television and saw a Red Cross nurse being interviewed during the Ethiopian famine. I was safe with my family and here were these children starving because of the country they were born into. It made a vivid impression on me.'

After a nursing Masters Degree from Nottingham University, she trained as a midwife in 2010, and joined Medicin sans Frontiers (MSF). By the following year she was the expat responsible for the female health of 30,00 refugees.

It was in Bangladesh that Anna fell in love and married Jafar Alam, a Bangladeshi man who is that country's champion surfer. They met when he was giving surfing lessons to other humanitarian aid workers. (What a life, and what a coincidence, from my perspective, that Kit, the heroine in *Monsoon Summer* marries Anto an Indian doctor.)

When in England, where Anna presently works with pregnant women and their families living with HIV, she and Jafar live on a narrow-boat home in Beeston Lock in Nottingham, and when in Bangladesh, she lives with Jafar's family, in Cox's Bazar – a coastal town in the South East.

When I asked her to describe the best thing about her work she said: 'Wow! I can't find the words. If a baby and mother is saved despite all adversity it is awesome. But humanitarian emergencies are so complex, and discharging that woman and her precious baby back to the war, or to the slum, or to the refugee camp. That's really shit.'

Haiti, where she went after a devastating earthquake, was a particularly traumatic time. She says in a typical understatement: 'Finding safe accommodation was challenging. I slept on the hospital floor for a week as the violence in the street blocked my exit. The hardest thing about that was knowing that the labouring women were also struggling on the other side of the violence to get to us.' A cholera outbreak, which in many cases led to spontaneous labour in the women, added to the challenges.

'Some babies survived, which was a miracle, and every success kept us strong for the multitude of losses. I will never forget the women and babies we were unable to save.'

Not being able to save a baby had heart-breaking resonance for

Anna and her husband Jafa last year when they were given the news that in her words 'all pregnant couples dread.' A routine antenatal appointment, at 22 weeks, detected that the baby they had longed for was in her words, 'very seriously poorly'. As they were guided through what she describes as a 'painful haze of disbelief' through scan tests, and MRI's by 'a compassionate and skilled team of midwives, sonographers, obstetricians and neurosurgeons,' their worst fears were confirmed.

'Our precious little baby would not survive, and there was no science or treatment that could change that.' She was advised that to continue the pregnancy would be dangerous.

In a letter, published in the Telegraph, shortly after, she wrote:

'We are still in the darkness of our grief, which I am told is normal. However, I do remember the endless support we received throughout the challenges of birth from staff, family and friends. My placenta did not deliver, so whilst I had precious time holding my daughter, I received emergency interventions to stop the bleeding. I later needed to go to the operating theatre to complete the delivery under a general anaesthetic with IV antibiotics to prevent infection.

'I do not have the words to express our loss,' she continued, 'However I am conscious of the things we must remain grateful for despite our sorrow, especially with the awareness of how many women and girls suffer in childbirth all over the world.'

'Nearly 1,000 women die every day from childbirth, all over the world' she tells me, 'Every day! We don't know how lucky we are. For a woman to die in front of you just because she happens to have been born into a poor family in a poor country, that is something you never quite get over. This should be on everyone's agenda, as it is almost completely preventable.'

What a cruel twist of fate though it still seems that someone who has done so much to relieve maternal suffering should have to endure the loss of her own child. But she displays no bitterness, only admiration for the National Health Service that saved her, and a determination to keep on working. 'Sorry,' she wrote to me at the end of a long and passionate email. 'I could go on. It means so much to me, hence why I am now involved in the teaching of midwives, and now that Bangladesh has highly trained midwives that are recognized as professionals, I am hopeful we will continue to see improvements.'

And there is a happy postscript. Half way through this interview,

I learned that Anna Alam Kent is now 24 weeks pregnant with a new baby, and cautiously joyful.

If you want to know more about the work of MSF please visit ww.msf.org.uk

STAY IN TOUCH WITH
JULIA GREGSON

To find out more about Julia and her writing,
visit her website www.juliagregson.net

Connect with her on Facebook/AuthorJuliaGregson
Or Tweet her @juliagregson

Make sure you've read her sweeping historical romances...

THE WATER HORSE

A sweeping historical love story

Catherine Carreg has grown up a tomboy, but is consumed by a longing to escape the monotomy of village life, and runs away to London. Alone in the unfamiliar bustle of the city, Catherine finds a position in a rest home for sick governesses in Harley Street, run by Miss Florence Nightingale. Then, as the nation is gripped by reports of the war in the Crimea, Catherine volunteers as a nurse – and her life changes beyond all recognition.

'Lively, atmospheric novel'
Sunday Telegraph

EAST OF THE SUN

**India 1928. A land of heat, dust and dreams,
and the promise of love...**

Three young women are on their way to India, each with a new life in mind. Rose, a beautiful but naïve bride-to-be, is anxious about leaving her family and marrying a man she hardly knows. Victoria, her bridesmaid couldn't be happier to get away from her overbearing mother, and is determined to find herself a husband. And Viva, their inexperienced chaperone, is in search of the India of her childhood, ghosts from the past and freedom.

Each of them has their own reason for leaving their homeland but the hopes and secrets they carry can do little to prepare them for what lies ahead in India.

'A rich historical novel'
Sunday Times

JASMINE NIGHTS

**A tale of decadence and destruction, of love and
of danger. It is the captivating love story set in
an extraordinary world.**

1942, and the world is at war. It is a war that has already shattered
families and devastated countries. But for some, it will also mean
the greatest of adventures. The world is on the brink of enormous
change. A beautiful young singer, Saba, finds herself transported
to the fading glamour of Alexandria and the heat and decadence
of Turkey. On the glamorous Middle Eastern social circuit, Saba
rubs shoulders with double agents and diplomats, movie stars and
smugglers. Some want her voice, some her friendship, and some the
secrets she is perfectly placed to discover...

'Exotic, decadent, dangerous and terrific storytelling'
Woman & Home